A SWANSEA CHILD

Geoff Brookes

AN INSPECTOR RUMSEY BUCKE NOVEL

Published by

Llyfrau Cambria Books, Wales, United Kingdom.

Cambria Books is a division of

Cambria Publishing.

Discover our other books at: www.cambriabooks.co.uk

Dedication

This book is dedicated to Paul Roe (1940 – 2020), my uncle and my friend, who was very sadly taken from us by coronavirus in November 2020.

I dedicate the book to him, with enormous gratitude for all the happy memories he has left behind. It was a privilege and an honour to know him.

In the same series

In Knives We Trust (2018)

Our Lady of Mumbles (2020) Published by Cambria

CONTENTS

Prologue April 1876

Constanta, Romania

It was time to go home, without a doubt. They had done the job, delivered the timber, and now it was time to cast off. Constanta wasn't a safe place anymore. Captain Butler took a last look along the quay, deserted now, the smell of burning and a sense of fear blowing between the tall sinister warehouses, sheltering threats in this darkest of times. He stood, with his gun at the ready, beside the deckhand, who quickly unfastened the hawser from the mooring ring. Everyone who worked on the quay had disappeared for their own safety, and so if they wanted to get the *Penrice Castle* away intact they had to do it for themselves. And they certainly wanted to get away. There was smoke, then flames. Now there was more gunfire; shouts. A scream. Butler nodded at the deckhand; it was time for them to get on-board.

Suddenly they heard a man running down the narrow incline that came from the town. Butler turned, watching the man's shoulders bounce off the rough walls on either side. He raised the gun in his hand, hearing the man panting as he approached the ship. He was carrying a large bundle. 'Domnule Butler!' he called. 'Domnule Butler! Please listen to me.' He stood in front of Butler, panting now, trying to catch his breath. The gap between the *Penrice Castle* and the quayside was widening.

Now Butler recognised him. They had brought a consignment of railway sleepers to Mr Abramovitch and he had invited Butler to his smart villa for an elaborate supper. That was where he had met this dishevelled man who stood before him. It was Raduta, Abramovitch's valet. 'I did not expect to see you here tonight,' said Butler. 'It is dangerous for anyone to be out on these streets. We were about to leave, Raduta.' He gestured at his ship and at the anxious faces of sailors looking down at them from the deck.

There was a loud explosion in the centre of the town and then the

1

disturbing sound of shouts and cheering.

'There is not much time,' said Raduta, still catching at his breath. 'Listen, please. This is Chana. This is the girl of Nicolae Abramovitch.' He pulled the shape away from his shoulder and Butler could see that it was a terrified child. 'My master says that you are a man of honour. So I ask you please. Take her, and her parcel. It is so difficult here. Nicolae Abramovitch asks me to do this. There is a fire. There is killing. Please take her. All of her is so precious.'

Butler was struggling to process all that Raduta was saying as the obedient stern of the *Penrice Castle* drifted further away from the quay. Then, when a burst of flames lit up the sky, he could see that Raduta's shirt seemed to be covered in blood.

'Please take her. Domnule Nicolae will come to find her. He will bring a doll with him. But it is not safe here no more.' He saw Butler staring at the blood on his shirt. 'A man attack us in the street. Chana is injured a little, too. This is his blood. Not hers. Quickly. Take her.' Another spire of flames plumed into the sky, turning it a dreadful red. 'They come for my master. There is no time. They look for me. They look for her. You must take the girl.'

Butler stared at Raduta. There had been tension in the town; he had seen angry crowds, he had seen the armed guards outside the Abramovitch house. Constanta had been on the edge of riot, he knew that. But take a child? How could he deal with a child?

'Skipper,' pleaded the deckhand. 'Begging your pardon, but I think we ought to be going.'

Raduta held out the girl to him. He could see wet blood across her left shoulder. She was shaking with terror and with shock. Raduta's teeth were clenched and he opened his eyes wide, pleading with him.

Butler reached out and took the child and then the grubby sack was thrust at him too.

Raduta closed his eyes and bowed his head. Then he turned and ran. As he disappeared back into the smoky haze of the town, Chana looked at Butler and began to cry.

*

It became a long and difficult voyage; the spring weather continued unhelpful and even when they reached the Mediterranean, it remained grey and threatening. Captain Felton Butler was unable to shift from his mind the memories of the things he had seen in Romania. But then, how could he? He had a permanent reminder; the child.

She had cried all the way and there was little that he could do to comfort her. He knew absolutely nothing about children and poor Chana had been inconsolable. Why had he agreed to take her? It had been such a stupid idea.

He was sure that he had never been intended by nature to be a father; he had certainly never developed any parental skills. He and Margaret were perfectly happy in their marriage; his long absences at sea worried neither of them unduly. Margaret was certainly not troubled by the disruption to their relationship, for she was always busy with her two boys. Felton had been a supportive stepfather, as everyone acknowledged, but then, they were his brother's sons and someone had needed to step in when Arthur had been lost overboard around Cape Horn. He had done his best, even though the call of the sea had been strong, and at least the boys had turned out well enough. But he had never had to deal with a baby before. He had persuaded himself that Margaret would be pleased to adopt a little girl. She had always said she wanted to have a daughter. And when Chana was thrust into his arms, Butler hoped at last that he would now be able to provide what she had wished for. But he soon realised that he was out of his depth. Suddenly his concerns had changed completely, for he was no longer concerned with how Margaret would react; now his greatest anxiety was whether the child would actually arrive in Swansea alive.

They had put into Constantinople and the first mate, Robert Beck, had tried hard to persuade him to hand the child over to a woman – any woman – but Butler was convinced that he was made of sterner stuff. However, it was another rough passage to Thessaloniki where they picked up a cargo of currants and, by the time the *Penrice Castle*

3

reached Valletta in Malta, he knew he had been terribly wrong. He should have paid someone to take her from him. But it seemed that when the sun finally emerged, the child seemed to settle. If it was the sunshine that had cheered her, thought Butler, then she was in for a particularly miserable time in Swansea.

Captain Butler wandered around the attractive old town for a while, enjoying the contrast between sun and shade in its narrow streets after such drab days. He listened to the plaintive sounds of caged birds hanging from doors and windows, a crucifix swaying gently beneath each of them in the breeze. He wondered if the birds would sing just as well beneath a Swansea sky. Probably not, he decided. He listened to their songs, sensing the sadness in them. Perhaps that was what Chana was doing, trapped in a cage called the *Penrice Castle*; she was crying for her lost freedom. He dismissed such nonsense immediately; he had never been fanciful.

The morning was certainly a taste of summer, although the vibrant Mediterranean scents of fruit and spice could never disguise the smell of corruption that hung over this idyllic place. Even the simplest of actions required urgent lubrication with a series of small bribes. He knew that when he had paid two men to watch the ship, he was actually paying them to ensure they did not attack it themselves. Butler had always thought Valletta was a beautiful place, but in his recent visits he had sensed something rotten at its heart. He watched the preparations for the imminent arrival of the Prince of Wales on an official visit. Would they take protection money from him too, he wondered?

Eventually he settled for a few minutes on the ramparts, eating an orange, looking out across the sea to the horizon and wondering what to do. He had given his word and that, for him was an unbreakable contract. But he had no idea how he was going to get the child back to Swansea – and none of the crew did either. He wondered whether he could hire someone in the town to care for her for the rest of the voyage. Money would get you anything in Valletta. But what if that didn't work? Perhaps he should never have agreed to take her – but really, what choice did he have? Nicolae must have been desperate

4

and Constanta had been a dangerous place to be that night. Something terrible was happening in the town and he was just glad to be getting away. Even a small innocent child like Chana had been hurt. No one now could know how Chana received the wound on her shoulder, but at least it seemed to be healing.

Butler sighed and finished his orange and looked for a moment across the red roof tops to the dome of St John's Cathedral. Valletta was his habitual place to re-provision. He loved the tall narrow buildings by the harbour, their honey-coloured limestone absorbing the warmth of the sun, and he wondered if the *Penrice Castle* would stay seaworthy long enough for him to come back. He didn't have a great deal of confidence. It was creaking and groaning more than he was comfortable with these days. Still, stranger things happen at sea.

He wandered back to the ship, resting at a wharf in the Grand Harbour, with a sense of foreboding. The prospect of more days at sea with a distressed child barely eating and the Biscay before them was dreadful. But strangely as he walked up the gangplank, all seemed calm. Chana was no longer crying and was playing, reasonably happily it seemed, though she still regarded the sailors who had gathered round to watch her with considerable suspicion.

'What's happened?' he asked Beck.

'Went through the bag that man gave you. At the bottom I found that doll she's got, Captain. She seemed very pleased to see it. Calmed her straightaway.' There was a small piece of cheese in front of her, with fresh bread from the town, the edges of which had been nibbled. Only a few currants remained in the bowl she had been given. 'Things are looking up, I reckon.'

Captain Butler looked at the doll. It was simple, made of rags, the limbs loosely tied. Nothing special, it seemed. He shrugged. He had always found children strange.

'There were other things in the bag too,' Beck added. They had not thought to examine it previously. He pulled it open and withdrew a necklace which he handed to Butler. It seemed old and was very heavy. It had a pendant which was large and circular, embossed with

5

a shining, raised, rectangular centre like a miniature shield, with a sparkling stone at its heart. He considered it carefully. It must be glass. Had it been a diamond it would be worth a fortune. He turned it around so that it caught the light. To the uneducated eye it would probably look as if it was made of silver, inset with garnets and pearls. But it couldn't be. It was merely a clever copy of something or other.

'Look at it, Captain.' He blew out his cheeks. 'That is worth a pretty penny, I'll be bound.'

Butler stiffened slightly. 'Like as not. But then I don't know. It was given to me in trust, Mr Beck, and it stays with the girl. I gave my word, and that has got to count for something. He trusted me with this poor little mite and I can't let him down.'

Beck laid a hand briefly on his forearm. 'I wouldn't expect thee to say anything else, Captain. The little lass is in safe hands on this old boat.'

Butler smiled at him, grateful for the support. 'I reckon she is safer now that she has shut up. And she will be a lot safer when I hand her over to Margaret,' he smiled.

Beck delved into the sack again. 'There is this too.' He produced a tube of stained fabric and pulled from it a thick length of ancient paper that appeared to be wrapped around two pieces of wood. It was certainly old and the edges of the paper seemed to be crumbling. 'No idea what this is supposed to be. Can't see our little Chana being too interested in it.' He slipped it back into the cloth bag.

'Did you look at it? Did you open it up?' asked Butler.

Beck nodded. 'Couldn't understand a word. Couldn't recognise the language. And anyway, you know what it is like with other people's handwriting. Not easy.'

Part One – Arrivals

One

She pushed her pram up the steep hillside to Pentrechwyth, the village poisoned by the copper works, where the vile smoke brought an early death to many and ensured that no plants could ever grow on Kilvey Hill. Amy walked past The Rising Sun, where inside someone was playing a fiddle. She always wondered how they did it and whether it was difficult. She thought she might like to try it. She turned to the left away from the road, down a mud track seemingly going nowhere. Hidden behind a pile of slag and waste there was a derelict hut, never intended to be a home – it had once been a storeroom or possibly a night-watchman's lodge – but this was where Amy lived. There was a serviceable door and the roof was largely intact, although the stonework around the window had fallen away and the jagged hole had long ago been covered with a threadbare blanket admitting no light. A faint trickle of smoke emerged from the chimney.

Down below her she could see the glowing fires in the copper works, something which always gave Amy a sense of comfort, especially on nights like this when the air was dry and still, so that the smoke from the chimneys went straight up and didn't wash over the hut and try to smother her. Even if anyone found the hut in this forgotten part of the shapeless industrial complex, it was unlikely they would ever imagine that it was inhabited. It was a lost place. Outside the door there were two fat jars about two feet tall, with handles on either side of the neck. One of them was broken. There was a small wooden barrel with a wooden lid. The ground was uneven, black rocks and sharp slag hiding in the dark, waiting for unwary feet.

Amy took Cat from the pram, where he had been keeping her battered rag doll warm and put him on the floor. That pram had been a lucky find, abandoned on the side of the North Dock, and she didn't even know that Cat was inside until he stuck his head out. He was her friend now and she watched him stretch, as he always did, before he

8

wandered over to sniff in welcome with the other two cats, before creeping off to explore in the corners.

Auntie lay, troubled in her breathing, in the low unstable bed pushed against the damp wall of the cottage. A thin fire was still smoking steadily in the grate, the only wood that Amy had found today proving rather too wet. The floor was covered in ashes and stained straw.

It had never been easy looking after Auntie, but things had become even more difficult when her brother Joseph disappeared. She didn't really know who Auntie was, except that Auntie had been here as long as she could remember and that she had always called her Auntie. She in turn called her Amy and so she assumed that was her name, although part of her was never really convinced that it was. But she was always certain that Joseph was her brother. Clever he was. She had relied upon him; they had both relied on him.

She missed Joseph. Whenever he came home, he always brought something for them to eat but she hadn't seen him for quite a while now. He must have found somewhere better to live and she was sad that he hadn't been back to see them.

Amy smelt the jug, wrinkled her face and then poured water from it into a shallow earthenware bowl. She dipped a dirty rag into it and then dabbed at Auntie's lips, trying to moisten them. It was difficult. Auntie had been very sick for a few weeks now and Amy wasn't sure what to do next. She didn't seem to be getting any better. Auntie turned on to her side and muttered disconnected words before her voice trailed away. Amy was extremely worried.

Auntie collected the urine from the cottages along Rifleman's Row and in Foxhole. She went from house to house with one of those large jars on her head and people would empty their chamber pots into it. Then she would go down to the Copper and the man there would pay her for it. Auntie said that they used it to clean the copper sheets they made, but Amy couldn't understand that. Why didn't they use water from the river? They wouldn't have to pay for that. Perhaps they were just being kind.

9

But then Auntie had got ill. She said that it was because her jar was cracked and all the pee had dribbled on her. So Amy had been doing the collecting instead. It was hard work and it made her smelly, though she soon got used to that. But couldn't balance that big jug on her head. She couldn't even lift it up. So she had put a barrel with a lid into her pram and took that to make the collections. The man at the Copper didn't give her much for it because he said her barrel didn't hold very much pee, so she had to go up and down the hill more times than Auntie ever did and she got very tired. But she needed, somehow, to find food for them to eat and so she had started to go down into town with Cat to see what see could get and also because she enjoyed the lights.

She had always liked it down there. There was always so much to see. In the nights there were lights and fights and many more people than she could ever count. She loved watching them and listening to their voices. She heard lots of things that she didn't understand, but it was fun to look at all the people. They were always doing silly things that made her laugh – like coming out of pubs and falling over and singing and shouting. Sometimes, men smelling of beer would give her pennies, but what she liked best was when women gave her things to eat or took her into one of the dark and smoky pubs that made her cough, so that she could sit by the fire. Sometimes she saw that nice lady with the ribbons. She always looked for her around town; she had seen her earlier. Perhaps she might help her with Auntie, if she asked. But she wasn't here and so Amy thought carefully about what she should do. She was sure there was a doctor in Hafod. He would help her.

But there was a problem.

The ferryman who took people across the river wasn't there in the nights. He started work early in the morning when the shifts changed over in the works, but in the night he wasn't there. How was she going to get Auntie to Hafod? She couldn't walk down to St Thomas to the bridge or up to Morriston either. All she could do, she decided, was to take Auntie down to the ferry and use the boat herself. She was sure Mr Clarke wouldn't mind if she borrowed it. In fact, she would take it back and he would never know.

People were always very kind, thought Amy. That lady she liked who she met in town tonight, the one with the straw hat and those ribbons, always gave her something to eat. Tonight, Amy had stood patiently outside the Mermaid Inn whilst the lady went inside and then came back with a pie and gave it to her, saying 'It's a present from the barmaid.' The barmaid sounded like a very nice person too, and she had brought the pie home to share with Auntie but it didn't look as if she would be able to eat it. She decided to eat it herself.

But there was an important lesson there, she decided. It was important that you found the right person, that was all, then everything would be alright. All she needed to do was find a doctor. Someone would know where he was.

She helped Auntie to sit up in bed and then pushed her boots on to her feet. She put her hat on for her, then she took the blanket from the bed and wrapped it around her shoulders. She hoped that the doctor wouldn't recognise it because she had taken it from a washing line in Foxhole one evening after Auntie had been taken ill. He might be too busy to notice, though.

They had needed another blanket because Auntie wouldn't let her share the bed with her anymore and Amy had been forced to make a new one for herself on the floor. When she examined the blanket more closely, she realised that it was unlikely that anyone would recognise the blanket now.

There was a commotion in the corner, a growl and a squeal. It seemed as if the old tom had caught something, but she couldn't stay to investigate.

It wasn't easy to help Auntie down the hill towards the river but it was dry and not especially slippery and Amy was able to support her most of the way by holding her hand tightly, though she stumbled and fell twice. It took a long time to get Auntie back on her feet. It was hard when Auntie was so much taller than you. Auntie's hat had fallen off and she couldn't reach to put it back on so she pushed it on to her own head. It sat there uncomfortably, like a bowl.

When Amy arrived at the river, where the flat-bottomed boat was normally fastened to a wire that stretched across to the opposite bank, there was a problem. The boat wasn't in the water. It had been pulled up on to the muddy bank and it wasn't attached to the wire.

Amy wasn't sure how important the wire was. She had seen Mr Clarke wiggle the wood that stuck into the water and that was how the boat crossed the river. She was sure that she could do it, for it didn't look difficult at all. It took her a while but eventually she managed to push the boat into the dirty water whilst Auntie sat on a piece of concrete in the mud. But it was difficult to keep it in place and to get Auntie into the boat at the same time, especially since Auntie could barely walk. Perhaps she was tired.

Eventually she managed to get Auntie close enough to the boat so that she could fall into it, and Amy pushed it further out into the river with the intention of climbing aboard. But the out-going tide caught it and it drifted away from her. She splashed into the water to catch it but it had gone far beyond her reach. Amy dragged herself from the water and tried to follow the boat along the slimy bank but it wasn't possible. There were more lumps of concrete and old tree trunks and they slowed her down too much. She stumbled and the hat fell off into the mud. When Amy finally saw the boat again, Auntie was disappearing downstream far too quickly, lying back and staring at the sky, with her hand trailing in the thick oily water.

Two

One of the younger reporters at the Cambrian, cleverly - in his own mind anyway - would later call her 'The Lady of the Tawe,' although Dr Benjamin probably beat him to it. Others identified her by her more familiar name of 'Auntie Pee,' once they had pulled her from the boat which had come to rest against one of the supports of the New Cut Bridge.

They found that Auntie Pee was dead.

How and why she had got into the boat and how she died were initially less important than the considerable confusion that happened when the shifts changed over in the copper works and many of the workers either couldn't get home or, more importantly, couldn't get in to work at all. This was a serious obstruction to production and an even more serious disruption to earnings. The walk up to Morriston or down to St Thomas was an unwelcome inconvenience, which was only resolved when Constable Davies finally returned the large and unstable rowing boat to Mr Clarke, the ferryman. Then, inevitably perhaps, someone mentioned cholera, an unfounded rumour that raced around the town, causing the utmost terror. Reassurance was vital and, once Auntie Pee's body was securely in custody inside the police stables, Doctor Benjamin was sent for.

He was a young man and thin to the extent that the ladies of the town were anxious to offer him both nourishment and an introduction to their daughters. But his blue, sometimes cold, eyes were not yet turned towards them. He had a fiercely engaged social conscience and his determination to find a place working amongst the poor had brought him to Swansea, where he had replaced David Beynon. He had left for Aberystwyth for a fresh start in cleaner air, where the family could try to find peace following the consequences of daughter Emily's terrible abduction.

His examination of the neglected body was thorough. His hands moved with knowledge and respect over the spare and emaciated frame, untroubled by the vile smell that hung over her like an evil

13

miasma. Eventually he nodded and stepped away. 'And so this is our very own Lady of Shallot, who probably created more of a stir this morning, in her death, than she ever did in her life. In my opinion there is no evidence that this is an example of suicide.'

'And did she have cholera, Dr Benjamin?' asked Bucke fearing the answer.

'No, Inspector Bucke. A sick woman without a doubt, but there is no sign of diarrhoea. There was a swelling in the legs but I would say that she was most likely killed by poverty alone, desperate grinding poverty from which there is no escape. I have seen it every day since I arrived here and I heartily wish that it was not allowed to exist.'

'I understand what you say, but at least you have provided me with a small relief, Dr Benjamin. A civic panic about cholera would be most unhelpful. We do not need any more hysteria in this town. There was more than enough for our needs last year.'

'The poor woman is dead and should not trouble the town, although we should be ashamed that someone as filthy as that should be living amongst us.' Benjamin shook his head. 'Shameful.'

Inspector Bucke rather liked the young man – his idealism burnt bright and although experience might soon knock the edges off that, nonetheless it was good that the poor and the overlooked had someone else to champion them. He had already established his presence at The Ragged School and Bucke had heard that numbers attending had increased as a result. After all, where else could the poor get free medical treatment?

They left the stables and walked over to the main building, their breath hanging in the still cold air and they pulled their coats closer around them. A pig screamed from the nearby abattoir.

'Do you know where she lived?' Benjamin asked. 'It is imperative that we ensure there were no others living with her in such a similar state. Must be upstream of the bridge, obviously.'

'The constables know her but not where she lived. She was known as Auntie Pee and she collected urine for the copper works.'

Dr Benjamin shook his head in disgust. 'And there are people who live like this? Who collect urine? In Queen Victoria's Great Britain? We should be ashamed. Do we think she had any children?'

'Not that we know of. Someone said that a young girl has been making the collections for the past week or so but who she is no one is sure. Perhaps someone is trying to steal the business, as if it is worth anything. I have asked the constables to keep an eye open.'

'It is beyond my understanding, Inspector, how in a place such as this, lives can be lived and can end without anyone knowing anything.' He shook his head slowly.

'The Ragged School does good works, doctor,' said Bucke. 'That should help, in the long run.'

Benjamin sighed. 'There is such a need. We have 110 children every morning. Of course many of their friends are at work and so we have 350 of them in the afternoons.' He turned to Bucke, his eyes bright with commitment. 'I am not stupid, you know. The children don't come for religious instruction. They come for the free food and the warmth. And I know that many of them are sent to us by their parents to save the expense of finding them food. But it doesn't matter. The need is real enough. It is the only place where they can find medical help.' He was suddenly angry. 'Of course, our duty is nothing more than to ensure that they are well enough to go to work to support the rich.'

Bucke opened the back door to the police station and allowed the doctor to enter. The young doctor was taller than him, for Bucke was little more than average height and he paused to look down at him and at Bucke's calm appraising eyes. Benjamin saw a powerful man but someone measured and controlled in all that he did. His hair was neat and clean and his trimmed beard covered the scar along his jaw which he had brought home with him from his service on the North West Frontier, the incident during which he had been separated from part of his left ear lobe. Benjamin saw enquiring and sympathetic brown eyes. He had never seen the lines of sorrow and darkness that had once gathered around those eyes and which were now so rarely seen in the warmth of his new-found love.

15

Benjamin paused in the doorway. 'These children are poor, but they can raise themselves to high positions and to the accomplishment of great things, if only we will let them. It cannot be right that such things are denied to them. It is a terrible waste of their potential, which is no less than that of the children from the wealthiest of families. I truly believe that, Inspector.'

'Ah, Doctor Benjamin, good morning.' It was the Chief Constable who was leaning against the counter, in conversation with Sergeant Ball. 'Inspector Bucke, a busy morning already, as I understand it.'

'We endeavour to keep busy, Captain Colquhoun,' said Bucke. They had become good friends in the months since his appointment. He was a compassionate and intelligent man, his face dominated by a generous moustache and penetrating eyes. Bucke knew that Colquhoun was always very aware of the political implications of his job but refused to allow such things to compromise his commitment to the absolute truths of right and wrong. He was close to all his officers, visiting them regularly, understanding their concerns and frustrations. His calm response to the emergence of a violent religious cult in Swansea and the trust he had placed in Rumsey Bucke to handle it, had drawn the force together and made it stronger. He had left his office in the Town Hall today because any inconvenience experienced by the Copper Masters was sufficiently important to ensure that he was fully aware at first hand of what steps his officers had taken. He was not there to offer criticism or advice; merely to be informed, so that he could manage the inevitable complaints.

When Dr Benjamin had left, to walk the short distance to Back Street and the premises of the Ragged School, Sergeant Ball reviewed the other events of a difficult night.

'Can't say there was much for anyone to get excited about. Another sack on the beach. Three now since Christmas, another baby. Boy this time, still with a cord attached. Looks like another still-born to me. Breaks me heart it do, Mrs Ball not having any children. Shocking times we live in. Been in the sand for a while they say. Doctor Sullivan's coming down later. It will be natural causes, you can be sure of that, just like the others.' He shook his head.

16

'There are some desperate women out there, Stanley,' said Bucke sympathetically. 'It is a crime to bury a body like that, we all know. But it is a tragedy whenever or why-ever it happens.'

Captain Colquhoun nodded. 'Anything else, sergeant?'

'Telegram from Bristol. Couple of robberies. Old man murdered and his house ransacked in Swindon. A lot of money taken, but they didn't send any more details, praise be to God. Then they had a vicar robbed and beaten on the Bath Road in Bristol. Did we know anything? As far as I know, we've heard nothing. Got enough villainy of our own as it is, without us troubling ourselves with someone else's problems, unless you lot are keeping things from me. Like you do.'

'Whoever it is, he has a distance to travel before he becomes an issue for us,' said Colquhoun. 'Anything else?'

'Constable Gill had a run-in with Vinegar Bridget. She was drunk and very disorderly. He had to put her in the wheelbarrow to bring her in. Not the first time.'

'What has she done this time?' asked Bucke.

'The usual – '

'Wait a moment. Please excuse my ignorance, but Vinegar Bridget? Why Vinegar?' asked Colquhoun.

'The sour old cow once drank a pint of vinegar for a bet in the Mermaid. The name stuck. Do anything that woman, they say. A face on which a blush is never seen. A real pest when she is drunk.'

'What happened last night, Sergeant? She been breaking windows again?' Bucke looked carefully through the logbook.

'Windows have been broken at the Royal Exchange, I grant you, but don't know for certain it was her. It was Gill who brought her in, as I said. There had been an argument with a gent called Jenkins from Jockey Street but then he had been stupid, as far as I can work it out. He said that she had taken his purse containing 4s.6d. He says he was out on an errand for his wife, to Moses Davies the chemist – except he was heading in the wrong direction. Stupid bugger says he got into

17

a conversation with our Bridget and she put her arm around him and suddenly his money had disappeared. Well, he has to tell that story, doesn't he? How else can he explain it to Mrs Jenkins? Bridget told Gill – before she fell over – that she'd done a bit of business with him. That is how she had the money. She spent it all and had a free ride in a wheelbarrow. I'll let her out when she has woken up.'

'And what about Milford then? Has she been in too?'

'Not since last week when she hit Edward Rees with a poker, but then, knowing him, he probably deserved it. Didn't press charges. Too risky. I have to say, Inspector, it is my honest opinion that Vinegar Bridget and Milford are the ones you should be looking at as regards that thieving that is happening at the Star Theatre. They have been seen.'

Bucke nodded. 'A possibility worth exploring, yes.'

'But Milford? Is there something else here that I should know?' Colquhoun was curious, though a smile seemed to sparkle in his eyes.

Bucke nodded. 'That is our very own Selina Coleford. Once met, never forgotten. Wouldn't want to fight her.'

'But why is Selina Coleford known as Milford? Or shouldn't I ask?' said Colquhoun.

Bucke smiled at Sergeant Ball's discomfort, for he was blushing. The Chief Constable went on. 'You see, we had a lady with a similar title in Carmarthen, where I served previously as you know, Inspector.'

'Indeed, Captain,' smiled Bucke.

'An unusual coincidence, you might think, is it not, Sergeant?'

'Yes, Chief Constable,' he replied, increasingly embarrassed.

'Ours was an industrious lady of mature years, I would say. I think she may have come from the town of Milford. And yours? I feel, as Chief Constable, that I should be informed,' he said with a smile in Bucke's direction.

'Well, sir, they call her Milford because she is always ready to be a haven for seamen, sir. That is what I am told. Not that I approve of such talk, mind you, sir. Wouldn't normally mention it, sir.'

'Of course not, Sergeant,' said Colquhoun, as he picked up his hat from the counter. He walked towards the door. 'I am pleased to hear it. Good morning to you both.'

It soon became a routine day. Ball set about arranging a pauper's funeral for Auntie Pee and Bucke continued with issues raised by the behaviour of members of the Militia in the town.

Bucke's problems with the Royal Glamorgan Artillery Militia began with a group of new recruits who were rather full of themselves, believing that their membership conferred rather more status upon them than the rest of Swansea were prepared to accept. Consequently, when they were mocked – as they were quite regularly – they had a tendency to over-react. There had been a spate of incidents, leading to squabbles, fights and general disorder. At an artillery practice on the Burrows, when they had marched up and down, full of self-importance, they were showered by abuse from The Hat Stand Gang, a loose collection of feral boys from St Thomas. They had secretly filled the mighty cannon with scraps of timber and when the gunners cleared it and readied themselves for the exciting moment when it would finally be fired and their status thus confirmed by a very loud noise, the boys had then taken it in turns to dance dangerously in front of it. Two of the recruits had levelled guns at them and their remaining dignity vanished as their colleagues tried - and failed - to grab the boys. It should have been an afternoon of impressive military precision, one that would reassure anxious Swansea citizens that the security of the town was in safe hands. Instead they were subjected to the unconfined hilarity of the mocking crowd. That had set the scene and in the evening there had been a large disturbance outside the Albany Vaults, when members of the Militia had been reminded of their inadequacies by a crowd of copper workers.

Such disorder was not good for the town and Bucke met with the elderly and ineffectual Colonel Ballard to urge restraint upon the recruits, otherwise there would inevitably be arrests. It was not an encouraging meeting; Inspector Flynn told him that he had never expected a positive outcome.

'It is like the constables in the end, Rumsey. The uniform alone doesn't bring respect, but the soldiers think it does. You have to earn respect. I keep telling the constables. You will, in fact, be mocked because of your uniform. To those in the poorer streets of town, it looks like you think you are better than they are, because you have shiny buttons. Not going to take that, are they? Want respect? You earn it by the things you do, that show you are better than the uniform. I tell you what, Rumsey. Those soldiers of ours are a joke. If the Germans or the French or whoever, land in Oxwich and fight their way across Gower, it is not the Militia who will save us. I'd send out the cockle women.'

Bucke had smiled and nodded. Flynn was right. They were hopeless.

*

There was a cold wind, bringing with it flurries of snow. It would be a tricky evening, Bucke knew, and not because of Constance, for he loved her with all his heart and treasured every precious moment with her. No, the problem would come later on, when he would have to return to his desolate room above the surgery of Mr Scott the dentist, on Fisher Street. On occasions like this, when they met, they were always careful that he did not stay too late. He knew that in his role as a police inspector, he needed the support of the people in the town to do his job, and that Constance too, in her position as a piano teacher, must remain above reproach if she was to be trusted with young people. So they were required to show the utmost propriety and thus their evenings had an unconventional shape, with their meal taken later, after they had spent some time together. Living without servants as Constance did, thought Bucke, had its advantages.

There was a remarkable depth to their love that neither had experienced before and would not be denied; they had taken an inevitable step after they had survived those near-death moments in the collapsing mine. After that, they had become addicts, and there

20

was no going back.

Constance's rooms on St Helen's Road were modest but comfortable. In the warmth of love she had created a home that wasn't yet quite theirs, but might soon be, for she was taking legal advice from Mr Strick about a divorce from her disappeared husband. It wouldn't be easy, but both she and Rumsey were determined to pursue it.

Constance White was short and slight, with large brown eyes and a slightly upturned nose. Her dark hair was rarely securely contained in the bun on her head and it would release itself in a moment, thus requiring endless adjustment. Legally, she was still married to William Bristow, but he had fled to America and in so doing had allowed Rumsey Bucke to change her life. She had discovered within herself courage and resolve which she didn't know were there. She had ferocious loyalty to Rumsey and had uncovered an unexpected passion for him so profound, that she regretted so many wasted years.

They lay together, the pleasant aroma of a simple stew on the stove eventually forcing its way between them and making them hungry. It was then that Rumsey spoke of Auntie Pee, the haunting image of neglect that she had presented fixed firmly in his mind. This was how he managed the details of his sometimes distressing days, for by sharing such things with her, he found it easier to deal with them. She, in turn, was fascinated by his work.

Constance stroked his hair gently. 'Do you know, Rumsey? Until I met you I never realised that such poverty existed here, so close to where I live. I saw the poor at the Church of Our Lady of Mumbles but they were in their Sunday best. I did not realise that there are people here who live like that.'

'Poor Auntie Pee.' He sighed, bitterly. 'The soul of Swansea – filthy, unknown, neglected. There are stories out there that would horrify all of us, and at the moment we do not know them all. In the market yesterday one of the constables confiscated a rotting rabbit from Mabe the Butcher. It was, by all accounts, green, falling apart and the smell was shocking. The constable didn't like handling it. He put it down – and when he turned round it had gone. Someone had

21

stolen it – to eat.'

Constance shook her head. 'I struggle, of course I do. It is hard to make ends meet. And yet I have all this.' She gestured around the simple bedroom. 'Others have so much less. I wonder how they survive. And Auntie Pee? Did she live alone?'

'We don't know. We hope there were no children. What state they might be in is impossible even for the constables to imagine.' He told her then about Doctor Benjamin and his mission at The Ragged School to help the poorest children.

Constance leaned over and kissed him on the forehead and then climbed from the bed. 'It is good to know there is someone else here in Swansea with a conscience.' She ran her hands through her hair, 'Come, Rumsey. Let me feed you now. It is cold outside and it has started to snow. I need to warm you before you go home.'

*

Amy felt that she could relax. She would have liked to have gone with Auntie but the boat had been too wilful. It didn't matter though. Someone would have found her and helped her. Soon Auntie would be better and she would come home. So until then, she needed to do Auntie's work for her. Because if she didn't then someone else would start doing it and Auntie would be cross. So she carried on all day, pushing the pram, filling and spilling the barrel, collecting the pennies. She was glad she had found that pram. It was very useful. And Cat had been inside too, and she liked Cat. But he couldn't help with the work, and it was hard.

But when evening came, Amy was feeling lonely and cold and hungry and sore and she really wanted to see that special lady with the ribbons and the straw hat, because she might be able to help her. She might be difficult to find but she could start in the places where she had seen her before. So she picked up Cat, put him in her pram to keep dolly warm and set off down the hill to town. She looked everywhere but didn't find her. A large lady outside the Ship and Castle on the Strand gave her a sandwich and Amy ate it straightaway. It was a cold night and there was snow blowing on the wind. The lady

22

tried to persuade her to go inside to get warm but she really wanted to find the other lady. Amy looked everywhere but didn't see her and eventually she had to go home.

Three

The man rowed ashore. Not very well and with little control but the tide did the work and the small lifeboat eventually grounded a short distance from the dry sand. It was dark and it was cold and snowflakes clung to his coat. He could see the faint outline of the ship drifting on in the westerly wind, sightlessly into the night, its masts pointing to the clouds as if seeking the stars. He watched until he could distinguish it no longer and then waded ashore, keeping his sack and his shoes above his head, out of the cold water. At least he would have some dry clothes to change into.

As far as he could understand it, from the rudimentary map he had drawn and from what the captain had said, this ought to be the southern part of Gower. He was still some distance from Swansea, but he was closer than he had been yesterday. He didn't know exactly where he was but that didn't matter too much. Walking into the sunrise, to the east, with the sea on his right, would get him there.

He put his sack on the sand, above the tide line and swept back his hair with both hands. He realised that he had lost his hat and clenched his fists in anger. He would never find it now. It could be in the sea. He wondered whether he should go and drag the boat up the beach, then he could turn it over and use it as a shelter. But he wasn't sure that he was strong enough. He looked around, his eyes adjusting to the darkness, confident that the clouds covering the moon would help to hide him. There were rocks and he could smell the seaweed on the wind. Over to his left he could see regular shapes that seemed man-made, and he was briefly alarmed that there might be houses. He had to find out, so he made his way slowly towards them, taking some comfort in the possibility that there might be outhouses in which he could shelter. But they were merely ruins and within them he found a sheltered spot where he could settle down. He changed his breeches, put his shoes back on, wrapped himself in his blanket and waited for dawn.

He must have dropped off to sleep because he could hear seagulls above the noise of the waves and when he opened his eyes it was light and the snow had stopped. It was still, and very cold. He looked down towards the sea and there on the beach he could see a figure digging in the sand, below the tide line. It was a man and he dug two deep holes and into each one he placed a small sack. Then he added some rocks and then replaced the sand. He watched him carefully until he disappeared from sight behind some dunes.

He leaned back against the stone wall. He was hungry but food would wait. What he needed more than anything was water. He rubbed his face with some dirty water from a puddle to wake himself up, making prolonged eye-contact with a seagull with a vicious beak that seemed to be looking at him with hunger. He smiled to himself; just another hollow-eyed killer. He waved his arms and the bird reluctantly flapped away, with a final squawk of contempt. There was clearly a village along the bay and he walked cautiously towards it, picking up a hefty piece of driftwood from the beach as a walking stick.

*

It was only a short while later that a horse stood patiently, impassively, whilst the man beat its owner to death with a rock.

It had still been quite early when he reached the village and he had stopped at the bottom of the steep hill by the church, wondering what to do. A horse had left a deposit in the track. It didn't look fresh and it hadn't been collected by a gardener. It seemed that no one had been outside yet, apart from that person he'd seen on the beach. But if anyone saw him, a stranger in the village, and so early in the morning, they might think he was merely another tramp, or suspect that he had come ashore in the night and he didn't know whether he wanted to plant such an idea – he could not be sure how common that was in this part of the world. But everything was quiet and then he heard the wagon coming and so he stepped to the side of the road. A man looked down at him and stopped. He had a lined and weather-beaten face, a flat cap and a thick woollen scarf against the cold, with fingerless gloves holding the reins of a healthy - looking brown horse.

25

A working man, wearing a leather apron, his wagon full of dripping seaweed. He was an affable and good-natured man it seemed, with a welcoming light in his eyes.

'Swansea?' he asked. 'Steep pull up this hill, let me tell ye. Hop in the butt if ye likes. Makes no odds to me. Walk it if you want. I gotta tek this jorum o' seaweed to Sketty Hall for the gardin, but I shall be a bit leery on the way home, zz'snow, so at least the hoss won't be cuzzening.'

The man smiled at him, threw his sack on to the bench and then climbed up beside the driver. He seemed grateful for the company and chatted away easily as they made their slow way away from the church.

He was right; it was steep. Water from the seaweed dribbled audibly from the rear of the wagon and its sweet smell enveloped them. The driver had a flask of water which he kindly shared with him. He nodded his thanks and watched the countryside open up before him, once the wagon crested the track from the village, holding the length of bleached driftwood between his knees. It was not what he expected at all. Pleasant green fields, an impressive hill to his left, small villages and the sea to the right.

'Not much to say for yourself, have ye?' the driver asked. 'As likely as not you has no idea what I am rabbiting on about have ye? Like as not ye a vurriner. Teks all sorts.' He turned and saw his passenger already looking at him. 'Don't trubble yeself, if you dint understand. Nice to have company.'

But his passenger understood well enough. He knew he had no choice, or there would forever be the risk of news spreading of a foreigner landing in Gower in the middle of the night. That was not what he wanted. So he leaned over and pulled on the reins and the horse stopped as the wagon approached a broken stone wall.

The driver smiled. 'Go behind that melted wall if yous wantin' a zig, but dint be shy, there is none around, like as not.'

The man made to get down but instead turned round and struck the driver viciously with the wood on the back of the head. He rocked forward, shocked, his hands going instinctively to the back of his head. The man pushed him hard on the side of the face with the stick and knocked him off the wagon. Then he ran around the back of the wagon to the driver's side and beat him repeatedly with a sharp stone from the broken wall until he was sure he was dead. He removed the leather apron then dragged the body to the other side of the wall. He changed his clothes again and piled lose stones upon the bloodstained waistcoat and breeches he had discarded, before pulling on the apron. Then he climbed back on the wagon and followed the road, soon joining more everyday country traffic heading into Swansea.

When he had judged that he had gone far enough he stopped at a pub called The Black Boy. He went inside and bought a pie and a pot of beer and sat in the corner, watching and listening, just an ordinary man dressed for work in a leather apron. When he had finished, he abandoned the wagon full of seaweed in a field close by and then walked into town, following the traffic.

He had arrived. And now he needed to find a room.

*

Elsewhere in Swansea, there was someone else moving into new premises.

Sarah Rigby had, eventually, found a room in Elephant Street. She had had to leave her old accommodation at the top of George Street when the cold January had taken her landlady, Mrs Eustace. She had always been so accommodating and Sarah, out of respect, had never conducted her business on the premises. However, Harold Eustace, the son who had inherited the house, was not at all disposed to Sarah living there, for no matter how much her stock had risen following her considerable heroism in the collapsing Calvary Pit, she could not escape the shame attached to her professional status. Sarah's exploits had ensured that she was much admired, though she knew that this would not last, for admiration would do nothing to feed her. She was, inevitably, asked to leave, since prostitution – even if never carried out on the premises – did not conform to Eustace's aspirational vision for his new property.

Her new room was even less inviting than her old one. It was bare, cold and rather damp, to the left at the top of an unstable staircase. There was a narrow bed, its stability barely guaranteed by lengths of oily rope joining the legs to the base. There was a battered washstand and a small grate full of ashes.

Sarah sighed. That it should have come to this. Her childhood had initially held out significantly more promise. Her comfortable and happy life in Bristol had changed without warning when her adored father, an engine driver, had died in a railway accident. Her mother had tried her best, but there was neither money nor comfort after he had gone. Mistakes made, unwise choices and now rooms such as this were her life and had become her prison. She knew she had to escape, though she knew of few women who had ever managed successfully to leave behind such a destructive life-choice. Sarah was determined though and had no wish to waste money on accommodation when she was saving all that she could to fund her emigration. At least the money she had painstakingly accumulated was safe at the moment, hidden beneath the sheet music in Constance White's piano stool.

The closeness that adversity and imminent death had brought to their relationship would not easily dissipate. Their relationship was important to both of them, based on mutual and genuine respect. It was sad however, that no matter how close they had become, there remained an enormous disparity in their social standings and the ways in which they were perceived by others. There was a tension too, since Sarah also, but secretly, saw herself as Rumsey Bucke's lost lover and envied Constance's place in his heart. Constance did not seem to be aware of it and, if Bucke sensed anything, he never said. But it was clear to Sarah that she needed a fresh start somewhere far away, where she didn't have to be what circumstances had forced her to become. But to do that she needed money. And how else could she acquire it?

Sarah's new home appeared unstable, precariously balanced, looking down on the Strand below and seemingly eager to slide down to become part of it. She heard the building creak, for it stood on top of a tall but poorly constructed and insubstantial stone wall, against which drunks on the Strand relieved themselves. She noted that none of the floors seemed to be level and that the window frame hardly fitted at all. It seemed to be a building designed by a distracted child.

She looked out through the scratched and pitted glass and sighed again, twisting the familiar ribbons on her hat between her fingers. This was not a nice place. She knew the couple who lived in the rooms opposite and that was not helpful, either. The woman was a music hall singer, Fanny Stevens, who used the stage name 'The Angel of Swansea.' It was a title she had unwillingly inherited from a ship's figurehead seen, apparently, offering a blessing to the town from the heart of a blazing fire, an arson attack intended to hide the body of a murder victim. Sarah knew that Fanny's most important attribute was not, however, her ability to remain similarly untouched in the midst of the fiercest flames. She was, as she understood it, an impressive performer with a remarkable voice, though Sarah had never heard her.

The man, presumably her common-law husband, was Jack McCarthy, and she knew too well that he was someone to be avoided at all costs. She'd had dealings with him before. He was regarded by many as clever, since he seemed to escape the closest attentions of the police, despite his dubious activities, but as Sarah knew too well, he was entirely unpredictable. The women on the street were certainly very wary of him, for he was spiteful, short-tempered and prone to violence. McCarthy was running at least two girls from a squalid house a short distance away on Mariner Street. Sarah could not condemn, of course not, and she knew, from bitter experience, that any woman could find herself in such circumstances. But it was hard to think of anything much worse than having him as your pimp. It was not the sort of arrangement she intended ever to get involved in, but it might be difficult to be lodging next to a man who not only knew her business but also knew her darkest secret, and the thought made her shudder. Could she really start her work again? She had no choice, but at that moment, for Sarah, it was as if she was starting out on the streets for the first time, looking for that first client and hating everything about him, but smiling nonetheless, because you wanted his money.

Down below on the Strand, she caught sight of the solitary and filthy little girl who she sometimes saw wandering around Swansea, pushing a pram. She strained her neck to watch her walk down past the sawmill and on towards the station. The girl troubled her for some reason; more so than any of the others she saw every day. Perhaps it was because she was so easily identified by the pram she pushed around, a symbol of the sort of childhood that the girl herself had been denied. How could she prevent the descent of an apparently lost child like her into a desperate future that might match her own. Who was she? Where did she live?

Had she once met her with her pram, outside the collapsing Calvary pit? Sarah couldn't be sure it was the same child. This one seemed younger. But she couldn't be certain. It wasn't as if she was the only child living in terrible squalor and poverty in the town. And in their hunger and their neglect, they all looked the same. But she had certainly seen the pram before.

Sarah realised that she had started looking out for this particular girl in the evenings, wanting to make her warm, sometimes giving her something to eat. There were so many lost Swansea children, wandering the streets and she could not help them all. But there was something about the girl that moved her more than any of the others she saw and she didn't know why. Perhaps it was indeed the pram, both a toy and a symbol of childhood, or perhaps it was the fear that she might share Sarah's destiny, and no one should experience that. Life on the streets was fragile- too many children, cold and starved, were found floating in the docks. A young girl had been dragged out of the North Dock at Christmas. She always wondered whether they fell, or whether they jumped.

Sarah lost sight of the girl and turned away, a cold draught persuading her of the need to urgently buy some curtains from Nellie Damms in the market. She needed to turn this shabby place into a home, but she was not sure that she had the energy to do so. Constance's rooms on St Helen's Road seemed palatial in comparison.

*

Selina stood on the corner of Mariner Street, watching people going by, waiting for business. She was quite tall and broad-shouldered, with strong arms and hands like shovels. Her greasy hair, cut short, was a greying brown and her once-notable face had been coarsened by the choices she had made. In her eyes there was still the lingering light of intelligence but her refinement had long since disappeared, a small shred thrown away with each empty bottle. Today she was not particularly hopeful; late afternoon was never a good time. A train had recently come into the station, all steam and hiss, but the passengers had hurried away down High Street, and those who did not were residents, who ignored her. There was only the odd little urchin girl with the pram outside the station and she merely stood and stared. She wasn't begging. She was just watching. Perhaps if she earned something Selina would buy the girl some bread or something. Perhaps the little girl's life was worse than her own – and if that was the case what sort of future did she have? If Jack got hold of her then she had no doubt that he would make it worse. Selina shuddered at the thought. You could never be sure what Jack would do.

Bridget came to stand by her. She was shorter than Selina, stocky and aggressive, her blotchy gin-infused complexion best seen in a darkened alley. 'Quiet isn't, though. You know what I say. No business, no drinking.'

Selina sighed. 'What's wrong with the men in this town? Don't they see quality when it's right in front of them or something?'

'Men? Pah!' she said with contempt. Then she reached out and held Selina's arm. 'Wait a minute, Sel. Look. Might be in luck here.'

Walking towards them, past a fresh pile of fragrant horse manure at the end of Ivey Place, was a young man in uniform, a member of the Artillery Militia. He was certainly looking at the two women, but turned his eyes away, embarrassed when they waved, coyly they believed, in his direction.

Experience had taught them that this was the most important moment of all. If he crossed the road or turned around, then they knew that they were not to prosper. The soldier certainly paused and looked around him. Then he seemed to polish the buttons on his tunic and kept on walking. He was a little more portly than he would have liked and his breathlessness on parade was one reason why the other recruits regarded him as a figure of fun. His tunic was straining across his chest, and his feet squashed into boots that were too small, meant that his attempt to walk with imposing authority fell a little flat.

Selina hitched up her skirt very deliberately and smiled at him. He stopped and Bridget stepped out in front of him. 'Afternoon, General. My, my! What an impressive uniform. Very smart, don't you think so, Sel?'

'Makes you weak at the knees, that do.' She raised her skirt a little more and her eyebrows still further, surely her most provocative signal. 'You know what, Bridge? This could be the General's lucky day, don't you think?'

The young soldier tried to look brave, tried to exude authority. 'Not a General yet, you understand,' he said, pushing out his chest. 'No. Just a sergeant,' he lied. 'But I think one of you two could be in luck, too.'

'One of us?' asked Selina scornfully. 'Surely you can't choose between us two beauties? That's not possible.'

'Tell you what, Selina. That would be a shocking insult, wouldn't it? To leave one of us on the street, don't you think? All jealous and ignored.'

'Shocking, Bridget. Shocking. Anyone would think he couldn't handle the two of us.' Selina dropped her skirt. 'And him a soldier.'

'Wasting your time, Bridget. No powder in his pistol, this one.'

'Too right, Selina. Calls himself artillery? Carrying a damp popgun, I reckon.'

The man was confused, embarrassed, unable to keep up with the practiced dialogue of these two friends. 'Wait a moment, please.' He was embarrassed and knew that he was suddenly out of his depth. But he was also aware of the terrible effect this encounter might have on his reputation, should news of it spread. These women surely didn't know who he was, did they? But he couldn't be sure.

'You get off home and rub your buttons, little boy. Women like us need a real man.'

'I didn't say I couldn't. I wasn't expecting it to be the two of you…'

Bridget knew now that they had him. 'And so you are saying you are ready to make a choice, then? Can't say I am happy with that, Sel.'

'Nor me, Bridge. Best get home before the toy soldier upsets us some more. Don't know what he is doing. Ask him to take his pick and this one would choose a shovel.'

'Have a care, ladies. You will be pleased beyond measure,' he said, in what he hoped were his most impressive tones.

'Really?'

'Don't you doubt it.'

'Best come along then, soldier. Whilst you are still in the mood,' said Selina with a wink.

He followed them, carrying his bravado as if it would protect him from their practised attentions. But a small part of him realised that he was snared and that there could never be any protection.

He followed them into the dirty house that smelt of damp and rodents. He suddenly knew that he didn't want to be there at all. His narrow eyes sank even further into his head.

'What's your name, General?' asked Selina.

'George. George Thomas.' He looked around him, trying, and failing, to find some courage within himself. 'Who is going first then?'

'Let's see the colour of your money then shall we, Georgie boy?' said Bridget.

'How much do you want?'

'How much have you got?' she asked.

He knew he was following their lead when he should have been taking control, as a real man would. It was time for a bit of male dominance, he decided. 'Never you mind about that. You will be ready to pay me, just you wait.' He grinned weakly.

Bridget laughed. 'Well, well. Who would have thought it? Can't hardly wait.'

He started to undo his tunic, smirking. 'Where's the bed then?'

'We won't be needing one of those,' said Bridget, laying a rough hand on his shoulder.

He realised that he could only see one of the women. The one called Selina seemed to have disappeared. He looked at Bridget now that she was closer to him and realised that really she wasn't attractive at all. Her skin was blotchy and sore, and her teeth unpleasantly discoloured, snaking at unusual angles into her bottom lip. Involuntarily he stepped backwards and Salina jumped on him from behind, pinning back his arms. Laughing, Bridget came up to him, twisted his nose harshly, then with familiar ease, worked her way through his pockets, removing his purse.

'Get off me, you bitch!' he shouted, struggling, but unable to free himself.

Bridget's eyes narrowed and she put her hands around his throat and squeezed sharply. 'Now you bugger off home, laddie, afore we really do hurt you.'

Selina, with a strength that frightened him, threw George across the room and he fell to the floor, stunned by this sudden and vicious turn of events. She lifted him up, gave him an evil smile and then kissed him violently, giving his lip a sharp bite. She pinioned him again. He squealed loudly but could only watch as Bridget took a knife from the table and sliced off some of his tunic buttons. She put them in his pocket and then pulled his cap down as hard as she could so that it was jammed over his eyes. Selina let him go and, as he struggled to remove the cap, together they threw him out of the house and on to the street, slamming the door after him. They decided that they wouldn't tell Jack about that one and explored the disappointing contents of his purse.

A young boy watched George crash through the door, put down the wheelbarrow of ashes he was taking to dump at the junction with High Street, and shouted gleefully, 'A bonneting! A bonneting!'

A mocking crowd gathered, as if from nowhere. Such a joy, this unexpected music hall performance on their dismal street. This is what happened if you entered a world where you did not belong. George, humiliated, rolled on the mud, pulling at his cap to the general scorn. One of the women took pity on him and helped him with it. He did not thank her. Seething with rage, he pulled himself to his feet and walked away from their pointing and their hoots. He needed revenge but he knew he could not go to the constables, no matter how close he was to the police station – the shameful display of his humiliation in a court case he was unlikely to win, was something he could not contemplate. The rest of the Militia would never forget. But then, neither would he.

Amy had wandered over from the station to watch the entertainment. She loved seeing the man in smart clothes rolling around in the mud. Everyone was laughing and seemed happy and friendly. She wondered why he had put his cap on in such a silly way but perhaps he just enjoyed making people laugh. There was another man there though, who she did not like. He was staring at her all the time. She had never seen him before and when he started to move though the crowd towards her, she turned and kept running with her pram into the maze of streets on the other side of High Street until she was sure she was not being followed.

Four

Jack McCarthy was waiting in the back yard of the Ivorites Arms on High Street. He was cold, he had been there for some time and he was not a man known for his patience. Selina had said she would be there by midday and yet there was still no sight of her. He was a dark man, muscular and powerful, the thick black hair sprouting around the edge of his habitual dirty cap. He remained clean shaven so as not to distract from the impact of that hair. He had deep-set eyes which were almost always without warmth or compassion. He was noted for his cruelty and his aggression, though he had two acknowledged children who he loved, in his own way. Timothy and Iris lived with their mother on the Strand and he saw them occasionally. It always amused him that she did not know that legally she had never been his wife at all, for their relationship was in fact bigamous and no one realised that he was already someone else's husband when he had married Violet. Jack always enjoyed a secret.

Selina eventually appeared in the yard. 'Where have you been then? You said midday. You are late.'

She said nothing and handed him a small canvas bag, which he put down by his feet.

'She give you the money?'

Selina nodded but Jack was unimpressed. 'Well?' he asked. She handed over a small cloth bag, bunched at the top with rough string. Jack weighed it in his hands. 'If you know of any, I got some gypsies over in Killay looking to buy a child, they reckon. Haven't seen their money yet though. Would prefer a girl, they say. If you do hear anything let me know. You understand?' Selina nodded. 'You and Vinegar earn anything yesterday?' Selina shook her head. 'I didn't hear you, Milford. I'm waiting.'

'No nothing, Jack.'

'Not what I heard. A commotion on Mariner Street, they say. Militiaman bonneted. Then you and Vinegar drinking in the Bush.

That is what I am told.'

'Well, what you was told is wrong, Jack. That ain't my fault, is it?'

Jack stared at her, intimidating. 'Watch it, doll. You have been warned. You are watched. Got eyes everywhere. And next time, don't keep me waiting.' He reached over, twisted her cheek and winked. 'Got it?'

*

It was in the afternoon when the news spread around the town and so they started to gather at Mumbles Head, ready to receive a gift from the sea. Some brought carts and others brought wheelbarrows, though most would be happy to take away anything they could carry. They stood watching the boat drift towards the rocks, where the sea broke itself into white foam, willing each wave to drive it ever closer. The Mumbles Lifeboat could get no response to their calls to the boat and they had to consider that it had been abandoned. The crowd on the shore cursed the attempts of the lifeboat to put men on board to save it, and then cheered every time their efforts failed. It would only be a matter of time they thought, and the crowd that had gathered along the tide line celebrated every creak and crack as the doomed ketch came ever-closer.

It was a bright afternoon, now that the snow had blown away, which provided a very pleasant backdrop for this free entertainment. The turret of the whitewashed lighthouse perched high on the summit of the rocks, reflected the sunlight and, by doing so, disguised the very real dangers of the place. Fortunately, the boat was drifting in the open channel beyond, teasing the spectators by its refusal to pass into the swirling waters that separated the rocks from the mainland. No one knew what had happened to the *Ann of Bridgewater* but they all knew what its future held and their greatest hope was that the shore would soon be strewn with wreckage. Whatever it carried would be of some value, surely. The waves would also obligingly dismantle the ship for them and they could take the timbers away. Nothing would be wasted.

But the *Ann of Bridgewater* was quite low in the water and eventually a couple of men from the lifeboat scrambled aboard, and the crowd groaned, sensing the inevitable, disappointing, outcome. The boat was taking on water and so, sensibly avoiding the rocks beneath the lighthouse for which Bucke was particularly grateful, the emergency crew ran it aground on the beach, where the police would find it so much easier to guard until the customs men arrived. The boat set itself at an ungainly angle, well embedded in the sand but largely secure, and it was now easy to climb on and off. The crowd, rather as the ship had done, began to drift away in disappointment.

The Militia men who had arrived, noisily, full of unwarranted self-importance, imposed themselves on the deflating drama before them, offering irrelevant supervision to the spectators, on the basis that the police could not cope effectively. They were generally ignored, though there was a minor scuffle with a group of local youths who were unimpressed by both their uniform and their presence. Bucke looked at the Militia and sighed. Why? What did they think they were doing? Their captain ineffectually tried to usher them back towards Swansea, whilst they ignored him and shouted loudly at any women they could see. How would he have managed without them, he wondered? He thought he should turn his attention to more important matters and reviewed what he knew as he walked towards the beached boat, indicating that Doctor Benjamin should accompany him. They could not be sure what they might find.

The *Ann of Bridgewater* had sailed out of Llanelly in the middle of the night after unloading a cargo of lime and was then seen drifting steadily along the Gower coast all day yesterday, apparently abandoned. The Swansea police had received both a telegram from Llanelly about the ketch and then a message from the police station in Reynoldston in Gower, when a constable had been unable to raise a response from it.

Consequently, Inspector Flynn had deployed Constable Morris immediately to Mumbles to help the local constables ensure there would be no interference from wreckers. 'Nothing more than theft, is wrecking,' said Flynn firmly. 'Taking away the wealth of others who has worked hard to make it. Like stealing a man's life.' He looked at

Morris firmly. 'Do your job properly, that is all I am asking. You were a sailor once. Get down there and don't let none of the buggers who turn up steal anything, not a plank, nothing.'

Inspector Bucke had agreed to take Dr Benjamin with him, in case there was illness or injury on board, and he was there himself to supervise the operation, should it be necessary. The presence of an Inspector would allay any fears the residents of Mumbles might have of riotous behaviour and disorder migrating along the bay from Swansea; they already had enough disorder of their own.

It seemed unlikely that the boat had been stolen but what had happened to the crew no one had any idea. The small two-masted vessel had been monitored constantly from the shore as it progressed all the way along the Gower coastline and no one had seen a thing. It would normally have a crew of three but there was no sign of them – apart, of course, from the body behind the crate in the wheelhouse.

Once the tide had receded, Jenkin Jenkins, the Lifeboat coxswain, helped Dr Benjamin up the rope ladder on to the ketch. Bucke followed them. The hull was a dirty white, the teak decking stained and the brass fittings tarnished, but generally *Ann of Bridgewater* appeared to be in a seaworthy condition. The wheelhouse seemed to be weather-tight and there was a long crate upon which, Bucke assumed, the captain would normally sit. Today, however, there was a one-eyed ginger cat and behind the crate there was the body of a seaman, tightly curled on his side, with arms folded across his abdomen. He was dressed practically, in oilskins, and the pool of dark blood that had settled beneath his head would never penetrate such garments. The cat continued to stare at Bucke with barely concealed contempt. 'Where, in the name of all that is holy, have you been?' it seemed to ask. It jumped off the wooden chest to allow Dr Benjamin to lean over, look at the corpse and confirm that the man was dead.

'He didn't do this to himself, that is for sure. The back of his head has been smashed in – the brain is exposed. Such an unpleasant grey colour, don't you find? There are many dangerous things on a boat like this.' He gestured vaguely at the masts. 'Large and heavy moving pieces of wood. Anyone of those things could have done it – but not

39

knocked him through the door and down here. That's impossible. I would suggest that someone did it to him. It is obvious to me. One of his crew perhaps? I don't suppose it is for me to speculate, is it?'

Bucke shrugged. 'In these circumstances, it is inevitable that every one of us forms their own opinion. We can see how he died. By whom and why are the difficult questions. They pay me to find those things out. Do we know who it is?'

'Looks like someone I seen around, Inspector. But I don't rightly know his name. Might be the skipper,' said Jenkins. He shook his head. 'A right mess, that's for sure.'

'And there are no other bodies on the boat?' asked Doctor Benjamin.

'Not found none, doctor,' said Jenkin. 'If there was anyone else on here, well they ain't here now.'

'But there must have been someone else here, mustn't there? To have done this. The victim has not done this to himself.'

Bucke called up two of the constables to remove the body whilst he wandered around the uneven deck. The cat followed him soundlessly, waiting patiently whilst Bucke examined something, and then moved on with him. The ship was bare. They had not been carrying any cargo, it seemed, for the hold was empty. An empty vessel, except for a dead body. Where had the boat been going? Jenkins came to join him whilst Benjamin supervised the constables, clumsily manoeuvring the corpse down the rope ladder to take it back to Swansea in the police cart.

'Have you noticed, Inspector? No rowing boat. It has gone, isn't it? Should be stowed over there,' he said, pointing to the stern.

Bucke had not noticed, he had to admit. 'And would you ever leave port without it? For any reason, Jenkin?'

'No reason I would know of,' he replied. 'Very foolish thing to do. I reckon someone must have took it.'

'And rowed away,' nodded Bucke. He went over to the ropes

where the rowing boat had been secured. They had been untied, not cut, so it did not appear to have been released in haste. And then there, beneath the gunwale, he found a dirty cap. Unexceptional, made of canvas that might once had been blue. He picked it up, the cat looking at him with what Bucke believed was encouragement, urging him to consider seriously such obvious evidence. He turned it around and examined the inside. There was a label there, with writing in no language that he could recognise. He folded it up and put it into his pocket.

When he climbed over the gunwale to climb down the ladder, Bucke scanned the deck for the last time and found himself looking eye to eye with the cat. Why was he suddenly so concerned with this particular cat? Swansea was full of them. But Bucke felt that, somehow, he had been selected by the creature, as if it were an honour. There was nothing that he could do about it, for it seemed that his fate had been decided. The cat walked casually to Bucke and waited to be picked up, settled comfortably whilst the Inspector struggled down the ladder and then sat imperiously on the bench in the police wagon as it made its way along Oystermouth Road. Bucke knew that he had been adopted and hoped very much that the cat would feel the same about Constance.

Back at the police station, Doctor Benjamin put the corpse in the stables and showed anyone who had the courage to look the extent of the injury. The victim had been struck very hard indeed by something very heavy. There was no evidence on the boat itself of anything that might have been used to deliver such a blow. But as Bucke knew, it might have been thrown overboard immediately after use. Benjamin's enthusiasm to teach the constables the anatomy of the skull was ended prematurely. There had been an accident at a house in Cross Street and he was required urgently. He walked away briskly, with the intention of returning to complete his work with the dead tomorrow. The living were more important.

The victim was identified as Samuel Allen, captain and owner of the *Ann of Bridgewater*. The mate was Tom Foster but there was no sign of him anywhere. Had he done it? Had he murdered the captain?

41

He had to be a suspect, thought Bucke. As far as those who knew them were concerned, and the ship was a frequent visitor to Swansea, they appeared to be the best of friends. The message Bucke received suggested that nothing they had done last night in Llanelly had raised any concerns. The two of them had been seen drinking together and then had seemingly sailed off into the night with the tide and now one had disappeared and another had died. Had there been a crime? Was this kidnap? Theft? Piracy? Was it murder? Was it all of those things? Or none of them? It was very strange. But how could he ever find out what had happened on a small boat out at sea with no witnesses?

*

He sat in the Concert Hall public house on Wassail Street, a few doors down from the lodging house where he had moved in yesterday, taking a bed from a landlady who had shown little interest in just another sailor, other than his money. He was nursing a jug of ale, watching and thinking, as always. This was a poor place, he realised. He hadn't known what to expect. He had always imagined it as a sleepy little fishing village; he hadn't anticipated such obvious poverty in Swansea. There was a great deal to see here and it was certainly a vibrant place, though dirty and dark. And there was danger here too, and that suited him perfectly. But in a place of this size, finding the child was not going to be as easy as he had hoped. He'd seen a girl with a pram who could have been her, but he had lost her in streets that were unfamiliar to him. He scoffed, silently. The idea that he might bump into her by chance in the street, on his first day, was plainly ridiculous.

There were a lot of poor people in the town; he had seen them fighting, arguing and drinking. He had seen the sailors and the prostitutes and he knew that their presence would help him in in his work. There were so many of them around. Ordinary people always know things that the police do not. Why would it be different here to what it was at home? He had plenty of choices and all he required was patience. But there was something he had to do to set his mission properly in motion, otherwise why had he arrived in the town in the way that he had? At the moment no one knew he was here, and that was good. He knew that in a place like Swansea, it would prove so easy to disrupt the fragile sense of order, to create doubt and fear, to distract the police so that he could do his work. So now, it was time; the time for chaos – and for pleasure.

He had a plan and he knew it would work. He had prepared it in his mind for such a long time and now he was here, it should begin.

*

Constance finished her lessons early because she needed to see her solicitor, Mr Strick, a desiccated and angular man, humourless and morose but exceedingly efficient. He was cataloguing examples of her husband's abusive behaviour – his neglect, his violence and, of course, his desertion. Constance did not relish these conversations – this was not the first time that she had seen Mr Strick – for she had to uncover the experiences she preferred to keep hidden. Her past was far less important to her than her future, but complete happiness in the future depended upon her dispelling the ghosts of an unrelentingly grim marriage and so she was willing to confront them. However, today Mr Strick was elsewhere on business and so she had to speak to one of his assistants, Henry Fry. He seemed very intelligent, although ridiculously young, and Constance could see that he found talking to an attractive woman about the details of domestic abuse very difficult. The incident when her husband had scalded Constance by throwing boiling soup at her, left him wide-eyed and shocked. She offered to show him her scars and began to unbutton her sleeve, but he shook his head and looked away. Poor Henry Fry, thought Constance, you have a lot of awful things to learn.

But the meeting hadn't taken as long as she had anticipated. Mr Fry, a little uncomfortable, had rushed through some of the details but really, he hadn't been as difficult to talk to as the generally disapproving Mr Strick. She would have to go back, and she knew that if the divorce was to happen then it would, of necessity, require a huge investment of time, but she was prepared to do it for her sake and for Rumsey's. So, with the unexpected bonus of free time, Constance walked up the Ragged School on Back Street, to see if there was anything she could do to help.

The destitution in the town had started to disturb her and she knew, in truth, that it was Rumsey's fault. During her marriage she had never had any contact with those who lived in poverty in Swansea, and there were hundreds of them, living meagre lives of toil and sickness, in squalor. Listening to Rumsey speak about his experiences in the police force had opened her eyes, and then, when he had asked her to undertake some surveillance work for him at the Chapel of Our Lady of Mumbles, she had seen the poor for herself. She had been shocked and remained appalled that such a world existed so close to her own, and was embarrassed that she had never previously realised it was there. It was the children that worried her, always the children, living cold and malnourished lives, dying too soon, too easily. So why hadn't she been to The Ragged School before?

The school day was drawing to a close and she had to wait a few moments whilst the children spilled out on to Back Street and then a little longer, whilst a boy with a battered dirty crutch and one leg hopped easily down the steps. Inside she found light and the warming smell of soup from the kitchen. She could imagine what brought the children here on a cold day. There were still some children inside, inadequately dressed for the weather she felt, playing in small groups, reluctant to leave. She looked around and saw a tall thin man, well dressed, applying a stethoscope to a boy's back, his hands moving respectfully, his eyes full of gentle concern. By his side there was a girl sobbing, clutching his leg and burying her face in his trousers. She introduced herself and Doctor Benjamin smiled at her warily. He put his stethoscope back in his pocket.

'Bronchitis. One must fear the worst.' A woman came and gently prised the little girl away from him. 'We are in a sombre mood today. This is a terrible moment for us, Miss White. One of our younger children, Mary Jane Dowling, merely three years old, has died of burns in the hospital this afternoon.' He shook his head. 'Lived on Cross Street, not far away. Mother went to the privy, left her alone in the kitchen and when she came back Mary Jane's rag doll had caught fire and it seems that she tried to smother the flames by hugging it. The poor girl had burnt herself so badly on the chest and arms. When

44

they fetched me I knew it was too late. This is what happens, Miss White. Young children die every day on this side of the town.'

Constance shook her head. 'This is terrible, Doctor Benjamin. That such things should exist within a prosperous town....'

'Miss White. I am comforted when people of some substance are prepared to look beyond their own concerns and consider the terrible conditions that exist all around us. I have my own patients, many of whom contribute handsomely to my mission here, but there is never enough. We have done little in Swansea to suppress the stench of poverty.' He threw his arms around, indicating the school room. 'This school was founded almost forty years ago. The movement started in London, did you know that? In Swansea, it seems, you cannot choose to rescue your own poor children until someone else shows you how to do it.' He looked at her fiercely. 'Do you know why we are called the Ragged School, do you? Because the most destitute children were often turned away from Sunday School because of their 'ragged' clothes. Apparently you could only come to God if you were well-dressed and clean. No one thought to tell the disciples of Jesus that, evidently.' He snorted contemptuously. 'Typically, that was what it was about, religious instruction. Starve and freeze all you like in this life, because your next one should be better. To be frank Miss White, I regard that as arrant nonsense. Does that make me dangerous, do you think? You might be wretched and destitute, you might live amongst vice and misery, but at least you can receive religious and moral instruction? Sorry you have no shoes. Sorry you will die before your time. Do not concern yourself.' He shook his head, his mouth tight. 'I hope this does not shock you.'

Constance smiled. 'I thank you for being so frank. The poor people of this town need as many champions as they can get, Doctor. What is important is the help they receive. You cannot afford to be choosy, can you? It cannot be tainted by whatever views you might have yourself. You must accept help from whoever offers it, surely?"

'We survive entirely upon public subscription and charitable donations, Miss White. Generally given so that the donors can feel better about themselves. But we cannot afford to be choosy, as you say. Are you one of those people, Miss White? Here for the thrill of seeing starving children in rags? We are not an entertainment, but if that is what you are, you will not be the first.' He looked at her defiantly, appraising her.

'I can give you only a little money, Doctor Benjamin.'

'I cannot afford to say no to any donation, no matter how small.'

'But what I would like to do is to offer you my time, on those occasions when I do not have pupils. Like your obligations to your patients, I think.'

'And what can you do? Read Bible stories? Tell them their lives will be better when they are dead?'

'I shall play the piano,' she said, keeping her temper. 'And the children can sing. Something different in their lives, perhaps.'

'And what will that be? Improving hymns?' he said scornfully.

'Doctor Benjamin. I would be grateful if you would not make assumptions about me. I am not here to be insulted or patronised by you. I am here because I wish to help the children. I was thinking of nursery rhymes or children's songs. Something they might enjoy. Something denied them, that other children take for granted.'

Benjamin studied her closely. 'That might work, for some of the younger children certainly. Please, Miss White. I am sorry to appear so cautious, but I will not have the children displayed as an entertainment for the guilty rich. For the most part, I feed the children, before I do anything else. They come here for warmth and food and to offer them God instead seems to be an insult, for he has ignored them so far, has he not? Though it would be so much easier if we could find another cook, now that Mrs Challis is leaving.' He smiled at her; it was the first time Constance thought that he looked honest and genuine; the first time his rage seemed to have relented. 'I shall look forward to your return, Miss White. Our piano isn't the best, but I am sure it will suffice.'

'Rather like my own,' she replied, attempting to diffuse the tension between them.

'You must excuse me, Miss White. I have a meeting with my medical supplier, Mr Morley, and there is to be a temperance meeting here this evening so I must empty the school of children. They must not be seen, lest they disturb our visitors. Even our two generals over there, absorbed in their manoeuvres, who are always so reluctant to leave.' He gestured at the last two remaining boys who were playing happily with a small handful of battered lead soldiers. 'Come, Andrew, Francis. Time to go home.'

Disappointed, they packed away the toys in a wooden box, reluctant to leave behind the warmth and the light and instead walk home in the cold up to Evans Terrace. But the Doctor ushered them out of the building, and Constance followed them on to Back Street and stood for a moment outside the brewery to watch the boys scamper away, still playing soldiers, shooting and shouting, bouncing off the walls, climbing up to look over fences. At least those two had shoes, though whether they matched as a pair was not clear, but so many of the other children had none. She turned away and walked home quickly, suspecting that Rumsey after an afternoon in Mumbles might be hungry and chilled. The streets were quiet and there was still sufficient daylight to remove any threats in the shadows and she made her way home purposefully through the busy town, leaving behind a disturbing world of which she knew little and returning to familiar comforts. But those comforts seemed this evening to be edged with the shadow of insecurities, seemed to be a little more fragile.

Five

It was when she realised that she was hiding from prospective clients that Sarah knew something was wrong. She had been standing at the corner of Tower Lane and High Street, near the Jones brewery, the sickening smell of yeast blooming, it seemed, from the frost that formed on the walls around her. Her work relied upon her being noticed and yet tonight she was fearful that anyone should see her, backing deeper into the doorway whenever she heard footsteps.

A man had spoken to her from the door of Glover's Oil and Grease Works; he had called her 'Sarah.' She must have known him but she didn't want to look, so she had sworn at him, the words venomous, hissed like a viper. He had walked away, leaving her to her tears. There had been plenty of tears tonight, the sort that she could not control, the ones that flowed ceaselessly down her cheeks. It was a very long time since she had cried, but now she didn't know how to stop.

Sarah realised that she could not go on, not with this vile occupation. 'But what am I to do? How else can I live?' She realised that she had spoken aloud, which was not a clever thing to do if you didn't want anyone to notice you. But hers was a lonely life. When she had stayed with Constance she had enjoyed the human contact, the presence of someone else. It was harder to bear the solitude now that the companionship had slipped away, as they returned to separate lives.

She could no longer allow herself to be pressed against a wall by drunken sailors. How could she have ever allowed men like that to come anywhere near her? What had she been thinking? 'But I was desperate... Oh shut up Sarah!' she said quietly, admonishing herself. She should never have kissed Bucke in the pit. It had been a mistake. Constance was her friend, someone who made no judgements of her. And yet she had kissed the man her friend loved and tasted all that he represented, of the life she could never have, and now her world could never be the same again.

She had come out into the clear frosty night beneath the shining full moon with every intention of working, but she knew that she could do this dreadful thing no longer. So what was the point of standing here in the darkness if she had no intention of working? She should go home. But she didn't want to move – there was a man on the other side of High Street who seemed to be watching her closely and her instincts, well-honed after years on the street, made her wary. She could not make out any details of him, for the light was so very poor here, but he hadn't moved for a while. Were there any other women around? She couldn't be sure. But he hadn't approached her; he just watched. She didn't think he was shy, waiting there whilst he tried to gather his courage. It could be that he was waiting for someone. But his presence unsettled her. There was something about the way he was standing, with his head slightly tilted to one side, which seemed to suggest he was studying her. She was sure he wasn't wearing a hat, which was unusual on a night as cold as this one. Who was he? Somebody? Nobody?

She could walk the other way, down Tower Lane and on to Back Street. But that would mean that he was behind her, and she didn't think she liked that idea. But did she want to walk towards him? On the street you always had to be extra careful. It was the only way to survive. She would wait a bit longer, see if he moved.

Sarah had her savings, of course, the ones that Constance was keeping for her, to fund her passage to a new life a long way away. She might have to spend it now, if she could not work on the streets any more. But how long would that money last? After all that time, after all the work through which it had been slowly accumulated, to suddenly to throw it all away when so very close to her escape, seemed stupid. And if she spent it, then what? Sarah was momentarily paralysed by a sense of desperation. No answers. No plan. Just an overwhelming need to stop. Now.

He was still watching. Waiting? And Tower Lane was dark and it was cold and the stars, though shining, were not looking at her. What to do? It wasn't far to Back Street. There might be more people around there. She would go. No hesitation. Just walk briskly and listen out for his footsteps. Done it before. Easy. There was nothing on these streets that she had not confronted previously. She took a deep breath and then launched herself from the shadows and walked briskly down the middle of the lane. Don't turn. Don't look back. Nearly there.

Suddenly her head shook and the world in front of her seemed to slip to one side and she stumbled against the wall. She knew immediately that she had been hit, though she felt little pain, rather a complete dislocation from reality. She found herself sitting on the floor and there was a man standing next to her, looking down. All this happened so very quickly, Her ear was burning where he had hit her. She knew then that she was about to die. She had felt this before in the mine, but here she was alone and vulnerable. The man wasn't going to leave her now. He started to lean over her; he made a guttural noise, a little like a growl; the moon cast the shadow of something in his hand on to the stones on which she sat.

There was a sudden clatter and the man seemed to stagger. He might have lost his balance, but he turned and snarled some threat Sarah couldn't hear. Then a small voice shouted, 'It's the police! They are coming!' and then he disappeared from her view. He must have walked behind her, Sarah thought, as she waited for the next blow. Nothing happened. And then there was someone tugging at her shoulder. She shook her head, trying to clear it.

'Don't cry,' said a small voice. 'The bad man has gone. I have some pie here. You can have some.' It was the small dirty girl who pushed the pram around Swansea. She put her hand into the pram, brushing aside the cat and, pulling out a morsel, offered it to her. 'You can have it. I am not hungry. Not that much.' When Sarah shook her head, the girl put it back into the pram. 'You can have it later.'

Sarah smiled at her. 'Thank you.'

'You've been crying. Your face is wet. You must not worry. The man has run away. I hit him with my pram. I can look after you. Me and Cat can do that.' The child nodded, as if it was decided. 'Me and Cat have been looking for you. And Dolly.'

Sarah rubbed her head. 'Why?'

'You gave me a pie before, the other night. Not this one, but another one. I remember.'

'I remember too. What is your name?'

'Amy. You are the lady with the ribbons.

Sarah smiled. 'You must call me Sarah.'

Amy paused. 'I think that is a nice name. Can I be your friend, Sarah? I will be a very good friend, I promise.'

'You already have been a good friend, Amy. You have rescued me. I would be very pleased to be your friend, as long as your mother does not mind.'

'I have no mother,' said Amy, blankly.

'I am sorry to hear that. Where do you live, Amy?'

'I live with Auntie.'

Sarah shook her head again and rubbed her eyes, trying to gather her thoughts. She had known that man was dangerous. Whatever his anger was, had he fully expressed it? Or had there been more to come that Amy had prevented? She had been hit before – an inevitable part of the path she had chosen – but never before quite like that. He hadn't finished, she was sure, and Amy had saved her. 'Where did that man go, Amy?'

'He was not a nice man, Sarah. He hit you and you had not done anything to him.'

'And which way did he go, Amy?'

'Down that way towards the High Street. He ran fast because he knew he had been wicked. He didn't like it when I hit him with my pram.'

Sarah stood up and leaned against the greasy wall. Her ears were still ringing, though she felt less dizzy.

'Where do you live, Sarah?' asked Amy. 'I can take you home.'

Sarah smiled at the puzzling little girl. Her clothes were rags, little more than shreds, but her eyes were bright. 'I now live on Elephant Street.'

'Are there any? I have never seen one.' She shook her head, sadly. 'I will take you home.' she said firmly. 'I want you to be safe.'

'You are very kind.' Sarah could not help smiling. 'How old are you, Amy?'

The girl shrugged her shoulders. 'I don't know. No one has told me.'

'Well, Amy. I think I should be taking you home. As you can see, the streets are not always a safe place. Where do you live?'

Amy looked at her carefully, unsure of how much to say. She made a decision. 'I live with Auntie.' She paused. 'Near the copper, that's where I live.'

Sarah hoped it was this side of the river, not the other. It was a long way to a bridge. 'Are these the only clothes you have? You must be cold.' Amy said nothing. 'Why did Auntie let you come down here tonight when it is so cold?' Sarah took off her shawl and wrapped her in it. Amy, wide eyed, drew it around her and absorbed the warmth.

'I came to get a pie. And the lady gave me one. You can have a piece.' Together they walked to the end of Tower Lane. 'I wanted to see your ribbons, too.'

Sarah was troubled by this frail, neglected little girl – a lost child, a Swansea child. She could not imagine what her home was like. She smiled at her and pulled a ribbon from her hat. She wasn't going to need them again. Sarah tied it to the handle of the pram whilst Amy looked on, wide eyed. She touched it, running it through her fingers.

'Can I keep it?'

'Of course you can. I have no more need of it.'

'I knew you were kind – it is good to be kind.'

'Will Auntie mind?'

'No. Auntie won't mind. Is it far to your house, Sarah?'

'It isn't far but it isn't a house. It is just a room, Amy.' Sarah paused. 'Would you like to see my room? I could like a fire.'

Amy was very tempted. She was very lonely and living on her own was so very difficult. But Auntie might be back, and she had to take Cat home. She wasn't sure what to do. They walked past Regent's Court where there was a loud crowd watching a domestic fracas and then along Ebenezer Street.

'You must come to my room, Amy. We need to warm you before you go home.'

Amy did not reply but kept walking resolutely until they arrived on Elephant Street, They stood outside the burial ground of Bethesda Chapel. A cold breeze suddenly disturbed her hair. She looked up at Sarah. 'Do you think they buried the elephant here?' she asked.

'It would be a good place, wouldn't it? Are you coming inside with me, Amy? I would like that.'

'No. Auntie wants me to be home. And Cat too. I said I would bring you home.' She nodded. 'I will come tomorrow to see that you are not hurt.' She turned and strode away.

'No, Amy. Don't go. Wait!' But she disappeared into the darkness.

*

For the rest of her life, Eunice Grimshaw blamed herself for Lizzie's death. No matter where she was, every day that she woke, Lizzie was there, smiling at her. She didn't seem to be blaming her, one bit. But that did not matter, for Eunice blamed herself. She knew that she was responsible for her sister's death and from that guilt there could never be any escape. It had happened suddenly, so unexpectedly, and now it would haunt her forever. Just a harmless bit of fun, just a drink with a couple of soldiers, that's all it was. But how could she have known?

'Come on, Lizzie! It will be a laugh. He has promised to bring his pal – he is a militiaman too. They are both militiamen. I bet he is real nice.'

'But I don't know him, do I? I have never seen him. He might look like an *asyn mochyn* for all I know. You haven't seen him neither.'

' Don't be dull. They don't have ugly ones in the militia,' said Eunice. Lizzie snorted. 'Lizzie, it will be a laugh. A drink in the Seabeach, that is what he said, that's all.'

'And more, if I knows a militiaman.' Lizzie folded her arms, looking stubborn.

'Well, you can always come home. It is not far, is it?'

'How long as you known him, anyways?'

Eunice looked coy. 'This afternoon. I was talking to him on Little Madoc Street when I was coming back after doing Mrs Reynold's laundry.'

'This afternoon! That long? And you want me to come along just so that you an' him can clear off to the sand dunes?'

'It is not like that at all. He is a very proper gent. Do it, Lizzie. Please. He is real nice. He is called John Elias and he comes from somewhere up the valley. Speaks Welsh and English. Very educated. He reckons his pal is even better looking than what his is, honestly. Please, Lizzie, for me. For your big sister.'

The evening was not a great success at all. Eunice and John seemed very -what was that word? - enthusiastic, thought Lizzie, though her sister was often impulsive and not always quite as discerning as she should be. Richard Walters, her own companion for the evening, was rough and coarse in appearance, manner and language. He was short and powerful and his narrow eyes hinted at aggression, the vile stink of his pipe hanging over them like a pig's caul. Within five minutes she was already unpeeling his wandering hands and squirming away from his hasty, lascivious embrace. What sort of girl had he been hoping for? And she felt alone too, for Eunice and John slipped further and further behind as they walked to the Seabeach Hotel.

Walters ordered two quarts of beer and brought them to their rickety table, where Lizzie edged away from him and he pursued her clumsily. She drank the beer, warily looking around, ensuring that she could get out of the bar as soon as was polite. But things changed quickly. There was muttering and significant looks and suddenly John and Eunice stood up and announced, rather too casually, that they were just going for a walk. Lizzie scowled at her sister. It was not what she wanted to hear. Walters grinned at her and winked, moving his stool still closer. Alone with Richard Walters was not a place she wanted to be. She watched Eunice leave and sighed. After another ten minutes of aimless and disjointed conversation and the chancing hands of an unsophisticated militiaman, she decided that enough was enough. She stood up. 'Well, it has been very nice meeting you, Richard, but I am afraid I have to go home. My mother is unwell and I must tend to her,' she lied.

'A bit early, isn't it? I mean to say, I bought you beer. I don't expect you buggering off home so soon, like, do I? I got a right to expect a bit of entertainment, now don't I?'

Lizzie turned and walked towards the door. 'I am not at all sure I want to understand what you are saying, Richard. Thank you for my drink.' She walked a little more quickly as she went through the door and on to the street. Her sister was nowhere in sight, so she started her walk home. Then the door of the hotel was thrown open loudly. She didn't turn round.

'Oi! Where do you think you are going? Get back by 'ere.' She ignored him. ''Lizzie!' he shouted. Then he ran after her and grabbed her by the arm, pulling her back.

'Let me go! You are hurting me!'

'You owe me! I bought you a drink? And then you walk away?'

' Leave me alone, Richard Walters!' she said loudly, in the hope that someone might hear his name. 'Your attentions are unwelcome!'

He hit her, punching her in the shoulder and knocking her head back against the wall. 'Bugger off home, if that is what you want. Who cares? You are an ugly bitch anyway.'

Lizzie held her head as Walters walked away purposefully, back to the Seabeach, and then she walked on a little further, determined to get as far away from him as possible. Her eyes were watering though, and by the time she reached the corner of Argyle Street she had to stop beneath a gas lamp and catch her breath. She had banged her head but she would be fine; it was just a rotten way to end a rotten evening. Bloody sister. She would definitely get it in the morning.

*

The man was in the shadows, breathless. He had run some distance through Swansea, blindly, and he found himself at the bottom of Argyle Street near the Royal Arsenal and now he was bent over, his hands on his knees, panting. He was angry with himself, angry with his lack of resolve. He felt so foolish, it was as if someone was laughing at him and he hated that more than anything else. Why had he let a bony child in rags, with a doll's pram, frighten him away? Why?

He started shaking with frustration and rage at his failure. He should have just swiped her with his cosh and then got on with the job. But he had panicked. His took the cosh from his pocket again for the pleasure of running his hands around it. It was a small billy-club, like the kind a policeman might have. It was covered in leather, it had been skilfully stitched and it was hard and smooth. He loved to touch it, he loved the feel of it. He closed his hand around it and tried to gather himself. It had all seemed so easy when he was standing in that doorway on High Street, watching her, and then he had hit the filthy whore once and it had been good. But he had lost his nerve. Now he wanted to do it again but he needed more resolve. Nothing else would satisfy him now. The idea had consumed him for such a long time and now he had tried – and failed- there was no going back.

It was dark here, with salt and seaweed on the breeze. It was as if he was at sea. And then he saw her. A solitary woman, picked out by a streetlamp. A woman alone? It was a sign; she had been identified for him. Now he knew his duty. He heard muttering and was momentarily alarmed. Then he realised it was himself. 'The bitch, the bitch, the bitch…'

Eunice and John came along past the Seabeach Hotel arm in arm. He had agreed to walk her home. 'After all,' he had said, adopting the role of the chivalrous lover, 'you never know what ruffians might be hanging around in this part of town.' Eunice had squeezed his arm in return. It was very pleasant to be here with him, in the moonlight.

As they walked slowly towards Argyle Street, trying to make the evening last that little bit longer, Eunice saw a figure sitting against the wall beneath the flickering gas lamp. When she realised it was Lizzie, she ran towards her.

Lizzie was dazed and she had suddenly acquired two black eyes. There was blood flowing steadily from her nose, and Eunice started to wipe her face with her cardigan. 'My poor, poor Lizzie.'

'Oh my God. What has he done?' Is she alright, Eunice?' asked John frantically.

Eunice helped Lizzie to her feet. Even in the uncertain light of the gas lamp she could see that there was a mark across her nose. Eunice examined the rest of her sister's head - there was a large lump on the back.

'Stupid-born bugger,' said John, shaking his head. He did not seem to know what to do.

'I'll get her home. You see if you can find 'im,'said Eunice firmly and then nodded for emphasis since he did not seem to understand. He looked around and then ran back the way they had come.

'My head hurts, Eunice. But really, I am fine. Honestly. Don't tell Mam, will you?'

'Was it Richard who did this, Lizzie?'

'I am not rightly sure, Eunice. It was dark.'

'And he didn't interfere with you, did he?' asked Eunice as they walked slowly down Rodney Street.

'No, he didn't. I didn't let him. That was the problem.'

When they walked through the badly-fitting front door Mrs Grimshaw was waiting for the two girls. She looked at Lizzie. 'Who was it? Who walloped you?' She did not pause for an answer.' Eunice, this is your fault! Taking your sister out and bringing her back like this! Get to bed, the pair of you!'

'It wasn't nothing to do with me, Mam. She's been hit by a militiaman!'

'Why? What have you two been doing? Get out my sight, the pair of you!'

In the early hours of the following morning, after a series of alarming convulsions, Lizzie Grimshaw died before they could persuade the doctor to attend to her.

Six

The parents of the two boys from the Ragged School were standing outside the police station. Francis Dolphin and Andrew Mazey had not come home last night and they had now been reported missing. It had already been a long and worrying morning without any news of them. Naturally, the boys were going to be in serious trouble when they eventually found their way home, and forceful punishment was being planned with such concentration that the parents had to be persuaded to step aside to allow other visitors access to the front door.

Constance had brought Sarah to the police station as soon as she could, insisting to Sergeant Ball that Inspector Bucke must know immediately about an attempted murder. Ball knew that Constance White was a force to be reckoned with and not always patient either. But he also knew that she would not come to Tontine Street unless she had very good reason. He was, though, surprised to see her in the company of Sarah Rigby. They certainly came from opposite sides of Swansea's social divide. He nodded to her, though since he had no idea what was going on, he did not make any of his usual flippant comments. 'I shall check that Inspector Bucke is available. Busy morning here, Miss White. Don't rightly know when we'll get our dinner. Murder last night, see.' He shook his head. 'Hell to pay. Soldiers, they say.'

'How awful,' said Constance. 'I had not heard.'

'Inspector Flynn is dealing with it. Might be tricky.'

Rumsey Bucke, of course was delighted, though perplexed, to see them together. Constance was at home in the office, relaxed and confident. Sarah less so, for her own experience of police stations did not involve comfort and security, rather trouble and arrest.

'Rumsey. You have to listen to this very carefully. Sarah did not want to come to see you but I made her. We came straight here as soon as the Burton child had finished her lesson. Sarah was attacked last night!'

'I see. I am very sorry to hear that. And how are you feeling today?' he asked.

'I am well thank you, Inspector. Angry, of course, and my ear is still sore. But I am otherwise uninjured.'

Bucke listened very carefully to what Sarah said, never doubting that it had happened, which she found comforting, since in her experience policemen did not take women like her seriously. He made notes and prompted her gently with questions – What time was this? Did he use his fist? What did he hit you with? Did he say anything? And there was nothing about him that you might be able to identify? Then he paused and leaned back in his chair. He looked at Constance and very slightly raised his eyebrows. 'Please excuse me, Sarah. This is a question of some delicacy, I understand that, but I have to ask it. Might it have been a client of yours, do you think? Someone from early in the evening, returning – for whatever reason?'

Sarah shook her head. 'I was untroubled last night, Inspector Bucke, until that moment. Half past nine it was, as far as I can tell. A few minutes earlier? I don't have a pocket watch.'

'So an unprovoked attack, as far as you are concerned.' He scratched his beard. 'Thank you for telling me, Sarah. It is important that I know about this. It would be sensible to warn your colleagues, in case we have someone with a grudge of some sort walking our streets. Naturally I shall instruct the constables.'

Sarah nodded and Constance waited for her to speak. When she did not, she decided to take the initiative. 'I think Sarah has something she ought to say to you, Rumsey. Isn't that so?'

Sarah closed her eyes and shook her head briefly. 'I have decided to abandon my disgusting career. I cannot face it anymore. The very thought of it turns my stomach. Once, I could tolerate it, but no longer. That is why I went to see Constance this morning, to talk to her about that, not about the man in Tower Lane. That has always been an occupational hazard in my dirty life.' Constance started to speak but Sarah held up her hand to stop her. 'Of course, Constance, typically, offered me space in her rooms but I cannot move in with

Constance nor do I want to.' Rumsey and Constance exchanged a glance but said nothing. 'I have some savings, as you both know. What I shall do when they are gone, I cannot say. But last night I was saved, by that small girl with a pram who we have all seen around town. She appeared by my side and the man fled. Why? I still do not know. She is called Amy and I know nothing about her and yet she came and saved me. She has less than nothing and yet she offered me comfort and food and made sure I arrived home safely.' She sighed deeply. 'How can I continue to throw my life away? My life has to better than it has been so far.' She closed her eyes and lowered her head.

'Sarah hasn't told you everything though,' said Constance, leaning over and placing a gentle hand on her arm. 'I think we may have found a job for her, in The Ragged School. We are going there now. They are looking for a cook.'

Rumsey took them to the front door, discreetly squeezing Constance's hand, as he held it open for them. 'A new start, Sarah. I hope most sincerely that it is a successful one for you.'

Sarah paused on the step and held his gaze just a little bit more than she should. 'As I do myself, Inspector. It is merely a possibility I have been presented with, but without it I do not know what I would do. Except perhaps descend into a drinker's death. But now of course, I must also look for Amy.' That quiet moment of reflection was broken by a disorderly commotion as Constable Payne dragged into the police station a young boy, barefoot and in rags, who struggled and fought every inch of the way. The two women stood aside and Inspector Bucke followed the wrestling pair inside and closed the door firmly.

Payne, slow of thought and quick of temper, threw the boy against the counter where, without a word, Sergeant Ball handed him a key. 'I'll lock him up for a while, Sergeant, and give him a chance to calm down. Our Lyndon, been nicking again. And I will tell you something for free, young man. That's enough of the language or you'll be crying.' He pulled the cursing boy, all flailing arms and kicking legs, through the door that led to the cells.

'One of our regulars, is it?' asked Bucke.

'Lyndon Griffin. Can't stop stealing. He'll take anything, though usually it is just food he's after. Don't know why Norman is so excited today. Lyndon must have said something. Tell you what. Inspector Flynn wants to have a word about that girl who has died. When you have finished, could you have a word with Lyndon? Put the fear of God into him or something? We have just about tried everything else, over the years.'

'I can try, Stanley, but I can't guarantee any more success than anyone else. James wants to see me, does he?'

'Yes. He is in his office with Bonfire Morris. He was the constable who was called when the poor lassie died this morning.'

'Stanley. Don't use his nickname. You know he doesn't like it.'

'Not here, is he. Here, read this before you go in. Doctor's report.'

Bucke leant against the counter and skimmed through the postmortem. There had been a massive haemorrhage, a clot in the interior fossae of the cranium, a fissure fracture of the skull. Probably the violent blow to the face had thrown her head back against the wall. She must have seen who hit her if she was thrown backwards, he thought. He knocked on the door and went into Flynn's office. He was a good friend, tall, clean shaven and always sensible and unflustered.

'Just going through a few things with Iago here. He knows the area. Knows the family. And as we know, there's a lot of unhappiness about the militia across the town, but especially down near the barracks. Carry on, Iago.'

Constable Morris nodded at Bucke and then continued. 'Lizzie Grimshaw was not a prostitute as far as I know, though they reckon her sister Eunice dabbles now and again. Goes to see Lambrick the Grocer and they say it is not just to do his laundry.' He consulted his notebook. 'Lizzie worked as a domestic for Sergeant Major McConnockie for a while, but the mother says that she had moved on to charring. Last night she went out with her sister to meet a couple of soldiers. They took them to the Seabeach Hotel. They weren't in uniform – well, likely to get better service that way. I took Eunice down to the barracks this afternoon and she picked two of the parade when they lined them up. No hesitation. John Elias and Richard Walters. Since Elias was with Eunice then it all points at Walters don't it? Not only that, but when I was bringing them in they was talking in Welsh. They didn't know I was Welsh too, did they?' He smiled a smile of triumph. 'Elias said *Ni ddylech fod wedi cyffwrdd â hi, rydych chi'n anghyfreithlon* and then Walters said *Ni fyddai'n dod â mi a beth bynnag rwy'n ei gwthio. Doeddwn i ddim yn taro hi.'*

'Good work, Iago,' said Bucke. 'But what does it mean?'

Morris shook his head. '*You should not have touched her, you idiot.* That is what Elias said. And then Walters replied, *She would not come with me and anyway I pushed her. I didn't hit her.* So he admits pushing her. Just not where she was found. Says he pushed outside the Seabeach. Fact remains someone gave her a right thump. Walters was there and he admits laying a hand on her. He done it, without a doubt.'

'And what time would this be?' asked Bucke. Flynn noticed that he was looking very thoughtful

'They all agree on that. They reckon it was about ten o'clock.'

'You see, the time is interesting. It complicates matters quite a bit. It might be that Walters is telling the truth. Perhaps he did push her outside the hotel. We can't say, but I will tell you what I know.' He reported Sarah Rigby's statement, and the assault that was carried out on her at the top of High Street at around nine thirty. 'Let's be clear. Walters could not have attacked Sarah Rigby. He was in company. Presumably we can place him in the area of the Seabeach Hotel at that time, Iago?' Morris nodded. 'So therefore we have either two separate individuals, attacking women in the same way on the same evening in Swansea, hitting them round the head. Or we have one. And that one can't be Walters. But it could be Sarah's assailant. He could have got down to Argyle Street in time.'

'Bloody hell, Rumsey. It is not what I want to hear,' said Flynn. 'I thought we had it all sorted.'

'But Walters does admit getting hold of her. He says he pushed her. But what if he is lying?' asked Morris. 'What if he hit her and slammed her into the wall? Then she staggered on a bit before she fell over. There might be two of the bastards in town. We don't know there are not,' Morris said emphatically.

'I agree, but Lizzie Grimshaw didn't say it was him,' added Flynn. 'You would have thought she would have.'

'She did say it was a militiaman, according to the mother,' added Morris, anxious not to lose his arrest.

'All I am saying, Iago, is that we should not close the case. That's all. We keep on looking.'

'I agree,' said Flynn. 'But we can still keep the bugger locked up until he goes up before the magistrates. Let them decide.'

'I need to speak to that little girl who wanders the street with a pram. She might have seen something,' said Bucke thoughtfully.

'Good luck with that. No idea where she is from. Foxhole someone said. But I will keep an eye out for you,' offered Constable Morris.

By the time they had got Lyndon Griffin out of the cell he seemed to have calmed down a little. He was no longer throwing his limbs around in a chaotic way, though he was still sullen and morose. His feet were black like shoes, his shirt threadbare and tethered to his thin frame by an inadequate waistcoat. There was a deep red and expanding stain of blood oozing through from his trouser pocket. Norman Payne stood by his side, ready to intervene, but it was highly unlikely that the boy would have the strength to do harm to anyone, other than himself.

Bucke looked at him; it seemed impossible to imagine a more poignant example of poverty than this. How old was he? He could not begin to speculate. Any age between nine and sixteen he thought. He looked at the blood stain, still expanding. 'Are you injured in some way, Lyndon? Do I need to summon the doctor?'

Constable Payne snorted. 'There is nothing wrong with him,

Inspector. Thieving little urchin.'

'Lyndon, are you in pain?'

'There is nothing wrong with him, Inspector. Lyndon, empty your pockets for the Inspector. Go on. Don't be shy. Show the Inspector what you have been doing. Caught the little bugger in the street round the back of the abattoir. Always hanging round there.'

'I ain't done nothing. I found them, that's all.' He continued to stare at the floor, much to Bucke's continuing concern. 'I didn't go into no abbey tywer. On my mother's life, I didn't.'

'What did you find, Lyndon?' asked Bucke.

'For Christ's sake, show the Inspector what you have been nicking afore I lose my temper, Griffin.'

'Please, Constable Payne. There is no need.' Bucke looked at him with disapproval; his aggression was unnecessary and was a serious impediment to helping this poor, wafer-thin child. There was suddenly a very wet sound, a unpleasant, slithering sloppy sound, and Bucke looked back at his desk. There on the corner there was a bloody mass of something. Lyndon sighed and pulled out some more from his pocket and added it to the pile. Bucke leaned forward, concerned, and prodded it with his pencil. It smelt of blood. He looked at Payne.

'See. Told you the little bugger has been nicking again.'

Liver, that was what it was. Liver. Bucke was not sure that he wanted it on his desk but Lyndon inserted his bloodied hand once again into his obviously large pocket and withdrew some more offal. This time he placed kidneys on the desk. They were unmistakably kidneys, last night's supper with Constance. Now Bucke understood the abattoir reference. Then he produced a heart that had been mauled by someone or something.

'He is always in trouble at the abattoir. Always loitering, always looking for scraps. Always chasing him off.' Payne gestured at the pile of organs on the desk. 'As soon as the butcher's back is turned. Had a sheep's head the other week. Tried to hide that under his shirt. This lot here?' He came closer to the desk. 'Pig that is, like as not. They has been sticking pigs and he has been pilfering.'

'I hasn't been stealing nothing. I found this lot. Honest I did. Didn't go in no abbey twyer. By a shed round the back I found them.'

'Little liar…'

There was a commotion outside, raised voices and suddenly the door of the office burst open.

'Some of the boys said he had been taken! I came as soon as I could. How dare you arrest this poor unfortunate! Release him immediately! I demand it!' It was Doctor Benjamin. 'It is help he needs. Not punishment!'

'He has been nicking, Doctor,' sighed Payne. 'Bits of pig.'

'Please, Constable,' said Bucke gently, trying to calm the situation.

'He does not steal! He takes food, that is all. He needs to live. He has a poor elderly mother to feed. What else is he to do? What else would you do, I ask you?' He went to the corner of the desk to point at the offal dramatically. 'And look at the scraps the poor boy relies upon.' Then he paused and bent down to examine them more closely. He looked up at Bucke and then withdrew a battered silver tongue depressor from his pocket and began to poke the pieces around, separating them. He turned to look at Lyndon. 'And where did you get these scraps from, Lyndon Griffin? Tell me the truth, mind.'

'Like I told the copper 'ere, round the back of the abbey twyer. Outside a shed. There was a pile of them. Dog must have 'ad 'em.'

'And you can show us where this is, Lyndon?'

'Surely I can.'

Doctor Benjamin nodded. 'Good boy, Lyndon.' He turned to Bucke. 'You see, you have a problem Inspector. These are not from a pig. They are human.'

*

Lyndon had taken them to the other side of the road from the

66

abattoir and through a broken piece of fencing into the premises of the Swansea Pottery. There were dogs outside a shed, fighting over bloodied fragments, so it was very easy to identify the place, though it took a while for the Constables to drive the hungry animals away with their batons. The ground was bloody, a chaos of organs and membrane. 'That is where I got them pig bits from. Dogs had had them but I chased them away with that shovel, there. I reckoned I could have washed them proper. That's 'ow I knew sommink was up. Heard the dogs, like. Didn't go inside. Didn't like to.'

The constables were backing away slowly from the door. They did not consider that going inside the shed should be considered as part of their duties and soon they were some distance behind the Inspector and the Doctor. Bucke turned around and saw the gap. He could not blame them.

'Would you like me to go inside?' asked Dr Benjamin.

'No, Doctor. As awful as it might be, it is my job.'

Benjamin nodded. 'Well, then we shall go together, Inspector. But prepare yourself. They were not the internal organs of a fully-grown adult.'

The door was hanging open, probably forced by the dogs. Inside, it was dark and smelt of butchery.

The bodies of two young boys were hanging from the same roof beam, their foreheads touching each other, as if they were engrossed in some obscene embrace. They were a mere six inches from the ground and there were clear signs that the dogs had been taking an interest in them.

Doctor Benjamin turned their heads gently, an act of love it seemed to Bucke. 'Oh no. It is Dolphin and Mazey. Oh no. My poor, poor boys.' He turned to look at Bucke, with eyes full of tears – and fury. 'The man who can do such a thing as this must be hanged, Inspector and I will do it, if necessary.'

'I will find him Doctor and the law will then decide. Not you. Not I. Not the parents. Otherwise we are no better than the person who

67

did this.' Bucke spoke quietly and calmly, though he felt that the doctor was not convinced. 'What can you tell me, Doctor? Before we remove their bodies.'

'There are too many bodies in your police station, Inspector Bucke. Andrew and Francis are dead. I last saw them alive when they left the Ragged School at, perhaps, five o'clock. I sent them home. They live on Evans Terrace, I believe.' He gently turned their heads. 'It may be some comfort, though I cannot see it. Both boys have been hit on the back of the head with something heavy. Could have been that shovel, I cannot tell. Look at the damage to poor Andrew's ear. I would suspect they were both stunned, like pigs, before their throats were cut, as you can see. Then they were strung up and their abdomens split open for their organs to spill on the ground to feed dogs - and almost, someone even poorer than themselves.' He stood up. 'Why would anyone do this? Tell me, Inspector. What purpose does it serve? Poor innocent boys, slaughtered like beasts.'

Bucke shook his head and turned away. 'A madman. Or someone who wished to be noticed. Are all their organs there, do you think?'

'There may be a heart missing, I think.' The doctor's head was bowed but Bucke could see tears dripping from Benjamin's cheeks. 'I will confirm that later. Perhaps a dog...'

'I will arrange for the constables to remove the bodies to the stables for your official examination. Ours is sometimes a hard path for us to follow, Doctor.'

There was nothing much else that Lyndon could add. He has seen an opportunity to pilfer a bit of food, that was all. It had not troubled him that the shed was in the pottery rather than the abattoir. There was no one else around, just the dogs, and he had managed to pull some scraps from them, defending himself with a shovel he had found. He had seen no one and had emerged through the fence at precisely the wrong moment, straight into Constable Payne on his lunchtime patrol.

There could never be an easy way to deliver news as hellish as this. Bucke always wondered if there was a better way in which the delivery

68

of awful news could be done, but no one had ever taught him. There was no way in which he could disguise it. He had lied about deaths before to save the feelings of grieving parents. But there was nothing he could do in this case. He could swear that he would track down the killer, but why should they believe him? What did he know? The families were bewildered. How could this be happening? Surely it was some kind of ridiculous mistake? The boys had been coming home, as they had done almost every night. Why now? Why here? Why pick them?

Constance and Benjamin had been the last to see the boys alive. The pottery was on their normal route home but no one had apparently seen them, dodging in and out of the shadows as they were, lost in their game. Whether they had been killed elsewhere and their bodies brought to the shed or whether somehow they had been lured there it was impossible to know. Perhaps their game had drawn them there for an infernal rendezvous? All things seemed possible at this moment, but he needed information and he was not sure where it might come from.

Bucke was always surprised at how quickly news could spread, uncontrolled, around the town. Within an hour, mobs of young men were patrolling the streets looking for foreigners. Two Chinese seamen were badly beaten on the Strand and soon all the ships were sounding their hooters, recalling their sailors for their own safety. The Hat Stand Gang, of which the two dead boys were aspiring members, searched for clues, but there were none. The constables themselves could not find anything at all. Their big boots and the foraging dogs had obliterated any footprints there might once have been. This was the sort of crime that could only be solved if someone had seen something. No one had. And so soon, it would be time to release the dead bodies of two little boys to their parents, to allow them to manage formalities they never thought would be theirs.

All this raced around Bucke's mind as he sat in his office in the police station, hoping that through his diligence, he would eventually be able to offer the families some peace, some comfort for a loss so cruel and undeserved, for something so hideous, inflicted upon their innocent boys. What was he to do? He needed to think.

There was a knock at his door and Constable Davies looked, unbidden, into the room. 'Dint want to bother you like, Inspector. But there is a man outside. Irish, I reckon. Name of Abraham O'Vitch. Wants to have a word. He has come to Swansea to look for his little daughter what has gone missing.'

Bucke's blood ran cold. 'Not another. You had better show him in, constable.'

Seven

The man on the other side of the desk was a surprise to Bucke. He was well dressed, neat, precise and very still. His clothes seemed expensive and well-cut, and he sat, a compact figure sitting upright in the chair, his hat on his lap and his hands resting together briefly on the top of a walking stick, held between his knees. He smiled at Bucke, then wiped his mouth with a handkerchief which he dropped into his hat. He seemed of average height, his broad shoulders suggesting the possibility of strength and power. His clean-shaven face was long and mournful, for his cheeks were hollow, and his narrow brown eyes were focused intently upon the inspector. He was calm and confident. Bucke judged him to be forty years old, perhaps a little less; he had an air of superiority, a man who expected to be obeyed.

'Please allow me to correct your constable. A foolish error for him. I am not O'Vitch, as he is saying all the time. My name is Abramovitch. Nicolae Abramovitch.'

'I apologise on his behalf, Mr Abramovitch. Yours is not a name with which he is familiar.' He nodded, in acceptance. 'I understand from what he told me that you are looking for someone here in Swansea.'

'Yes, this is so. This is my daughter who I seek. She is called Chana and now, already, she will be seven years old.'

'I would like to help you as much as I can, Mr Abramovitch, especially since you are looking for a child so young. But you will understand, I am sure, that I must know much more. It would be helpful if you could tell what has happened that makes you believe she is here. You are not from Swansea, as I understand it.' Bucke sat back in his chair, waiting.

'But of course, Inspector, sir. That I understand. It is five years ago now when Chana was given to one of your sea captains for safe keeping and now is when I am here to recover her and return her to her family.'

'And what is the name of the sea captain, Mr Abramovitch?'

'He is called Captain Felton Butler. I need to see this man very immediately. He has been a good man and I must reward him now for his help, but my Chana must now come home with me to her family.' Abramovitch smiled faintly and nodded, then waited expectantly, as if he believed that Butler was hidden beneath the desk.

'It is not someone I am familiar with, I am afraid, but of course I will ask my officers.' Felton Butler was an unusual name, not one he would have forgotten. 'Tell me, Mr Abramovitch, why did you hand over a young child to a Swansea sea captain, and then not come to collect her for five years? It does seem a bit of a puzzle to me.'

Abramovitch waved a hand dismissively. 'To understand that, Inspector, sir, you must understand my country very much more.'

'And where is that, Mr Abramovitch?'

'Romania, Inspector, sir. Now we are a new country and proud to be, for we have struggled against the Ottoman and today we are our own Kingdom. But the war of independence was brutal and we have very much the help of the Russians in our fight. In our town there was much suffering. I am from near Constanta. There are many Greeks there, there are many Turkish also. They come after your war in the Crimea. Sultan Abdulaziz he builds there a mosque. But then they say that our village of Mamaia is only a poor fishing village, only for Turkish people, and so we should go because we have too much money. I am a Jew. They say I am a Russian spy. But I am Romanian. My mother is Romanian, She called me a Romanian name, Nicolae. This you know already. But my father, he is a Jew. They do not like Jews. I am educated. They do not like educated. My father made money when he builds the railway to Cernavoda. They do not like the railway. My father he helps to build a lighthouse, The Farul Genovez. They do not like that either. They do not like our beautiful house in Mamaia. And so they burn it. And they kill everyone. Their wish is to destroy our family. The fire reaches to the stars. And I can smell it now, too. Where my wife dies and my brother also. It is a terrible day.'

'But you survived, it appears.'

'Yes, I survive. I run away to make the Turks chase me, to help the others. So I hide in a ditch and they cannot find me. But I send my servant man, Raduta, with Chana to the harbour and he gives her to my friend Felton Butler and he takes her to keep her safe. But Raduta comes back and he too is killed and so I am alone and now I am here to collect her. I remember so well holding her close to me. There is blood. She is cut on her shoulder. She sleeps. I think she is dead. She is not dead and Raduta he takes her and I hope I have not lost her, for I trust Captain Felton Butler. He is a good man. She will be seven years old and Captain Butler will have told her of me, I know he will. He will have told her to be patient. And now I am here.'

'Thank you, Mr Abramovitch. This is a very dramatic story, and a sad one too. I hope you can find Captain Butler. Do you think you will recognise your daughter, Mr Abramovitch? It has been five years now and she will have changed. All children change as they grow.'

'Of this I am sure. A father will recognise his daughter, Inspector, sir. Perhaps you have no reason to know that.' Abramovitch tapped his cane on the floor for emphasis.

'I hope you are right. It would be dreadful if she did not recognise you. I hope you have considered that. Or if you were to be mistaken about the girl you find.'

'It will not be the wrong girl. I have the ways in which to recognise her. Chana came here with three things. She has her own special doll, her companion always. I have one with me that is the same in all ways. These dolls were twins, for her. I have one and she has the other. I told Captain Butler to return Chana to the man who comes with the doll. But it is not a man, it is not a messenger. It is better, it is me. It is her loving father. She also has a heftel with her, what you are calling a necklace or a pendant, I believe. It belonged to my mother. It is a trifle but I shall know it. But she has also a scroll of parchment which is very important to all of us in Romania. I send it with her to stop it being burned by Turks. This is so important. And when I see that, I shall know she is Chana.'

'Important to Romania, you say? Why, Mr Abramovitch? '

73

'Perhaps you are knowing that Constanta was, by the Romans, called Tomis?' Bucke wondered why he should know, but said nothing. 'It was the place where their poet Ovid was, as you say, exiled. To Tomis.' Bucke shrugged. 'But you must understand, this is important, you see. Very important. I am a scholar. I study very many ancient texts. I study the work from the Synagogue of Aleppo, of course I do. But also I study many Romans. Horace. Virgil, Ovid, especially. In my house there was a copy of the work by Ovid that so many they say is lost. But it is not lost. We had it and I sent it with Chana for it to be safe. It was his tragedy, called *Medea*, a great drama. And it was in my house, in his own hand, the hand of Ovid. A great treasure. I must take it home and Romania will rejoice, for it will be back where it belongs.'

'I see.' Bucke was sceptical. 'I will do whatever I can to help, though I do not quite understand why you should give away something so valuable, along with your child.' If Abramovitch was waiting for a more enthusiastic response, he was disappointed.

'I had no choices. But for your help I am very grateful, Inspector, sir. You are the police. This is your town. The people will do as you say and so you will help me find her, I know this. I have money.' Abramovitch seemed to think that the meeting was over and began to rise from his seat.

'One last question, Mr Abramovitch. One thing that puzzles me. You see, your daughter left for Swansea five years ago, and I hope to God that she has arrived safely, but if I may ask you, where have you been? Why has it taken you so long to get here?'

Abramovitch sat down again. 'Your question I understand, Inspector, sir. A sensible question. When I was coming here, I was arrested and put in prison in Budapest in Hungary. They believed I was a spy sent by the Russians to murder Emperor Franz Josef but I am not. That is why I am taking so long. I shall return tomorrow at this time, Inspector Sir, for more news.' He stood up again.

'Wait a moment, please. One last thing.' It was impulsive but Bucke felt that he had nothing to lose. He pulled from his drawer the cap he had found on the *Ann of Bridgewater*. 'Can you tell me anything about this?' He handed it to Abramovitch.

He gave it a cursory glance. 'It is a hat. What is it you do not understand?'

'Please, Mr Abramovitch. Look at the label. What does it tell you? I do not recognise the language.'

'It is a hat. The language is Hungarian. It is a hat made in Hungary and so I do not see why...' His words tailed off and he frowned. 'Tell me please, Inspector, sir. With respect I ask you. Why do you keep this hat? It begins to trouble me a little, this Hungarian hat.'

'We found it, Mr Abramovitch. On a boat. And I would very much like to speak to the gentleman who was wearing it.'

'Why should there be such a hat as this, from Hungary, here in your town?'

'We have many visitors here, Mr Abramovitch. Sailors from all over the world. I wondered where it had come from, that is all.'

'Hungary has no sea. It has few sailors. Only on the river.' Bucke was watching Abramovitch closely as he paused and closed his eyes. He seemed to make a decision. 'You must see, Inspector, sir, why I am troubled in this way. For as I tell you, I am in prison. They take me in Budapest as I journey here for my daughter. They say I am a dangerous man sent by Russians. I am not, but it is what they believe. They say I am there in Hungary to make unrest. To make a revolution. They put me in prison. I make roads. With these hands they ask me to make roads. The hands of a scholar?' He held out his hands for Bucke to see. 'Look at these hands. It is ridiculous. I carry stones. I break rocks. And so then, after so many years I escape. They send me to collect more stones but I hide in the cart of a farmer. And this hat? What it tells me, Inspector sir, is that the Hungarians have sent a man here in this town of yours, to kill me.'

'I see. I can understand why you are worried,' Bucke said soothingly. 'But how would they know that you are here? If they have been following you, why wait until now? They could have attacked you in France or anywhere.'

75

Abramovitch rubbed his eyes. 'They take me to prison and hurt me very much. All I can do is tell them the truth – it is always easier to remember the truth than any lie you have made. And so they know I am coming to this distant town of yours to find Chana. So they have sent their murderer Czibor, and he is here before me. He is an evil man, a lunatic killer. He has been sent to kill me and to steal Chana from me so that they can steal the scroll of Ovid and destroy the history of Romania.'

Bucke considered Abramovitch very carefully. It sounded so implausible, but he had had recent experience of foreign agents in the town. 'And this writing is an object of value? Would its value justify the considerable expense of coming here?'

'You do not understand. This object, as you call it, is a sign. It does not mean wealth. It means power. It has influence. The scroll is a relic of Romania. It is ours and is for no one else. It is part of our culture.' He paused again. He stood up. 'I have a room at your Castle Hotel. Please keep me informed of any news you are having of this Hungarian. You must believe this very seriously. I know these people. He will be sheltering amongst the poorest in this town of yours. Czibor is here before me and it means great danger for me. I know this. I think you have very many of these poor people in your town with whom Czibor could hide. And you must know, without a doubt, that he kills children. For no reason, he kills children. He is so very sick in his mind, for that is where the devil lives. But also, he is a government agent, that is why he is here. You must believe me. You must find him before it is too late.'

Bucke was not at all sure how to interpret this. Was this a key piece of evidence with which he had suddenly and unexpectedly been presented? Had he been given the name of a suspect for the murder of the two boys? But why was it that he was not convinced? 'I shall instruct the constables to keep a careful eye out for this Hungarian. Thank you for the information, Mr Abramovitch.'

Abramovitch dismissed his comment with a casual gesture. 'It is important that you seek out this Hungarian very quickly. I come here by train and I arrive at my hotel and the manager he already tells me that you have many murders in this town. There are children murdered, he says. Now I know why. You must do everything to detain Czibor the Hungarian, for he shows no mercy. He is truly a monster. Already he has started his work. And so you must find Chana, before he takes her too.'

Bucke took him through to the front door and shook his hand. 'We will do our best for you, Mr Abramovitch. We will begin our enquiries as soon as we can.'

He nodded, restored his gloves and handkerchief to his pocket, put his bowler hat on his head, tapped it in place. 'Please. Find Czibor the Hungarian., He is an evil man,' he said. 'I shall need your protection, inspector, sir,' and then walked away.

As he watched him go, Bucke considered an irony that had wandered into his mind. The people of Swansea, for whom he worked, eagerly considered all crimes to be committed by foreigners. And yet here was a Romanian who was doing exactly the same thing.

Sergeant Ball leaned across the counter as he came back inside. 'Very dapper, I must say. Different from our usuals isn't he? Who was that, Inspector?'

'Interesting story, or so it appears, if we take it as the truth.' Bucke went through Abramovitch's story as Constable Morris wandered in from his beat. He stood by the counter, listening carefully, rubbing the tattoos on the back of his hand with his thumb. He was suddenly alert when Bucke mentioned the name Felton Butler.

'I know him. Well, leastways I knew his brother better, Arthur. We shipped together, round the Horn, until the stupid bugger fell off. Felton married his missus. Well, there were children see and Felton and Maggie knew each other. And he was away at sea most of the time. Lived in St Thomas. Sebastopol Street, nice little house. Never went there myself, mind.'

'Really? And is Felton Butler still there?'

'No. Afraid not, Inspector. Went down with the *Penrice Castle* in the Bay of Biscay. Leaky old tub that was. A couple of years ago.

77

Might be three. '78? Can't remember. Poor Maggie. Two husbands lost at sea.'

Did they have a young girl there? Adopted?'

'Don't rightly know, to be honest, Inspector.'

'And is Maggie Butler still there, Iago?' asked Bucke.

'Don't rightly know, really. You lose track, don't you? Leastways, I do. I think I heard that she had remarried. Well, a woman needs to live, don't she? Don't know his name though. Tell you who might though. Felton's sister. Old Mam Saunders. Still around. Tell you what, Inspector. Not my place, I know. But why don't I take you down there? I knows her. I see her in the chapel sometimes. Lives in Miers Street and she is always a bit more comfortable in the Welsh.'

Bucke smiled and put a hand on his shoulder. 'Iago, let's go. Oh, and Stanley, can you send Davies across to the train station. See if he can find out what time our friend Mr Abramovitch arrived.'

*

It wasn't far to Miers Street and it was a small house, pleasantly warm and cosy with its glowing stove and Mam Saunders sat comfortably in her chair, wrapped in a shawl, her lined face making her look even more like an engraving of a traditional Welsh woman taken from an illustrated magazine.

She looked suspiciously at Inspector Bucke, unhappy with the presence of a police officer in her house, though mollified by a Welsh-speaking constable smiling encouragement at her, someone who had known her two brothers, someone who had been there when poor Arthur had been lost. As the two of them spoke, Bucke smiled, trying to catch occasional words. He drank the tea she had made for her guests, served in her precious cups and saucers, and looked at the cat sprawled in front of the stove and wondered if Constance's new companion was equally as relaxed.

'Nawr yna Mam,' began Morris. 'Nid oes dim yma i boeni amdano. Ychydig o newyddion yr ydym yn chwilio amdanynt, am deulu Arthur.' He started by asking about Arthur's family, as he later reported to Bucke, putting

78

the emphasis on their shared past at sea. Bucke was impressed, for Morris had shown a subtlety he never thought that he possessed. He listened carefully as they walked back to the police station late in the afternoon.

'Well, Inspector. There was a child. A beautiful girl she says. It was like she was used to something better, to a different life. Cried a lot when she first came. But Mam said nothing about no jewel or no paper. Her brother Felton definitely brought her home from somewhere, she knows that. But what has happened to her, she doesn't know. Mam never liked Maggie, she says. Didn't like her when she was married to Arthur and didn't like her when she was married to Felton. He was away a lot, but he did a good job looking after Arthur's boys. He always worked hard. Always brought home the money. None of that drinking, she says. And this girl started to learn and could talk proper Welsh. But then, when Felton was taken, Maggie married again. Some man or other with a few kids, a widower. You know, Inspector, the same old story. Moved away, Mam Saunders not fussed where she had gone. And then she hears that Maggie has upped and died. Two years ago. So where the girl is now is anyone's guess. With her widower father, who isn't her father? Or with his new wife, who isn't her mother either? Trail has gone cold, I reckon.'

Bucke shook his head. 'Don't you find all this so terribly sad, Iago? All that sadness and loss?'

Morris turned to him. 'Suppose I do. But it is normal. Lots of stories like this in St Thomas, let alone in Swansea. Some a lot worse too.' They were at the bottom of Wind Street now, surrounded by carts and noise and the smell of the brewery. 'Not sure how you go about finding her. She could be anywhere. Any little girl you see might be her, living with her mam and dad who aren't her mam and dad at all. Might not even be Swansea.'

'Not easy, is it? At least we know that she was here, that she was cared for. We know that this part of the story might be true. But to track her now? And then perhaps to tell her she is not who she thinks she is?' Bucke turned to Morris. 'Thank you for your help this

79

afternoon. It was much appreciated.'

It was a very difficult enquiry. If they found a girl, Bucke wondered, could there ever be proof of who she really was? Could those two objects be regarded as proof? There were plenty on the east side of Swansea with births that had never actually been registered. Did that mean that they didn't really exist? And was it ever enough to hope that a dream could become real, merely because you wanted it to be? Could that ever, actually, be enough? How could Abramovitch find a girl and know that she was his? Or was he capable of finding a girl who could have been his daughter but then deciding that actually she wasn't?

It was Friday night and the newspaper seller was shouting loudly. This was Paul Roe, a man of forthright views, who stood at the bottom of Wind Street every night offering a commentary on the day's news, expressing dangerous thoughts, as far as Bucke was concerned. He sometimes wondered whether he should arrest him for sedition, but offering his interpretation of the news was not, as far as Bucke knew, a crime. Here, Roe was amongst his own and those on their way home stood around for a few moments most evenings to listen to him. The factory owners would never hear Roe calling to those like himself from Hafod and from Greenhill, but as far as he was concerned he was planting seeds that might one day germinate. "Starving girl dies collecting cinders on tip owned by the richest man in Swansea,' he shouted. 'Police say no crime was committed,' he added loudly, looking Bucke straight in the eye as he bought a paper from him.

Bucke skimmed through the pages, looking for the story. Ann Wood was one of the many who were sent out to pick cinders from the tip. It was her daily duty to inspect its black desolation for scraps which, once accumulated, might provide some warmth for the family and allow them to cook. In her search she had wandered into the most dangerous part of the tip and it appeared that she had been overcome by fumes from smouldering material deep within. There, unconscious on the tip, she had burnt to death. Accidental death they said, just another accidental death. Could she have been Chana?

Possibly too old, but who could know?

Bucke closed the newspaper noisily. Ann Wood, dying when she should be playing, another child lost somewhere, starting a new life far away from where she was born, and two boys horribly murdered. What a time to be a child. What a place to be a child. 'Two boys from Mount Pleasant brutally murdered,' Roe shouted. 'Police no idea. Waiting for prayers to be said in church.'

Bucke nodded to him. 'Stay warm, Paul.'

'Thank you for your concern, Inspector Bucke. Better off you just find the bastards, eh?'

On their way back to Tontine Street, Bucke took Morris with him to Tower Lane where they examined the scene of the assault on Sarah. There was little there, just the usual litter – a dirty chewed carrot, some feathers as if an animal had caught a bird, a blackened banana skin and a battered brass button, which Morris picked up. It appeared to have been trodden on. Perhaps something had been driven over it. They could have no idea how long it had been there. 'Waste not, want not,' said Morris. To which Bucke replied simply, 'It might be evidence.' There was nothing else, just the fading tracks left by the wheels of a small barrow – or a pram, perhaps.

It was foolish to think that they might have found some crucial piece of evidence, reflected Bucke. It was so hard when you could not go back in time and watch what had happened as an observer. But then, if that were to happen, then much of the work that he did now, carefully trying to re-assemble a strange story from apparently unrelated fragments, would be unnecessary. That was never going to happen, he realised that. No one would ever be able to see what had happened in the past.

'Let's get back to the station, Iago,' he said. Then he reached out a hand and grabbed Morris's wrist. 'Look! By the brewery. There she is.' They saw the girl with the pram, a ribbon trailing from the handle, walking away along Back Street. He called to her. 'Amy! Amy! Can you help me, please?'

The child turned briefly as if to check who he was, and then ran

81

away as fast as she could, up past the entrance to the sawmill and then to the right into Regent's Court. Amy would not have recognised that this was one of the most notorious places in Swansea, squalid and lawless. All that she would say was that the people here were nice. There was a group of women standing around idly in their aprons, their washing hanging limply on knotted and frayed washing lines.

'The coppers is after me!' she said breathlessly, and without a question or indeed without any word at all, they allowed Amy and her pram through and then removed their clothes props so that the lines descended and obscured the view. By the time Bucke and Morris came into Regent's Court they could see nothing but threadbare washing. The women, adept at dealing with the police, something that they did most days, were adamant that they had seen no one. 'A girl with a pram? Here? Yous off yer 'ead.'

By the time the policemen had fought their way through the sheets and drawers, Amy had made it through and had managed to slip on to the High Street and then headed north, slipping from sight into Powell Street and into the maze of narrow alleys and courtyards that now seemed to have been squashed even more closely together by the development of the railway.

Bucke emerged from Regent's Court but could see no sign of the girl. His only possible lead had vanished once again. He asked another newspaper vendor if he had seen her but he shrugged, clearly not a man who wished to be seen speaking to the constabulary in any circumstances.

There was no news from Inspector Flynn either when they returned to the police station. Whoever had killed the two boys must have been covered in blood, but no one had seen or heard anyone or anything. The superintendent at the abattoir reported no missing knives and no sign of intruders.

Eight

Bucke leaned against a pillar at the rear of the small, cramped Star Theatre, watching what he could only consider to be an act of desperation on the small stage in front of him. No one in the audience had yet thrown anything at the plate-spinner, but it could only be a matter of time. His own concerns had little to do with theatrical inadequacy and more with law and order. There had been an increase in the number of thefts reported recently and an enhanced police presence might be useful. He was not inclined to ask Sergeant Ball to station a constable here permanently. It would not be a sensible use of a constable and the theatre was a place where they could be so easily targeted. After the day that he had experienced, he certainly needed to do something different and, perhaps, clear his mind.

It was full tonight, as it often was, and the air was thick with smoke and the scent of stale beer. The audience was screaming at the juggler on stage constantly, some in an attempt to provide sufficient distraction to make him drop the balls, and others to draw his attention to the precarious balance of the plates he had spinning on sticks. They were so close to him that they could see the cracks in his thick plaster of make-up; they could smell the fear. This was a moment of colour and malevolent entertainment, a chance to mock and humiliate a stranger at the end of a grey and mundane day, but a distracted audience enjoying themselves, could easily be relieved of the few valuables they had by an opportunist or two. Bucke looked around but could see no sign of either Vinegar Bridget or Selina, in his mind the most likely suspects.

Next up was another inadequate performer, this time Harry Boston, 'The Singing Painter - Artiste Extraordinaire,' - who produced on stage portraits in broad rapid brush strokes, on paper stretched tightly across a frame. The design had been previously punctured in the paper with pins and, as long as the light was good, Harry could get away with it. But it was not gripping entertainment to see a man paint a second-rate portrait of the Prince of Wales at speed, and the audience, as they always did, soon became restless and abusive. They were confident they should be allowed their criticism, for they had paid for a ticket and believed in their right to express their dissatisfaction. Thankfully, Harry had chosen not to sing tonight, preferring to get off the stage as quickly as possible and so did not detain them for long; he took a bow and then scurried off stage as quickly as he could, with his easel and paint, happy to escape without the traditional barrage of orange peel and apple cores.

Bucke knew him vaguely as a desperate man, barely holding penury at bay with a second-rate theatrical act, who was frequently found drunk in the steep lanes between the High Street and the Strand. It would all unravel soon, thought Bucke. The lights and the make-up and the dubious glamour could not disguise the smell of failure that hung like a cloud around his shoulders. But tonight everyone in the theatre seemed good-natured and he could see no one sulking around, ready to dip into pockets. He pushed himself away from the pillar. He had done his duty; he had been seen and offered as much reassurance as he could in this diverse and unpredictable environment. It was time for him to go.

The Master of Ceremonies clapped his hands, hoping to restore order. 'And now ladies and gentlemen! For your delight and back by popular demand! Yes! Tonight, I can announce the return of Fanny Stevens, The Angel of Swansea!'

There were cheers and Bucke leaned back against the pillar. He could spare a few more moments and he didn't want to miss this. It was a shame that Constance was not here with him to see her. He had heard her before and her performance would be the only highlight on this thin and uninspiring bill. The audience knew it too.

A confident, self-possessed woman walked out to the middle of the stage and stood, hands on hips, commanding the theatre, defying the audience, driving them almost instantly into silence.

Such a small auditorium brought everyone so very close to the stage and they could see the power in her eyes. The Star had the intimacy of a public house and was often just as raucous. Fanny knew this and was adept at using the proximity of the audience to her own advantage.

She undoubtedly had presence: within the briefest of moments the audience was hers. She was of average height but her hair, studded with pearls, was carefully sculptured and made her seem taller. It had an attractive red tinge, though Fanny always regretted that the sheen it had in her younger days had gone, a consequence of too little washing and too much dirty air. And yet in this filthy place she could produce such a wonderful sound; the sound, it was said, of an angel. Fanny had a powerful chest able to sustain a note for long enough to draw attention to her impressive bosom and to inspire applause. She had a pretty face, with inviting lips, perfect teeth and full cheeks, though her skin suffered for spending too long beneath heavy stage make-up. And whilst it was a face that had seen trouble, sometimes a warmth revealed itself in those eyes that could not be extinguished. Usually though they were cold and unapproachable, for they had seen too much cruelty and betrayal. They had watched her talent squandered, they had watched her sink into a cheap, squalid variety theatre, singing to raucous miners and giggling shop assistants for a pittance. It should have been so different.

A voice shouted from the gallery. 'Get on with it, then!' There were some hisses and a sound like a slap being delivered. Still she waited, even the foreign sailors who had been a little bemused by painting and plate spinning and had gossiped and leered at female members of the audience without pause, now settled, aware that something special was going to happen. They recognised that Fanny had an aura, on stage at least. The light caught the pearls around her neck and her glittering earrings when she moved her head, as if a divine light was playing around her.

This was her place, this was her world. Here she was in control. As the silence took hold, she looked across the auditorium with barely concealed contempt. She glanced up at the gallery, sneered at the lecherous men in the boxes. She would start in her own time.

Tonight was one song only. She was here as a favour – Benjamin Bevan, the baritone from Bangor, booked at some expense, had failed to turn up, indisposed they said, though his reputation suggested that he was probably blind drunk in a railway hotel somewhere en route.

Harry Boston would accept any offer of employment, out of necessity, and had rushed to the theatre as soon as he had the invitation to fill-in. And Fanny? She needed to be on stage. She never said no. The Star Theatre might not be much but it was all that she had. She lived for moments like this, when she commanded the audience and people listened to her, when the stage was hers alone.

With the slightest inclination of her head, the band started and there was an audible intake of breath. It was the introduction to the crowd's favourite, and Bucke recognised it too, the tragic ballad *The Children of the Wood*, a real tear-jerker, written solely, it seemed, with the purpose of making drunks weep.

Fanny took the song slowly – the band were ready for this - enunciating the words clearly to focus on the narrative and to squeeze every drop of melodrama from it. Her audience could not hear it too often – a brother and sister placed into the care of their wicked uncle following the tragic death of their parents, who plans their death to steal their inheritance. Their murder is thwarted, but they die abandoned and forlorn, their bodies covered by leaves laid by grieving robins.

Everyone knew the story so well but it never failed to touch an audience; perhaps, thought Bucke because childhood and happiness were so fragile in their own lives. It was a melodramatic story in every way, but one which carried with it that uncomfortable truth. And Fanny's delivery was perfectly judged. There were those who would come to The Star solely to hear her sing this song, to wallow in its emotional vortex, like addicts, allowing their eyes to brim with tears and relishing the thrill, because they knew it wasn't real.

Bucke watched the enraptured audience, some of them mouthing the words as Fanny took them through the story. The dying father, faltering, said to his brother

'Look to my children dear;

Be good unto my boy and girl,

No friends else have they here.

And the whole audience, even the few who had never heard the song before, even those who did not fully understand English, knew the poor father was deceiving himself.

When she sang the line about the children taken into the wood, chattering happily, *To those that should their butchers be,* the audience drew in its collective breath, responding, perhaps, to the emerging news of those terrible deaths in a dismal shed at the Pottery. The tension of the song increased with the insistent drum under-scoring the plight of the children in the wood. Then a trumpet mimicked a hunting horn, the music stopped and Fanny sang of the death of the children unaccompanied. Her voice had such expression, such range.

Thus wandered these poor innocents,

Till death did end their grief;

In one another's arms they died,

As wanting due relief:

No burial this pretty pair

From any man receives,

Till Robin Redbreast piously

Did cover them with leaves.

No one moved. No one stirred. All that could be heard was the sincere purity of Fanny's voice, the sound of heaven briefly filling every part of this tawdry theatre. Then the drum returned and soon the instruments followed, as the punishments inflicted upon the wicked uncle were listed. The line, *the heavy wrath of God* was greeted with approval. The deaths of his own two sons were applauded as just and appropriate, and by the time Fanny reached the end of the ballad, the moral compass of a fairy tale world had been restored.

It had been a cathartic experience and, as the audience burst into wild applause and as Fanny offered the audience her contempt and the briefest of bows, Bucke slipped outside, grateful to breathe the fresher air from the sea. It was quite a performance. He might have heard her before but knew that he could never tire of that remarkable voice. And tonight, with the macabre deaths of the two boys still fresh in his mind, her song had touched him deeply. He knew that it would haunt him for days to come. No one could escape the mesmeric qualities of her voice or the depth of her expression. Or indeed escape the way in which she seemed to reach deep inside your soul. Fanny never failed.

In the box to the side of the stage, another member of the audience was completely transfixed, lost entirely in the magic of that moment. It was the first time that Henry Fry had come to the theatre and he was entirely overwhelmed. How glad he was that he had allowed himself to be persuaded.

*

He would learn something, he might even grow up, said Maldwyn Leyshon, a regular who enjoyed the thrill of stepping into the slightly dangerous world of the music hall. He had booked his habitual box and had sat leering at the chorus line on the stage, making lewd comments designed perhaps, to further unsettle a younger man who was always so embarrassed when he showed him his collection of mildly erotic *cartes de visite*. 'I can get you some, you know. Artistic,' winked Maldwyn.

Henry shook his head. He was twenty two, though he appeared much younger. To his colleagues he was a young man, naïve and inexperienced, and they rather enjoyed making fun of him.

His physique was still not completely formed and he remained boyish. One of the office cleaners said of him that he had a face so young, hair would be embarrassed to grow upon it – he was certainly clean-shaven and how often he had to shave was the subject of whispered conversation when work became particularly boring. There was no question about his intelligence or about his diligence towards the driest of contractual details, but what he knew about people came from books, not real life. Nevertheless, his clients were beginning to realise that shy though he was, Henry Fry understood all of their papers.

88

His colleagues teased him without mercy, ready to make him blush whenever Mr Strick was out of the office fulfilling his regular duties as a coroner. His embarrassment proved that he knew even less than they thought they did themselves about the world. Henry Fry's innocence was, for them, self-evident. It was obvious to everyone that he was much more comfortable in the world of books, for he was an avid reader. That was his world, where things were so much more predictable and more easily controlled. The real world was disorganised and unexpected.

Henry had always worked hard, doing what he was told at home and at school and eventually qualifying to work as a solicitor. He was, like his parents, proud of his achievements – their only son a professionally qualified gentleman, with prospects. His father had found him a position with the notable firm of Strick and Bellingham and was in the process of reaching an agreement with Doctor Sullivan of Sketty concerning his daughter Harriet, a quiet, unassuming girl of little conversation but much money. Everyone was sure that it was a good match; Henry just wished she would let him hold her hand sometimes on the way home after chapel on Sunday afternoon. He didn't think it was too much to ask. If he was honest, he had always preferred Emily Beynon, who was much more lively and very pretty. A bit moody at times, he would have to admit, and he would have had to wait a while, for Emily was still quite young. But something had happened, some sort of scandal and the family had moved quite suddenly to Aberystwyth, of all places. And so now he was expected to marry Harriet Sullivan.

He was regarded as good-looking by the girls who gossiped together after church in the Uplands. He was quite tall and his dark hair had an appealing curl. A faint smile would sometimes play across his lips when he thought no one was looking, but the girls saw it and speculated frequently about why it happened. He was regarded as a desirable catch, his shyness providing an interesting challenge, even though he seemed to be properly spoken for and thus out of bounds, even for Faith Bishop, the vicar's daughter. She was a generously proportioned young lady, more enthusiastic and uninhibited than the others, who swooned occasionally at Henry's brown and soulful eyes which, she claimed, had once looked straight into hers when they reached the line, *I will fear no evil: for thou art with me* during the singing of *The Lord is My Shepherd.*

Some of them privately thought that Faith was making it up but they decided that even if it was true, Henry was much too shy to do anything about it. His parents had decided his future for him and he didn't seem strong enough to stand up to them. Harriet Sullivan might be boring, but she had money and so Faith sighed, her friends comforted her, and then she found her comforts elsewhere. It was a heartless world.

Tonight, Henry would probably have agreed with her. There was neither heart nor soul in the Star Theatre. He had never been here before and, if he had been honest, he would have agreed that he wasn't that keen. It wasn't his world, but Maldwyn felt that a visit should be an essential part of his on-going education, as if he were some kind of guide and mentor.

Henry wasn't stupid, far from it. He was socially clumsy and inexperienced but there were times when he showed an acute awareness derived from his reading. As he sat looking down on the stage at a man pointlessly spinning plates, he wondered what really motivated Maldwyn. Why did he come here? Was it just to shout loudly at the performers? Why would you do that? And why did Maldwyn insist on bringing him to the Star Theatre? To make himself feel superior, more experienced? What was the point of that? To give him the chance to show off? To allow him to play the part of the man about town, perhaps? Or did he need someone with him in order to make his experiences seem real? In some way to validate them and then to indicate his own superiority? Was Maldwyn merely trying to embarrass him by introducing him to a world that he knew nothing about? Or was he trying to make himself more attractive to the show girls by standing next to him?

Henry was never sure and he would be able to think about it more carefully at home, and so create a narrative from all these unanswered questions. But suddenly in the twilight world of the foggy theatre, these things ceased to trouble him, for Fanny was singing and Henry

Fry was mesmerised.

He knew immediately that he had never heard anything like it before and he was spellbound by an unexpected and unfamiliar narrative, something that the audience of working people from the wrong side of town all seemed to know very well and yet it was something that had been denied to him. He had never anticipated that he would ever find anything to rival the power and immersion he experienced in the novels he consumed, and certainly not tonight. But the simple power of this ballad, emphasised by the insistent rhyme, the rhythm and the music, took his breath away. Fanny's command was absolute and he was drawn into her voice and her presence. He knew almost instantly, and he could never explain why he knew, that this was a life-changing moment.

Henry was convinced that at one point in that small grubby theatre, she had looked at him alone and directly, and he fell, lost, into those blue eyes shining up at him from the stage. His stomach did somersaults. When she sang *And he that was of mildest mood Did slay the other there,* he was certain that she had seen deep into his soul and had seen the inevitable triumph of the quiet unassuming man, and that she had recognised him as such.

The show was over. Nothing could be expected to follow Fanny and her performance and the audience began to leave, waving and calling to each other as they spilled out on to York Street. Henry stared at the empty space on the stage where Fanny had been standing, as Leyshon stood and stretched himself.

'Did you hear her? What a voice.'

'Oh yes, fair play. Very good. Of course she is. But don't worry about her, Henry old lad, she is past it, an old boiler. Come with me - the chorus girls are much more fun. You won't be disappointed.' He winked. 'Might cost you a few shillings but...' Maldwyn nudged him heavily with his elbow and winked again. 'Come on. Let me take you backstage.'

'You mean, you can really get backstage?'

'Of course I can. You'll learn. Just need to know the right people in life, that is all. Come on. These girls can show you a thing or two. Don't doubt it. Very willing.' He winked.

He led Henry downstairs but instead of following the crowds, Leyshon dragged him through a very narrow alley and into a yard that the theatre shared with the Albany Vaults. This was a convenient arrangement, particularly for the members of the band who could slip into the Albany for refreshment between songs. There was a doorman who sneered as Leyshon slipped him some coins but stood out of their way. Then they were in a corridor with a two shabby dressing rooms, with their doors wide open. Girls were changing their clothes, laughing and shouting. There were people pushing everywhere in the confined space.

Henry had never been anywhere quite like it, amongst such a number of casually undressed women. He was wide eyed, alarmed and thrilled at the same time. The grinning Leyshon was like a young boy at liberty in a sweet shop. He reached out and put his hand on a passing shoulder. 'My goodness, but you are a pretty young thing. I couldn't take my eyes off you on stage. How do you manage to kick your legs so high?'

'Wouldn't you like to know,' the girl replied, twisting her shoulder from his grasp.

Leyshon laughed as if it was the funniest thing he had ever heard in his life. 'You minx!' He tried to grab her again but she slipped away from him. 'You see, Henry! They are so sprightly.' He raised his hand to his hat and touched the brim. 'Good evening, dear,' he said to a small dark girl who was pushing past him.

'I've heard about you,' she announced and wiggled her crooked little finger at him. 'Tiny Tim, they calls you. Takes all sorts, don't it?'

'You saucy piece! Come here, my girl!' But she wiggled that finger again and slipped back into the crowd. 'You see, Henry! That's how it's done. Watch what I do and you can't go far wrong.'

Henry was paying little attention to this tiresome performance but instead was looking along the corridor, trying to see if he could find

92

Fanny Stevens. He was sure he caught a brief glimpse of the naked breast of a girl changing against the wall. Another girl from the chorus pushed past and Leyshon put his arm round her waist and pulled her to him. 'You have such splendidly long legs, my dear. Did you know that the ruffians in the stalls can see such a long way up them and yet a gentleman like myself, in his box, has to imagine all those treasures!'

The girl twisted from his grasp and faced him, bored by the familiar courtship rituals. 'Look, sir. I am tired. Let's just say it will cost you, shall we?'

Maldwyn Leyshon stepped backwards, knocking into the juggler, leaving with his plate spinning poles beneath his arm. He was shocked by her frankness. 'I say! Have a care, madam.'

'Well? Is it a yes or a no? I don't have all night.'

Then Henry caught sight of her through the door of one of the changing rooms, carefully trying to comb out her hair. He forced his way up to her. 'Please excuse me, Miss Stevens. I am terribly sorry but I ...' He lost his words suddenly. He realised that she was a striking woman of attractive maturity. She carried on fighting with her hair, waiting for him to finish his sentence, appraising him with such penetrating eyes.

'What I was trying to say was that I ...' He lost his words again.

Fanny sighed. 'What did you want to say? Just say it. It can't be that hard, surely?' She turned and went across to the small dirty table that was pressed into the corner of the room and drank from her generous glass of brandy, which she always claimed soothed her throat, Then she picked up a rag and with it she began to wipe her face. Inexplicably, Henry had followed her. Speaking to her back suddenly seemed easier.

'I just wanted to say that I enjoyed your performance tonight. I thought it was wonderful.' She continued to wipe the paint from her face. 'I thought your phrasing and the variation in the tone really captured the drama of the story. I thought it was really well done. I just wanted to tell you myself.'

Fanny turned, surprised at what he had said. It wasn't normally the sort of thing she heard from stage door creeps. She looked at him properly, aware of his nervousness and his youth. 'Thank you, sir. You are very kind.'

Henry blushed. 'I just thought it was wonderful. One of the finest things I have ever heard. I wanted to tell you. I didn't expect to hear something quite so beautiful in a place like this.'

Fanny raised her eyebrows, then smiled at him. 'You are not like the other men who hang around the stage door, are you? Do you really think that you should be here?'

'No, not really. Another clerk from the office brought me. I didn't know what to expect.'

'That surprises me greatly. Most men come here because they see girls from the stage as girls having a certain reputation. Isn't that why you came?' She started to gather up the artificial pearls from her hair and put them in a box.

'Oh that isn't why I came here. I mean I just saw you and...' His words faded away again.

'And are you married Mr...'

'Fry. Henry Fry. I have an understanding with Miss Harriet Sullivan of Sketty.

'I see. It depends what you both understand, I suppose.' She looked at him 'This isn't a place for you. Surely you know that? It has been pleasant meeting you, Mr Fry but I fear I ...'

'May I invite you to accompany me for a drink, sometime? This evening, perhaps?' Henry's face flushed suddenly and vividly. 'Oh my goodness. I am so terribly sorry. I don't know what came over me. Please forgive me.'

Fanny looked at him carefully, as if for the first time. Then she smiled at him and allowed him to see warmer eyes. 'You certainly don't lack courage, Mr Fry.'

'I hope you can forgive me. I had no wish to embarrass you,' he said, reddening still further.

'Mr Fry. I would be very happy to accompany you.' He gulped and Fanny realised that she had to manage his hesitancy if she was to avoid a total disaster. 'And where shall we go, do you think?'

Henry had no idea. He had not planned any of this. He said the first thing that came into his head. 'The Mackworth Hotel?'

'Your intention is to take a music hall girl to a hotel? How bold you are, Mr Fry! What has got into you?' He looked terrified and Fanny briefly regretted teasing him. She smiled and laid her hand lightly on his arm. 'Come with me. I know somewhere a little more lively.'

*

If she were truthful, she would have to admit that the conversation was not especially stimulating that evening. They had sat in the corner of the Adelphi and he had talked of his work as a solicitor, dealing with contracts and business agreements. He was shy and uncertain, a pleasant young man – and certainly a number of years younger than her – but someone who had suddenly found himself in an unknown world, full of curious thrills and mysterious threats. Fanny had warmed to him, although he appeared very inexperienced and a little immature. Why should she not accept his nervous invitation? Anything was better than going straight home – she knew what to expect there. But as she walked home she found herself, curiously, smiling and thinking about young Henry Fry. He was not old enough to be away from his mother, she was sure of that. But he was a nice boy and for a few moments his polite and clumsy attention made her feel good. She laughed silently and bitterly. Here she was, thirty-five years old and enjoying the attentions of a man who was little more than a child.

She continued walking up High Street and shook her head. *Ah. Don't be stupid. You are too old for this. Too old for him.* But the other voice in her head, the one that was still alive, despite everything else, reminded her that Henry had asked to see her again, and she had said yes and had smiled inwardly. She knew she had better compose herself. It wouldn't do to go home smiling, not if Jack was there.

Men were always hanging around the stage door, always pushing in. She had become used to it, never gave the toffs a second thought. But Henry seemed different somehow unless, of course, she was the one who had changed. As she had grown older she wasn't harried quite as much as the younger girls. Times were hard for everyone and no one should be surprised if the girls did what they thought they had to do to survive. She had done it herself and she couldn't blame others for it. She didn't regard it as a mistake, more of a necessity. And it certainly wasn't her biggest mistake. Oh no. Her biggest mistake was Jack.

As she walked past the end of Tower Lane she thought she heard a voice, a single word. She looked around her. There might have been a figure in the shadows, seen in the corner of her eye, but no solid shape formed, as far as she could see. Fanny walked on briskly. She had heard there had been an attack on a woman here recently. Best not linger, she decided.

She stopped briefly outside the railway station, enveloped in steam and smoke, and checked behind her again. There was no one there. She looked across at the police station at the corner of Tontine Street. Odd, she thought, that it should have been in a police station, of all places, that it had started.

Seven years ago it was. Fanny had witnessed an attack on one of the drummers in the theatre band. The local ruffians were always ready to prove their manhood, as if in some way assaulting one of their friends would impress the dancing girls. Fanny had grabbed hold of the assailant, banged his head forcibly against the wall - she was a lot more confident then. She was at the old police station to identify him, which was easy; since she had not let go of him, there could be little debate about who had done it.

But Jack was there too, arguing with the desk sergeant, denying accusations that he had assaulted a woman in a doorway on Wind Street. He had smiled at her and foolishly she had smiled back, possibly in relief that the tension of the rest of the evening had dissipated. And so he had taken her to the Bush Hotel and very soon

96

afterwards her enslavement began.

Jack was cruel, domineering, unpredictable. She would stop sometimes and wonder how it was that a strong independent woman as she had been, was suddenly a victim. What had happened? She was trapped, abused, beaten, humiliated, controlled. It was as if she had become two people – one at the theatre and then another at what she bitterly called home. Her casual arrangements with wealthy patrons were soon replaced by more regular obligations, enthusiastically arranged by Jack.

She walked on. Why hadn't she left? Perhaps because she didn't think she mattered much anymore. Her life was filled with aggression and squalor. She had been beaten and brutalised. Her will and her spirit had been burnt away. She ate little and was frequently locked in deep, very dark moments, hating herself beyond measure, accepting the abuse and the violence because that is what she deserved.

Fanny was only ever alive when she was on stage, when she was singing in front of an audience, in front of flimsy scenery and beneath inadequate lights. Her only escape, the only time she was truly free. She would run away tomorrow if she could, for she knew she could only ever revive her singing career if she left Swansea. She was Swansea's very own angel, apparently. But what did that mean? If she was an angel, how had everything gone so wrong? And so now she was reduced to drinking with a nervous child, grabbing crumbs from someone else's table and yet happy to do so. She sighed once more. She hoped that Jack had some brandy. Tomorrow was Saturday and she had to do a matinee and an evening performance and so brandy would help her preparations, she told herself. Henry had said he was going to turn up to one of them, which she thought was sweet.

She entered Bethesda Street and walked along through the dirt and around the pools of mud towards their mean rooms in Elephant Court. She hoped, as always, that Jack wasn't there.

Nine

It was a silent breakfast, but then it was always a silent breakfast. Perfunctory morning prayers had been abandoned long ago and had now been replaced by habitual, but impossible, fantasies of freedom from a desiccated marriage. The dish of devilled kidneys waited for them in the middle of the table whilst they waited for Faith to appear, a morning ritual that contained a bitter irony that was not lost upon Cyrus, her father. Hilda was staring at her lap, as if in prayer, though Cyrus knew that was not the case. He looked to the left into the mirror, in which he could see the garden, brown and bare, desperate for spring; he could also see the reflection of a thin man with a thin neck and a prominent Adam's apple, a man with large teeth, spectacles, dark hair and whiskers. If he looked to the right, straight out of the window, he would inevitably catch a glimpse of the sideboard on which a brandy bottle stood, perilously close to empty. He bit his thumb nail. Perhaps Jack would call this week. Cyrus was always waiting for something or other. This morning? Waiting for Faith. But then, he was always waiting for faith.

He spent his afternoons in his study, apparently writing out his thoughts on the back of small cards, as an aid to memory, he said. He liked to consult them during sermons. Today was Sunday, the day he had to perform before his congregation. The brandy bottle showed that he had been trying his best to prepare some important words for them. He had to admit that he hadn't been feeling too well for a week or so and he had drunk rather more of the brandy than he should, in order to control this vague abdominal pain. Hilda had bought him some pills, Roache's Liver Pills, and they were there on the table before him, next to his fork. He poked the box. They didn't seem to be working too well. Perhaps they needed more time. He had hoped that it might stop his hair from falling out. He had been passing blood too, but he hadn't bothered to tell Hilda. What would be the point?

There was no sound, just the clock which always had the capacity to distress Cyrus, each second another wasted moment in a wasted life. Cyrus Bishop? Vicar of Llwyn y Bryn? And that was all he would ever be? He touched the cards in his pocket.

'Faith is a long time coming,' said Hilda.

Cyrus snorted derisively. Stupid woman. How didn't she know? Faith had left him years ago. This can't go on, he thought. And then he realised that it could. He reached out to lift the lid from the tureen, the faint but penetrating scent of urine indicating that the kidneys were still warm – just. Where was the child? It was the same every morning. He looked at Hilda, his wife, sallow and bitter. Was her life any different from his? No more productive, it seemed. Hilda, the perpetual and notorious shopper, who would patrol Swansea every day, rather than stay in the vicarage. Were they just torturing each other? Is that what life was destined to be?

Hilda sighed and adjusted her sleeves. Then she paused, suddenly alert. 'Cyrus. Did you hear that?'

'Did I hear what, Hilda?

'That noise.'

Cyrus was irritated. 'I could hardly smell a noise, now could I? What noise was it?'

'There. That noise.' It was the unmistakable sound of a baby crying. Hilda looked confused, bewildered. 'Where is that coming from? Where is it coming from, Cyrus?'

Cyrus closed his eyes. He knew. It had been inevitable.

The door to the dining room was flung open and Lily the housemaid stood there, breathlessly. 'Vicar! Mrs Bishop! Come quick! Please! There's a baby on the floor!'

They ran upstairs to Faith's room. She was sitting on her bed, shaking, her knees drawn up to her chest. There was blood everywhere. She was sobbing, panting, her auburn hair dishevelled and sticking in strands to her sweat-stained face. 'Oh my God! Oh my God!' There on the floor was an apparently healthy baby boy, crying robustly.

Hilda leaned against the door frame, unable to process what she could see. 'Faith. Where is this baby from?'

'It is from me! Don't you understand, Mamma? It came out of me!'

'Yours? How is that possible?' Hilda's hands covered her mouth.

'Who is the father?' whispered Cyrus.

'How should I know?' sobbed Faith.

Then Hilda began to shake and she clutched at the door frame desperately. 'Cyrus, do something.' Her voice was barely audible. 'What will people say? What about the neighbours?' The baby's cries tried to speak to the heart of their common humanity – but Hilda was unmoved and she raised her voice above it. 'Do something, Cyrus!' She pointed at the child. 'Get it out of here!'

He looked at his daughter as if she was a stranger. 'Does it belong to Luther Atkinson?'

Faith shuffled further back up the bed, her face locked in terror. 'It came out of me! Take it away!'

Cyrus persisted. 'Is Luther Atkinson the father?'

'I told you! I don't know!'

Hilda suddenly engaged with what her husband had asked. 'Luther Atkinson? The grocery boy?'

'Take it away from me!' screamed Faith. 'Make it shut up!'

'Cyrus! Do something. Think of your position.'

'And what would you have me do, Hilda? With our grandson?'

'Get rid of it!'

Lily bent down and wrapped the baby in a towel. 'There we are, my handsome.' He stopped crying and locked on to her eyes. She rocked him gently. 'He's a beautiful little thing, and no mistake. Look at 'im, Faith.'

'No! No!' Faith gathered herself at the bed head, trembling in fear.

'Please yerself.' Lily shrugged and turned to the vicar. 'Excuse me

100

for bein' forward, Mr Bishop, but my sister can sort all this out for you. Our Mags knows what to do. She could feed the poor little mite on account as she has just had one of her own. Mags could tidy up Faith as well, sir. Make sure she is alright. And she could take care of the boy for you, make sure he's well arranged for, sir. No questions asked, like.' She laid the baby on the bed and the towel fell open. If they didn't agree she wouldn't pick him up again, and she knew they realised that. Lily was shrewd; they had to accept her offer or pick up the baby from the bed and, by so doing, accept its presence. Were they prepared to pick him up?

Faith screamed out again. 'Look there is an animal! On the floor! It came out with an animal!'

Lily shook her head. 'Calm yerself, Faith. That's the after-birth, I reckon, Never got to see me sister's.' She paused and looked at the vicar and his wife, as Faith from the top of the bed, continued moaning, unwilling to look at her son. 'What would you like me to do, sir? For a consideration, of course. If you are interested, sir.' She was a pretty girl, shrewd and confident, and she also knew that Cyrus Bishop was frightened of what she might say about him.

Cyrus Bishop knew he wasn't going to get a better offer. He admired her practicality. He nodded at her.

'I'll crack on then. I shall go and get my sister. Be about 10 minutes, if you are lucky, sir.'

Hilda stepped into the room, away from the doorway and pointed an angry, accusatory finger at Faith. 'A Home for Fallen Women, that's where you are going, young lady! Far away!'

'And then we will have lost faith a second time,' laughed Cyrus Bishop hollowly.

*

Rumsey Bucke ate his breakfast as he walked through the Sunday morning streets, cheese and stale bread, on his way to the town hall to see Captain Colquhoun. He needed to see him before the Chief Constable went to church, to ensure he was informed of the state of

101

investigations, should the mayor speak to him after the service.

They sat together in his office, listening to the sailors unloading a consignment of timber from a ship in the South Dock, the clatter of the wood as it was dropped on to the quayside and the raucous shouts of the dockers, reminding them of their duty to maintain an orderly town. Bucke did not think they were making a very good job of it at that moment.

'As you know, Isaac, it has not been an easy few days. We have had six deaths - that we know about anyway - in a very short period of time. I am not sure how much of a link there is between them, though some of the victims seem to have sustained serious head wounds. Four murders, definitely. Probably five. The other might be manslaughter. I don't know.'

'Six? That many? I know about the Grimshaw girl, those two unfortunate boys and the Captain of the *Ann of Bridgewater*. What are the others?'

'Samuel Allen, he was the captain of the *Ann of Bridgewater*. The owner too. I am, as sure as I can be, that he was murdered. Well, yesterday, the body of the mate, Tom Foster, was washed ashore at Rhossily. He'd been in the water a few days but he had helpfully had his name tattooed on his arm.'

'A helpful custom if you are planning to drown,' added Colquhoun.

'His head was, they say, badly damaged from the rocks, so it is hard to know what happened to him. The rowing boat from the *Ann* was found washed up at Port Eynon. Neither of these things leaves us any closer to knowing what happened.'

Colquhoun nodded, thoughtfully. 'Someone killed Allen but if it was Foster, why did he leave the boat? Why didn't he dump Allen's body over the side?'

'Exactly. Why?' asked Bucke. 'Unless of course there was a third person on board.'

'Apart from the cat, as I understand it,' said the Chief Constable.

102

'Apart from the cat - and then later in the day Constable Hamley from Reynoldston found the body of a farmer from Port Eynon. Behind a wall in Penmaen. Rhys Matthews. He had been beaten to death, a bit like Allen it seems. He'd been taking seaweed to the gardener at Sketty Hall and his cart was found in a field in Killay, its load still intact. His leather apron was missing and there were some bloodstained clothes hidden under a pile of rocks. But no one saw anything, not anyone who has come forward so far, anyway.'

The Chief Constable flicked through the reports on his desk. 'A lot of head injuries here, Rumsey. It seems that whoever it is has more success with male victims than he does with female.'

'If it the same person. I fervently hope there are not two of them out there, but the way the cases are spread out it implies that there might be. We are in that terrible situation that until he strikes again, then we have so very little to go on. Unless someone has seen something, and that is what the constables are concentrating on at the moment.' Colquhoun nodded. 'It is the murder of the two young boys that disturbs me most. I will tell you why, Isaac. A feeling. I have no evidence. I felt it when I saw them hanging from that beam. It was very carefully staged. Deliberately so. It is hard to put it into words. But I worry that it was made to look as if we have an insane man with a knife in town. To me? I thought it was calculated. The bodies were too identical. Too symmetrical. And perhaps that makes it worse.'

'Insane people do not have the same mental processes as the rest of us, Rumsey. They are insane. Some revel in such extreme precision.'

'I know, Isaac. And it would be easier to assume that it was a moment of lunacy. It was a full moon, after all. But it felt, what can I say? It felt too precise.'

'All I can say, Rumsey, is trust your instinct. But don't let it blind you to the truth. The most important thing is to make sure it doesn't happen again and that you catch whoever did it. Stupid thing to say, I realise that. But we both know that murders happen generally between people who know each other, in whatever way. This, Rumsey, seems completely unprovoked and irrational. And therefore

103

unpredictable. You are right to be worried.'

'Unless those boys were killed for a purpose. And at the moment we have no way of knowing what that purpose might be. They would have nothing worth stealing. Unless they had seen something that they should not have seen, and even if they had, why silence them in that way? There is something else that troubles me too, Isaac.' Bucke went on to outline the story he had been told by Nicolae Abramovitch.

'How unusual. I can understand why you have doubts, Rumsey. But in a war in which your own home and family are threatened, who knows how any of us might react? To give your child to a stranger? I am not sure myself, either. It is interesting of course, but his search cannot be your priority.'

'Certainly not whilst we have murder on the streets, Isaac, I agree. I have confirmed those parts of his story that I can. He did arrive at Swansea High Street Station in the late morning on the London train, making a great deal of fuss about luggage and directions. No one could miss him. Now he has a room in the Castle Hotel. But his daughter? I suspect that whoever has her now, has no idea where she has come from or who she might be.'

'They might think she is theirs, Rumsey. Why shouldn't they? And then what? We couldn't just hand her over to a stranger, could we?'

*

Jack McCarthy leaned against the wall outside the Seabeach Hotel, waiting for the constable to move along his beat. He had his wheelbarrow and a shovel with him. It had been a busy few days, the seeds planted in the warmth of last May had reached fruition, with consequences that could no longer be easily ignored. Jack believed he was offering an essential service as far as his customers were concerned. It wasn't for him to question or to disapprove. Others would do that. He did as he was asked and earned his money.

When the constable drifted out of sight, Jack marched purposefully across the road. He had always found that digging on the beach during the day attracted less attention than it did in the

104

evening or the early morning. Everyone who saw him would assume that he was stealing sand, for building or something. Of course he wasn't supposed to do it, but most people turned a blind eye. He didn't go back to the same places if he could avoid it – and sometimes, if he thought someone was taking too close an interest, he would take a cart out to one of the beaches in Gower.

There were few people around today. It was clear and dry, another day in this long and featureless winter, though the breeze was pleasant. He preferred it when it was raining, because people hurried past, heads down, but so long as he did not look furtive he would not be questioned and indeed barely noticed. On a Sunday morning many would be in chapel. It was a good time to be on the beach.

He walked about twenty yards down towards the sea and then dug a deep hole, quickly putting into it two hand-sewn bags which he had already weighted with stones. They would never float to the surface, if they were left undisturbed. He filled the holes quickly, eyeing the two unpleasant dogs scavenging further down the beach towards Black Pill and then threw some sand into his barrow. It wasn't his place to offer any sorrowful words or funeral rites. For him it was more important to get off the beach and then dump the sand in someone's garden. It might be an unexpected bonus for someone. For Jack it was another job done, with the prospect of more to come.

As he crossed Western Street he saw Vinegar Bridget leaning against a wall. 'What are you doing here?' he asked aggressively. 'Someone asked you to spy on me, have they? Or couldn't you get a seat in chapel this morning?'

'Just waiting for you, Jack. You know I can't manage without you. Got some business for you, if you is interested. Some boys just run down with a message from me cousin, Mags.'

He put down the wheelbarrow. 'You could have found me earlier. Just come back from the beach. I don't want to go back too soon.'

'Yes, well this time, I got a live one. Born this morning. You might not be needing your shovel. Out at the Uplands, nearly. Plenty of money for it, but you need to move quick. Vicar's daughter. Up by

Llwyn y Bryn. She didn't tell no one so it was all a bit of a shock, I've heard. Healthy it is, though. A boy. I am on my way to fetch it. What do you want to do?'

This was an opportunity not to miss. A fee for collection and then possibly he could sell the child on. But they had to get a move on and Vinegar Bridget had to keep the boy alive; she didn't have such a good record at that.

'Know anyone, Jack?' She didn't like it when they had to drown one.

'You go and fetch it and I will see what I can do. There is a woman in Morriston, been on at me for a while.'

'I'll get off up to Mags then. I will see you back at Mariner Street.'

Jack nodded.

A Militiaman walking towards the Arsenal whistled across the road. 'Vinegar! Me old love! Are you working?'

'Yes, but not with you. Bugger off, John. Go and play with your rifle,' she replied as she walked away and Jack hurried off to Morriston. He knew a garden where he could dump the sand.

*

Abramovitch sat in a chair outside the Castle Hotel, a cup and saucer in his hand. It was a relaxing Sunday morning and the air seemed a little fresher today, as if it had been filtered. It was important that he was seen, that his appearance was commented on, that he became a talking point in the town. He smiled at everyone who came past, offering them a cheery good morning, taking a particular interest in any children who wandered by. A policeman saluted him respectfully, which Abramovitch enjoyed. He had to be patient, he knew that, and it was useful to form an impression of this place that he knew nothing about.

There was plenty to see. He watched a grey old man beating an emaciated donkey, in a vain attempt to make it pull a small load of ashes that was clearly too heavy for such a threadbare creature, even if the incline at the top of Wind Street was a slight one. He saw an over-weight man in a dirty tweed jacket and a sailor's cap pushing a barrow full of apples, stopping occasionally to shout a raucous invitation to buy. Abramovitch could see juice dripping steadily from the barrow as those at the bottom, not fresh enough to be seen, were pressed by the slightly better fruit in public view. The man hurried on when he saw the policeman. A young man with an advertising billboard over his shoulders was standing on the other side of the road, outside Mr Fuller's, the pork butcher, closed for the day. 'Cabinet and Furnishing Department at B. Evans and Company,' it announced on the front of the sign. When he turned to go down the street opposite, Abramovitch could read 'Carpets, Linoleums, Floor Cloths, Mattings, Curtains.' That was Caer Street, Abramovitch noted. He needed to learn these things. A drunk was slumped in the doorway to Mr Oliver's, the bootmaker, a forgotten remnant of a Saturday evening, devoted to oblivion, and the policeman was now trying ineffectually to move him on. He noticed that there was a gap amongst the buildings, like a missing tooth, the legacy of a recent fire, or so the manager of the Castle Hotel told him. Thin, irritable dogs were roaming fruitlessly through the ruins. The unimpressive castle was ruined too, the stones darkly stained with soot.

He watched a boy driving a hoop down the hill where the cab stand would be, if it wasn't Sunday. The boy lost control of it and watched anxiously as it ran away, straight into a prosperous-looking man standing outside the newspaper offices. He caught hold of it and held it out for the boy to collect. The newspaper? Now why hadn't that occurred to him before? Certainly worth a try.

He had yet to see anything exceptional, though. This was a town like any town, Abramovitch decided, though not in one important respect. As if to remind him of it, there was a hoot from a ship on the river down behind him. Swansea was a busy seaport and that might bring significant advantages when he finally needed to leave. He would certainly have to explore the docks as soon as he could. A job for this afternoon perhaps, he thought.

He finished his tea, ridiculously adulterated by milk as far as he was concerned and stood up. What he needed to do now was to get a better idea of the town and its lay-out, to find his way around it more easily, to see what he could see. A walk would be a very good idea, he decided. It had turned cooler, but he had experienced far colder, and it was dry. The perfect opportunity. He might even see a girl.

Abramovitch could hear singing in a chapel further up the road towards the station. That might be a good place to start. He could stand outside for a while, listening to the music, perhaps. Wait for the congregation to emerge, watch where they went. He would be inconspicuous, too. He went into the hotel and collected his hat and cane, then sauntered casually towards the singing. The town seemed well-blessed with chapels, all of them to his mind doing good business. He acknowledged those people he passed cheerfully and, eventually, selected the premises which appeared to be creating the most noise. He stood some distance away, ready to mingle with the people. He saw that he was on College Street now and, as he assessed the area, he realised that he was not alone. There was another figure in the narrow doorway of a public house, The Wyndham Arms. He was wearing a long dark coat, the collar turned up and with a scarf drawn across the bottom of his face. He seemed to be banging his fist repeatedly against the wall. He started to sway. Abramovitch watched him closely, wondering what he intended to do.

The doors of the Methodist Chapel opened and families started to emerge, gathering in small groups to be sociable, oblivious to the man in the dark coat moving quietly amongst them. Abramovitch watched him working his way towards a group of girls, who appeared to be fifteen or sixteen, laughing together a short distance from their parents. Abramovitch watched him closely, trying to interpret his furtive actions. Then the man turned and saw that he was being watched. For a brief moment their eyes met. Abramovitch did not flinch, did not blink. Then he raised his hat. The man turned sharply and walked quickly away, tripping on the uneven pavement and staggering for a moment into the wall. Some of the congregation muttered disapprovingly and their opinions were there, in their eyes, for all to see - to be drunk outside the chapel at this time was, frankly, deplorable. He disappeared from sight.

The crowd began to break up and make their way home. Abramovitch followed one of the larger groups that strolled amicably down into the town, on to Gower Street and towards some impressive residences, accepting as a new member of the congregation this well-dressed, confident-looking man, who was a short distance behind them. Their Sunday-morning smiles indicated their intention to introduce themselves at their earliest convenience. Abramovitch himself had already acquired some interesting information, but he was more pre-occupied with the man prowling in the crowd. That had been especially interesting, he thought. Not at all what he had expected to see.

Ten

Constance was not completely sure what to do about the gift of the cat. She thought that it was a heartfelt gesture on the part of Rumsey, at least she hoped it was. But she was not an animal person. They had kept a cat in the school in order to control the mice. But here? In her own rooms? She was not convinced. The animal was very demanding, distracting her Monday morning pupils by walking across the piano during lessons, a distraction they were eagerly prepared to embrace. He was forever troubling her bread to the extent that she considered nailing it to the ceiling. Then, Constance briefly considered nailing the cat to the ceiling but decided that this might upset Rumsey. She hoped that he hadn't intended it to be a Valentine's Day gift. Oh no, the cat was not the most welcome addition to the household, even if on Sunday afternoon he had made them laugh by sitting at the foot of the bed and looking disapprovingly at them with his one eye.

By midday on Monday, Constance was certain that their relationship was not going to prosper and she expressed her concerns when Rumsey dropped in briefly at midday. ' I have to say that this cat behaves like a sailor on shore leave. He won't leave the female cats alone and he spends the rest of his time fighting with the boys, then he comes home to worry my bread. Do you know what I will call him, Rumsey? Black Bart.' She looked thoughtful. 'I think I will see if the doctor will let me take Black Bart to the Ragged School. The children might get pleasure from his company, for he is undoubtedly a character. I said I would go there anyway to play the piano this afternoon and to see how Sarah is settling into her new job. She has been there for three days now. You never know, she might like Black Bart too.'

'But the cat isn't black, Constance. He is a ginger cat. I thought you might have noticed.'

'He is indeed ginger. But he is a pirate.'

'It is Valentine's Day after all, Constance. Surely Black Bart has a right to look for companionship on a day like this?'

Constance smiled, then tugged gently at her ear. 'Mrs Damms has been to see me. This is her favourite day of the year, she loves all the gossip. She tells me she has heard a story from her cousin who has told her that her sister in law's friend knows of one young man who has, this very morning, sent his beloved a kipper.'

'So I understand it, Miss White. I have heard the same story.'

'Love moves in mysterious ways, Inspector.'

'It's wonders to perform.'

'A mis-quotation I am afraid, Inspector Bucke.'

'Of that I am aware, Miss White.' He waited, holding her gaze. 'One hopes that the young lady was able to enjoy an unexpected and untroubled breakfast. It must have provided her with plenty of time to think deeply about her beloved.'

Constance pushed a strand of hair back behind her ear. 'Thoughts that will have lingered with her all day, of that I am sure.'

'Do you know, Miss White, that today the Post Office delivered over 20,000 items. Normally they deal with a mere 6,000 letters. The Postmaster told me so.'

'Clearly there is a lot of love here in Swansea today, Inspector Bucke.'

'And perhaps there are some living here who have some choices to make.' He paused again. 'I have always believed that one card should be sufficient. If it comes from the person you love.'

It was now Constance's moment to pause. 'I feel that you should know that the postman brought me a card this morning. A Valentine's card, Inspector Bucke.'

'I hope it had a stamp on it – so many of them do not and the love expressed might struggle to triumph over the embarrassment of an unexpected fine.'

'I can report that it carried the correct postage and, within, there

111

was a most heartfelt message.'

'I am not at all surprised, Miss White. There is no one I know who is more worthy of such a letter.'

'You are so very kind, Inspector Bucke. I had but one card. It may be important for you to know that.'

'I would like to think that one card was enough.'

'Oh yes, indeed. I could not ask for more. Should you wish it, I can show it to you.'

'Please do not trouble yourself, Miss White. I might previously have seen something similar.'

They looked at each other, neither of them saying anything. It was Constance who eventually was brave enough to break the silence. 'Perhaps I should make a cup of tea, Inspector.'

*

When Bucke returned to the police station at lunchtime. Inspector Flynn told him of a discovery on the beach, opposite the Seabeach Hotel. Two weighted sacks had been uncovered by some dogs and inside them were two small, perfectly formed but dead babies, one still with the umbilicus and placenta attached. Still-born possibly, though a post-mortem would confirm it. The bodies hadn't been there very long, it seemed. It wasn't unusual to find bodies on the beach but Bucke could never take such discoveries for granted. A child, perhaps created in love, had now been found dead in the sand on Valentine's Day. No one might ever know the extent of the tragedy that had been uncovered.

Bucke ran his hand through his beard. 'You know, James. I have been thinking for a while that we have a baby farm somewhere in the town. Whenever we find babies like this they seem to be in groups, not often alone. Method is the same too. Weighted sacks spread along the bay.'

'It is a wicked trade, Rumsey. Wicked.' Inspector Flynn held up his hand to stop Bucke's reply. 'I know we have so many women who

112

find themselves in a desperate condition, but it is wrong to my way of thinking that anyone should be making money out of it. It is all I am saying.'

'Someone must know who to contact if you want such a thing carrying out. There will be parts of the town where such things are not a secret. The hard part is finding someone who will tell us about it. No one likes the business but there are many who will tolerate it as a necessity.' He shook his head. 'So much of our work depends upon nosy neighbours.'

*

It was hard work; there was no doubt about that. She had to be in school early in the morning to begin the preparations, to chop vegetables and stretch out the insufficient fragments of meat for the ubiquitous cawl. It was easy to prepare, it was warm and it was nourishing and it would be available for any child throughout the day, with some judicious topping up. The Ragged School was busier in the afternoon on most days, for many of the children went to work in the mornings before arriving, hungry, at lunchtime and by then, the school would be awash with its welcoming aroma. She also had to receive the bread from Eynon's Bakery, she scrubbed tables, she washed. Her hands were suddenly raw, her hair steamed constantly above the pans.

This was Sarah's new beginning, her new life. And it was hard and she worked all day. The Ragged School survived on charitable donations and so there would be little money to pay her and what they had would always so uncertain. But for the first time in her life Sarah felt proud of what she was doing. She was making a contribution, helping others; finally, after her shameful years, those years of frustration and anger at the injustices of society, she had found a way of fighting back.

In Doctor Benjamin, Sarah had found a kindred spirit, someone committed to the poor, untroubled by the religious priorities of many of the sponsors. He wanted to work with the poor and offer them realistic help - and now, after three days, so did she. He was certainly decisive. He had appointed Sarah immediately he met her, knowing nothing, as far as she knew anyway, about her background. He asked her to start the following day – 6.00 am on Saturday. Perhaps he recognised her talents; perhaps he was desperate. Constance had given her a clock, just to make sure she wasn't late.

The children were small and vulnerable, sometimes living in quite terrible conditions which remained beyond the understanding of most other people, barely surviving in abject, relentless poverty in an otherwise prosperous town. Sarah understood Benjamin's rage and was determined to do everything she could to make their lives better. But she knew that she could only do part of it – her own life wasn't a great deal better. She knew that the impact she could have was limited, that she could do little directly to change their futures, but she also knew that feeding them was an important start. Benjamin, forthright as always, was adamant that it wasn't religious instruction the children needed – to believe in a benevolent God when they lived in such dire circumstances seemed ridiculous to him. But Sarah saw that he was driven to change their lives. She had never met anyone quite like him before. He was an intense man, angular and often humourless it seemed to her. But he was without doubt very committed to the well-being of all the children and ready to devote all his time to them, treating the debilitating illnesses of poverty and neglect. He was easily moved to tears by what he saw.

It was difficult for her, too. She had shadows enough in her own past that haunted her and the death of children that she had met in the brief time she had been in the school upset her greatly. This was a winter culling, two children dead so suddenly. And for Sarah the hardest thing was the way in which the other children accepted it. No shock, merely resignation.

Constance arrived in the afternoon to play the piano and the children really enjoyed singing loudly and in an uncontrolled fashion. Their version of Ring a 'Roses, with actions, was riotous. Their pleasure and energy were infectious and brought a smile to the school which, in its relentless conflict with disease and poverty, had been previously absent. For a few verses of whatever song it was, the children were set free and together with the warm smell of cawl, it helped the school to feel briefly like a home. They played happily and appeared to look at the blackboard on which the alphabet had been chalked with rather more determination than normal. Benjamin stood at the side of the classroom and felt that suddenly, there was progress. There was a different atmosphere and the children seemed happier. Sarah, arms folded across her apron, felt there was, at that moment, a sense of pleasure and enjoyment that the Ragged School sorely needed. She thought she might ask around for some old rope so that the children could skip, though some seemed so frail it was a wonder that they could walk.

Benjamin stood by her side. 'It is the size of the task that is so overwhelming, Miss Rigby. So much is wrong and so much needs to be done.' He pointed, suddenly animated. 'Look at those two girls there, playing with those dolls. They have no shoes. Never worn any, ever, they say. Can you believe that? It is scandalous. Here is Queen Victoria's Empire, here is Swansea in 1881, and there are children with no shoes, walking the streets in February.' He turned then to Constance. 'Thank you, Miss White. I must admit that I was sceptical of your request to play the piano but I have to accept that it has made a huge difference.'

'Thank you, Doctor Benjamin,' nodded Constance. 'The children seemed to enjoy it.'

'God knows that they have little to enjoy. If, of course, God knows anything at all. The terrible murder of those two innocent boys still hangs over us. What sort of demon could have done such a thing?'

'The police will find him, Doctor Benjamin,' soothed Constance, 'I am sure of it. May I return, later in the week with a friend of mine, whom I am sure the children will enjoy?' She smiled at Sarah's obvious surprise.

Benjamin raised his eyebrows. 'I shall look forward to meeting them, Miss White. If you will excuse me, I have an appointment with Mr Morley, my medical supplier.'

The children began to leave, Benjamin pleading them to be careful on the streets. 'Stay together,' he urged, though it had done little to keep Francis and Andrew safe.

*

At the Star Theatre, preparing herself for the evening performance, Fanny sat at her dressing table with her habitual glass of brandy and smiled. She had Valentine's cards every year and she and the chorus line would sit together and compare them and giggle at the absurdity of it all. It was the most ridiculous custom. But this year she had received one that was different. This one was not anonymous. It was the first one she had ever received that had been signed. By Henry Fry, in a flowing hand. Silly boy, she thought, and smiled before she put the card safely away in her drawer.

*

Jack McCarthy had never been impressed by Valentine's Day. He preferred dealing in cards of a different kind. He was standing on Wind Street, near the offices of the Cambrian newspaper, waiting for his contact to arrive. It was a simple and profitable trade. Captain Diogene Morin from Brest, a name which always amused Jack, was a regular visitor to Swansea, who came to collect coal and brought with him passable brandy and those much sought-after *cartes de visite*, erotic postcards from Paris, featuring outrageously exotic underwear. As Cyrus Bishop, the vicar of Llwyn y Bryn said to Jack when his last order was delivered to him, 'Such joys are so rarely seen on the banks of the Tawe.' They were such scandalous images – and there was an eager market for them too, amongst the more sophisticated and discerning gentlemen of the town. Any man who had the money and the inclination could enjoy the secrets of the Parisian boudoir in miniature, and in private.

Jack enjoyed this profitable and simple business. He loved the way it took him into the wealthier parts of town and provided him with a fascinating and potentially lucrative seam of compromising information. He could not believe that the men who collected the cards sold by Jolly Jack McCarthy never seemed to consider, for a moment, the dangerous position in which they were putting themselves. He kept all his clients isolated, so they never knew who else was implicated in the trade and was confident they could never

116

gather against him. He regularly scanned the family announcements in the newspapers, especially engagements and marriages, and was always ready to suggest that a modest consideration could prevent any potential embarrassment that might develop as a consequence of any injudicious purchases that may previously have been made. They could cast such a dark shadow over nuptial planning. It was a pleasant and uncomplicated way to earn a little money. The first *cartes de visite* he had traded had been quite small and many of his clients rather enjoyed discreet pocket-sized aids to relaxation, but now Morin occasionally brought cabinet cards which were larger and allowed the appreciation of finer details. They were significantly more expensive, but some of his clients liked to pay closer attention to the overall artistic presentation.

Dai the Potato wheeled his baked potato cart and oven down towards the corner of Green Dragon Street. It seemed to Jack to be such a hard way to earn a living, out at all hours, in all weathers, merely to sell potatoes, often to drunks who might then try to steal his money. Life could be a great deal easier, and when he looked around him, and saw Captain Morin approaching, a grey satchel over his shoulder, containing his new stock, he smiled in anticipation of profit.

Morin was a morose man, unkempt, wearing the dirt and grime of five days at sea. He grunted a multi-lingual greeting, his English was not a gift he was always ready to bestow on Jack McCarthy. He opened his bag and handed Jack a collection of small cards, who flicked casually through the delivery. It contained the usual carelessly placed veils and fans, the stockings, the pearls. He handed them back. 'You promised me better. Not paying any extra for these.'

Captain Morin smirked and withdrew some larger pictures from his bag. 'From Paris. Very new. A few days ago. Some no clothes.'

Jack looked more interested. 'From the front?'

'And back also.'

This was what he wanted. He looked through them. Morin was right. They were considerably more candid – and he knew he could sell them. It was what some of his customers were waiting for.

117

They argued about the price, of course. It would have been rude not to. He objected to a couple of damaged corners; Morin talked about rising costs from his supplier. It went on for a good five minutes until they eventually agreed a price. Jack knew it was all about creating a compromise that would let both of them think they had won. So Jack threatened to buy elsewhere and Morin threatened to find a different market. It was a ritual, a transaction based upon the understanding that both of them were eager to cheat the other - that is what made the wheels of business turn. Soon Jack was counting the cards and Morin was counting the coins in the cloth purse he was given, their backs turned to the busy street and the horses shuffling and snorting in the cab stand. They shook hands and Morin confirmed that he would return in a month. There was no brandy this time – they had been a lot more vigilant in the docks recently and he wasn't prepared to risk it. He put the coins in his waistcoat pocket, pulled his jacket closed, handed the purse back to Jack and set off to the Albany Vaults where he would celebrate another successful business deal.

Jack watched him go and then nodded to Selina, who had been waiting on the other side of Wind Street, next to Dai Potato. It was a worth a try.

Selina walked briskly after Morin and then walked around him and stood in his way. With practised charm she laid a hand on his shoulder. 'Good evening, Admiral. A fine man like you, alone in the town? Don't seem right to me. Surprised you haven't been troubled. Some very undesirable women 'round here, you know.'

'*Comment?*' asked Morin.

Selina laughed, her right hand wandering, exploring his pockets. 'Foreign too? You want to be careful. Tell you what, Admiral. Take me for a drink an' you can have a bit of company an' I can give you a few tips, like.' She found where the money was.

He knocked away the hand on his shoulder. '*Merci beaucoup mais je ne comprends pas. Si vous veux bien m'excuser...*'

Selina quickly slipped her hand into his waistcoat pocket and,

118

grinning, pulled out some coins which she put into her mouth.

Morin was suddenly confused. What was happening? He did not see Bridget approaching behind him, ready to empty his pockets whilst he was distracted. As this little drama unfolded, Amy who had emerged from Salubrious Place, pushing her pram, was watching closely. She was fascinated by the way the two women were manoeuvring themselves into position, though she didn't much like the way they seemed to be picking on this man. He didn't seem to realise that there was a woman behind him. She moved closer to get a better view.

Morin moved after Selina, who was backing away from him waving her hands, teasing him.

'Donne-moi mon argent, salop! Maintenant!'

She fished a coin from her mouth, her cheeks still bulging, and offered it to him on her palm.

'Mon argent!' he shouted again.

Bridget was getting closer and Selina crooked her finger to indicate that he might like to pull out some of the coins from her mouth.

'Je ne mets pas mon doight la-bas!'

Amy could see what was going to happen next because Selina, walking backwards and enticing the man, slipped off the curb. She tumbled, the money spewing from her mouth. Morin fell upon it, scrabbling desperately with the two women, especially with Bridget who was pushing and shoving, trying to extract coins from his pocket at the same time.

A noisy crowd formed from nowhere and Amy, reacting swiftly, ran through the crowd and grabbed a couple of the larger coins. She didn't know what they were but if these people were fighting over them, they must be worth having. Amy turned and ran away from the wrestling adults up Wind Street, the ribbon on her pram handle fluttering by her side. Morin and the two women stopped their struggle briefly to shout after her but it was too late. The crowd cheered, for they saw in her timeless qualities that they recognised –

119

she was opportunistic, brazen, defiant - and they celebrated her small triumph as the wresting on Wind Street resumed.

Amy ran on, through the High Street, avoiding horses and carts and snapping dogs, until she arrived at the Bethesda Chapel, where breathless, she waited.

Sarah and Constance had tidied up the kitchen at the Ragged School and then left for home, in different directions. They said nothing to each other, even though they were apprehensive at parting, given the assault on Sarah last week. But it was early and there were plenty of people moving around and the streets had felt convivial, rather than dangerous, as Sarah reflected as she entered Elephant Street. Then she saw Amy, wrapped in the shawl she had given her and holding on to the ribbons on the pram.

'Amy! Oh my goodness! Where have you been? I have been looking for you.'

'Why?'

'Because I have been worried about you.'

'Why? What have I done?'

Sarah smiled. 'Amy. I need to make sure that you are properly cared for. You looked after me when I was in trouble and I want to do the same for you.'

Amy seemed confused. 'I am not in trouble, Sarah. I have something for you. I wanted to give you something because you were hurt.'

'That is very kind of you, Amy. Have you had anything to eat today?'

Amy shook her head faintly and then pushed out a closed fist and emptied into Sarah's palm two half- sovereigns. 'My goodness, Amy! Where did you get these?'

'I found them. They were on the street. I thought you would like them.'

'This is extremely kind of you, Amy. Perhaps we should use one of them to get you something to eat. What do you think?'

The child, independent and yet desperately vulnerable, looked thoughtful. 'I think that is a nice idea.'

They walked together back down the High Street in a companionable silence to the Welcome Coffee Tavern, stopping on the way to buy some shoes and a jacket for Amy from Michael Riley who dealt in second-hand clothes from a barrow at the end of Morris Lane. Sarah used her own money, since she did not want to excite Riley with a glimpse of a half-sovereign. She would use that in the coffee tavern. As she paid, an older, well-dressed man, examining clothes on the other side of the cart, came round to them and smiled. For a moment Sarah thought she had slipped back into her previous life. He had a bowler hat sitting darkly above a face that seemed made entirely out of shadows, his eyes shining from tunnels. He looked carefully at Amy and then ran his hand over her hair, withdrawing it quickly when he realised how dirty it was.

'What an engaging young girl.' He leaned down towards her. 'What is your name? I would like to know.'

Amy snarled. 'Go away, you old goat. Leave me alone.'

The man's face was expressionless. He turned to Sarah. 'This is your daughter, I think. How old is she? I need to know very importantly.'

Sarah took Amy's hand. 'Good evening. We have an appointment,' and they walked briskly away down High Street. She was all-too aware that he was watching them.

'Why did you call him an old goat, Amy?'

'It is what Auntie used to say about men like him.' Amy realised she had made it sound as if Auntie wasn't there anymore and was cross with herself.

In the Tavern, Sarah watched as Amy ate a pasty so very quickly that she had no choice but to buy her another. That one did not rest long on the plate, either. Amy pulled her doll from the pram and sat it on her lap and then drank warm milk with honey, holding the cup as if it was a holy relic.

'Cat ran away,' she said finally.

'I am sorry to hear that, Amy. Perhaps he will come back.'

'I don't think so. I think he was hungry. If someone feeds him he will love them better than me. He wasn't mine anyway. I found him when I found the pram. It was all alone on the side of the North Dock. I waited for ages but no one came to find it and so I took it and I found Cat inside. But he's gone now.' She looked wistfully out of the window. 'I think Dolly still loves me.' She looked round in wonder at the tavern, at the tables, the iron stove, the lights, the steam and was wide-eyed when Sarah bought her more milk.

What was she going to do with Amy? She couldn't let her go, could she? She was such a little scrap.

'I have an idea, Amy. This money you have given to me? Well, it is the best present I have ever had. Do you know what I will do? I have a special purse here. I shall keep that money in here and I will only spend it when we are together. What do you think of that? We could come here again, if you wanted.'

Amy nodded slowly. 'I think that is another good idea. You have lots of good ideas.'

'Who do you live with, Amy?'

'I live with Auntie.'

'Do you have a mam? A mamma?'

'No. I have an auntie.'

'And is there anyone else there?'

'No.' Amy looked uncomfortable. 'I had a brother, Joseph, but he isn't there anymore.'

'I see,' said Sarah. 'Will Auntie mind if you come here with me? Do you think?'

'Auntie won't mind.'

122

'I have another idea, too.' Sarah looked into Amy's large and trusting eyes. Who is this child, she asked herself?

'I like your ideas, Sarah.'

'Good, Amy. I hope you will like this one. I have a new job, you see. I cook at The Ragged School. I am sure you would love the school. There are lots of other children there. I know you would enjoy it. There is food and there is playing and there is singing.'

'I thought your job was doing that thing with men.'

'No, Amy. Not anymore. I work at the Ragged School now. Come along tomorrow morning and see if you like it. Lots of children come every day.'

Amy shook her head. 'I can't, Sarah. I work in the morning.'

'I see. And what is it that you do, in the mornings, Amy?'

'I collect for Auntie. And then I take it to a man and he gives me money.' Amy could see that Sarah was disappointed. She was sorry too. 'But I will come in the afternoon. I promise.' She tucked the doll back into the pram, along with her new shoes.

Sarah could see that Amy had decided that it was time to go. She was a worldly little girl, though there were so many of them, old before their time, their childhood stolen from them, their lives incomplete and cruel, victims with no future. Not all of them could be saved, but Sarah knew that she should do all she could to rescue this malnourished girl. She asked to walk her home, but Amy refused, of course, and hurried away down Welcome Lane, a child who knew too much, who had seen too much and who had lost her childhood.

Sarah watched her, her head full of questions. It wrenched at her to see Amy walk away, to return to goodness knows what, and to do nothing about it. But how could she? She lived with Auntie. But where? In what conditions? Amy was so obviously neglected and seemed wary but so bright. Perhaps she should follow her but Amy turned the corner at the bottom on to the Strand and Sarah knew she'd never catch her now. But there were other questions too. Who was Amy? And then that other question, the one that haunted Sarah, the one that might explain why she was so drawn to her, why it was this child, out of all those who lived on the very edge of life, that so haunted her dreams, the one question she dare not ask.

Amy was consumed by sadness, too. Her dirty hut was dark, for she had no candles left and the meagre embers she had brought home in a metal can from the copper works glowed faintly, offering little heat and no light. She liked Sarah very much, she always felt safe when she was with her. She was always talking to Dolly about her. She used to talk to Cat about her too, and she missed him now that he had gone. She had to go to work in the morning. It is what Auntie would have wanted her to do. Amy had heard at the copper that a woman had been found in the ferry boat on the river, so it wouldn't be long before someone made her better and she came back. But she still thought she would go to see Sarah at the school in the afternoon.

Eleven

Rumsey Bucke lay in his narrow bed, holding the Valentine's card in his hand. He'd been awake for quite a while now. It was still dark but he didn't need to see, to feel the love in the card. His emotions were in turmoil again. It happened sometimes, though less frequently now, but he was still vulnerable to these occasional, but disabling, storms of guilt and sorrow.

The last Valentine's card he had received had been two years ago, when they had all been living happily as a loving family in Henrietta Street, before everything went wrong. At that time, he had had no reason to think that in six months his two children would be dead from measles and that six weeks later his wife Julia would be taken by diphtheria. How could you ever anticipate that?

He climbed briefly from his bed, went instinctively to the wardrobe and pulled out Anna's doll and Charles' wooden sword, the only reminders of his children, other than such vivid memories. He missed them terribly and he missed the life and the love they had shared. Of course, quite unexpectedly he had a new love and those clouds of sorrow no longer obscured the sun permanently. But sometimes the pain came back to him and then he felt guilty about finding such profound happiness - and the love and the passion. And so he lay back on his bed, the sword in his hand and the doll clasped to his chest, ashamed of his new love, ashamed to have betrayed the three people he once loved more than anything else in the world. But he also knew that now, the only thing that could make him feel better was seeing Constance. It was such a set of contradictions. He shook his head and wiped the tears away with the corner of his dirty sheet.

The dark window rattled gently in the breeze. Bucke's room was poorly-furnished, with an ill-fitting window, bare wood, the intrusive smell of damp and decay, and the imprint of the pain inflicted by Mr Scott, the dentist downstairs. It was narrow and cold, a room with neither warmth nor purpose, just a washstand, a chair, a wardrobe and the bed. Should he ever move away from here, there would be nothing for him to take with him. This was the place where he slept and it had never become his home, nor was it ever likely to be. Now his home was wherever Constance was, but it hadn't always been like that. It seemed wrong to find solace for his lost life through the company of another woman, something he could never have contemplated previously. He accepted that life moved on for everyone, and perhaps Julia would have done the same, if circumstances had been reversed. But he could not think his way out of his sorrow alone.

He made a decision and got out of bed, replacing the sword and the doll. He would go to the cemetery and speak to the grave that the three of them now shared. He hadn't been for a while and he felt guilty about that, too. Bucke swilled his face quickly in the cold water at the washstand and dressed. He had time for the visit before he reported to the police station.

There were plenty of people around, heading for work, and they greeted Bucke cheerfully enough, despite the early hour. He was well-respected in Swansea, a reassuring presence rather that a threat. To see him patrolling the streets was sufficiently normal for it to be unremarkable. The streets seemed purposeful and comforting, with the smoke from the coal fires, revived for the day after being banked-up overnight, drifted down from the chimneys and swirled in the cold air.

When Bucke arrived at Danygraig Cemetery he was alone and he followed the familiar path to the gravestone. He did not need the light to find it; he knew it far too well. He stood in the darkness with his hand resting on the cold damp stone, his head bowed, tears flowing. Just beneath him were Julia and Anna and Charles, just as cold as their impassive memorial. He apologised for his absence. He had been busy but he promised to come back soon. He'd bring flowers.

He looked up at the sky; it was getting light. He needed to see Constance but he was already late. He took some deep breaths to compose himself and walked back to the entrance, wiping his eyes with a rag from his pocket.

When he got back to the entrance, Florian the gravedigger was there. He was a short, dark eyed man, strong, powerful and invariably

126

silent. He was ready to do the most unpleasant of tasks for anyone, as long as he was paid in advance. Bucke had employed himself, to memorable effect, when he asked him to create a rat-king. Florian was from Central Europe somewhere, no one could be completely sure, for he spoke as little as possible, though he understood English perfectly well. Perhaps most of the things said to him were not worthy of a reply.

Florian stood by the gate, leaning on his spade, watching the Inspector approach and, when Bucke saw him, he realised that he might be able to help with one of the many puzzles he was dealing with.

'Good morning, Florian. I hope the day finds you well.'

'There is no rain,' he replied tersely.

'You must have plenty to do at this time of year.'

'There is work, always.' He studied the Inspector carefully. He knew he wanted something.

'I have a small job for you, Florian. It won't take you long.' Florian said nothing. 'Can you read Hungarian?'

Florian's eyes flashed. 'I am Hungarian. Is it an idiot you are thinking I am?'

'I am sorry, Florian, I didn't know where you came from,' said Bucke, trying to soothe him. 'I never meant to suggest that you cannot read.' There was no reply. Bucke realised that he hadn't managed the conversation very well, he hadn't been concentrating. He handed over a couple of small coins. 'I would like you to read something for me.'

'And this is all you offer me?' Florian sneered at the paltry payment.

'It is only four words, Florian. Next time you are passing call into the station and I will show it to you. I would be very grateful for your help.'

Florian looked dismissively at the money. 'But not so much grateful, I can see.' He paused. 'Perhaps me too you can help,

Inspector.'

'I would be glad to, Florian. Of course there is no charge for my help,' said Bucke, briefly lifting his eyebrows.

He offered the inspector the faint smile of a practising strangler. 'Someone here. My work they have been disturbing in the cemetery. There is digging. Your constable I have told. There was a new grave. It was opened. Not by me. A baby in a bag was put inside. I found it. This person you must stop.'

At the police station the story was confirmed. Constable Payne had been called yesterday afternoon to the site of the disturbed grave, which initially looked to him like an exhumation and therefore not his responsibility. Alas, Florian revealed to him a sack containing a newly-born baby, in earth still soft from the original burial.

Inspector Flynn raised an index finger. 'Baby farm, Rumsey. No question.'

'Nothing to identify the poor child?' asked Bucke.

'Not a thing. Still born, the doctor says. Could have come from any part of town, I reckon. I have asked the constables to ask around. Sometimes there is a nosey neighbour, someone with a grudge or someone keen on doing God's work. You know how it is, Rumsey.' Flynn was exasperated, 'They should help the poor woman, shouldn't they? That would be better, wouldn't it?' An altercation began in another part of the lobby.

'Whoever is burying these babies is very careful. Doesn't leave anything behind. Nothing here, nothing on the beach. Seems to have been quite a lot recently, too.' The argument was becoming louder.

'We'll get a lead soon enough. Rumsey. And we will get them. But it won't solve the problem, will it? Won't stop the lassies having babies.' There was loud shouting now, two men confronting each other. There were threats and insults.

'Burying still-born babies is one thing. It's the ones they murder – and we know they do it. That is what we need to stop,' said Bucke above the noise.

Flynn turned round. 'You two! Less of the noise, if you will! This is a police station, not the Strand! What's going on, Sergeant Ball? Who are these clowns, disturbing the peace in our happy police station?'

Ball pointed a finger at the taller of the two men. 'I've warned you. You'll be in the cells, if you are not careful. I won't have you upsetting Inspector Flynn.'

'What have I done, like?' The man cast out his hands in supplication. 'It's him!'

Ball turned to the other man.' And as far as you are concerned, Albert Lee, I've had a guts full of you and it's not even eight o'clock!'

Lee was unshaven, dirty and shifty, his hands squeezing and twisting the sleeves of his greasy jacket. 'Begging your pardon, Sergeant, but I dint do it. Wasn't me.' He tugged the disintegrating collar of his thin colourless jacket. 'Everyone's got it in for me.'

'Of course they have!' shouted the taller man. 'That's because you are a bloody tea leaf.'

Ball was getting exasperated. 'How many more times, Ford? Now stop it!'

'But the bugger killed my chickens!' shouted Ford.

'No I didn't, Sergeant. May God strike me dead if I did.'

'Shut up, Lee! God's got better things to do than strike you dead!' said an exasperated Ball.

'What about the one I caught you with, you bugger?' Ford was trying his hardest not to hit Lee.

'I found it!'

Flynn had heard enough. 'Lock 'em up, Stanley. Let's have a bit of peace.'

Ball opened the flap of the counter and gestured to the cells. 'Come on, you two. We've all had enough.'

'But I have done nothing wrong! It is my chickens the bastard has

129

killed!' Ford was incredulous.

'I never touched none of 'em! I want to see Inspector Bucke! I got news for him. It's important!'

Constables Davies and Gill bundled the two men down to the cells, still protesting and Ball turned and spoke to the room in general. 'A word of advice, gentlemen. Never move to Bowen Street in the Hafod. That bugger Lee would steal your teeth if he could. Found early this morning in Willie Ford's garden with one dead chicken and a lot of feathers. Sure, he did it. We'll bang him up for a while and then the bugger will come out and do something like it again.'

Peace had descended and Bucke and Flynn sat in the corner of the lobby, running through their current concerns before they both departed to the courts. This was not the most interesting of weeks, for the Assizes were in progress at the Town Hall and they were both required to attend and look suitably stern whilst justice in all its splendour was bestowed upon Swansea. Everything seemed to take such a long time. Amongst the most serious and unpleasant cases, there were a great deal of bankruptcy cases and a long argument about William Lynch, who had been indicted for sending a ship to sea in an unseaworthy condition and then there was an extended dispute about who precisely owned a cow.

The constables gathered at the counter putting off, for a moment, their own departure for the streets.

'Afore you go, lads. Just a reminder. Nick the Holly is due for release from Cox's Farm soon and I don't reckon he will have seen the light, so watch out for him.' The constables groaned. 'And neither will Frankie Starr and he is due out soon as well. Can't say we have missed 'em.' They were both habituals and both tiresome. 'I shall be keeping a couple of cells warm for the buggers.' He looked down at something in front of him. Something he didn't recognise had appeared there and he was irritated, for he prided himself on a tidy counter.

'What's this then?' asked Sergeant Ball, turning over a small box in his hand that had been left there. 'Roache's Liver Pills?' He shook it, hearing it rattle.

'That will be mine, Sergeant,' said Constable Davies. 'My mam swears by 'em. I said to her, 'me bowels are troubling me something shocking this morning,' an' she says 'these will sort you out.' She's on to her second box now.'

'That's not your liver that's the problem, Constable. That's your bowels, like you said. These are Liver Pills.' Ball read the box carefully.

'Cures everything. See what it says.'

'I'll wager it doesn't stop you farting,' said Constable Gill. 'You have been at it all morning.'

'American sugar-coated pills,' read Ball. *'Purely vegetable and guaranteed not to contain one particle of mercury or other deleterious poison used so frequently in other remedies.'* He paused. 'Very reassuring, I am sure. *These pills are a sovereign remedy for bilious disorders, liver complaints, dyspepsia or indigestion.'*

'See. My mam won't hear a word said against them. See what it says? *A sovereign remedy.'* Davies nodded his approval. 'You can't go wrong.'

'You believe all this nonsense?' Ball put the box back down on the counter.

'Look what it says on the back.' Davies picked it up and read from it. *There is no illness to which flesh is heir, that these pills cannot cure.* And they come from Swansea. Couldn't be better, could they?'

'Where do you get 'em from then?' Gill folded his arms, looking sceptical. 'I haven't heard of no pill factory in Swansea and walk all over its bloody streets.'

'There's Mr Wardle on Waterloo Street. He's a herbalist,' said Davies.'

Gill shook his head. 'Calls himself a Medical Botanist, now. Ridiculous notion. But I have never heard of no Roache.'

'Well, my Mam gets them from the newspaper. She don't need to go to no shop. There is an advertisement and she sends off a letter with 12 stamps and then they come back. Easy.'

Gill picked up the box now and snorted. 'You didn't read this out though did you? *'Females will find them most invaluable and should never be without them.'* He threw down the box in triumph.

'Well, see. That proves they work, don't it? Cos my mam never farts.'

'Women's pills? You will be taking in washing next.'

'Gentlemen, please. Let's get back to work, shall we?' Ball slid the pills across the counter to Davies. 'Put 'em away. You've got villains to catch.'

Davies slipped the box back into the pocket of his tunic. 'A couple of these little beggars an' we'll be fightin' fit. None of them villains will stand a chance.'

The constables started to disperse and Flynn and Bucke stood up, ready for a long day in court, As they did so, the door to the station opened and Bucke was surprised to see Nicolae Abramovitch standing there, as well presented as before, removing his gloves and dropping them into his bowler hat, smiling at the policemen assembled in front of the counter. 'Good morning, gentlemen. To see you all is so good. A fine body of men.' He took out a handkerchief and wiped his mouth carefully.

Bucke greeted him. 'You are out early today, Mr Abramovitch.'

'It sometimes is good to walk the town early, Inspector, sir. When the air is fresh. If ever it is fresh in your grey town. Passing by I was, and so I was thinking perhaps that you might have important news for me.'

'Please, Mr Abramovitch. Perhaps you would step into my office for a moment?'

'I do not see a need for such formality. All you must do now is offer me the direction to my daughter's home. That is all.'

'I have no news for you at the moment, Mr Abramovitch. I shall bring any news to you the moment I receive it.' Bucke watched him closely.

'No news? What sort of town is this, Inspector, sir? That you cannot find a young girl? It is quite easy, surely?'

'Quite simply, Mr Abramovitch, there is so much that we don't know and I apologise for that. We are looking and the constables have been carefully briefed, but we don't know that she is still here. We don't know if she knows who she is or indeed if those who are caring for her know that either.'

'So Chana is a feather blowing in the wind, that does not know it belongs to a bird? Is that what you are saying? And you cannot help? And have you found this Hungarian who is killing people?'

'Our enquiries continue, Mr Abramovitch.'

'This is most unsatisfactory, Inspector, sir. It would not be allowed in my country. Do you not keep records, here in this town?'

'The census is in a few months,' said Bucke, gently. 'They are every ten years. Your daughter is too young to have appeared on the last one.'

'You must hasten. Do you not understand? My daughter is in very grave danger, as I have told you. Czibor the Hungarian. And I am sure I have seen him, Inspector, sir, and yet you say you cannot find him. This worries me, for he is looking for Chana. This I know. Listen to me. I have seen Czibor. He is walking around silently, looking at young girls. I know that he is doing this. He is waiting for me to do his work for him; he wishes me to lead him to her. Then he will strike, for himself and for Hungary.'

The police station fell silent. Abramovitch had seen him? Perhaps this was the breakthrough they needed.

'And so you have a description of him that will help us with our investigation, Mr Abramovitch? Where do you think you saw him?'

'I know I see him. I have not seen him before but I do not need to see him before. I knew straight away when I saw him. He is a famous killer but he is not well disguised. Outside a small church

133

amongst many people. On your College Street. He is young. He has a dark coat. A dark hat that is flat.' He shrugged. 'This is a great trouble to me, for you say you cannot find him, yet I have seen him, Inspector, sir. You cannot, it seems, find anyone.' He turned and walked imperiously out of the police station.

'Job done then. Shouldn't be hard to find,' declared Constable Gill. 'A man in a dark coat and a flat hat.'

The silence lifted and the constables began to leave, grumbling about the day ahead. Inspector Flynn looked at Bucke perceptively. 'What's the problem, Rumsey?'

'I don't know, if I am honest, James. But there is something about the man that doesn't convince me, but I don't know what it is. You see, if he saw this killer, this man with Satan in his soul or whatever he said to me, why didn't he tell someone? Why wait until today? And how can you positively recognise someone who you have never met before? Perhaps a day sitting in the Assizes will help clear my mind.'

*

It didn't. But nonetheless Bucke was certainly grateful for the opportunity to escape from the Assizes early when it came, for he needed to write a report for the Watch Committee about the number of babies that had been buried on the beach. He was making quite good progress too, when Sergeant Ball put his head round the door. 'Sorry to trouble you, Inspector. But I thought I'd have a quiet word.'

'Come in, Stan. What's troubling you?'

Sergeant Ball leaned across the desk. 'Nothing, Inspector. Nothing at all. It's Albert Lee. He reckons he wants to speak to you. Says he has vital information for Inspector Bucke but he won't say nothing to me.'

'Let him wait a bit longer, do you think, Stan?'

'Well see, Inspector. I am going to release him. Willie Ford's not pressing charges . He got his dead chicken back and Mrs Ford has boiled it. I reckon she plans to give Albert a slap on the sly. That is how they sort things out, on Bowen Street. I wouldn't like to be in

134

his shoes when Jemima comes to call. Anyhow, Albert doesn't know this yet. He thinks that if he speaks nicely to Inspector Bucke, then Inspector Bucke will let him go. What do you think?'

Bucke smiled. 'That is an interesting opportunity, Stanley. Bring him up. Stay close to the door. I might be calling for you.'

Ball winked.

As Bucke feared, Albert Lee was no cleaner than he had been in the morning. He stood nervously, scrunching his sleeves between his crossed hands again. 'I have some information for you, Inspector Bucke. Some important information. I knows you will find it interesting. But fair's fair, like, isn't it? You scratch my back and I will scratch yours, that is what they say.'

Bucke leaned back in his chair. The idea of scratching Lee's back, especially through that jacket, was not appealing. 'It all depends what you have to say, Albert. Remember, withholding information from a police officer is an offence; it could, in fact, be even more of an offence than the reason why you are here already.'

'I never did kill that chicken, Inspector. God's honest truth. I found it dead, didn't I? Scrawny bugger, anyway. I found it in the street. Dog had had it, I reckon. And I don't need to be taken into no custody and presented afore the magistrates on account of a dead chicken what I didn't kill. I can't afford no fine.'

'You have been inside before haven't you, Albert?' asked Bucke, speculatively.

Albert looked offended. 'Yes. And I don't want to go back. I will tell you something else, Inspector. I never insulted a postman or interfered with a policeman called Parry. Them is all lies. I had a solicitor an' everythin'. He said it were a stitch up. It were Dick Burke did it. Everyone knows. But I was not from Cardiff, was I? So it had to be me, didn't it? Hard being English in Wales. Always picking on me. Innocent I was. Still am.' He sighed at the injustice of life for a petty thief. 'But I sees things, see. I sees a lot, here and there.'

Bucke raised his eyebrows and decided that he wouldn't try to

135

untangle whatever it was that Albert had said. 'We all see things If we look, Albert. What did you see?'

'You'll let me go? If I tell you?' Bucke said nothing and raised his eyebrows, inviting him to begin.

'Well, it were last week.' Albert stopped to bite the corner of his lip and looked shiftily around the room as if he was concerned they could be overheard. He scratched at his arm vigorously. He probably had fleas. Or lice. 'Last Thursday it was. I was up by the abattoir, see. In the dark, it was.'

'Perhaps you'd better sit down, Albert.' Bucke was suddenly alert.

'Thank you, sir. Very kind of you, sir. You see, I knew you would want to know. Serious business is murder. And dangerous. Puttin' myself at risk, by even talkin' to you. Bear that in mind, Inspector, if you was ever thinking of a cash consideration, like.'

'What were you doing up there, Albert? The truth, mind. Or you are back in the cells.'

Albert took a deep breath; the truth did not come easy to him. 'I went up to see if I could find a chicken, sir. To see if any of 'em had got out, like. Trying to get away. I would if I were a chicken.'

'So you were stealing, is that right, Albert?'

'It is all words, Inspector. When it comes down to it. Nothing but words. I was seeing what I could find, sir. Stuff that had been forgotten, sir. Sounds nicer. I mean, a chicken could have got out, when you think about it, like. But they hadn't. That is why I ended up back on Bowen Street, Inspector. Missus wanted a chicken.'

'So you were at the end of Ebenezer Street, is that what you are saying?'

'Yes, but I couldn't get into the slaughterhouse, could I? It were all fastened up. But then, you see, I looked at the fence round the Pottery, see.'

Bucke continued to watch him carefully. 'But there is no food in the Pottery.'

'You know what it is like, Inspector. You'll look anywhere when you are hungry.' Bucke didn't know, but said nothing. 'And then I noticed that the fence was shaking like, so I stepped backwards where I couldn't be seen and a man comes through the fence, don't he?'

'Can you describe him?'

Albert thought that the question was ridiculous. 'It was dark, Inspector.'

'Was he tall? Was he short?'

Albert shook his head, puzzled. 'Like everyone else, I reckon. Didn't see his face. He had a hat and his collar was up. He had a jacket that was dark and he was wearing one of them aprons. Leather, I should think.'

'Was he carrying anything?' asked Bucke.

'Not that I could see. He went off up Dyfatty Street. Towards the Golden Lion.' Albert screwed up eyes as tightly as he could, to indicate that he was thinking hard.

'And what did you do?'

'Obvious, innit? I looked through the fence. But I didn't see nothing that looked like you could eat it.'

'You wouldn't. Not in a pottery. And what time was this, Albert?'

'I reckon no later than seven. I don't remember hearing no bells until a bit later, see.'

'So that's it? You saw a man come through a gap in a fence? And you didn't go inside? You didn't look inside a shed? You saw nothing else?'

'Inspector. It is where them boys were murdered, you know that. I think I seen the man. I knows which way he went. Every little bit helps a policeman, they say.' Albert stared back at Bucke, defiant, confident.

'This is not very much from a man who wants me to let him go free, is it? You saw a fence. You saw a man. And?'

137

'You asked me to tell you the truth and that is what I has done. It might not be exciting but this is all the truth,' he pulled at his jacket again and grimaced. 'Never exciting, the truth. Is it?'

Bucke said nothing; this was so inconsequential it was very likely the truth. But he had seen the hint of a glint in the corner of Albert Lee's eye. Perhaps there was more. 'Well, if that is it, I'll call Sergeant Ball and you – '

'There is something else. May God strike me dead if I tell you a lie. Might be important. Not for me to say, is it? But I found something, didn't I?' Bucke waited, saying nothing. 'A very important something, I should say, even if I am no policeman.' Albert put his hand in his pocket and produced a dirty rag. 'Found it, didn't I? On the floor when the man come out. When I first had it the blood on it were still wet, but it has dried now. It were real, Inspector.' He placed the rag on the desk. 'Real blood.'

Bucke moved it around speculatively with his pencil. The killer must have dropped it. There was no other explanation, if Albert was telling the truth. He looked at Albert, letting him know that he was not ready to be fooled, then carefully unfurled it, tattered and battered as it was. The handkerchief was dirty and there was a great deal of what looked like dried blood on it. There was some rough and untidy embroidery in the corner, inexpertly applied. BUDA it said.

'Told you. Told you I had something,' said Albert with pride. 'Vital, I'd say. Man's name, I shouldn't wonder. Worth a tidy consideration.'

'Thank you, Albert, I am very grateful.' Bucke called out. 'Sergeant Ball!' The door opened immediately. 'Please Sergeant, I should be grateful if you could escort Albert here off the premises. He has been very co-operative and I would be happy for you to square things quietly with Mr Ford.'

Albert grinned in relief as Ball took him by the elbow. 'Albert Lee, you are a lucky bugger and don't you forget it. Behave yourself now. Inspector Bucke has been very kind and as like as not won't be so generous if you turn up here again. So hop it!'

'Much obliged, sir. I shall take heed, sir. Never doubt it. You can rely on me, sir. Whenever I am needed.'

Would that were possible, thought Bucke. But he had learned something, though he had no idea how important any of it might be. He knew now that the two boys, Dolphin and Mazey, had been murdered within an hour of leaving the Ragged School, by a man wearing a leather apron who, it seemed, had dropped a blood-stained handkerchief inelegantly embroidered with the word BUDA. Was it really a reference to the capital of Hungary, he wondered?

But perhaps more importantly, was it genuine, dropped careless by the killer, Czibor the Hungarian? Or had it been picked up by one of the boys from the street? But then, thought Bucke, it could have been planted there deliberately to mislead. More questions. Always, more questions.

Twelve

It was not the happiest of mornings at Danygraig Cemetery, where there was another unfortunate incident, one which did little to improve Florian's temper. It was eventually confirmed that two funeral corteges had both left the Uplands at about 11.00 am. One was that of Emrys Lansey of Hanover Street and the other was for the respected widow, Mary Fleming of Westbury Street. No one seemed to have noticed, least of all the man himself, that Reverend Cyrus Bishop, the vicar of Llwyn y Bryn, was officiating at both funerals, both of which had been unfortunately arranged for the same time.

Vicar Bishop's name was a joke that never wore thin amongst some of his more elderly parishioners and meant that they were inclined to give him a little more latitude than perhaps he deserved. This, however, was an occasion designed to test their patience. They accepted graciously that, by all accounts he was more distracted than usual by other, private, issues at that time, but his part in what was to follow could not be readily forgiven.

Florian, in response to the clear instructions he had received, had only dug one grave and he stood to one side and sighed loudly whilst he watched a most inappropriate squabble. When the much larger group of mourners for Mary Fleming arrived, they found the grave already occupied by the coffin of Emrys Lansey. His relatives, very eager to show themselves worthy of a legacy, despite having left it a little late, defended the plot aggressively. A brief fist fight developed when two of Mary Fleming's older mourners jumped into the grave and tried to remove a coffin that was obviously too heavy for them.

'You may as well stay down there, grandad. You won't be too long yourself,' someone shouted and other mourners started to throw earth on to them and then prevented them from climbing out. More blows were exchanged when an attempt was made to startle the horses drawing the Mrs Fleming's hearse. There was a deal of inappropriate shouting, amongst which some unfortunate vocabulary was heard.

Mr Bishop stood to the side, wringing his hands, calling for restraint and being completely ignored. He was missing his carelessly forgotten hipflask a great deal. He had no idea at all over which coffin he should be conducting a ceremony; the pressure upon him to exert an authority which he did not possess in such chaotic circumstances was too much for him. The police were called and they restored order, with the mourners on both sides over-wrought and dishevelled.

Florian had already started to dig a second grave on his own initiative before the police arrived, the physical labour, however welcome, doing little to obscure this additional confirmation of the unremitting stupidity of human behaviour.

*

Amy was, for a few moments, overwhelmed by the Ragged School when she tentatively walked in. If she had thought Sarah was not going to be there, then she would never have had the courage. It was bright, it was colourful, it was noisy, it was so different. But the warm smell of the soup was irresistibly welcoming. She saw some children sitting down at old desks, waiting for their lesson to start and looking at a board with some white marks written on it that looked quite familiar to Amy, although she didn't know what they were. Others were playing with toys. It was a bewildering place.

And then Sarah appeared. She had been waiting for her at the side of the room. She was pleased to see her, Amy could see that, and she took her through to the kitchen. She was talking, though Amy couldn't hear. It was such an unexpected experience; she wasn't used to such a noisy environment. Some of the children looked at her pram with interest as she pushed it through the room and one girl came up and touched the ribbons attached to its handle. Amy knocked her hand away and glared.

In the kitchen Sarah gave her a bowl of soup. It was very nice, very warming. There were round orange-coloured things in it which she wasn't sure about but she tried them because she didn't want to upset Sarah. They were a bit strange but she ate them anyway. She finished one bowl and Sarah refilled it.

What a place this was. So many people, so busy. Amy looked around, at the wooden floor, at the ceiling, at the tall windows and, as she became more familiar with the room, she finally began to hear Sarah's voice, for she had continued to talk.

'...Constance will be here soon, I think. We are going to have singing again. Black Bart is around somewhere. Now you have had something to eat we can go and look for him. He is our cat. He hasn't been here long and he is still getting used to us. He is a bit grumpy. So you be careful, he has already scrammed some of your new friends. Leave your pram here. Dolly will be quite safe.'

'She isn't called Dolly anymore. She is Sarah now. Sarah Dolly. I can talk to her in the night now.'

Sarah blew out her cheeks and then wiped her brow with her apron. 'Let's go into the schoolroom, shall we?'

Amy saw the cat almost immediately, prowling around the edge of the room. She went straight to him and he arched his back as she stroked him. 'That is really good!' said Sarah. You are the first person he has allowed to touch him since he came to the school. What an honour!'

Other children gathered around to watch and the girl who had fondled the ribbon stood by her side. Then suddenly, as children do, their hands touched, held and then together they skipped away. At that moment Sarah knew that Amy was now part of the school. She returned to the kitchen to her work. Amy wouldn't leave without her pram. Then, as she finished the washing up, Amy returned and pulled Sarah Dolly out of the pram. 'Myra wants to see her,' she called as she ran back to the schoolroom.

The kitchen had been surprisingly untidy that morning when she arrived, especially since Sarah was sure she had put everything away last night. There was sugar spread across the table too, which she couldn't explain. But someone could have been using the school for a function or something. She was the new person in The Ragged School and it was not her place to question anything. She didn't want to upset anyone – she really needed this job. Sarah smiled as she hung

142

up some wet clothes that the children had brought in to dry by the fire, then went out to see what Amy was doing.

She found her sitting intently with a slate on her lap and a piece of chalk in her hand. This was truly magical. By making lines on the black slate you could leave a mark that looked a bit like the thing you were looking at. Myra was very good at it and she had made some marks that looked like Black Bart, and then she put a patch on his eye. Amy really hoped that she would be able to do something like this herself one day. When she looked at the blackboard she realised that the shapes on it were the same as those that were outside some of the shops in town. That was interesting. This school was a place full of surprises.

When Constance arrived at the piano, Myra took her to sit at the front for the singing. Amy wasn't too sure what was happening but she soon picked up the words in the songs and the actions too.

Whilst the children were singing and laughing, Dr Benjamin brought in a well-dressed visitor who surveyed the room very carefully. Sarah saw him, a man with a cane, in a suit, carrying a bowler hat. Visitors from the more prosperous side of town were a regular occurrence and Benjamin always hoped for a donation from them. This visitor moved amongst the children, stroking the hair of some of the girls, who flinched from his touch, instinctively. He stood behind the group in front of the piano, tapping his foot. Of course, Sarah had seen him before. This was the man she had seen at the second- hand clothes barrow, the one Amy had called an old goat. His smile was still thin, still insincere. Benjamin took him into his office and Sarah hoped he got a generous donation from him. There was something about him that she didn't like; Amy's comment about him might contain the perceptive power of an innocent child. The old goat.

As the afternoon drew to a close, Sarah's anxieties increased. Amy had settled, she was playing very happily with some of the other girls. A little lost girl, suddenly able to escape briefly from a demanding and dangerous life. Sarah sighed and Constance, sensing her worries, came to stand next to her. 'Her childhood. This is it. She has found

143

it. This is what she has been missing. I hadn't realised what an insubstantial thing she was.'

'Poor thing. I really do not want to let her go, Constance. Not now. Look at her. Finally the child she ought to be. And if I let her go, what am I sending her back to?'

'Do you think she will come back?' Constance looked at Sarah carefully. 'You are worried that one day she won't, aren't you?'

Sarah made no reply and they watched her. In a room full of dirty children, she was by far the filthiest. But her eyes were bright with intelligence and hope, it seemed.

'I have an idea, Sarah. Let's take her home, back to my rooms. We'll get some clothes from Michael Riley and then we can bath her. She needs a new beginning. She needs to wash away her old life.'

*

It became a wonderful occasion, blissful, unlike anything Amy had ever experienced before. She had the attentions of two loving, giggling women, enjoying themselves, and she was at the heart of it all. It was something that she would never have thought possible. The kitchen was steaming with hot water that was being collected in a small tin bath. There was a black iron stove behind it, with proper glowing coal, not miserable scavenged embers. There were new clothes waiting for her on a chair. The room smelt clean and warm. Amy had no doubt. This was the most beautiful place she had ever seen.

She was reluctant to take her clothes off but, as Constance said, if she was going to wear her new ones it was what she had to do. Amy was surprised when the two women recoiled at the state of the undergarments and threw them immediately on to the fire. Sarah and Constance began by washing her hair, which they said smelt like a stale unemptied chamber pot. She wasn't really sure what they meant. The dirty water they threw away. They said that it wasn't something she should be sitting in. Sarah said she was using the rosemary-infused water to cut through the dirt, though she was not sure what that meant. She said that Amy's hair was much lighter than they had both

144

believed. Was that important? She trimmed the ends of her hair with shiny scissors whilst it was still wet but that was fine because it didn't hurt.

Amy wasn't sure at first about the warm water. Again she was worried that it might hurt, for she had never sat in a bath before. Constance let her put her hand in it. Amy admitted to herself that it felt very nice. There was soap that smelt like flowers in the market and it slipped so happily across her skin and that made her laugh. They persuaded her to stand in the bath first and then, once they had washed her legs carefully, soothing the cuts and grazes on her knees, she sat down and they poured water over her shoulders and washed her back. Constance and Sarah seemed so happy together and seemed to enjoy it as much as she did. When they had finished and she was wrapped in a large flannel shirt she felt happy and sleepy and she sat comfortably in front of the fire. It was a beginning. She had been re-born.

There was a knock at the door and Constance jumped up. 'That will be Rumsey. He will be so pleased to see you.'

Amy froze. She was suspicious by nature, for her survival had always depended on it and she had been tricked, and trapped now, inside a strange house. She knew this man's name. It was one she could remember. She didn't like men very much. Auntie said they were goats and she had heard some people on the streets saying that policemen were evil. So why had Sarah and Constance brought him here? What were they going to do to her?

Sarah leaned across and took her hand. 'Amy, don't look so worried. Inspector Bucke is a fine man. He is a very special friend, to Constance, especially.'

'He is evil. All policemen are evil. People say so. I have heard them.'

'No he is not, Amy. Do you remember last year when I met you outside that coal mine?'

'No. That wasn't me. I have never been outside no coal mine,' Amy said, moving uneasily in her seat.

145

Sarah wasn't surprised. Amy seemed much younger than the other girl who had a pram and who she had spoken to outside the Calvary Pit. 'But you have heard about it, haven't you?'

Yes, I have. I heard some men talking about it.' Amy glanced towards the door nervously.

'Constance and I went into the mine to help some people and then the roof began to fall down. And we were inside.'

'Were you very scared?' Amy was shocked. 'Did you get hurt?'

'Only a little bit but we were very frightened. It was dangerous and we nearly died. And who helped to rescue us? Rumsey Bucke did. He held my hand and pulled me out.'

'Did he really?'

'Yes, he did. He is a good man. Do you like Constance, Amy?' Sarah was stroking her hand gently.

'She is my friend. You are my friend, too. I like you very much. You are my best friend.'

'I am very pleased to hear that, Amy. So you must try to trust him, too. Do you think you can do that? He helps lots of children. He helps everyone. Do you promise not to worry?'

Amy was apprehensive. 'I shall try but he is chasing me – '

The door opened and Constance brought Rumsey into the kitchen. Amy's alarm was obvious.

'Good evening, Sarah. How very pleasant it is to see you here. I hope your day has been a pleasant one?' Bucke said nothing to Amy.

'Of course, Inspector. May I introduce to you our new friend, Amy? She has been at the school with me this afternoon.'

Bucke bowed his head slightly. 'Well Amy, how nice it is to meet you at last. I have seen you before of course, but never in a place so comfortable. That's a fine shirt you have. I used to have one like that, very warm. Did you meet Black Bart today? How did you get on with him?'

146

Amy suddenly found herself being drawn into a conversation but she couldn't stop herself. 'You know about Black Bart?'

'Yes he does,' Sarah said. 'In fact, the Inspector rescued him from a boat.'

'Rescued him? Was he in trouble?'

'I think Black Bart is always in trouble. He was on a broken boat and when I turned up I think he decided that I was going to be his servant. But Constance, I am hungry. Shall we have something to eat? I am sure that Amy will help me lay the table and I will tell you all about the old villain. The first thing we have to do is to get rid of this bath full of water. I have brought some ham for our supper and we don't want to drop it in the water, now do we? Did Constance play the piano at the school today? Did you sing? Perhaps she will play for us later if we ask her nicely? What do you think?' And so by not giving Amy a moment to object to anything, a friendship was born.

Later, Amy, tired and comfortable, fell asleep on some cushions on the floor and the three adults considered her. Without the thick film of dirt she seemed more frail than ever, vulnerable, in peril, though there was a strength about her, a determination, a resourcefulness. She was a pretty girl, her blue eyes when she had looked around the table, had been even more pronounced now that her face was cleaner, although her body, as Constance and Sarah could confirm, she was scarred in any number of places. Her shoulders were bruised and coarsened by whatever it was she did.

'What a treasure she is.' Sarah bent down and moved a strand of hair from her mouth.'

'She will have to stay here tonight,' Constance said. 'We can't possible disturb the poor thing, not now. She looks so peaceful. Where does she go, anyway? You had better stay too, Sarah. Amy will be happier waking up here if she sees you.' Sarah nodded.

'It is a shame she did not see more when you were attacked,' said Bucke as he went through what Amy had said.

'I don't think she said much that was new,' said Sarah, rubbing her bruised ear where she had been hit.

Constance put her cup and saucer on the piano. 'Amy heard the man muttering bad words, she said, when she first walked past him.'

Bucke scratched his head. 'Which is interesting in itself. Because he showed no wish to attack her. His anger – and he is obviously angry – is directed towards women alone.'

'He didn't creep up on Sarah, either. Amy saw him run up to her,' added Constance.

'Quite a distance too. To succeed he really should have been closer. That doesn't make sense to me,' said Bucke. 'Do you think he used something when he hit you? A weapon of some kind? A piece of wood? A tool perhaps?'

'I can't be sure. It was a hard blow but I didn't see anything. Amy hasn't mentioned it either. She does remember buttons. She said they were shiny. I think I remember buttons, too. Although when he hit me everything was spinning round.'

'We found a button at the scene, but generally a button is just a button.'

'It is a start, Rumsey,' said Constance. 'You just need to look for someone with identical buttons or a man with mismatched buttons. No man likes mismatched buttons.'

'Why didn't I think of that?' asked Bucke, shaking his head.

'What do we know about Amy?' asked Constance. 'She is a strange little thing. There is hardly anything to her and no one seems to know where she lives.'

Sarah sat forward in her chair. 'I don't know where she lives or who she lives with. She isn't the girl I spoke to outside Calvary Pit. She was older I think and what happened to her I don't know. Amy found the pram with the cat in it. The same pram, but now owned by just another Swansea child. Amy keeps talking about Auntie. She says she had a brother but he isn't there, wherever that is. Whenever I ask her about her mother, she just talks about Auntie.'

Bucke looked thoughtful. 'And the child was very smelly, you say?'

'I have not experienced anything like it,' said Sarah. 'Like a chamber pot. On Monday when I took her to buy shoes from Michael Riley, this well- dressed toff with a cane and a bowler hat touched her hair and then backed off. He turned up at the school this afternoon too. Amy called him an old goat.'

'Now that is interesting. At the school today? I know who that is. And he was interested in Amy you say?' Bucke thought about that for a moment. 'But I can tell you a little more about Amy, I think. Because I think Auntie is dead. She is the woman who was found dead in the ferry boat last week. Aunty Pee. She collected urine for the copper works. So that means Amy is completely alone. When she wakes up I suggest that you ask her about the boat. I think she is an orphan and you have rescued her in time, thank goodness.'

Amy was not used to sleeping so comfortably and she stirred little throughout the evening. But Constance's home was unfamiliar and she woke up suddenly, initially disorientated and confused and very wary. Sarah, who had been watching Amy carefully, gave her a cup of warmed milk and soon she persuaded Amy to talk. Yes, she had helped Auntie into the ferry boat that she had borrowed, but it had been too heavy for her and had drifted away. But she had to go back now, ready to get on with their work in the morning, collecting. Auntie would be cross if she didn't.

Sarah as firm. 'You must not go, Amy. It isn't your job anymore. I had a job once, you know that. But I have a different job now. I go to school. You don't have to keep on doing the same job.'

'But I only have one job,' said Amy stubbornly, trying to push past Sarah. Constance came into the room and leaned against the door.

'No, Amy. No. You cannot live on your own. You are not old enough. You should be with people who love you. ' Sarah paused. 'Auntie isn't coming home. She wasn't very well, you know that. It is very said but she died. Inspector Bucke said. You know what that means, don't you?'

Amy nodded and lowered her head.

Constance pushed herself away from the door. 'Look, Amy. Inspector Bucke sent one of the constables to see me just now. He went to see the man you sell your collecting to. He said he had found someone else. He said you were very good at the job but he needed someone taller. So he said thank you and sent you a shilling, here it is.' Amy said nothing, but it was clear that she was wavering. 'Amy. I have an idea. Why don't you go to work for Sarah in the Ragged School? I know she will pay you and you can help her with the cooking and all those other jobs. You will pay her, won't you Sarah?'

'Of course, Constance. And I have an idea, too. One of her jobs could be looking after Black Bart. I think he likes you.' Amy smiled.

'A capital idea!' Constance clapped her hands.

'And just to make sure you get to work on time, because no one likes someone who is late, you can move in with me. Then we can go to work together. How about that? We can start in the morning. You should go back to sleep, really, Amy. It's going to be a busy day.'

*

The man stalked the streets. He was good at it, slipping in and out of doorways, staying in the shadows. He stood quietly to one side as a young man strode confidently down the middle of the uneven pavement towards a theatre, where crowds had already started to gather. He was well dressed, confident, happy it seemed, carrying a large bunch of flowers. He smiled and watched this prosperous man, off to his leisure. But the watching man knew there were many others he saw in this town, with lives that were so very different, and also he knew that fear and confusion could be created so very easily in a place with such obvious and unbridgeable divisions between rich and poor. He had spent some days observing them, his own cynical view of the world drawing him to those who preferred to remain unnoticed and hidden, like himself – the pickpockets, the robbers, the burglars – those who did not wish to be noticed at all, walking close to the walls. And those who were lucky and comfortable, believed people like these, who lived such unimaginable lives of need and disease, were just waiting to pounce on prosperous men walking down the middle of the street carrying flowers, foolishly believing themselves safe. It

150

made him smile, for the confidence they displayed was so fragile, so easily punctured. Who, in reality, was at home on streets like this? Who owned them, made them their world? It certainly wasn't the rich. And he knew without a doubt that the terror and fear that were within his gift, were his most important weapons.

So he remained patient, watchful and wary. And then, finally, in the middle of Temple Street, he saw the opportunity for which he had been searching. A Swansea child.

There was a young boy, short, under-nourished but bright-eyed, selling newspapers outside The Three Lamps. He still had a few left but he seemed pleased with himself. Why not? He had had a good night and suddenly here was another man wanting to buy a paper. He fumbled with the change, dropping a couple of coins, because his hands were cold.

'Why not go inside?' the man suggested kindly. 'You will be able to warm your hands up. Perhaps you will be able to sell some more newspapers. The barmaids will not be minding.'

The man was very persuasive and led him inside. And it was warmer, like he said. And another man bought a paper. This was his best night ever, selling papers. And then the man gave him a drink. Don't worry he said. You have deserved it, he said, selling all those papers and I will pay for it. It was a bit sour, he thought, and the pot was huge but the other men in the pub cheered when he finished it and someone slapped him on the back and suddenly there was another big pot of beer in front of him. Someone shouted something about him climbing in and there was a lot more laughter. He felt a bit dizzy but then it was very warm in The Three Lamps. No wonder men came in here, out of the cold. He realised he could not remember what he had done with his newspapers. Were they on the floor? He wasn't sure but the men started cheering again and then they were clapping and they laughed as he drank the beer. Some of it spilled down his chin and into his muffler and really did feel dizzy now and the room seemed to be moving around him all the time and the big red faces of the men laughing seemed really close to him. He must have said something. Perhaps he said he wanted to pee but he wasn't sure. But the man helped him to his feet and everyone was shouting and cheering, but he couldn't walk properly because the floor seemed to be very uneven and so the man put his arm around him and his leather apron felt hard and damp and the man took him outside. The air was so very cold and he stumbled and fell. He lay on the ground and was sick and the man helped him up and then they walked for a while. He wasn't sure where they were going. He seemed to be walking downhill. Then he heard voices and some laughter and he seemed to be lifted up and very soon he was swaying slightly, which made him feel sick again. He must have fallen asleep he thought, but even when he opened his eyes everything was still very dark and he thought he was walking again. Then he banged his head on something and it hurt, so he closed his eyes and it was still dark and he felt as if he was spinning round and round really quickly into a darkness that seemed eager to consume him.

Thirteen

When they found him, there was dirt all over his body, as if he had been dragged through the street; there was still thin blood coming from his mouth which had trickled into his hair; his left eye was open and sightless, and there were lesions on his head. It was an infernal sight but it was easy to interpret. He had been beaten to death and then afterwards he had been strapped like a starfish to the large wheel of a hansom cab, which had been paraded silently through the town by a blinkered, plodding horse. His fingers and toes had been worn away by their contact with the rough ground.

The horse had finally come to rest at the stables that served the Mumbles tramway, where it stared impassively at a wall until the night watchman of the Swansea Hospital found it, believing that the badly tethered horse had run away. He called for the police immediately.

It was Patrick Connor, still only 10 years old, his small body broken on a wheel. Many people knew him – they had, indeed, bought newspapers from him. A small boy below average height and weight, even in Swansea terms, dressed in his thin clothes and tattered fingerless gloves, with an unerringly quick mind for small change. Here he was, now a fingerless corpse, displayed, abused and violated for the constables. Bucke, who had been called from his bed in Fisher Street, and was now grey-faced and grim, bent down to place his face close to the boy. There was a lingering cloud of sour beer surrounding him. He stood up and stepped back.

This was truly insane. Why would anyone do something like this? Who could ever believe that their life's destiny required the gruesome murder of a child? It is a transgression, that is what it is, thought Bucke. A rejection of one of the things that makes us human, the instinct to care for and protect children. If we dismiss that, then what does that make us?

And then, Fanny Steven's song, *The Children of the Wood*, came unbidden into his mind once more and that particular line from it that appeared to speak to him personally, telling him to find '*those that should their butchers be.'*

'Didn't strap himself to that wheel,' said Constable Davies, shaking his head. 'There must have been someone else involved, to my way of thinking.'

Bucke took a deep breath. He didn't think he could cope with Davies, just at the moment. 'Patrick worked on Temple Street, didn't he? Go and ask some questions, Evan. See if anyone saw anything, will you?' Davies nodded and walked away, a man on an important mission.

You might beat a boy for many reasons, none of them particularly worthy, but why would you do this? Bucke walked around the cab. What was the point of tying a boy to the wheel of a cart? And his mind went back to the boys in the shed, Mazey and Dolphin. It was either insane or it was calculated, such attention-seeking images intended to create the maximum effect, to spread alarm and horror. Was it possible to use logic in trying to unravel something that actually defied logic? It was something that Bucke asked himself much too frequently. He looked at the boy again. It had to be nothing more than a macabre coincidence, surely, that Patrick's body was found upside down, just like the other two.

They released Patrick's body gently and then two constables, led by the night watchman, carried him into the nearby hospital where an examination confirmed that he had been beaten viciously around the head and then strangled with his own muffler.

'Who does the cab belong to, do we know?' Bucke examined underneath and gestured to Payne to check the cab. Constable Gill walked around the cab and checked the number.

'That, I reckon, is the cab of Iestyn Godfrey, Inspector,' he said. 'Wonder what has happened to Iestyn? Decent sort he is. Not like him to leave his cab go wandering like this.'

'He's here. Inspector.' Constable Payne leaned out of the cab. 'Here. In the back. And he hasn't bought no return ticket, either.'

Iestyn Godfrey was slumped on the floor of the cab, his once-lively, intelligent eyes now sightless, like pebbled glass. There was blood in a pool beneath him as a consequence of a serious head wound. However, the cause of death was likely to be his cabman's whip that was wound tightly around his neck. Patrick and Iestyn, killed in the same way. Bucke climbed back down and leaned against the cab, closing his eyes. Why? What was the purpose of this?

'There's a lot of it about, Inspector,' said Payne.

'Yes, constable there is. Too much of it.' Bucke bent down to check beneath the cab once again. He had noticed something on the other side and he wanted to be sure. There was indeed sawdust stuck beneath it. If it had been raining, it would have washed off. But there had been no rain. He squeezed underneath and then rubbed the sawdust between his fingers. It seemed fresh and there was no sign of any recent carpentry that had taken place on the cab. It must have been picked up from the ground, Bucke was sure of it. He allowed Payne and Gill to take Godfrey's body into the hospital whilst he checked the cab for himself. There was nothing unusual to see, though there was no sign of any money either. Was it still somewhere on Godfrey's body? Had money ever been the cause of his death? It seemed highly unlikely. A cabman's earnings?

He sat in the cab. It must have been somewhere discreet where Patrick's body had been attached to the wheel. But why? Why had he been there, wherever that was? Who was killed first? Patrick or Iestyn? Did that matter? And how had the horse found its way to this spot, not far from Constance's rooms and the street where he once lived, rather than anywhere else?

Gill and Payne came out of the hospital. 'Doctor confirms he is dead, sir. Pity that. Was hoping to ask him who did it.'

'Please, Constable Payne.' This was not a good moment for levity.

'Sorry, sir. Just trying to be cheerful.'

Bucke accepted his apology with a nod. It was a dreadful thing to have to see and people reacted in different ways, 'Which stand did he usually work from? Do we know?'

'Wind Street. That is where I normally see him,' said Gill.

'That makes sense. Patrick would have been there too, on Temple Street. I suggest we go up there.' Bucke paused. 'Constable Payne, can you ask on the road. Shops, usual sort of thing. Did anyone see or hear a cab? It would be good to know what time it turned up here.'

When Inspector Bucke arrived on Wind Street, he found the cab men who had returned at such an early hour, standing together, shocked and mourning Iestyn. When did they last see him? Must have been 7.30 pm, something like that. What did anyone see? That Godfrey had been on Wind Street, waiting his turn in the rank. A man had hired him; someone said he might have been wearing an apron. Someone else said he had a lad with him who seemed unwell, but no one was paying much attention. He had set off with his fare up Castle Bailey Street. Another said that he thought he'd turned on to College Street but no one had seen him after that. Must have had to go a distance, was all they all thought.

The apron again. Bucke noted that. He couldn't find Davies, which was probably for the best and so he and Constable Gill considered what they knew. Bucke was silent, considering the cracks in the pavement thoughtfully for a moment, until he nodded as if to himself. 'Tell me,' he asked Gill. 'How do horses walk?'

'I can give you a stupid answer, Inspector, if you want, but I don't think it is what you require. I would say in a straight line, sir. Until someone tells them not too.'

'Right, Constable Gill. And so do we have a straight line, for a horse to walk along, do you think? Here in the centre of Swansea?'

'Well yes, sir. Obvious, sir. College Street, Gower Street, on to St Helen's Road.'

'Yes, constable. Now think. Is there anywhere on that route where you could hide a cab, whilst you tied poor Patrick to the wheel, where you wouldn't be disturbed? Anywhere at all?'

Constable Gill patrolled those streets every day and for a moment he considered his beat.' There is only one place I can think of, sir,' he said eventually. 'The Tannery. On Gower Street. They are doing some work there. New roof on one of the sheds. Might have left the gates open, you never know. Stinks up there, mind.'

He was right, of course. When they arrived, the smell of rotting flesh and concentrated urine was like a curtain that had to be parted for them to gain entry. It was one of the least attractive places that Bucke knew. Of course, everything in the courtyard had been trampled, for the men replacing the roof had already started work. And Gill was right. The gates were not secure, for they had been damaged during a delivery of timber. But amongst the sawdust there was blood – unmistakable, and a great deal of it, too. Was it human? Possibly. There were also the faint tracks of wheels, though he had to admit that he could not say with any certainty that they belonged to Godfrey's cab. But he was as sure as he could be that this was where Iestyn and Patrick had died. Take a cab to Gower Street, go into the tannery, close the gates…Then point the horse down towards Heathfield Street and see where the mood took it. Bucke scraped up some of the blood-soaked sawdust and put it in a matchbox.

When they returned to Temple Street there were two constables waiting for Bucke, ready to report to him. Payne had little to say. No one had heard or seen anything on St Helen's Road, though the cab was not there outside the tram depot when Mr Smitham had come into work to feed the horses at about 4.00 am. It was when Constable Davies started to outline what had happened that Bucke started to get angry, and the more he heard, the angrier he became.

Initially his feelings were tinged with shame, for he had been unable to prevent the death of another innocent young boy. This was his job – to protect the people of Swansea, sometimes from each other and sometimes from themselves – and in this he had failed. But it was worse than that – much worse. Because in those moments before his death, Patrick Connor had been an object of cheap entertainment.

He had been seen on Temple Street in is habitual position and so Constable Davies had begun his inquiries in the Three Lamps. When he reported his findings to him, Inspector Bucke went inside to explore further the sorry tale.

The licence holder, Mr Savours, adopted a lofty, disdainful attitude, one not likely to soothe Bucke's temper. He hadn't been in the bar, he was upstairs in the billiard room. He knew nothing about what had happened in the bar. Of course, he did not countenance what must have happened but obviously he couldn't be blamed. He couldn't be everywhere, now could he? He called the barmaid, Celia Jackson, who had a room on the premises.

It took a while to get to the truth but Bucke recognised her evasions and was patient. Patrick had indeed been given beer, there was loud cheering, it was a huge joke, an entertainment. It had been a great laugh. Everyone knew boys drank beer at home. Then a man had taken him away. Just a bit of fun. Can't have done any harm, surely not?

Except he was dead. Bucke was calm and measured in the face of this shocking condemnation of the town in which he worked. Who took him outside? Celia didn't know. 'Did he come back? The man? Did he come back? Did he come back into the bar?'

Celia shifted in her seat. 'Not that I noticed, sir.'

'So he took the boy outside and didn't come back?'

''That's right, sir. Yes, sir.'

'And what did he look like, Celia? This man who didn't come back?'

'Ordinary, sir.'

'How tall was he?'

'Normal. sir.'

'And his voice? How did it sound?'

'Normal, sir.'

'There was nothing about him that you noticed?'

'Not really, sir. He had a flat cap like most of the men do. And he was wearing a leather apron. Lots of men wear aprons, too.' Bucke showed no emotion. It wasn't much, but it was something. A link, however slight it might be.

'And what did this ordinary man do, Celia? When he was in the bar with Patrick?'

'Like I told you afore, sir. He was his friend, sir. They were playing. He was buying him beer.'

'And did you serve him, Celia?'

She paused and her eyes lowered. 'Yes, sir. I did, sir. But it was all in fun.'

'But he got him drunk, Celia, didn't he? And you served him.'

'He only had two full pints, sir. And some mouthfuls.'

'But he got him drunk, Celia,' he repeated slowly.

'It wasn't nasty, like. More of a game. Everyone was cheering, sir. Everyone enjoyed it.'

'Do you think Patrick enjoyed it, Celia?'

She bit her lip. 'I don't know, sir.' She paused. 'He might not have.'

Bucke felt no obligation to spare her feelings. 'And now he is dead.'

Mr Savours took him outside, blustering, saying how young lads should be in the Band of Hope, not drinking in pubs, because beer turns them into little beasts. Or little corpses, thought Bucke. He promised to dismiss Celia Jackson and Bucke, unusually, didn't care. It had been a serious, disastrous mistake. Unforgivable.

At least he had a lead, a very slender one, and in some ways unhelpful, but a leather apron was beginning to feature in what he was told. It was common working attire, but it wasn't a jacket or top hat and tails. What did he have? A leather apron, and an embroidered handkerchief. Was it really time to start to believe in the Czibor the Hungarian?

*

159

His case had finished very quickly but since Mr Strick would be out conducting the inquest into the death of the poor boy who had been strapped to the wheel of the cab, Henry Fry didn't need to rush back to the office immediately. It was a cold day and some people said they thought it might snow later; men in carts were said to be gathering, in the hope of employment removing it from the streets. Henry was not convinced, for the clouds did not look dark enough, but in truth he didn't much care, for his mind was spinning and he was finding it difficult to concentrate. He had done his best during the morning but in the afternoon he knew he would stare at his papers without achieving a great deal. The Angel of Swansea, Fanny Stevens; that was all he could think of.

He had hoped he would be able to see her twice on Saturday because she was singing in the matinee and in the evening. But there was a function and he was obliged to attend, with Harriet, his intended. Shy, innocent, rather boring Harriet. And this was to be the rest of his life? A comfortable house in Sketty? Two dogs? A housemaid, children and days filled with contract disputes? Is that what it had to be? And so tomorrow it had to be afternoon tea at the Vicarage. Were wedding plans really that advanced? If so, no one had told him. Or if they had, he hadn't been paying attention. But it was all probably inevitable now.

Vicar Bishop was a strange man, reflected Henry. He was known for standing uncomfortably close to women and for showing little appetite, or so it appeared, for the obligations of his job. The incident in Danygraig Cemetery yesterday had already achieved legendary status in the town and hardly inspired confidence in those who used him. Henry's imagination took off suddenly. Perhaps Vicar Bishop would book two weddings at the same time. Why not? He now had a reputation for such things. And then Henry would find himself married, irrevocably, to the wrong bride.

Now, that was an interesting idea, quite exciting when he thought about it. He could find himself married to Harriet's cousin, the radiant Alicia Southwell. Or to a conjurer's assistant, ready to travel the world. But then a very different and disturbing possibility confronted

160

him - Nancy Norris, the girl with too few teeth who dribbled and had visions in church. When he had thought that, he realised he could not unthink it; the image was now lodged in his head. No, he decided, It would be too much of a gamble. Someone had said that Faith Bishop, the vicar's daughter, had gone away to stay with her aunt in Staines and wouldn't be back for a while. He was quietly relieved she wouldn't be there on Saturday. She was, he found, a little too forward, a little too knowing.

He looked around him. This was the ordinary world. People engaged in their business on Wind Street, hurrying between banks and shipping agents. This was a different place at night. More dangerous, much more exciting and yet, not all that long ago, he had neither known that it existed nor indeed the nature of the people who were at its heart. .What did the French call them? *Demi-monde?* People living on the edge of respectability? That was about right. It was a lot more exciting than contractual disputes.

Henry had been to see Fanny six times and she had let him visit her in her dressing room on three occasions. She knew where to find him in the audience now, too. He always went to the same seat in the front stalls where he could see her better. He could see other things too- like the air of frantic desperation that settled around the Singing Painter, who could neither paint nor sing – but he was there only for Fanny. And on Saturday? He might miss her altogether. Even if he escaped the vicarage, he would still have to go back to the Sullivan's and make small-talk whilst Harriet stumbled her way through some simple piano pieces and then he would be obliged to lead the polite applause. He disapproved of the sort of robust musical criticism that involved throwing a dead cat on the stage, but at least you knew where you stood.

What if someone went to see Fanny after the show, and she, lonely and disappointed because he wasn't there, accept his invitation and went for refreshment with him? A soldier perhaps? No, worse. A cavalry officer. Bright uniform, handsome, shiny boots. Aristocratic, even. Their eager eyes met in the flickering candlelight, her heart pounding beneath her straining bodice…He sighed. Sometimes an imagination was a curse.

Too much information could be, too. He knew certain information, not fit for the public ear obviously, about Hilda Bishop, the vicar's wife and her rather uninhibited shopping habits that the vicar needed frequently to resolve with irritated shopkeepers. How could he look at her and pretend he didn't know? She was a difficult woman anyway, intense and irritable, what his own father described as highly strung. It was not going to be a stimulating afternoon. The vicarage or the music hall? It would never be a difficult choice. Perhaps it would snow. And what difference would that make?

He had hoped that he would see Fanny hurrying to rehearsals but, of course he didn't. That had been a foolish idea, the sort of happy coincidence that only happened in novels. He had to get back to the office. Perhaps it wouldn't be that bad. Presumably Maldwyn would nudge him repeatedly, winking, offering to show him his exciting new *cartes de visite*. It was especially tiresome and of course today he had appeared for the first time in court in a criminal case and his client had been found guilty, so he knew he would be mocked about that, though really the verdict had been inevitable. He had been required to defend young James Edwards, a stupid boy who had been charged with throwing oil of vitriol into the face of a housemaid. He had admitted the offence and so all that Henry could do was plead for mitigation.

Edwards had been 'larking about,' as he called it, in a neighbour's farmyard in Llandeilo on Bonfire Night, making a noise, throwing mud, chasing chickens in the dark. The sort of thing bored country boys do, apparently. Jane Marks, the housemaid, had leaned out of her bedroom window to shout at them and Edwards had picked up a bottle he said he had found on the step and threw the liquid it contained into her face. It was oil of vitriol. Her skin had burnt, her skin remained patchy and one eye was still sore in the corner. In truth, she was very lucky it hadn't been worse. All Edwards could say was that he had thought it was water and all Henry could say was that there had been no motive for the incident; it had been stupid and thoughtless. It was the best he could do.

The judge, His Lordship Sir William Dentris-Field, smiled thinly. He condemned acid attacks in general, this 'filthy practice of foreign importation,' and sentenced Edwards to nine months, with hard labour. Edwards broke down in tears and was led away. 'Thank you, Mr Fry,' said the judge, meaning, Henry supposed, 'you've done your best,' and the court moved on to the next case.

But even in court, even on this important professional moment, his first appearance in court, he could not shake Fanny Stevens from his mind. For he remembered clearly the last conversation he had had with her as they edged slowly ever closer to each other around the table at the Adelphi and as they shared more personal details of themselves. She had been talking about Jack, the man she lived with and had said, almost casually, that he had once threatened to throw vitriol into her face. Henry was shocked, both by the threat and by Fanny's acceptance of it.

He went the long way back to the office, through Salubrious Place and as he turned the corner into Fisher Street he raised his hat politely to Inspector Bucke who was heading in the opposite direction. He acknowledged Henry with a brief smile. Henry wondered whether Bucke knew anything about Jack. Perhaps if he got to know him better, he could ask, for he was concerned for Fanny's safety. What sort of life did she actually lead? He realised that he felt a need to protect her and then had a such a sudden revelation that he had to stop and stare sightlessly into the dirty, impenetrable office window, of Richard Park, the horse dealer. What he really wanted to do more than anything else, was to liberate her, to set the Angel of Swansea free.

*

This wasn't usually something that he would do. He would much rather send a constable to look at the problem. There were murders in the town and the defacing of books in the library was less important, in his opinion. But Bucke was now more attuned with the intricacies of local politics than he had been. The Vice Chairman of the Library Committee, Mr Edward Bath, managed daily affairs but the Chairman was the Lord Mayor and so any problem encountered was quickly escalated beyond constable level. Bucke sighed as he walked and hoped that he wouldn't be detained for too long. There were others he was far more interested in detaining.

'Such a busy morning, Inspector Bucke. Most challenging. A foreign gentleman. Very smart. Very good English, thank goodness. Wanted to know if we had any ancient parchments. In Latin. I told him. The oldest item we have is, what is alleged to be anyway, an original copy of *Oroonoko* by Mrs Aphra Behn dating from 1688, though I have my doubts. But the gentleman wouldn't believe me and it was the devil's own job to get him out of here, I can tell you.' Bath sighed and mopped his forehead. 'These are difficult days, Inspector Bucke, difficult days,' he said, looking out of the window of the library down on to Goat Street, seeking out potential abusers of books.

He was a stout man, squeezed unhappily, and not always successfully, into clothes that were too small. He negotiated the gaps between the reading desks with only occasional success and was invariably out of breath. 'This correspondence in the newspapers. Entirely unnecessary. You may have seen it.' Bucke shook his head, gently. 'In the letters. Most unfortunate. Mrs Bishop, the vicar's wife, has been accused of taking books, by those we might wish to call busy-bodies. You must have seen it. Most vituperative, both ill-informed and unnecessary. Poor woman is accused – by people hiding behind a pseudonym I might add - of taking sixty books from the reference library. A complete lie. Look at the shelves. Is there room for sixty more books? Of course not.' He hesitated, 'it helps stock you see, if some volumes are kept away from the shelves. Eases space. She doesn't take them without permission. Of course not. A vicar's wife.' He smiled unconvincingly.

Bucke knew all about Hilda Bishop the Untouchable. Most people did. She had become far too important to be arrested. She was forever stealing things. It was said she had the biggest collection of umbrellas in Swansea. Her husband, Cyrus, was more well-known than perhaps he should have been to the watchful traders in the town. Bucke had no wish to deal with her compulsion today. Or any day, really. The woman needed the kind of help that he could not provide. He tried to keep his patience. 'I see. Your Christian opinions reflect no less a sense of charity than I would expect from Swansea's leading librarian.' He smiled. 'And it is your belief that I can help you with this? In some way?'

'Oh, no. Forgive me, Inspector. Of course not. No, we have a different problem altogether. You see, many of the newspapers and magazines we buy for our readers are being wilfully mutilated and defaced. The regulations are quite unequivocal.' He gestured at a poster displayed on the wall and then read it out aloud, as if he could not be sure that Bucke could read. 'Any person who shall wilfully damage any of the books, newspapers or indeed, any property of the library shall pay for every such offence a penalty of £2.' Quiet clear, you might think, and quite punitive. But you see, we have someone here who cares not a fig for such regulations.'

'And do you have any thoughts about who it might be?'

'None at all, Inspector. Of course not. We have many visitors here, as you can see this morning. My readers are truly gentlemen, and it is not my place to be standing over any of them, as if any of them were a common felon.'

'At least one of them isn't a gentleman, Mr Bath.' Bucke looked around the room. It was the early afternoon and after a morning of confronting horror, he had little patience with events in the library. There were about eight or nine men, sitting at desks, reading, glancing up at him out of curiosity and with irritation at the sound of their muttered conversation, particularly a militiaman, sitting by the window, the sudden sunshine catching the buttons of his uniform. So they were back then, thought Bucke. The Militia had been away for a few days firing their cannons near Brecon. No wonder the town had been so quiet.

'Sunshine eh? Doesn't look much like snow, whatever they say,' said Bath looking out of the window. 'But you see,' he resumed, 'it is not just mutilation. Oh no.' He dabbed imaginary sweat away from his forehead. 'We have volumes of fine art reproductions in the catalogue. Very expensive and popular volumes, as you can imagine, Inspector. But I can tell you that someone has been removing

165

illustrative plates, especially of classical Greek female statuary. The library has always been noted for its collection, splendidly bound and elaborately illustrated, and all once in excellent condition. Now they are being desecrated.'

Bucke glanced round the room at the men bent over their books. 'And these illustrative plates, Mr Bath. Were the statues clothed or naked?'

Bath snorted. 'Naked, largely. As you might expect. The Greeks believed that the human form was the most important subject for artists. A large number of illustrative plates are missing.'

'I see.'

'But it gets worse, Inspector. Someone has been writing in books as well. Frightful things. Filthy suggestions. Additions to line illustrations. Obscene drawings. It is quite a puzzle, deciding what I should do. I was of a mind that we should preserve these things so that we can, in the future, measure the improvement in educational standards.'

'How, Mr Bath? Through their accuracy?'

'No, sir.' He sounded irritated. 'Through their absence. But the Lord Mayor was anxious that I should contact you immediately.'

'Can I look at some of the examples you have saved?'

Bath went to the counter and spoke in a whisper to the librarian, Mr Thompson, who quietly withdrew a copy of *Vanity Fair* and then glared around the silent library and coughed, encouraging the readers to return their eyes to their books. He lowered his voice. 'This is the worst example I have, Inspector.'

Bucke looked through it carefully. The early chapters were unsullied, but as he progressed, he found words written in the margin. *Bitch WHORE Mutton* appeared most frequently. The end pieces were covered in crude, badly executed drawings by someone, he thought, with no skill but an unhealthy mind. There were female torsos with exaggerated breasts. In one a headless torso was transfixed by a sword which had been drawn so aggressively it had ripped the page.

'And obviously you don't know who did these things? You have no record who removed this book from the shelves?'

'Inspector. This is a library.'

And then, on the very last page there was a drawing of a small truncheon or cosh, if the proportions of the hand holding it were to be believed. There was what he imagined represented blood, dripping from it. 'I would be obliged, Mr Bath, if I could take this book with me, please.'

Bath shook his head. 'I am afraid you have to be a member of the library, and in any case this is a reference book. It cannot be withdrawn. No matter what the popular press would claim.'

'Mr Bath,' said Bucke patiently. 'This is evidence. I need it for my investigation. I am taking it with me. Is this your only copy of *Vanity Fair*?'

'We have three, of course. The other two are unsullied. A public library is like a gentleman's library, you see, Inspector Bucke. One must have three copies of any book. One to show, one to keep and one to lend.'

'And would that apply to women too, do you think Mr Bath?' It had, in truth, been a difficult day.

'Pardon, Inspector?' Bath looked puzzled.

'Just speculating, Mr Bath. I shall be in touch'

Fourteen

It didn't snow. Not in the afternoon, not in the evening and not overnight, and so the men with eager shovels and carts drifted away like the clouds, disappointed. A dusting of snow might have helped, thought Inspector Bucke. It would have brought a freshness and a purity to the streets, a welcome other-worldliness, for the real world had become, once again, brutal and vicious. But it was not to be and Swansea passed a troubled weekend. Tension, fear, distrust. It did not help that the Militia had returned.

Swansea might, perhaps, have pined for its absent heroes for three whole days, but now the Militia were back, after the excitement of firing their cannons imprecisely in the direction of someone's sheep in the fields outside Brecon. It was a splendid Friday night and the Militia were in town, ready to reclaim the ownership of the streets which their fine uniforms indicated was their birth-right. And so of course there were squabbles and fights with those young men from places like St Thomas and Cwmbwrla who felt they had something to prove. There was a rolling fight that began at the Adelphi and ended up in Castle Square. As Inspector Flynn pointed out, who could be surprised? It added to that sense of disorder and unease, a state of alarm at the murders of three young boys. It was only a few months ago that the dark cloud of a religious cult had smothered parts of the town in terror with a series of rapes, murders, and suicides; and now, suddenly, no one felt safe once again.

It wasn't just that three young boys had been murdered; it was the way in which their young bodies had been displayed with such contempt, as if they were the remnants of a sacrificial ritual. Not only that, but also the shocking details could not be hidden and they passed from person to person through the town like a virus, whilst the parents, who found it hard to confront the anguish in their minds, let alone see it displayed in the daily gossip and in the press for all to see, endured an unspeakable horror. Bucke could not imagine how terrible that must be, for the newsprint gave inescapable substance to their darkest imaginings.

The newspaper quite naturally looked for its own perspective on the murders. For them, it was all about the failure of the police to provide adequate security. Paul Roe broadcast it loud and clear from Wind Street. 'Maniac on the loose!' he shouted. 'Rich boys kept at home! Poor boys die on the streets! Read all about it!' Roe waved a newspaper in the wind. 'Are our lads safe?'

If he was honest with himself, that was a question that Bucke could not answer, for they had no real leads to explore. But the failure to make progress troubled him and when Constance finally asked him on Sunday why he was so distracted, his anxieties and concerns quickly emerged.

'Dr Benjamin feels it is more likely that it was human blood that I recovered in the sawdust, rather than anything else. There was blood in the cab also, so I would surmise that Godfrey was killed inside the cab and Patrick in the yard of the tannery. But I can't be certain and I have no evidence that tells me in what order the deaths occurred, though unless in some way Godfrey was involved, which seems unlikely, the cab driver would have to be silenced first. If Patrick was as drunk as they say, then he wouldn't have known what was going on. Cold comfort for the family, but that is all I can offer them at the moment. He was intoxicated and then led away.' He paused and rubbed his forehead aggressively with his palm. 'Three boys killed, Constance. Three young boys. Innocent boys. And I did nothing to prevent it. That is my job.'

'Do not punish yourself, Rumsey. No one could have known that these things were going to happen. It is horrible, they have been such cruel murders, they have been completely unpredictable. No one sane could ever anticipate something like this. And so, for me, these boys have been murdered by an insane person. What you have to do is to make sure it doesn't happen again. It is not as if someone told you it was going to happen and you did nothing about it. You feel the deaths of the boys acutely, of course you do, We all do. But other people died recently. The man on the cart, the men on the boat, the cab driver. They were tragedies too, for their families.'

'It is hard because the murders of the boys appear to be entirely unprovoked, unless there is a connection with the attacks on women that we can't see. But why is it happening now? And that is a dangerous question, Constance. Because it is so much easier for everyone to think such horrible things have been done by a stranger, not by someone you might have bumped into in the market. So yes, Abramovitch's idea that it is this the work of a Hungarian murderer who is pursuing him is certainly attractive. It would explain why it is happening now. But it doesn't explain why he is doing it.'

'Remind me, Rumsey. If someone kills a stranger, why do they do it?'

'Strangers? Four reasons generally, Constance. Insanity, revenge, to silence them, or for robbery.' He thought for a moment. 'You see, Godfrey's money is missing. His wife told us that he carried a leather pouch in which he kept his takings and we could find no trace of it. But I can't see robbery as a motive. He was not going to be carrying a fortune, was he? A cab driver in Swansea? It can't be the explanation – why take an intoxicated boy with you, if it was just a robbery? And then kill him in that way? There was no need. The money could only be a welcome bonus, nothing more in my opinion. In the dark yard of the tannery Godfrey died because the murderer wanted his cab and therefore it follows that the boy was abducted simply to be killed and in that particular way. It wasn't accidental. So does that mean that I am left with only one motive? Insanity?'

'But you are not convinced, are you? I can tell.'

'I am not sure what to think. If it is the work of a maniac then I cannot counter him with logic, because he has none. I need to believe that there is something else that shapes all this. Something that I can try to understand and unpick.' He shifted uncomfortably in his chair. 'No outrage was committed upon Patrick. He was beaten, he was strangled, he was displayed for all to see. But he was not raped.'

Constance took his hand. 'Time, Rumsey. That is all you need.'

'And that is what I haven't got. I cannot allow another death to happen. The murder of children increases the pressure on the police – there is the danger that we rush to a conclusion because we need to show we are not incompetent, not because it is right. That has happened before. Arrest someone, anyone, preferably either poor or foreign, and then it is solved. These murders have created an atmosphere. No one feels safe. I am looking for a pattern that could lead me closer to the truth. But it isn't easy to find. And then yesterday there was a report from Port Eynon. You mentioned Matthews the carter, delivering seaweed to Sketty, who was beaten to death in Penmaen?'

'Yes, I remember. Very sad. A father, I believe.'

'Well, someone saw a man sitting next to him in the wagon as it pulled out of the village. A man out early, feeding his pigs. Didn't know who it was. Believes it was a stranger. If it was a stranger, then where had he come from, in Port Eynon, early in the morning?' Constance watched him as he seemed to pull together the strands inside his head. 'I can't help myself but I am plucking clouds out of the sky and using them to weave a story. I have no evidence other than a stranger in a wagon.'

'Tell me your story, Rumsey.'

He drew encouragement from the confidence she had in him. She allowed him to speculate without fear and to make mistakes; she gave him strength. He stood up and began to pace slowly around the small room.

'Very well. A man comes ashore. I don't know why. He has killed the captain of the boat he was on. I don't know why. He might have killed someone else, the mate, but I don't know. Why was this man on the boat in the first place? I don't know. He then rides in a wagon from Port Eynon until he kills Rhys Matthews in Penmaen. I don't know why he does that, either. That is the beginning. It could be complete nonsense, a garment knitted out of spider webs. But whether it is true or not, after the murder of Matthews there are two attacks on women in Swansea, one of whom dies, probably accidentally. And on top of all this, we have the murders of the boys, which in their evil way, seem to be different from these other attacks.

171

They seemed to have stopped.' He stopped pacing and moved the curtains to one side to look out of the window at couples walking along St Helen's Road. 'You see, perhaps it was a sailor and he has now sailed away. If he has, well, it is all over, unless he comes back to do it all again in a few weeks' time.'

Constance hooked that irritating strand of hair back behind her ear. 'So you think there might be two stories here? Two killers? Or more. And that you are forcing them together, when they don't connect at all?'

He turned away from the window. 'That, Constance, has become my greatest fear, because that could make our work so much harder,' he replied. 'But you see, is any of this connected to this mysterious Hungarian that Abramovitch keeps talking about? It is a complication that I don't need. Unless it is true.' He began pacing again. 'I don't know what to think. I ask myself, does he really exist? And if he does, is he actually murdering the boys. And why? If he is a Hungarian secret agent or something, then why has he travelled all this way to Swansea to do it? You can see my problem. I have invented one incomplete story and nothing else that happens after the death of Matthews fits into it. It is so untidy.'

Constance scratched he head. 'I wonder, Rumsey, whether you need to break it down into smaller pieces instead of trying to make one story that contains everything. Remember when you were looking for Daniel Guy? You were told then that there could only be one murderer. But they were wrong and you were right. It was never one murderer. Remember that, Rumsey. And have faith in yourself. Everyone else does. And your Romanian friend, Abramovitch, who turned up at the Ragged School last week. There is something about him that unsettles me but I can't tell you why.'

'He troubles me too, you see, prowling around the town as he does. I don't know why, either. But he talks to me about Czibor and I feel that he is trying to do influence me, to control the way I am thinking.' Bucke shrugged his shoulders. 'He certainly doesn't have a very high opinion of any of us. To be honest, the feeling is mutual.'

'If he is looking for his lost little daughter then perhaps he is just nervous and anxious. You know, he has come so far, he is so close now and he can't find her. I need to be more charitable. I do try,' Constance sighed. 'Perhaps that is why he is difficult. But how does this Hungarian murderer fit into his story?'

'Abramovitch wants me to believe that Czibor is waiting for him to lead him to the heiress and the treasure she is supposed to have, which she might not know anything about.'

Constance reached behind her and took Friday's Swansea Evening Telegraph from the top of the piano. 'Have you seen the paper? Page 5. Your man Abramovitch has been interviewed.'

Bucke looked at it quickly. 'He must have turned up and offered J.C. Manning a story. A ha'penny newspaper and a ha'penny story.'

'Look at it later. It is all there. Everything you told me. Except now it is a lost Balkan princess. Living in secret in Swansea.'

Bucke groaned. 'That will not help anyone. There will be a whole ragtag collection of girls brought to him, their parents ready to hand them over for profit, hoping that a heftel and a scroll are not too important.'

'Is that all he wants, do you think?' she asked. 'Just a child? I can understand that.'

'I have no idea what he wants, to tell the truth.'

Constance was suddenly animated. 'But you see, Rumsey, you are looking for a pattern, you say. You cannot find one, you say. But when did all this start? Think about it. At about the time your Romanian gentleman came here. And he says someone else is here to kill him? I am just a piano teacher but I find this hard to understand, Rumsey. If there is someone here to kill him then why hasn't he done it yet? Everyone knows where Abramovitch is. He lets everyone know. So if this secret agent wants Abramovitch to lead him to the missing girl, then why is he so conspicuous? Why has he put all his details in the newspaper? When there is a murderer looking for him? Or for her?'

*

173

Sarah had been at the Ragged School for a week now and was as happy as she had ever been, working constantly and hard, earning little. She had begun to expand her daily repertoire by offering the children stewed American apples which she was able to buy in one gallon tins from Taylor and Company on Walters Road. There were more children attending now, increasingly drawn by the prospect of warm food, which made Sarah feel that her work was worthwhile. Of course, she had Amy by her side. This was not only a new job, but also a new life. Now she had an urgent reason to work – to provide for Amy.

Sarah was proud to walk down to the pier on Sunday morning and feel that those who saw her assumed, if they noticed anything at all, that the little girl holding her hand was her daughter. Amy asked questions about everything. Sarah was amazed at how quickly she learned, as though her mind had suddenly been liberated. She had borrowed a slate and chalk from the school so that Amy could practise her writing. Amy mastered her own name very quickly; after all it was all straight lines. Sarah's name was a bit trickier – there were lots of curves – but it didn't take her too long. She wanted to write it, for Sarah was the most important person in her world. Amy had no one else and she followed her everywhere.

Amy talked about the bath a lot; about how nice it was. Sarah herself saw it as a ritual They had washed away Amy's previous life. Now she could never go back. This was a new beginning. The terrible pressure of looking after herself had gone and Amy had been released, suddenly secure and loved. She had a bed on the floor next to Sarah's and the room in Elephant Court became their nest, the door closed against the rest of the world. Then, as dawn began to break, Amy would climb up into bed with Sarah, sigh and then go back to sleep.

*

Other children in the town, however, were not so settled. The Hat Stand Gang, a notorious group of boys who lived in that grey but profitable area between enterprise and crime, were deeply unsettled by the murders. They had an energy and an insight that could be properly and creatively harnessed, as Bucke had done once before.

174

But things were different now. They would never admit to being frightened – but they were. Three boys? Who was to be next? Who was stalking the boys of the town?

They threw stones, they shouted obscenities at men they didn't recognise, in a town in which they no longer felt comfortable. They clustered together, always looking over their shoulder. These were their streets, where they pilfered and ran errands and took messages. But suddenly these streets were not safe. On Sunday they shouted loudly at people going to church. They seemed reckless, breaking windows, throwing stones, running at speed through the narrow streets, knocking into people, accusing them of being murderers. The congregation at Trinity Chapel on Park Street was trapped inside by the boys throwing stones at the door until Constable Payne came to chase them away. They broke into the Industrial School in Bonymaen and urinated into the headteacher's teapot. They had once searched diligently for clues after the murders of Mazey and Dolphin, boys they knew who wanted to be accepted by them. But those deaths had occurred out of sight; Patrick Connor's body had been publicly displayed and even the strongest of them now felt fragile. They were a silent and unexpected presence on Monday morning when it was time for the funeral, a bleak, dismal, unforgiving occasion.

The men of the Irish community gathered in St David's Church to mourn Patrick, regarding Bucke with suspicion and hostility. Their rage was barely suppressed. How could such a thing happen?

'I'll find him,' he said repeatedly, as he worked his way through the crowd, shaking hands, offering condolences.

'As you say,' was the cold-eyed reply from Patrick's father, a man who had been crying for longer than he ever felt was possible. Bucke had to be there. It would have been a terrible omission for Patrick to have been ignored, an official presence was vital, no matter how uncomfortable it was for Bucke. Relations between the police and the Irish community in Greenhill had been brittle for many years and the potential for trouble in those dirty streets and unsatisfactory, unsanitary houses could not be ignored.

The relatives had already threatened vigilantes, their trust in authority shattered, not just by the murder but by the manner of it, though no one had any idea who they were looking for. But they gathered together to swear that they would neither cease nor relent until they had tracked the murderer down and fed his entrails to their dogs. Their anger emphasised Bucke's own sense of failure.

The Hat Stand Gang followed the cortege, uncomfortable about joining the adult world like this, not sure how to behave in such formal circumstances. They stayed silent and watched. The men walked in a solemn procession to Danygraig Cemetery, where Father Wade did his best to offer some hope in such inexplicable circumstances. It was the coffin of a child that he watched them lower into the grave, a life closed before it had properly started. There was no life to celebrate, just a death to mourn, in anger and with revenge in the hearts of those who stood around him.

Bucke watched them all, hoping against hope that an unknown figure would be seen at the edge of the mourners, none other than the murderer come to see the consequences of his handiwork. But this was real life and it didn't happen. The men dispersed as the grave was filled in and left to drink in the pubs of Greenhill. How the Hat Stand Gang would react to this emotionally charged occasion Bucke had no idea. He hoped they would not cause additional problems in a town that was already so uneasy.

*

Vinegar Bridget was looking for a gift and she knew where to find it. She had gone into Gladwin's Ladies Outfitters on Oxford Street, a superior establishment run by two sisters, Mary-Ann and Harriet, and not one in which she would generally be seen. But she needed some baby clothes of quality for the little boy from the vicarage. She couldn't pass him on into the tender mercies of Mrs Workman stark naked, now could she? It didn't seem right that a child should be taken to Slate Street in Morriston without one decent garment. Life was going to be hard enough as it was for the poor child. So Bridget wanted to do her best for him and, after all, he was a fetching child. 'Good as gold,' is what Mags said. 'Feeds and sleeps. I would keep him if I could.'

Bridget, violent and gin-soaked, had a good heart sometimes, though she possessed few morals to see her through a life in which the need for survival superseded every other consideration. She was a skilled thief and generally careful from whom she stole. She could deal with the consequences of being caught if it was the police who got her, but it was those unacknowledged retributions that took place out of sight that could be difficult. Gladwin's was fair game though, offering fine clothes for mother and baby from the west, the prosperous side of town, not for those from homes which still had mud floors.

They eyed her suspiciously when she went through the door. She was immediately recognised as someone whose custom they would not welcome, though, of course, money knew nothing of social class - clean or dirty, the coins were worth the same. Nevertheless, Harriet Gladwin watched her carefully, whilst Bridget occasionally sneered in return. How Harriet longed for a return to those days when customers had to make appointments to enter the shop and were kept at a considerable distance from the merchandise itself. She watched uncomfortably as Bridget examined the displays of embroidered waistcoats and ridiculously priced dresses, ready for a spring that seemed a long way away. In the corner, at the front and unfortunately next to the counter, were the baby clothes. Bridget could not afford to be too choosy. It was a case of whatever she could reach. She smiled at Harriet and saw in the corner of her eye the shop assistant moving towards the door to block her escape. Or try to block her escape. If the young and worried-looking girl wanted a fight, then Bridget was ready – and confident. After all, she had planned this carefully.

There was a nice white gown, edged in blue. It was quite startling to see something so clean. Could she reach a vest too? Or, even better, an embroidered indoor robe? They were a little higher, that was the problem. She toured the shop again, as she planned her next move.

'Is madam looking for anything in particular?' asked Harriet. 'We have some charming –'

'Just looking, ain't I?'

Bridget had a carpet bag with her and anyone could see that it had plenty of room in which to slip items of interest. The bag was large and Bridget was small – it looked like the place in which she slept. Olive, the shop assistant was uncomfortable, considering what the bag might contain. Neither she nor Harriet were sure that they wanted to confront an aggressive and powerful looking woman, with dirty calloused hands and a face that looked like a wave-pitted pebble. Harriet, however, was joint-proprietor and she had a responsibility for the preservation of the stock.

'I would be grateful if you would not touch the display. If you would like some help –'

The door opened and the bell ran loudly. This was not good news. It was Harriet Gladwin's considerable misfortune that both Hilda Bishop and Vinegar Bridget had turned up in the shop at the same time. It was a circumstance that was never going to lead to a happy outcome.

Hilda's narrow eyes scanned the shop, taking in the dirty woman by the counter who, even from a distance, smelled of poverty. Then, when Bridget turned, the two shop-lifters stared at each other, joined together in a moment of instant recognition.

'Good morning, Mrs Bishop. I shall be with you presently,' smiled Harriet, as cheerfully as she could manage, knowing that she was being wildly optimistic. Olive was confused, unsure who she should watch.

'I think I would like to look at your sanitary towels,' announced Hilda, choosing a product unlikely to be on display, her eyes concentrating on two silk scarves on the counter right in front of her. 'For my daughter,' she added, trying to make her request sound more convincing.

Hilda was notorious throughout the town and this had become a tiresome ritual. Shopkeepers would have to assess what she had taken, then send a runner to fetch the vicar who would pay for it. Hilda knew very well that this happened, but for her it was all part of the game. What she liked best were those occasions when she had things that were unacknowledged. Umbrellas, oddly, were the best. Walk in without one, then take one with you when you left. She often got away without Cyrus paying for an umbrella.

She stood, waiting to be served. 'Miss Gladwin, your sanitary towels, if you please. I have an appointment.'

Suddenly Bridget grabbed the gown, tried for a vest but dropped it, and headed straight for the door.

'Madam! Please!' shouted Harriet, ineffectually, whilst Olive moved towards the door, with little enthusiasm. She was too late and Bridget was suddenly outside where she immediately attached an old rope with a hook to the door handle and then hooked the other end around the lamp post outside. It took seconds and she fled, leaving the women trapped inside. It would only delay them for a moment, but it would be long enough. She walked purposefully across Oxford Street and into the market. Once inside, she disappeared amongst the stalls and was soon heading for home.

At Gladwin's the women were freed by a polite man with a bowler hat and a cane, but by then, of course, it was much too late. Olive was sent to look for a constable.

Mrs Bishop was outraged. 'Disgusting, a woman like that in a shop like this. One despairs. The distribution and availability of constables is a disgrace! I shall speak to the Chief Constable at the earliest opportunity. A personal friend of my husband, you know.' She looked sympathetically at Harriet. 'You must be so distressed. Still, your sanitary towels, if you please. For my daughter.' She pointed at the top shelf behind Harriet. 'There they are.'

*

When Bucke got back to Tontine Street, he found Abramovitch waiting on the steps for him, effectively barring his entrance. 'There you have it, Inspector, sir.' He leaned on his cane and looked down from the top step.'

'Have what, Mr Abramovitch?'

'The proof. Last week you have another murder, I hear. A terrible

179

circumstance. Another boy. Not a girl. It is the Hungarian, as I told you, Czibor is his name. It is a sign. It is a threat. He does not only kill boys. He kills girls. I know this. He is looking for a girl, my girl, and so he takes your town into hell.'

Bucke looked up at him. His confidence in the face of the death of children seemed entirely misplaced. 'There is no evidence that it was this Hungarian of yours, Mr Abramovitch. Why would he kill anyone, if all he wants is to find one particular girl? Or if he wants to kill you, then why does he kill someone else? I am not convinced by what you are telling me. I have to say it. None of what you tell me makes any sense, not to me.'

Abramovitch smirked and shook his head. 'You do not know these Hungarians. There is one here with a duty to make disorder wherever he can. Czibor will stop at nothing. This is his duty. Such murders will not end and so you must hurry to find my daughter, before he finds her.'

Bucke could not see any logic in what he was saying, except perhaps for the intense illogicality of an anxious father.' I cannot question every parent in Swansea and ask them where their daughter came from.'

'So you cannot find my Chana? And you cannot tell me she is safe? Is that what you are saying? Then, Inspector, sir, I must continue to look for myself. I am telling you I have already started. There are those here in your town who will help me. This is what I know.' He touched the brim of his hat with his cane and walked down the steps past Bucke and turned towards the High Street.

'Strange man, that one.' said Sergeant Ball, as Bucke walked into the police station. 'He has been waiting for you.' Ball was in front of the counter, picking up something from the floor. 'Dropped his handkerchief. I shall keep it for him. He is bound to be coming back. Not going to leave us alone, is he? The street boys have started to call him The Skull. They don't like him.'

'They are frightened of everyone at the moment.'

Sergeant Ball told him about a robbery at Gladwin's, smiling in spite of himself at the ingenious escape employed. 'From the description it sounds like Vinegar Bridget. Though poor old Harriet had her hands full. Hilda Bishop's been shopping, too.' He flicked through the papers on the counter. 'Oh yes, and we have had another telegram, this time from the police station in Newport. Another beating and a robbery, this time in Magor.'

'Getting closer, Stanley,' said Bucke. 'What is it? Swindon, Bath and now Magor? When was it?'

'A couple of weeks ago, I think. Gets on my nerves, this sort of thing. I mean, why tell us about it? Can't they sort it out for themselves? Too easy, it seems to me, to send out a telegram. They should be getting on with some proper work.' He blew out his cheeks. 'All these new-fangled things they expect me to do. They will have me talking down wires next. Ridiculous.'

'It's the modern way, Stanley.'

'Well, they can keep it Inspector.'

Herr Goldman, who ran the Photographic Co-operative Company on Wind Street came to see Bucke later. He was a man with bright intense eyes and greasy hair pulled carefully across his forehead, who had shed an unappealing layer of dandruff onto his shoulders that could have been a scarf. He had come to see Bucke to offer to take photographs of the next corpse the police found. 'I regret very much that I did not consider such an offer sooner, for I am sure it would assist you in your work. It would have helped in your investigations into the death of that poor unfortunate last week, if I could have taken a photograph.'

Bucke had never heard of anything quite so repugnant and told Goldman so.

'No, no Inspector. I am afraid you are quite wrong. This is the future. A photograph, properly lit and properly taken, would act as a record of what you found at the scene. It will help with your enquiries. Remember what it says in my advertising, Inspector Bucke. 'Outdoor Photography executed at the shortest notice.' I will be ready for you, always.'

'Mr Goldman. I saw Patrick's body. I don't think anyone else should have to see it. Certainly not the parents.'

'Inspector Bucke, this is the modern age now, This is 1881, not 1781. Just think about it. You will have the evidence before you that you cannot store in your eyes. You will always have the picture of what you saw, as you work your way methodically towards catching the murderer. I know that you do this, Inspector. You are highly regarded. But think. You can look at the picture, you can turn it upside down, you can take it home with you and then you will see things differently. Sometimes it is what you need. What we all need. It is the modern way, Inspector.'

Bucke could see, despite his instinctive resistance, that Goldman had a point. He knew that some police forces were planning to take photographs of felons that they could circulate to their colleagues. Bucke had never had his own photograph taken and he was sure it wouldn't hurt. And then another thought flew, unbidden, into his mind. If Julia and the children had been photographed, he would still be able to see them. 'I will think about it, Mr Goldman. I know where I can find you.'

'Think very carefully, Inspector. This is the future and you cannot stop the future happening.'

Bucke wished him a good afternoon and returned to a report for the Watch Committee. They would be just as much a part of the anxiety and fear in Swansea as anyone else. So he was lost in his work when Ball knocked and put his head round the door.

'What is it, Stanley? I am rather busy.'

The sergeant looked embarrassed. 'There is a lady here, sir.' He blew out his cheeks.

'Yes?'

'She says she wishes to make a complaint about a piano teacher.'

Fifteen

'I am Inspector Rumsey Bucke. What can I do for you, madam?' His heart was pounding. How could he deal with this?

'It isn't right, Inspector. And if something isn't done about it then I can promise you that my husband will go looking for the bugger. We thought it best to let you have first go at 'im, but if you don't, then we will go and get 'im. It isn't right what he has done.'

He had to stay professional but he could not suppress the sense of relief that surged when she used the word 'him.' He forced himself to look at the woman firmly. She didn't look like a vigilante, for she was what others might describe as matronly. But she did give him the impression that she was someone with whom you should not trifle. She had fierce eyes that flashed in her anger, with the broad-shoulders and forearms of a washer woman visible beneath her woollen shawl and her dull-coloured hair emerging from beneath her tight head scarf. 'I think I need a little more information, Mrs…'

'I am tellin' you, Inspector. It is 'im. And if you won't do nothing, then you will find the bastard floatin' in the dock, isn't it?'

'Please, Mrs…'

'I am sorry, inspector, but I am proper wound up, I am.'

'I am sure it is quite understandable; in whatever circumstances you find yourself. Now let's start at the beginning, shall we? Your name, please.'

'Fair enough, but you better get the bugger, sharp like. I am Elizabeth Dacey and I lives on Oxford Street with my husband Bill. His sister lives next door, don't she? An' I looks after her little girl, like, on occasion. Lovely little thing is our Jane. Bright as a button. Makes 'er auntie dead proud, she do. Well, this afternoon she 'ad a piano lesson with that devil–born bastard Barree, an' if you don't sort 'im, I'm tellin' you, you is lookin' at murder.' She screwed her hands into fists and shook them at him.

'Stay calm, Mrs Dacey and tell me all about it.' Bucke took a sheet of paper, ready to make notes. But the story that she told him was so terrible, so awful, that he wrote only occasionally, for he preferred to maintain eye-contact with her. He realised very quickly that he had to take full responsibility for the case immediately, for otherwise there would indeed be murder and those wishing to carry it out would have formed a queue so long and hostile that the police would have difficulty dispersing it. As Bucke told Captain Colquhoun later, it was a story so detailed that he never for one moment doubted that it was genuine.

Jane Probert attended piano lessons every week with Louis Barree, the well-known and much respected music and dancing teacher in the area. He was an accomplished musician, but, sadly, Jane was not, nor was ever likely to be, and her lack of aptitude led him to suggest to Jane's mother that she would be better accommodated by Miss White, whose musical accomplishments were less elevated. After all, Louis Barree held concerts in the Assembly Rooms and at local regattas. He was leader of the local Harmonic Society and involved in Eisteddfodau and he sold expensive pianos from a shop on the High Street.

'It seems clear to me, Isaac,' explained Bucke to the Chief Constable once Barree was safely in the cells. 'That he believed teaching scales to a ten year old girl was beneath him. But Mrs Probert liked the idea of Jane taking her lessons with him. I think she thought that since Barree is involved in most of the musical activity in the town, the girl would prosper. Though from what I hear, he is not a very good teacher. He can play the piano, but he can't teach it.'

Colquhoun cleaned his spectacles on his handkerchief. 'You have your sources, I am sure, Rumsey.'

Bucke nodded. 'Well, Jane has been a pupil with him for about a year. Not making much progress by all accounts. No piano at home, so every lesson is like starting out afresh. I know what that feels like.'

'Where does he teach her? At his home?'

'No. He rents a music and dance place in the Assembly Rooms.

That is where Jane went this afternoon. Her aunt, Mrs Dacey, took her. When she arrived, there was another lesson in progress so the girl had to wait and Mrs Dacey went off home. Well, all the next part comes from Jane herself. This is what she said to her aunt.'

The Chief Constable took a deep breath. 'Very well. Go on.'

'Barree took the previous pupil and her mother to the door. Then he came back and took Jane to the fire and encouraged her to warm her hands, which little Jane thought was a bit strange because she didn't think they were cold.' Bucke paused. 'I haven't spoken to the child, and in fairness to Barree he has admitted it all, which saves her having to explain it again. This comes from Mrs Dacey, because Jane went home and told her all about it. I wrote down some of what the aunt said at the time and filled in the details later. It helped that Barree confessed.'

Colquhoun said nothing and listened attentively as Bucke read from his notes.

'*He started to touch her and to rub her through her clothes. He then took her to the piano stool and sat by her. He lifted up her clothes and started rubbing her again*, I did ask, but it is not clear whether he put his hand inside her undergarments or not.'

'Very well, carry on, Rumsey.'

He went back to his report. '*Then he told her to play the piano with one hand. He then laid hold of her other hand and indecently applied it to his person.* And then it seems that he raped her.'

'Oh my good God.' The Chief Constable put his hands to his forehead. 'I don't suppose there is any chance that this is all a fabrication, is there?'

Bucke shook his head. 'None at all. As I said, he has admitted it. The poor girl felt sick and when the next pupil came, she ran home to her Auntie Elizabeth and told her everything. So then you have the father and the uncle shouting up and down Oxford Street and sharpening knives, ready for a castration. At least Mrs Dacey had some sense. She came to see me before things got any worse.'

'Is there anything else?' The Chief Constable continued to clean his spectacles as he considered all the implications of what had occurred. 'Any possible mitigation?'

Bucke looked down at his notes. 'Not really. Barree used to be quite cruel to her. Jane remembered him saying she was a *dull and thick-headed mortal* but in January he started to call her *little dear* and then started to touch her, holding her hand, that sort of thing. She didn't say anything at the time, more's the pity.'

'The poor scrap is just 10 years old, for goodness sake! I have seen a great deal in my job, as you have too, Rumsey. But it is hard to imagine a worse case of depravity. How is the child?'

'She appears well, as far as we can ever know. Doctor Benjamin will be examining her. She seems confused and rather frightened by all the fuss. What is going on in her mind we can never know. We will keep Barree locked up of course, for his own safety as much as for anything else. The Probert family have been far more decent than he has a right to expect, by letting us deal with it. And we are also protecting him from the enormity of Mrs Barree's wrath.'

Both men took a moment to reflect. There were times when their duties as policemen brought them into contact with the very worst aspects of life. Bucke realised that he would never forget that moment when he and Sergeant Ball had walked into the lounge of the Barree home on Cradock Street to arrest him and had seen the look of resignation in his eyes. This was the very moment when the life of the Barree house was to be destroyed forever. There was horror on the face of his wife Mathilde and also, Bucke thought, a suggestion that she was not completely surprised by what he had done. It was clear too, that Mathilde immediately recognised that her social standing has been completely destroyed. And no one else could ever share any of the responsibility for what had happened, for it was Barree's alone.

And then there was the housemaid, Elodie, who had not left after showing them into the room but instead had stood next to her mistress, with a supportive arm around her waist, looking at her master with such an insolent and unutterable contempt, it could only be completely expressed when she mimed a copious expectoration as

Sergeant Ball led him past her. How could anyone have imagined that he might entertain designs against the purity of a ten year old girl? What other secrets lurked within his past, ready to appear like mushrooms from a drain? The Probert's had not been neglectful. They had trusted Barree and he had betrayed them.

Bucke kept asking himself the same questions. Why? Why had Barree done such a thing? What was happening inside his mind? Was he consumed by some kind of abominable sickness? It surely could not be normal for a man to find small girls attractive in that way? Or was he merely a fifty-year-old man locked in his own world, one where he was convinced of his own inviolability, certain that, by right, he deserved to live above all social and moral norms? Bucke knew that Barree would never escape from the consequences of what he had done; on that grey late February afternoon he had defined his own future.

The following morning Bucke returned to Cradock Street, bringing Constance with him. She and Mathilde had occasionally met socially and he felt that she might be more comfortable with her there. She was a severe and humourless woman, with an unshakable belief in her own superiority. Such a ridiculous notion now lay shattered around her and she sat, much diminished, in front of a cold empty grate, hollow-eyed after a sleepless night. Her life in Swansea had been destroyed; it could never be repaired. And now she was married to a news item, to a man most people would like to mutilate.

'Elodie is going to leave, you know. I am sure that she will be offered a new position. News travels so quickly in this town. She will go to Singleton Abbey; I am certain of it.'

'I am sorry to hear that,' said Constance gently. 'You will miss her.'

'It is more important you understand, Constance, that I cannot afford her anymore. This house, too. I cannot afford this. I must leave. Now I must find employment, for I no longer have a husband. I have exchanged him for a convict.'

'Poor Mathilde, what a terrible thing that has happened.'

Mathilde picked constantly at her ear. She mused upon the perfidy

187

of men, as she had done throughout the night, and wiped her eyes with a much-used lace handkerchief. The man she had lived with, with whom she had shared a house and a bed, was suddenly revealed as a mystery to her. They had led separate lives, locked together in a fruitless loveless relationship, based upon mutual dislike. Now he had destroyed her. Mathilde resumed her sobbing. 'No one can ever understand the pain that I have.'

Constance said nothing. Her husband had run away when he wrongly believed he had been accused of murder, but Mathilde was generally wrapped up in herself to such a degree that she was rarely aware of the circumstances of others. She was hardly likely to see that there was any connection in the ending of their marriages. Constance reached out across to her and laid a supportive hand upon her forearm. It was as welcoming and unresponsive as ice.

Bucke sat forward a little in his chair. 'Did what happen yesterday come to you as a complete surprise, Mathilde? Had there been any indication that this might happen?' She shook her head. 'Have there been other of his pupils in whom he has taken an unnatural interest?'

'No, Inspector Bucke. But I have been in his own room this morning. And in the bureau I found these…these things.' She threw a pile of small cards on to a side table in disgust. 'My husband was a madman. That is clear.' The cards spilled on to the floor and Constance gathered them together. They were Parisian *cartes de visite*, showing models wearing underwear and pearls.

She passed them on to Bucke. 'How exotic.' She tried not to smile. 'Those pearls could cause some unpleasant chafing if they ever got caught in the mangle when madame was doing the washing.' Mathilde was especially unamused.

Bucke flicked through them. He had seen much more explicit images when he was in the army. These were rather tame. 'Did you know about these, Mathilde?'

'Of course not, Inspector. These are disgusting. To imagine that they were here in my house. Now I shall never be able to sleep in this house again.'

'Where did he get these pictures? Do you know?'

'I do not know. How could I? He lived his own life. How could I know that his interests should lie in this direction? How should I know he desired young girls? Children. She was ten years old.' She paused and wiped her angry, tearless eyes. 'That my life should come to this.'

'I shall take these cards away with me, with your permission, Mathilde.' She waved a hand vaguely in assent and Bucke put them carefully in his pocket. 'Has he had any callers who may have sold these cards to him?'

She shrugged. It had never been important to her. 'A man comes sometimes. He is no musician, but I do not know who he is. A rough, unpleasant man. He was of no interest to me.'

They walked back to St Helen's Road together, a snatched moment before Bucke returned to the police station. The destructive effect of what Louis Barree had done in that single moment overwhelmed them both.

'You see, Rumsey, what is hard here is that everything becomes concentrated upon Mathilde. The poor woman, her life destroyed, her descent into poverty, her husband a secret monster. All that is true, of course. It will be the talk of the town for weeks. Women who have never met Mathilde will talk of her as their best friend, who confided in them about the devilish needs of her sinister husband. I know too well. It happened to me.'

'And then just when they have forgotten, Louis Barree will appear at the Assizes and all the gossip will start all over again.' Bucke paused. He thought he heard a distant police whistle.

'And what do you think will happen to him?' asked Constance.

'A minimum sentence would be a year, with hard labour, I would say. I think he deserves more and if that is what he gets that he should think himself very lucky. A professional man you see. If he was a labourer in the copper works he might get five. Wrong, Constance but that is how it is. And then when he is released he will have to move away somewhere, far away and try to start again and hope that his neighbours don't find out. But they will.'

'What upsets me, Rumsey, is that the real victim isn't Mathilde, whatever she thinks and however much I feel sorry for her. The real victim is Jane Probert and I am sorry that Mathilde did not find a moment to ask after her. It is a terrible thing that she will have to carry with her for the rest of her life. And what did she do wrong? Nothing. Except want to learn to pay the piano.'

'She should have come to you. Did you hear something? Like a whistle?' They both paused.

'I don't think so. In which direction?' A cart full of bricks lumbered past, clattering on the road, masking all other sounds.

'I must be imagining it. The problem is that at times like this I am expecting to hear it. The town is so unsettled.'

'There are no whistles, Rumsey. Calm yourself. You are not alone. You have constables and the people of Swansea support you.'

They saw a queue of people outside Mrs Scribben's Servants Registry Office, the usual collection of domestic staff seeking a new position. 'Is Elodie there? I can't see her,' asked Bucke. 'It is a respectable agency, by all accounts.'

'I don't think she will need it. Lady Vivian at Singleton Abbey approached her some time ago. Once she knows she is available.... Her gentleman works there too, as I understand it. She will be well provided for.' Constance said, noticing that outside her own rooms there was another, if smaller, queue of young girls and their mothers.

Bucke smiled. 'I see news of Barree's disgrace has spread. I think business may be improving. Your reputation continues to grow.'

'I suppose every cloud that settles over a person, no matter how dark, can be tinged with sunshine for someone else. I can't take on too many, though. I need to keep time for the Ragged School. That isn't work in any way – and I enjoy it.'

They stopped and Bucke turned to her and bowed his head

slightly. 'I wish you a good morning, Miss White. I may call later, when I may have important issues to discuss.'

'I am grateful that you have warned me. I shall try my very best not to be intimidated.' She watched him stride away, towards another day confronting human frailty. Poor Rumsey, she thought. He often seemed so vulnerable, though he was slowly becoming more resilient.

Constance looked at the queue of expectant pupils, spying an opportunity. With any increased income she could look to make her domestic life a little more comfortable. A choice. Laundry service or her very own mangle? She would choose the former; a mangle of misery did not appeal.

*

It was the end of another long and happy day and Sarah and Amy were on their way home. They had been to examine Michael Riley's clothes barrow but they couldn't find him, so they had gone to Mrs Raatz on Waterloo Street who had a better range of sizes. Sarah wanted something better for Amy for a stroll down to the pier on Saturdays.

Sarah felt as if she had emerged from a long and relentless nightmare and, with her position at the Ragged School, she felt that her life had restarted. One thing puzzled her though, and she wasn't sure what to do about it. She didn't yet feel confident enough to broach the subject with Dr Benjamin. When she arrived at the school in the morning the kitchen always seemed to have been used. She always left it clean and ordered and yet some of the work had to be repeated every morning. She would speak to him in a few more days, she decided.

When they arrived home, Amy was in the middle of her daily speculation about what exactly happened to the Elephant after which the street was named. Jack McCarthy was standing outside, smoking his pipe. He seemed to be in an unusually reflective mood, for the world was treating him well today, it seemed. Sales of the new *cartes de visite* had gone very well. He had sold out and he was looking at a handsome profit. He had also been down on the Strand to see his children. No matter how much he had lost his moral compass, he still loved his children as much as an absent father could. He and his wife could barely speak to each other, even when drunk, but he had heard of a job that might suit his son, Timothy, working with horses at Sketty Hall. A couple of the men out there were his clients and had only yesterday taken possession of some of the highly detailed cabinet cards. They would soon realise that they owed him something. Life was good today and he greeted Sarah affably enough. 'Evening. Still working, Sarah?' He ran a hand through his thick hair and scratched his scalp.

'Don't be ridiculous, Jack McCarthy. It is a foul trade and you know it.'

He shrugged. 'If you are short of business, I could sort it for you. Be pleased to help. You can rely on me.' He winked.

Sarah decided not to respond. She looked at him and made a decision to speak to him. This was as good an opportunity as she might ever have, and she had to do it. 'Here, Amy. The key. You trot off upstairs for a moment. I will be up presently. I need to speak to Mr McCarthy.'

Amy looked suspiciously at Jack, concerned that she should not leave Sarah in his company. But the smiles and nods she received from Sarah seemed to satisfy her.

Jack watched her run up the stairs, holding the key proudly and with Dolly Sarah beneath her arm. 'Who's that then?'

'An orphan, Jack.'

'Are you keeping her then?'

'Of course, Jack. She has no one else.'

He looked thoughtful. 'How old is she, then? Do you know?'

'Eight? Possibly seven, I don't know. Why do you ask?'

'Just wondering.' He put his pipe in his pocket. 'If you don't want her, I can get rid of her for you. Not a problem.'

'What are you saying?' she hissed. 'Are you some kind of monster?' She clenched her fists.

'You heard,' Jack replied casually. 'You know what I am. I can sell her for you. Like I done before. Remember?'

Sarah bit her knuckle briefly. 'Yes, I remember. And that is what I want to ask you about.' She looked uncomfortable. Jack said nothing, waiting, arranging his hair and studying her face. 'It would be about seven years ago. You helped me out.' Jack nodded. 'I got caught. And that was a girl. My baby. My daughter. And you took her away. You said you knew someone who wanted a baby. And now I need to know. Do you remember who you gave her to? This is very important to me. My baby. Who had her?'

Jack laughed. 'It was seven years ago, you say? How do you expect me to remember?'

Sarah was persistent. 'Did you give her to a woman in Pentrechwyth? I need to find out!"

'I don't know. Why should I?' Look, don't let it eat you up. You'll never know. That is it.' Jack, unusually, tried to be sympathetic. 'Look, Sarah. What difference would it make now? You would be a stranger to her. She lives with someone who she believes is her mother. Why would you want to turn all that upside down? How could you prove you were the child's mother, anyway? You made a decision seven years ago and that is it. Can't be undone, now can it?'

Sarah looked up the stairs. 'But she is mine. And I need to know where she is.'

'You gave her away. And if I do not know where she went, then you don't either. She could be any seven-year-old girl you see in the street.' He held out his hands, palms up. 'The child was healthy and well, as far I can remember. That is all I can tell you. I swear to you that she didn't die, not when I had her. You gave her a different life, and perhaps it was a better one. But it was your choice.' He reached out and stroked her hair and then tugged on her ear, gently. 'That's life, isn't it?'

She knocked his hand away and sighed. 'I know.' She walked slowly up the insecure staircase which creaked alarmingly, as Jack walked off briskly down the street, whistling. He hadn't said what she had hoped he would say. But then, he hadn't shattered her dreams either.

Part Two – Departures

Sixteen

The pavement at the bottom of St Helen's Road was shocking. They really should do something about it. Elodie had lived in Swansea for quite a few years now and she still didn't know who 'they' were. Did anyone? It was stony and rutted, completely unfit for pedestrians. Her boots slipped and squelched loudly in a puddle, and even if, briefly, the world tilted, the street in front of her still appeared deserted.

It was an easy walk from the Abbey, all on the flat, and she had done it so often that it had become quite boring. Still, she wouldn't be doing it for much longer. She was betrothed now to Frederick Goodman, the butler at Singleton Abbey, a marriage that would change her circumstances completely. She was going to leave Madame Barree, of course. Lady Vivian had offered her a post as a lady's maid, with a particular responsibility for hair dressing. In the circumstances of Louis Barree's disgrace, it wasn't such a bad thing. It was time to move on, Elodie decided. She had enjoyed her work; Mathilde could be difficult at times but they had been able to resolve their difficulties together in French. Louis, she had always recognised, could be a little predatory but she had never struggled to deal with him. She had never been his victim but it had become clear to her that he had chosen them very carefully.

It would be very different working in a large house with a great many other staff, being part of a small self-contained society. But it was time for a change, she knew it. Fred was a little pompous at times, but that was part of his role at the top of the heap in the Abbey, she recognised that, and generally he was a good sort, really. It was going to be an arrangement that would suit both of them, she was sure. Elodie stepped carefully around another puddle. Why was it called the Abbey? She had often wondered about that because it didn't seem a particularly religious sort of place.

She wondered about calling in to see Constance who lived just a short way along the road, but it was getting late and she needed to be back at home. There was a horse and cart in the distance. It didn't seem right to Elodie that the roadway was well made but that the pavement barely seemed to exist at all at this point. She stepped off the pavement on to the more secure footing of the cobbles. The bottom of her dress was filthy and she was sure from the smell of her dress that it had trailed in something left by a dog. *Merde* she thought. It started to rain, so she stopped and organised her umbrella. She later speculated that this might indeed have saved her life.

Elodie unclipped the fastener, cursing the Swansea weather, and began to unfurl it, glancing back down the road to look at the clouds scudding in from the west on the tide. As she did so, Elodie caught a hint of a movement in a shadowed doorway and heard a deep voice muttering. She turned towards it and saw a man coming towards her, his hand raised to strike, vile words spilling from his mouth. Elodie, always so self-possessed, lifted her umbrella and allowed him to run straight into it. He was caught in the middle of the chest and the force caused both of them to stagger apart. Elodie was able to keep her balance on the more solid footing of the road but the man lost his balance and fell on to his back. Elodie regretted the absence of a spike on the end of her umbrella but the groans and curses he was making certainly suggested that he had been hurt. She remained calm and quickly assessed her options.

She could run to Constance's rooms but her dress might slow her down and she had no idea whether he was faster than her. If she had been wearing a skirt she could have taken it off. Why was there never a constable around when you needed one? It might be, she reasoned, that if she hurt him some more it might dissuade him from following her, as well as slowing him down, so she stamped as hard as she could on his ankle. It did hurt him because he shouted loudly but she was aware that she hadn't broken a bone, rather just pushed it into the mud. She thought about trying again but decided it would be unwise to linger. She looked at him more closely. She couldn't see his face, lying in the shadows, but she could see what looked like two brass buttons on his coat and a shape next to his hand that looked like a gift from a dog. '*Vous etes une crotte de chien!*' she snarled and stamped on his shin for emphasis and then turned away, walking as fast as she could.

Elodie had heard of some women concealing a poker inside their umbrella for just such an occasion and wished she had done it. She stopped outside Constance's front door but there was no light in the window. She looked behind her. There was no sign of the man and the cart she had seen was coming towards her, offering more security and less isolation. She wondered what Fred would have done in these circumstances and realised with shock that she did not know. Surely he would have protected her, wouldn't he? She pushed the idea aside, though remembering that Fred had never offered to walk her home. Tonight he was busy giggling with that grubby, unpleasant man who visited him sometimes, the one who also visited Louis Barree. Why did she think Fred was buying something from him?

She looked into the darkness again. There was no sign of her attacker, but this was not a moment to take risks. Madame Barree would not be the most sympathetic listener, locked as she was in her own bewilderment and anger. She wondered about going to the police station to report the attack. It would wait until the morning. The cart almost next to her now and all seemed clear behind it.

But as she walked on, Elodie realised that she owed it to all the women of Swansea to speak to the police as soon as possible. So, when she met Constable Gill standing at the corner of Wyndham Street, she asked him to escort her to the police station.

She was pleased to see that Inspector Bucke was still there, for she felt comfortable with him. He listened intently to her story, pausing once to dispatch a constable to examine the scene of the attack.

'It was over so ver' quick. I was not expecting it.'

'How could you be, Elodie?'

'It is what I was thinkin' about, after. There are things I wish I had been doing to him. But I had no time. I should have done more, Inspector. After all, m'sieur, he is a large piece of lard and I should have stamped on his head.'

'I think you have done very well, Elodie. What you have told me is very useful. I regret only that you did not incapacitate him.'

'I apologise, Inspector Bucke. The state of the pavement is so shockin' down there.'

'What I am interested in is the weapon he was carrying. You say it was like a small stick. Perhaps to fit in the hand, would you say?'

Elodie nodded. 'It was like a piece of a dog's shit, I am thinkin'. I told him so.'

'Quite, Elodie.' Bucke opened the copy of *Vanity Fair* on the desk and pushed it across the desk to her. 'Did it look like this? What do you think?' He pointed at the drawing of a cosh.

'This is very much a child's drawin'.' She flicked through a few pages. And it is the drawin' of a boy. A young man. They are not very good. He knows little of a woman's body, you can see that.'

Bucke drew her attention back to the cosh on the last page of the book. 'What do you think of this?'

'That is the weapon that the man 'ad. That is what it looked like. Exactly. The best drawin' he has done.'

'Thank you, Elodie. And you say there was something on his coat.'

'They were shinin'. Buttons I think.'

'That is very useful, Elodie. Thank you.'

'There are many buttons in the world, Inspector. I could not see them ver' well. It is dark down there. Something should be done.'

'And did you notice an apron? Was he wearing a leather apron, perhaps?'

'No. That I did not see. But I think you must teach your boys to draw somethin' they understand. And I warn you, if he tries it again I shall put ma parapluie in 'is eye.'

Elodie showed no reluctance at all to speak to the press about the attack, especially since it gave her an opportunity to complain about the state of the streets. She became the *Plucky Housemaid* and her name was accompanied by the humorous suggestion that the police force should employ her to confront footpads and ruffians. It brought her a brief celebrity that made Lady Vivian a little uncomfortable, for she preferred discretion in all things. But another consequence was that her assailant was given a name. The Evening Telegraph thrust him firmly into the popular imagination by calling him 'Cosh Boy.' And so, as a consequence, a campaign was born, to find Cosh Boy before a French lady's maid found him, so that his subsequent public emasculation could provide something of interest, as well as a powerful ritual to ensure the early arrival of spring. Of course there was a more serious consequence, though. Women were even more wary of the streets – and they had never been the safest of places. The pressure was on the police; it was their duty to soothe anxieties, and to ensure security and safety by catching Cosh Boy.

*

There had been an immediate response to his own appearance in the Swansea Evening Telegraph; Abramovitch could not deny that it had created a stir across Swansea. Illiteracy did not inhibit families, for the feature was read aloud in shops and pubs to all those who would listen. Naturally it was not completely understood, with some suddenly convinced that their daughter was being personally invited to become a princess in a land far away and that her parents and siblings would become respected retainers and live an indulgent life that was somehow their birth-right. The need for a doll as identification was not regarded as a difficulty and the idea of a scroll was not understood at all and therefore regarded as irrelevant. A brooch was not a problem and the age of the girl was considered to be negotiable.

Girls were brought to the Castle Hotel throughout the morning and Jack McCarthy watched them as he sat on a half-burnt plank in the ruins of the shipping office, eating biscuits from the adjoining shop, the John Dennis Biscuit Warehouse. It was now a dilapidated and smoke-blackened building, its exposed wall, that would never again be properly vertical, was supported by wooden props that seemed to be the strongest feature it had. McCarthy mused upon the inconsistent quality of the biscuits and considered his options carefully, sensing in the advertisement and in the atmosphere of hysteria created by the recent murders, an opportunity. He saw a couple walk out of the hotel with young girl. The father cuffed her around the head, said something and then snatched a doll from her and threw it dramatically into the road. Not a successful visit, then. Long may it continue, he thought. Perhaps they should be trying on slippers, like in that play that Fanny was always banging on about. Wouldn't be hard to find a girl with the right-sized feet, would it? Something about a ball, wasn't it? He couldn't remember. Then he saw Inspector Bucke walking down Castle Bailey Street. He didn't think Bucke knew him, but he felt it best if he were to slip away. Always best not to attract attention, in his experience.

Bucke was going to the Town Hall to see Captain Colquhoun so that he could talk to him about the newly-christened Cosh Boy – or, as he would have preferred, Button Man. It was a pleasant morning and he enjoyed the sun on his face and this opportunity to walk quietly through the town and order his thoughts, as much as he could. At the moment he could not see any links between Cosh Boy and the murders, but that didn't mean there were none. He had quietly considered whether the assailant was one of the constables, for the shining buttons that had been reported could suggest a uniform. The constables of Swansea did not have a convincing record of staying on the right side of the law. However, he could not place any of them in the areas where the attacks happened, not officially anyway, but he was not ready to rule out the possibility. Those buttons and the gap between the attacks also suggested to him the possibility it might be a sailor, someone perhaps who sailed locally, returning to Swansea regularly. Inspector Flynn said that he would take a walk down to the harbour master, to see if any departures and arrivals tallied with the attacks.

When he arrived at Castle Square he looked around and remembered the fire that had lit up the November sky. The rubble-strewn gap that now stretched between two unstable buildings was a constant reminder of a terrible night when the discovery of the body of a murder victim had set in motion the destruction of a family; a night when it was said, an angel had appeared in the heart of the flames.

Bucke saw a man he recognised as Jack McCarthy leaving the rubble. He didn't know him very well, for he had never dealt with him directly. He knew that he operated on the margins and what he did was always unclear. Bucke had never been comfortable with the regular meetings McCarthy used to have with the previous Chief Constable, John Allison, or the conspiratorial nature of their relationship. He had always believed that something was going on and that eventually McCarthy would become a person who might interest him. He had never spoken to him but Bucke had the impression that he believed he was clever enough to keep himself out of trouble; he knew that he certainly could not be trusted. Bucke wondered why he was here and about his decision to get up and walk away so briskly as soon as he saw him, which only added to the sense of suspicion.

'Good morning, Inspector, sir.' Abramovitch emerged from the Castle Hotel carrying a cup and saucer. 'Perhaps you can tell me why you people insist in putting the milk into your tea.'

Bucke shrugged. 'I imagine we are not familiar with the requirements of visitors from your part of Europe, Mr Abramovitch.'

'I have many requirements, Inspector, sir, and your town seems unable to satisfy any of them.' He drank from his cup, grimaced and emptied it on to the pavement. 'I have many visitors here. They read of my story in the newspaper and so they bring me their daughters. Have I told them that I wish to buy a child? Any child? Of course not, it is ridiculous. But they do not understand. My home is destroyed, my family is murdered and they think that I want their daughter, not my own.'

'If Chana is in Swansea, Mr Abramovitch,' said Bucke, 'it might be that those who have her, don't know who she is. I do not know how we can help you, not without further information.'

Abramovitch put his hand on the dark chipped door frame of the hotel, squeezing it as if from it he could extract water. 'It is ridiculous you have no records, Inspector, sir. What if the Hungarian finds her before you do? Tell me that.'

'Have you seen this man again?'

Abramovitch snorted. 'No. Czibor is too cunning. He is a secret agent and he has been trained well. You do not know he is there and then he kills.'

'If you do see him again, please inform a constable immediately.' Bucke could not hide his scepticism. 'If you do feel in danger, Mr Abramovitch, you might reflect that your newspaper article has attracted attention to yourself. Your Hungarian knows where to find you. I advise that you review your own security arrangements.'

Abramovitch dismissed his comments with a casual wave of the hand and Bucke resumed his walk.

*

Sarah assessed the kitchen carefully. Nothing was out of place; everything had been put properly away. She'd check in the morning. Now it was time to collect Amy go home. She was still in the schoolroom, playing with her friend Myra. She didn't have her pram with her. It had been such a struggle to get it up the stairs to the room that she hadn't taken it out for a while, but she had promised Myra that she would bring it again for her to have a proper look at it. They were teaching the alphabet to Sarah Dolly and her new best friend Molly, Myra Kealey's rag doll. They were so absorbed in their play that they did not notice that Dr Benjamin was standing at the other end of the classroom, with that well-dressed man who had visited the school last week and who was watching them closely.

'We do our best here, of course, Mr Abramovitch, but I cannot correct the considerable injustices of the society in which I live. The neglect of the children here is an enormous stain upon my country's conscience. We presume to be the most advanced country in the world, leading an empire of millions, and yet we allow such poverty to exist in the heart of our prosperous towns. It isn't just Swansea, Mr Abramovitch. It is everywhere.' He closed his eyes and raised his face to the ceiling in distress, whilst Abramovitch discreetly looked at his pocket-watch. 'There are children living in conditions that are impossible to comprehend – and dying too – whilst lords and ladies ride around in carriages.'

Abramovitch shook his head in sympathy. 'It must be very difficult for you, Doctor, sir. I wish that there was more I could do to help you but, alas, I am a poor foreigner only, looking for his daughter.' He stared at Amy and Myra. 'And you do not believe you can help me, you say?'

Benjamin laughed bitterly. 'Many of our children do not know who their proper parents are. There are some who live in places we cannot imagine, with people you would describe as strangers. Our refusal to help them condemns us all.'

'Your work must be so difficult. Perhaps what you require is a revolution to sweep away the corruption that murders the poorest children.' He nodded his head in emphasis. 'I wish you every success, Doctor. Be strong, always.'

'That time will come, I am sure of it, Mr Abramovitch. I would not normally advocate any sort of civil disorder, but I believe that it is inevitable. Do you think, from your experience of Europe that…'

'But my daughter you do not know?' Abramovitch had not been listening and looked beyond Benjamin. He watched the two girls closely, the last two children left in the school. Abramovitch moved imperceptibly to the side to get a better view of them. 'A young child looking for her parents, lost and confused in a strange world?'

'Family ties are often very vague on this side of town, Mr Abramovitch. But if you will excuse me, I have an urgent meeting with Mr Morley, my medical supplier.'

'Naturally, Dr Benjamin.' Abramovitch shook his head sadly. 'It would delight me beyond measure to make a further donation to the school, but alas…' He let the words hang in the air as he walked towards the door. Benjamin nodded and followed him as good manners dictated, this was the kind of disappointment to which he had, too frequently, become accustomed.

Sarah emerged from the kitchen, ready to take Myra home first to Greenhill and then return with Amy to Elephant Court. She saw

Abramovitch and glared at him. The man from Riley's clothes cart; the man who visited the school last week; the man she did not trust. He made eye contact with her and she responded, to show that she could not be intimidated. Then Abramovitch smiled. She could not know that he had decided that he would not follow her; not tonight.

Doctor Benjamin closed the door as Abramovitch left and turned back towards Sarah. He seemed uncomfortable, as if he were keen for Sarah to leave. 'You must have so much more to do now that your work here in the school is concluded. It must be a difficult life, Miss Rigby, but I thank you sincerely for all the work that you do for our poor children.'

She was holding the hands of both Myra and Amy and she raised them together with a smile. 'Call me Sarah, please. The children do.'

'Of course.' He seemed to blush. 'Please take care, for our streets are dangerous, as we know.'

'I have lived on them long enough,' she replied, elusively. The doctor looked at her quizzically and she hurried the conversation on, before it entered areas which she had no wish to explore. 'There has been something that has puzzled me, Doctor, and I have been meaning to ask you about it.' The two girls looked up at Sarah, waiting patiently, holding her hands. 'You see, Doctor Benjamin, my last task in the evening is to prepare the kitchen, ready for a new day tomorrow. Putting everything in the correct place, cleaning. This is what I have just done.' She broke off to wipe Myra's nose with her handkerchief. 'Excuse me,' she smiled, 'And yet you see, in the morning the kitchen appears untidy, a little disordered, as if someone has been using it. I don't understand. Please don't misunderstand, I don't mind, but...'

Benjamin looked uneasy, thought Sarah. Nervous. 'Of course, Sarah. It is very remiss of me. I should have said something. I apologise most sincerely.' He ran his finger round his shirt collar, as if loosening it. 'In the evenings I often come down to the kitchen to carry out my researches, for I am trying to develop...' he paused, as if he was thinking of a word, she thought...' an effective cure for...for...measles which, as you will know, takes so many of our

205

children. I believe I am very close to success.'

'That is excellent news, Doctor Benjamin. It will be a considerable triumph.' She watched him carefully. 'What an achievement that would be. If I can be of any help at all in your work…'

'Thank you, Sarah. I work long into the night, weighing, mixing, assessing, recording. It is exhausting work but as I intimated, I firmly believe that soon there will be a breakthrough. I clean the kitchen as best I can, but always when I am tired, and I do not have your facility. So please accept my apologies if I am making your work harder than it should be. But I am doing it for the children, who give us the passion that drives us forward.'

'Please, Doctor. Do not apologise. I was merely curious. Now I know, I will be happy to clean up for you. Leave things as they are and I will do it.' She was sure he was hiding something. She was merely the cook – but why, she wondered. did he feel the need to deceive her? She continued to watch him carefully.

'I take supplies from Mr Morley and it is so very expensive, as I am sure you can imagine. But it must surely work and then so many lives will be saved. I correspond with others across the world. Mr Morley kindly visits the post office for me almost every day. You see, I believe that the alkaline saline solution, normally recommended, eases the eruptions but does not cure.' He looked around the classroom. 'My medication contains no opium and …I will do my best to ensure that the kitchen matches up to your exacting standards, Miss Rigby, … sorry, Sarah. But please excuse me.' He turned abruptly and went into the kitchen.

Sarah smiled at the girls. 'Come on then. Let's get home shall we? And then back tomorrow for another wonderful day.' The three of them ushered out an eager Black Bart for his nightly patrol and at the same time, Sarah again wondered why the doctor had been so evasive.

Seventeen

Bucke arrived in the police station quite early. He needed to get on with his report into the attack on Elodie. He was hoping that in the process of writing and by structuring the evidence, he would find links to the other attacks that had so far eluded him. Then he could go out into the town and discover if anyone had anything they wanted to say to him. They often did. And then he would make an arrest and everything would be solved. So, lost in his fantasy, he was surprised to see Florian waiting for him in the lobby, sitting neatly, patiently, with his hat resting on his knees. As soon as he saw him, Bucke felt guilty. He had forgotten that he had asked him to call. 'Good morning, Florian, I am very pleased to see you.'

Florian looked at him impassively. 'You are late.'

'But I didn't know when you were coming, did I? But I am very grateful that you have found the time.'

'Promise,' replied Florian tersely. His eyes, beneath those heavy brows, seemed to slip even deeper into his head.

'Come into my office. I want you to look at something for me.' Bucke led him into his office. He could see that Florian was uncomfortable at being indoors.

'I have little time, Inspector. I must go to work, also.'

'Of course, Florian.' Bucke sat down and took out the hat from the *Ann of Bridgewater.* 'Look at this. What does it tell you?'

Florian looked at Bucke and then examined the hat carefully, turning it round in his hands. He was not to be hurried. 'It is a hat. A fisherman's hat? But a hat. I am sure.'

'Would you like to have another look?'

Florian raised an eyebrow, said nothing. He looked at the hat again, then put it down. 'What you want to know?'

Bucke was trying his best to be patient. 'The hat. What does the label say?'

He put the hat on the table. 'You think I know? How?'

'Florian, you told me you could read Hungarian.'

He snorted derisively. 'Hungarian I can read, Inspector Bucke. But not this. This is not Hungarian.'

He was suddenly alert. 'Do you recognise the language, Florian?' Bucke picked up the hat and looked at the words once more - *Magazin Pălărie Mangalia* - and offered the hat to him again, but Florian did not take it.

'Romanian, perhaps. What it says I do not know.'

'You sure? Not Bulgarian, perhaps? Turkish? Greek?'

'It is Romanian, I think. A strange language.'

Bucke looked at him carefully. He had no doubt at all that he was telling the truth. This was a very significant moment. Abramovitch claimed to be Romanian and yet had not recognised his own language. Why? 'There is something else you might be able to help me with. A name. Does the name Czibor mean anything to you?'

Florian did not react. 'It is a name. In Hungary. Of a horse? A man who sells cakes? I do not know. I have not heard it for a long time.'

'And you have heard of no one with this name, Czibor, in Swansea?'

'Of course not. I know Hungarians. Can I go now?' Florian flicked his eyebrows.

Bucke reached into his pocket and pulled out a coin, a shilling. 'Thank you. This is very useful indeed. I am so very sorry that I was late, Florian.'

He examined the coin, turning it over in his hand. Bucke was surprised that he did not test its authenticity between his teeth. 'I to work must go now,' he said eventually. 'Soon I join the Hatstand Gang. Their pay is better.' Florian stood and adjusted the thick string that held up his dark and dirty trousers. He nodded to the Inspector and left the office. Bucke remained at his desk, deep in thought, for quite a while. He thought he should begin his report but, as he did so, Sergeant Ball came in with a letter for Bucke which they had received from the police in Bristol. They had previously telegraphed a general enquiry to Swansea and had now sent more details of their concerns in a letter. It was signed by an old army colleague of his, Arthur Gordon; they had served together companiably in India and it was pleasant to hear from him. He too was now a police inspector and his request was intriguing.

Concerns had been raised by Mr Herapath, the public analyst in Bristol, about Roache's Liver Pills that were advertised in, and sold through, the newspapers and which originated in Swansea. Did he know anything about them, asked Gordon? They seemed to be made from some kind of organic material rolled in sugar, though they were not what Herapath would describe as 'wholesome.' He didn't think that they would cause any harm as such, though he would not take them himself and neither did he think they would do any good. Gordon went on to write that they had been reported to the analyst because a user had become unwell. Scientific analysis was continuing but Gordon was keen to know if Bucke knew anything.

Bucke didn't know anything at all. But the name was familiar. He hadn't heard of a pill manufacturer in the town and neither had the constables when Ball had asked them. They knew nothing, apart from Evan Davies, whose mother was an enthusiastic customer. It puzzled Bucke, something like this happening in Swansea and him knowing nothing about it. He prided himself on his knowledge of the town and he was rather affronted by his own ignorance. But it wasn't difficult to start to uncover it; after all, the advertisements necessarily included an address. Orders were sent to Box 51 at the Post office in Swansea – so that would mean the one on Castle Street. Consequently, someone must collect the orders from there and also dispatch the pills. Customers paid with stamps, so possibly the same someone had to bring them in to turn them into cash. All it would require was a simple surveillance operation and he was sure that one of the constables would be able to carry it out, though perhaps it would be best if he went down there himself first. He owed it to Gordon to do this properly. The report would have to wait for a while.

At the post office the manager knew very little, which was not a surprise, for it was a busy place. One of the assistants though, dealt with a man in a dirty and rather threadbare jacket, who came in on Wednesdays and Fridays with boxes to be posted. The Inspector had probably just missed him. The boxes were already stamped and then he would return unused stamps that the clerk would buy back. Today he had handed over to him a little over 10 shillings. But he didn't know who he was. He was just the man with the stamps.

Bucke was intrigued. It would be good to write back to Gordon with news of an investigation completed. There seemed to be precious few of those at the moment. When he came out of the post office he looked at the dark stained door of the Castle Hotel. Abramovitch was filling his mind again. What was he doing? What was his intention? He had never been comfortable with him and now he didn't trust him at all. Bucke needed to speak to him, to confront him, and he knew that the best place to do so would be in the police station, not in a place where Abramovitch might feel in greater control. He'd send a constable to request he attend at Tontine Street tomorrow morning. He didn't want to see him until he had worked out a clear strategy.

*

It was another Friday night in the Star Theatre and, not unexpectedly, things were not going very well. Their act was an unsophisticated one, tiresome at best, and Minx and Stinx were never very popular. Fanny stood in the wings watching a bored audience taunt and abuse their habitually desperate performance. Their tired humour was based entirely upon one familiar and over-used premise. Minx was a high-class lady – you could tell this from her parasol and her bonnet. Stinx was a tramp with a clown's face, seemingly devoted to Minx, an unattainable vision of beauty, but his love would always remain unrequited. It was an uninspired narrative and a tedious and amateurish act, relying entirely upon poor stage lighting to disguise the inadequacies of their performance. Minx was a thin, fading beauty, once a chorus girl and now a gin queen who could no longer dance.

Her husband, Stinx, was much older than her, his face blotchy from too much make up and too much alcohol, forever destined to tour the country seeking success with an act that would always be greeted with contempt.

Harry Boston, The Singing Painter and Artist Extraordinaire, had seen the audience and had refused to go on stage following such a disaster, fearing his inevitable humiliation in front of an agitated audience. So Fanny would have to be the one to go on and try to calm them. She shook her head as orange peel was thrown on to the stage. At least tonight there was no sign of a repeat of the legendary dead cat. She saw that Stinx was a clown without a circus, a small-town entertainer. Was this her fate too? Fanny shuddered.

The act ended with a knife-throwing finale where Stinx stood in front of a wooden screen, apparently oblivious to the knives thrown at him by Minx, whilst he released doves hidden in his costume. She missed by such a huge margin that the only tension that they could ever generate was whether the knives stuck in the screen or fell out. The audience jeered mightily and drunks in the stalls offered to throw the knives for her, promising enhanced accuracy.

The stage was now covered in feathers because one of his three doves had died. The poor bird had been hidden beneath Stinx's arm and, in avoiding the only knife that came anywhere near him, he had pressed his arm too fiercely against his side and squashed it. The last time they were in Swansea he had sat on one. The dead bird fell out of his jacket and Stinx threw it into the air to simulate flight. The audience howled with derision when it plummeted back to the boards with the aerial grace of a stone. The couple trooped off the stage, Stinx dragging behind him the dove, which had been attached to his jacket by string to prevent an escape. It was an ignominious retreat and the stage was covered in feathers and abandoned dreams.

Fanny shook her head firmly when Stinx asked her if he could 'trouble her brandy,' and strode purposefully to the apron in order to restore order. It took a while. A drunk at the rear of the stall continued to offer his services as a skilled thrower of knives and Henry Fry, in his habitual position at the front, stood up and turned to glare at him.

Fanny smiled at his efforts, which touched her very much; however she was far more direct and far more effective. She picked up a knife from the floor and threatened to cut his lights out and burn them on the stage if he didn't shut up. The audience cheered, Henry sat down and the drunk backed off. Fanny stuck the knife into her belt and soon had the audience singing raucously along with her in the chorus of *The Rat Catcher's Daughter*.

*

He slapped the cosh into his left palm, enjoying the sensation, enjoying the rhythm. 'Bitch,' he repeated with every stroke. He was powerful, he was the Avenger. But he knew that he was really a failure. He wasn't sure he had killed anyone yet. The woman in Tower Lane was still alive. He had lost his nerve and run away. Yes, the one down on Rodney Street had died, but she had been alive when he ran off. He knew that because she had been swearing at him. Perhaps someone else had finished her off. The newspaper said they had arrested a man called Walters for her death. A militiaman? He smiled. He was in the clear, it seemed. But he hadn't seen anyone die yet.

He rubbed his chest. 'Bitch. Bitch. Bitch.' It hurt. Thank goodness the umbrella didn't have a spike at the end. It was quite an extensive bruise. Perhaps when he was more skilled, he would go looking for her again. She wouldn't be so lucky then. 'Bitch. Bitch. Bitch,' he murmured as he worked the cosh a little harder.

The Evening Telegraph had started to call him Cosh Boy, demanding the police do something, put more constables on the street, urging women to stay at home. He laughed and increased the rhythm to two strokes into his hand, one for each word. 'Cosh Boy. Cosh Boy. Cosh Boy.' It was good to have a name, it made him feel important. And he was clever, he was one step ahead of the stupid policemen and they would never catch him. He had heard others talking about Cosh Boy too. They thought they were clever, saying that Cosh Boy had killed the captain of the ship that had washed up in Mumbles. Well, he hadn't. Cosh Boy didn't go to sea and he didn't want anyone stealing his triumphs either.

There was cloud again tonight, making the dark streets still darker.

Just as Cosh Boy liked it. Perfect for his work, cleaning the streets. Cosh Boy would go somewhere different tonight, somewhere the police would never expect. He thought about walking up to Sketty and waiting outside the Bush Inn but it was a bit far and he was tired after a long day. Where should Cosh Boy go, he wondered? A theatre! That's where. Those dancing girls were the absolute filth from the gutter. Good idea, Cosh Boy. Plenty of choice. No one would miss a dancing girl. No one.

*

Fanny gathered her handful of belongings together. The rest could stay in the dressing room, for she had a rehearsal in the morning and she was singing again tomorrow night. Melville, the manager of the Star, was desperate to keep her, she knew that. Fanny was quite a draw and his greatest fear was that she would move to the Swansea Music Hall or somewhere, so he kept her in his shows. If that was what he wanted, he ought to pay her more, thought Fanny.

Henry had been in the audience, defending her of course, but he hadn't been to the stage door tonight and she was surprised at how disappointed she was about that. He had become quite a comfort to her. But she remembered that tonight he had to go and attend some sort of function with his parents and his prospective in-laws. His fiancée, the homely and unexciting Harriet would be there and Fanny had felt a surge of jealousy that she had not experienced for many years. Henry had seen her performance and that gave her comfort. But it involved a deception of course, it had to; Henry was working late on complicated property disputes and so would be late to the function, but that was very little consolation to her. Just another of those falsehood that littered her life, just another reminder. He provided a window into another world, more comfortable, less dangerous, with quiet days measured by the snores of a well-loved terrier, rather than by incident, conflict and drama. She knew she could look through that window, but she also knew that those curtains would one day be drawn and she would be shut out. That world would never be hers and Fanny wondered when in her life she had reached the precise point when it was decided that such things would, in a future that had, by then, already been mapped out for her, always remain out of reach. Was it actually when she was born? Or could she have made a different decision at some unidentifiable time, which would have seen her tonight in her best dress in someone's drawing room sipping sherry? Were grubby theatres and dangerous streets all that were ever intended for her? All she did know, was that such a leisured life was not hers and never would be.

She said goodnight to Mr Pugh the doorman and walked through the passageway on to Little Wind Street. It was dark and cold but a brisk walk home would warm her and if she was lucky, Jack would be out. She hadn't eaten for a while but perhaps that could wait until tomorrow.

York Street was surprisingly empty and Fanny turned on to Fisher Street. It was a starry night and so the pubs were warm and busy. There had been a good audience tonight and she had performed two more ballads, both in English, after she had steadied the auditorium with her rousing version of *The Ratcatcher's Daughter*. It was always successful. Tomorrow morning, she was meeting the conductor of the band to rehearse a couple of songs in Welsh. It was time for her to expand her repertoire; she was getting bored.

She stopped to re-adjust her shawl and saw a cat slip silently across the street, its belly close to the ground, disturbed, it seemed, by a figure that had slipped into the doorway of the horse dealer's in front of her, as if trying to make itself inconspicuous. Fanny looked around. There was no one else in sight. She decided to go on but focused her attention on the doorway. There was someone there, she knew it. She also knew that she did not want that someone behind her in the dark. She crossed to the other side of the narrow street to give herself more space. Should she speed up and so signal her fear? Or should she slow down and make herself vulnerable? She slowed; she wanted to be ready for whatever might happen. From this side of the street she had a better angle. There was a figure there, there could be no doubt.

'Well? What do you want? I know you are there. 'She took another step. Then another. 'If it's money you want, I ain't got none.'

A man charged out of the doorway at her, shouting wordlessly.

214

His right hand was raised and he brought it down towards her with tremendous force. Fanny stepped backwards and felt the disturbance of the air as a cosh flashed past her face. The man stumbled and tried to recover, preparing himself for a lateral blow.

Fanny put her hand to her belt and pulled out the knife she taken from the stage. She had lived in Swansea for a long time and knew that every woman out at night needed some protection. 'Now you hurry on home, little boy. Or I shall cut your tiny balls off.' Perhaps she should not have insulted him but there was no point in trying to calm him down now. She took a step forward, pointing the knife at him. He was panting heavily and then started to mutter the word 'Whore,' repeatedly. He raised his hand again. She knew who he was.

'Have you ever been to the music hall, Cosh Boy? You remember the man with the knives? I'll wager you have seen him. You must remember. Comes on after the dancing girls. Remember?' Fanny moved the knife slowly backwards and forwards in front of him, never taking her eyes away from his. He was swaying now, perhaps ready to attack again. 'He throws knives. One of the girls stands against a board and he throws knives. Can you remember? Pretty she is. Feather in her hair. Big tits. You can see them from the stalls. You can see her legs too. All the way up. You like her, don't you? You can't take your eyes off her, can you? I know. I've seen you. And then the man throws knives at the pretty girl, doesn't he? You have seen that, too.' He was staring at her, still muttering. 'And do you know? He always misses, but the knives always stick. Have you noticed that? And do you know something else? This is one of his knives.' She turned her hand so that he could see the edge. 'And I will tell you something. I never miss. And this knife always sticks. Goes deep, too. Have to pull on it very hard to get it out.'

Fanny continued to face him and started to walk backwards up the empty street, away from him, the knife still outstretched. He watched her and followed her for a short distance with his hand still raised, but then wavered. As soon as Fanny judged that there was sufficient distance between them, she hitched up her dress and ran as fast as she could. Behind her she could hear the sound of windows smashing.

Fanny stopped outside the Cross Keys. There were people inside and she felt that she was now safe. She leaned against the rough wall smelling the beer, tasting the smoke. She was out of breath but at least that stopped her from crying.

Eighteen

He threw out his hands in exasperation. 'You have a murderer in your filthy little town and you cannot find him. So I tell you who it is. Then you still cannot find him and so you worry about a hat. You call me up here to your police station to talk about a hat? Why? I have told you what is happening. Czibor is here but if you do not wish to believe me, then what is it that I can do? I must protect myself if you will do nothing to protect me. I shall take measures.'

'When we met, you told me the hat was from Hungary. You said the label was printed in Hungarian. That you could not read it.' Bucke studied him closely.

'You are mistaken, Inspector, sir. I did not say it was a Hungarian hat. I told you it had been worn by a Hungarian. His name is Czibor. If you did not hear me properly or if to understand me you find difficult, then why should it be my fault?' Abramovitch leaned back in his chair and sighed, shaking his head. 'I tell you again, there is this Hungarian man in the town who is here to bring you anarchy. He kills children and then in the midst of it all he will seize my Chana and attempt to strike me down, whilst you and your pathetic officers are distracted. It is obvious. But you must decide that he is a Romanian? I do not understand you.' He laughed bitterly. 'And if this Hungarian should buy a hat in a second-hand clothes shop – and I see many of them here in Swansea – if he finds a hat, it would not concern him if it was made in Romania. Why should it? Would it make him any less of a murderer? Of course not. So he buys a hat. So you have the hat. But you do not have him.'

'And so you can read the label, Mr Abramovitch?'

'But of course I can. It is Romanian. The Mangalia Hat Shop. Mangalia is a place. South of Constanta. It has a hat shop, so I must think. Why is this important to you?' Abramovitch went on before he could answer. 'Who told you it was Romanian? What else did he tell you? That this hat was the most important thing in the world? Is it someone you can trust? What is he doing? Ask yourself that. He is

217

trying to distract you – to turn you away from your search for Czibor, the murderer from Hungary? He is trying to tell you that there is no man from Hungary but he is in league with him. He might even be him.' Abramovitch smiled. 'This is what he is doing, telling you to look for a Romanian, when you should look for a Hungarian. You see? He is tricking you. Your town is in chaos and so you worry about a hat? It is easier for you, perhaps, this worry about a hat. You have found a hat, you have not found a man, but you are pleased.' He paused. 'Inspector, sir.'

Bucke still said nothing. He knew he was making Abramovitch uncomfortable. There was little sense in what he was saying. He had lied about the hat. What else had he lied about?

Abramovitch needed to fill the silence that had dropped upon them, one that emphasised their confrontation. 'I tell you this now. He waits for me to find Chana. It is clear. Then he kills me and then he kills her. He wins. The Hungarians have the great Scroll of Ovid. It is part of a plan. Remember, he was here before me. We know that. The two boys murdered before I am coming here. And he does these things for the pleasure and for the chaos that he can cause. Cannot you see this, Inspector? He turns boys upside down; he turns your town upside down.' He sneered and threw back his head in contempt.

Bucke watched him carefully. 'You see, Mr Abramovitch. I don't know what to make of all this. You regard us here in Swansea as stupid, and you say there is an assassin here to kill you but then you draw attention to yourself. You talk about him as a man called Czibor, but no one has seen him. You don't even know what he looks like but you say you have seen him. I wonder, I wonder…' Bucke allowed his words to fade away. Then he added, 'Mr Abramovitch, why are you lying to me? I wonder what you are hiding from me?'

'You are being very foolish, Inspector. You do not know Czibor as I know him. Let me tell you. He murdered a beautiful woman, in Buda. Veronica Pesek and her daughter, Rosa Budai. She was only eight. I told you, he kills children and yet you do not take me seriously. He is here now, I tell you. This Hungarian killer. I know him but you do not. He is a brutal man and his killing here has not finished. Czibor is an evil man but also he is a government agent. He is useful to them. For he knows no compassion and so he is perfect for them.'

'And when did these murders happen, Mr Abramovitch? Of the woman and the child? The ones that Czibor committed, you say.'

Abramovitch waved his hand vaguely, as if detail was not important. 'In the autumn, it was. A terrible moment. Buda is a place of complete anarchist agitation but even that stopped for a moment at this horrible strangling of a woman. Blood came from her eyes, they say. Not tears. They came from everyone else, at such cruelty. And you see, then there was her beautiful child, found drowned in the Danube, innocent of all crimes but her life taken from her. There is nothing this Czibor will not do. This is why the government use him for their agent. He feels nothing. The whole of Europe is looking for this man, but they waste their time, for he is here, and yet you do not believe me.'

'And do you wish me to inform the Austro-Hungarian authorities, Mr Abramovitch? That Czibor is here?'

'No I expect you to capture him. Before it is too late.' Abramovitch stared back at him impassively. 'But this is not important to you. No. All you want of me, is this. For me to tell you about a hat. And so I tell you and so now I go. I have a meeting with Mother Superior Hillereau at your Convent. She does much good work, I am told, amongst orphans. She might be able to help me with my search for my daughter. You do not wish to do so.'

'You will find the convent on Convent Street, Mr Abramovitch. It is how we arrange things here.'

'I know this, Inspector, sir.' He collected himself and stood up. 'Good morning to you, Inspector Bucke. I wish you every success in your search.' He leaned forward slightly. 'It must get better. It cannot go any worse, surely not?'

Bucke, his elbows on the table, rested his chin on his interlocked

219

fingers and smiled. Abramovitch paused as if about to speak and then turned and walked out of the police station. Bucke followed him to see which way he went and watched him walk towards Carmarthen Road. At least he was going towards the convent. What sort of game was he playing? He had unsettled him, he knew that. How would he react? Bucke turned to go back into the police station and saw Amy and Myra coming from the direction of the abattoir, pushing the pram together, giggling.

'Good morning, Amy. No school today, I see.'

Amy sighed at his apparent stupidity. 'It is Saturday, Mr Bucke! Me and my friend Myra are playing today.' Myra was unsettled by Amy's familiarity with a policeman and tried to pull the pram away.

'I am pleased to hear it. You are looking very well, Amy.' And she was. Even in the short time she had been with Sarah she looked so much better, less malnourished, less neglected.

'We are taking Sarah Dolly and Molly Dolly, that is Myra's doll, for a walk –'

'They are princesses and we are their servants,' added Myra, for clarification.

'I see. And where do they want to go today?' asked Bucke.

'They want to see the ships,' Myra's involvement in their play conquered her fear. 'They have got treasure on them, to be sure.'

Bucke squatted down to look the girls in the eyes. 'You stay away from the docks, please, young ladies. It can be very dangerous down there.'

Amy nodded. 'We won't go to the docks, Mr Bucke. We will go to look at the treasure ships from the pier.'

'You promise, Amy?'

'I promise.'

'I shall have my constables watching out,' he said firmly.

Myra's eyes opened wide at this completely unexpected exchange and shook her head. 'We won't, I promise too.'

'Sarah said we needed a constable this morning, Mr Bucke. It was difficult to get the pram down the stairs. Sarah and I can do it together,' said Amy proudly, 'but we made a big noise and that man shouted some bad words but I had heard them before so it was alright but Sarah wanted a constable to give him a row.'

The two girls skipped away. At least someone's life had changed for the better, he thought.

*

'Fanny, I had no idea.' He kissed her forehead.

'You will get the hang of it. You will be a quick learner, I am sure of it.'

'And was all that normal?'

'Absolutely normal, Henry.'

'And it could happen again?'

'As many times as we wish.' She stroked his hair.

They lay together, entwined, in the narrow untidy bed. Their clothes were scattered across the room. Henry propped himself up on his elbow. 'You know much more about this sort of thing than I do, Fanny. Not that I mind, honestly. I didn't know, that's all. No one told me.'

'But now you do know.' She leaned up to kiss him. 'You are very sweet.'

'Am I?'

'Oh yes.' He was certainly not as she had expected and she was moved by how tender and gentle he was. He needed leading – now –

221

but not for long, she was sure. This had not been any kind of planned liaison. Fanny had been to her rehearsal and had met Henry accidentally, as far as she was concerned anyway, on Wind Street. He had insisted on walking her home and she had spoken to him about the attack on her the previous night. She needed to tell someone, but she had not been prepared for his reaction. He had been obviously upset, ashamed of his failure to look after her.

'I cannot allow you to walk home alone again. That would be entirely reprehensible.' Fanny raised her eyebrows. 'Well, perhaps not all the way. Just the darkest parts. I know it would be awkward for you to be seen with me. I can bring you so far, I am sure.' His eyes had become suddenly wet.

'Henry, that is so very kind of you. But I can look after myself. Because I have always had to look after myself.' She already knew that he came from a different class where such things did not happen, but she didn't feel she could leave him tearful on the street and so she had invited him in, since Jack was out…She realised later that they had both needed comforting.

He was hesitant, she was nervous. He said, red-faced, that he was inexperienced. She laughed and said that she had more than enough for the both of them and then realised that it might not have been a helpful thing to say, but he did not seem to notice. She soon realised that it did not matter. He treated her with such tender respect. He admired her. He loved her. She was absolutely sure that Henry was sincere. If she allowed herself to dream, she could imagine that he was holding open a door for her that led into another world, into another life. Would she ever be able to walk through that door? But she felt such a profound peace about the time they spent together on a sagging, lumpy mattress. For Fanny this was so completely unusual, quite beyond any of her previous experiences. It confused her and the introduction of hope like this into her life shocked her more than anything else. It was a unique moment.

Perhaps, in time, she would love him too. Perhaps it didn't matter too much.

She showed him her small catalogue of her press reviews. 'What's this one? *The Princess of Trebizonde?* Never heard of it.' He smiled at Fanny and then read it. *'Sparkling music, songs well performed by a talented young lady.'*

'That's me, Henry. I have done all the roles, you know. Comedy, farce, pantomime, burlesque. All of them.' She kissed his cheek.

'Look at this one. Oh I say, *A singing voice of good tone, much precision and delicacy of execution.'*

'And I had a shocking cold when that was written, too.'

'It says you have *a natural aptitude with posture and gracefulness of carriage*. How could they ever say anything else?'

'I sang *When the Heart is Young*. It was much commented upon.'

'I am sure that it was.' His hand fell on to her breast. 'Oh. I am so sorry. I didn't mean…' He pulled it away.

Fanny held his hand and put it back. She kissed him gently. 'I have to go soon. Matinee today, remember? Are you coming? It would be good to see you in the stalls. But I still have some time and there is something else I want to show you. Something you can think about when you see me on the stage.'

Later he walked happily down the narrow, pitted staircase which seemed to be caught up in one of those gales in the Bay of Biscay he had been reading about. He barely noticed the belligerent-looking low-browed man in greasy clothes who pushed past him. Henry stood on the unmade pavement, breathing in the dirty air, looking at the back of the Bethesda Chapel and thinking that the world was a wonderful place. He was as certain as he could ever be, that Maldwyn was full of hollow bravado. He had no idea what he was talking about when he looked at his little pictures and talked about the chorus girls. But Little Henry did. Little Henry knew and he would never be the same again.

Fanny had heard the familiar footsteps on the stairs and very quickly slipped her dress back on, roughed up her hair even more and then lay down on the bed as if snoozing, hiding how untidy it was.

'Who was that toff on the stairs, then?' Jack demanded immediately he opened the door.

'Don't know what you mean. I have been sleeping.' She looked away though the dirty window as if it looked out on to beautiful meadows and mountains.

'There was a toff on the stairs. You haven't been entertaining, have you? Because you know what will happen if you have. How much did he give you?'

Fanny swung her legs round on to the floor and sat up. 'No one has been here, Jack. I have been having a rest before the matinee. It is hard doing two shows in one day, and rehearsals too. Perhaps he was here to see Sarah Rigby.' She hated having to implicate someone else, but she was frightened of him.

'I thought our Sarah had gone all respectable now? Perhaps times is hard, like.' Jack had seen Amy playing out in the street, so it was possible that Sarah had sent her out whilst she did a little entertaining. But he wasn't sure. He looked around the cold unwelcoming room. 'You best be telling the truth. Because if you have been working, then that money is mine. You know that. And I shall have it. You know what will happen, don't you?'

'Yes, Jack. But no one has been here. I have been asleep.'

'So what is there here to eat?' he asked.

'Where have you been anyway? With that Selina? The Queen of Slime? Are you pimping her?'

'What? Like I pimped you?'

'Not anymore, you don't.'

'You were useless anyway.'

'Well, I have moved on.' Fanny felt unusually defiant. 'Remember what they said about me in the paper? Remember? Here. I still have it. What did they say about me? Eh?'

Jack walked round the bare room, looking for something to eat.

'Who cares?'

'Here it is.' She opened a yellowing copy of *The Times*. '*She has a voice of remarkable power and sweetness and who is everywhere received with unlimited praise.* There we are.'

'And?'

Fanny's eyes shone. 'I can do something. I can sing. I don't sell ridiculous postcards to old men. I don't bury dead babies on the beach. I do something, something other people care about. I can be a success if only I –'

'Yes, *if only you had a chance*. I have heard it all before, Fanny. But you ain't ever going to get a chance, are you? It has gone. You are just a tart. That's all. Still seeing toffs, I shouldn't wonder. And I am telling you now. If I find out that you are, you know what will happen.' He stared at her intently. 'You know, don't you? I will bust your nose. You are up to something, I know it.'

'And so are you. You are always up to something.

He stepped closer to her. 'Answering back now, is it? Just be careful.'

The light in her eyes suddenly dimmed and her head went down. 'Yes, Jack. Sorry, Jack.'

*

As the afternoon turned to evening, as they sipped tea together, Bucke had an opportunity to explain to Constance the unpredictability of police work. He had told Amy that the constables would be keeping an eye out for small girls playing on the docks, but of course he had no reason at that moment to assume that he would spend his own afternoon there. He was pleased to report that he hadn't seen Amy at all, in spite of the considerable and sometimes nightmarish drama that had unfolded and which had drawn so many ghoulish bystanders.

'You could never have anticipated anything like this. I was called to a ship in the South Dock. *The Maryland.* Came in on the tide this

225

morning. A cargo of wines from Spain. Some sherry too. In casks. They had been loaded in – I am not sure where. As I think about it, I didn't ask – Cadiz perhaps. But the point is that the hold was sealed. The casks on board and the hold sealed. Keeps the customs officers happy. But it was a difficult voyage. The *Maryland* was caught in a storm, they had to put into Lisbon, the Biscay was even rougher and they had to shelter somewhere in France. The captain told me all this. So they eventually tie up at the South Dock and they go into the hold.'

Constance put her cup and saucer down on the piano. 'I don't think I am going to like the next bit, am I?'

'No Constance, you are not. They had packed the hold properly, but the storm threw the barrels around. Rolled everywhere. And there, in amongst them, were two bodies.'

'Oh no.' Constance closed her eyes, as if this would stop her painting the scene that must inevitably follow in her mind.

'Yes. Stowaways. A mother and her child. Africans, from what I could see. Whether they knew where the ship was going, I cannot say. Did they choose the ship? Or did they pay someone to put them on a boat, any boat? A thief? A docker? One of the crew? But however they got on board, they were crushed by the barrels. Or at least, I hope they were crushed by the barrels. Because their bodies, when they were found, had been partly eaten by rats.'

'That's horrible, Rumsey!'

'Oh it was. They can be fierce, those ship rats. I won't describe what the sailors found, but they are a hardened bunch and even some of them were a bit queasy. If the poor souls had cried out they probably wouldn't have been heard. I want to believe that the casks got them first.' He sighed. 'It is such a terrible thing. They had travelled - goodness knows how far they had come. Escaping from something? Running towards someone? We will never know. There was nothing to identify them but someone loved them. And now they are gone. I don't suppose they wanted to come to Swansea particularly. The woman was a desperate mother trying to get a better life for her daughter, the child she loved, and then she traps her in a place from which they cannot escape, the place where they will die. She was such a pretty girl too. The rats hadn't touched her face. Not like her mother's. Sometimes my employment is difficult beyond measure.' He leaned back in his chair and closed his eyes. 'Swansea, a place where children are lost in the woods and then they die.' He sighed a sigh that came from deep within him. 'Do you know? I went looking for a rat so I could kill it, but I couldn't find one.'

Constance put her hand on his knee. 'That is such a sad story, Rumsey. There is so much suffering around us, here in Swansea. More than we can ever understand. And yet there is a whole world of it out there. Every day seems to bring more.'

'And do you know something else? When word got around – and it does spread so quickly, somehow people know these things almost before I know them myself – the quay was lined with spectators, desperate to see whatever they could see, and if they couldn't, well they could invent their own details. If it had been a longer voyage there might have been even less to see. And do you know, Constance, so many of the men who turned up, wanting to be a part of a mother's tragedy, they were wearing leather aprons of all kinds, dirty, oily, bloodstained, cracked and smooth, and yet I have to find one, just one, but it has to be the right one.' He looked up at her, his eyes full of sorrow. 'Please Constance, for a moment. Please hold me.'

*

His meeting at the convent had been brief and unproductive. Mother Superior Hillereau knew of no orphan girls who had passed through the convent who could possibly have been Chana.

Abramovitch had thanked her politely and expressed his admiration for her work, which he believed 'was sorely needed in a town such as this.' But really his mind had been elsewhere then and for the rest of the day too. He was becoming very concerned about Inspector Bucke.

He seemed to be very sceptical and perhaps a little too clever, far too eager to question and doubt what Abramovitch said. He was becoming an obvious danger and so something needed to be done. It was time to move on, he decided; time to slip away out of sight. After all, a man must protect himself in a dangerous town, especially where the police are fools.

So, in the late afternoon, Nicolae Abramovitch slipped out of the back door of the Castle Hotel and into Castle Lane. Once he had turned the corner into the Strand he was away, to his new room on Recorder Street, close to the prison wall. He would now become a Polish sailor called Andrzej Szarmach. He had recovered the grubby pouch containing his money from beneath the mattress and which he had now hidden inside his clothes.

But he was at least able to reassure himself. He was now as sure as he could be that there could be no rival claims ever made against him. The real Chana, if she was still alive, was not going to emerge from some diseased Swansea slum and claim her inheritance. He was sure now that this was the case. She was dead, or she did not know who once she had been. She was unquestionably lost. It made things so much easier. A blank canvas. How convenient.

And the town was so unsettled, so unhappy, so fearful.

Czibor? He smiled.

Nineteen

Hilda had enjoyed her afternoon a great deal indeed. It was Monday and the shops were always such a great relief after the tedium of church on Sunday. Today, she had managed to obtain an impressive box of handkerchiefs at D.T Edwards on Park Street, which had been very straightforward and a pair of shoes from West's on Oxford Street, which had been a bit trickier. They didn't fit, but you couldn't have everything, now could you? Brown too, not her favourite colour, but never mind. She would put them in the cupboard. She had been delayed too, at that ironmonger's, where her attention had been caught by an especially shiny pair of large dressmaker's scissors. None of the other customers seemed capable of distracting the unusually efficient shop assistant, who had stood by her, distressing Hilda with his unsightly acne, eagerly trying to help. It was only when she showed an interest in a display of trowels at the furthest end of the shop that he left her for long enough and she had the chance that she needed. When he returned she apologised, saying she thought they were polished cake slices and left, rather imperiously, she thought.

But it was all part of the game – and the pleasure. It meant that she would be late going home but that was not a problem. Hilda's afternoon, like all her afternoons, was empty and being somewhere, anywhere, was infinitely better than being in the heartless chill of the Vicarage.

She decided to take coffee in the Oxford Street Coffee Tavern. It is what sophisticated ladies did when they went shopping, wasn't it? Meeting friends. Being seen. Allowing others to admire their clothes. She had to pay for things, which was irritating, but on reflection she decided that she ought to do this sort of thing more often, nodding politely at casual acquaintances, with her shopping bags next to her, just a few trifling purchases, as befitting Mrs Bishop. Unless, of course, real ladies had all their shopping delivered. She thought they probably did. She picked up her cup and took a sip. It was such a pity that Cyrus had shown no interest in bettering himself, in making a proper career. Bishop had such an appealing sound. She would be properly valued then, moving in an influential social circle, not smiling vaguely at minor weddings and in vacuous suburban Sunday services.

Still, Hilda thought, smiling at the prospect, things might change, yet; she was very hopeful. Hilda put down her cup and dabbed delicately at her lips with a lace handkerchief. It would be good to feel that she had some status in the town, to be able to examine goods and shop without the tawdry encumbrance of cash. Yet Cyrus, for reasons which she could not understand, had refused to open accounts for her at the most respectable establishments in Swansea. It was a decision that still gnawed away at her. She gathered her bags and the waitress held the door open for her and bobbed respectfully as she left. Quite rightly so. She deserved no less.

Hilda walked along Oxford Street to find a cab. The cab drivers were more wary than ever of their passengers now, though Hilda Bishop was no risk, even if they had to go back later and call on her husband to collect the fare. The vicar's wife needed to travel in style, always, and when the cab eventually made its very slow way along Mansel Street in the early evening gloom, she looked out of the window, imagining that she was a duchess and waving casually at pedestrians, wondering what it must be like to be poor. Cyrus would be at home, shut in his study perhaps, doing whatever it was that he did in there. Perhaps he was writing another of his meaningless sermons; they seemed to take him ages. Mercifully, they didn't seem to be that long in church. Perhaps she had just got used to it. She hoped he'd remembered to take his daily dose of Roache's Liver Pills. She nodded casually at Doctor Sullivan's wife as she passed but could not remember her name. She had been to afternoon tea at the vicarage recently, hadn't she? A wedding or something? She could not remember. She would remind Cyrus about his liver pills. He would not have forgotten it was laundry day though, would he? He never forgot when Eunice was coming, did he?

The journey seemed to be getting slower and slower and soon the cab stopped altogether. She sighed with irritation. Really this would not do; it would not do at all. The cab driver climbed down from his seat and knocked on the door. 'Begging your pardon. Ma'am. But the hoss can't go no further, like. Gone lame. Been a bugger all day, it have. It won't go no further at all. Had a guts full. I can send for another cab, like, but it will be a while.'

'Never mind, never mind. This is most irregular. Please do not expect me to pay for an incomplete journey, my good man. That would be entirely ridiculous, as well you know.' Hilda leaned out through the window of the cab to orientate herself. She was at the top of Westbury Street. 'I shall walk from here, but please do not expect me to use your cab again. I have taken note of your number.'

'Yes, ma'am,' he replied, though his thoughts were different. *No Ma'am. I shall go and see your husband, ma'am.* He held the door open for her as she stepped down and handed her the two shopping bags. 'May I accompany you home, madam?' he asked.

'No thank you,' Hilda replied brusquely. 'That will not be necessary. I do not have far to go.' She examined the horse contemptuously. 'That is not a horse. That is a pot of glue. You should attend to it immediately and prevent it from soiling the public highway.'

'Yes, ma'am. Thank you, ma'am.' He would definitely be calling at the Vicarage in the morning.

Hilda walked down Westbury Street. The shopping bags were not heavy, though the very idea she had to carry them along the street was most demeaning. Having to walk the last part of her journey was entirely unacceptable and Cyrus must certainly do something about it. It was completely undignified.

It was dark as she turned the corner into the narrow lane that led to the vicarage. The gas lamps hadn't been lit yet and the heavy cloud made it a gloomy February evening. There was no one around, as far as she could see, and suddenly she rather wished that she was at home in the vicarage. The shopping bags were a little irritating now, banging against her legs. Proper husbands ensured that there was always a maid to carry bags; a lady should never have to carry her own. Still, things would be changing soon. She was sure of that.

Suddenly, quite unexpectedly, the image of her daughter, Faith, jumped into her head. She hadn't thought of her for a while, she realised. Hilda put the bags down and flexed her fingers. She had always been a demanding girl who seemed to want to do her very best to bring shame and dishonour upon all of them. How could she do that to her own family? There were occasions when she missed her, at breakfast especially, when conversation was sometimes difficult. But really, her behaviour had been so disgraceful. She had shown absolutely no consideration for her mother at all. As she bent down to pick up her bags again, a man leapt out in front of her.

'Really! Have a care, sir. You startled me. I have a mind to report you to the constable.' How unrefined the lower classes were, she thought. Then, Hilda focused on the figure from the shadows in front of her. He was panting in a most unsavoury manner and his eyes seemed lost in dark bottomless holes. Hilda was suddenly very frightened. Perhaps she should drop her bags and move backwards out of the lane.

He hit her in a wild swing across the nose with his cosh and blood exploded over her face. The man gasped and watched Hilda stagger. So he hit her again from the other direction and her bags fell to the ground. This was good. The woman was dazed and fell to her knees in front of him. He raised his hand again and, with confidence born of success, he swung the cosh freely into her temple. There was a crack and another spout of blood. He wanted to hit her again but she fell forward on to the ground. He was sure that he had killed her and he felt an unrivalled surge of pleasure. Smashing those shop windows had obviously improved his swing. Now he knew what to do and he was so proud.

At last. At last. He had not failed. He was now a man, a proper man, someone to be respected by other men. Women had every right to be frightened of him now. He tried to control his breathing but couldn't and he started to laugh. He looked down at her, not wanting to leave the scene, but knowing that he should, and quickly. She had not moved nor twitched nor groaned. She must really be dead. It would be good to see what happened when someone found her, but that would be a very stupid risk. If he pretended that he had found her, he might have to answer some questions and he didn't want to do that. His new notoriety was something he appreciated and now he would be feared as a proper murderer should, as an avenger. The other attacks had been rehearsals. This was a proper beginning. He thought about hitting her again but he was strong and pulled himself away from the scene of his first triumph and walked casually away down Westbury Street.

It was Mr King who found her, on his habitual constitutional walk home after a long day at the Swansea Savings Bank on Heathfield Street. He saw a figure lying face down and his first thought was that she had tripped, an inevitable consequence of how untidy the lane was, but as soon as he struck a match, he could see that it was much, much worse than that. He immediately ran back to Walters Road and waved down a cab. A constable was found and within minutes a group of policemen had begun to gather around Hilda, some carrying oil lamps.

Hilda still had an extremely faint pulse and so was taken at speed on a police cart to Swansea Hospital, just a short distance down the road, though regrettably she died en-route before Cyrus could be brought down to see her.

Her head was a frightful mess – a broken nose, a smashed eye socket, a fractured skull, all of which had caused both external and internal bleeding. Bucke arrived from Tontine Street, cursing the inadequacies of the gas lighting, for there was little chance of finding anything in the dark. The constables searched the area as best they could in the circumstances, but they found nothing, other than Hilda's shopping bags and her blood, seeping into the ground. They would have to search again in the daylight but they had no expectation of finding anything remotely useful. Hilda had left a reasonably busy street in order to cut through into the vicarage and, even though it was a busy time, with people going home from work, no one had seen anything. Mr King remembered watching a man on the other side of the road who was whistling as he walked, but he could offer no descriptive details. Just another man walking along the street; there were plenty of them. The constables called at houses, asked passers-

233

by, but learnt nothing. Will Nicholas, the cab driver, was easy enough to find. He came forward as soon as he heard the news, shocked to learn that, apart from the murderer, he was, it now seemed, the last person to see Hilda alive. It was not an honour that sat lightly upon him and Will was very eager to point out that there had been nothing amiss, other than an unhealthy horse, which was the reason why she had stepped out of the cab. He had seen nothing, of course, concerned as he was with leading Flash, the horse, down to the blacksmiths. Hilda Bishop had appeared irritable when he had told her that he could go no further, but he had no reason to assume that this was unusual. He hadn't seen anyone apparently lying in wait for her. If he had, he would have done something about it. How could anyone have thought otherwise? Bucke thanked him and reminded him to be vigilant in these difficult days.

Bucke walked back through the town slowly, reflecting on the case. He was sure that there was no suggestion that Hilda had been followed by someone solely focused upon her. She had travelled up from town in a cab, which made that highly unlikely. Therefore he reasoned that this had been another random act, a woman inadvertently walking too close to a murderer, a woman in the wrong place, at the wrong time and, wrongly, alone.

Was this Cosh Boy's work? Who else could it be? The press would be absolutely certain that it was and the only consolation, as far as Bucke could see, was that they would surely, now, stop regarding Cosh Boy as some kind of inadequate comic figure. An innocent – and respectable - woman had died and now Cosh Boy must be found, for he was a murderer who still, Bucke was convinced, had more work to do.

Bucke leaned against the wall of the hospital, watching the carts go past for a moment before he went inside to see Hilda's body properly. The attacks seemed to have nothing which connected them, other than the victims being alone during the evening. He was aware of four attacks on women- there may have been more, for the victims might not have come forward. These were women finding themselves, through no fault of their own, in a place where they became a part of a stranger's fantasies. The man seemed to be acting at random, without a pattern, apart from choosing women as his victims. He was ready to assume that the attacks were carried out by one man and the cosh was becoming an increasingly important detail and it linked him, perhaps, to the attack on library books. He could not see a connection with the murders of the boys, which seemed more calculated, deliberately dramatic, not just a random assault; they had been killed for a purpose Bucke had yet to identify.

That meant that he couldn't think Cosh Boy was responsible for the death of Iestyn Godfrey, the cab driver. Because, he was sure, that was about the murder of Patrick; Godfrey was just necessary to make the boy's death happen. His last fare had been a man in a leather apron, they said. Was that important? Such things were easily acquired and just as easily disposed of. Anyone could wear one. But, at the moment, that was all that identified the child murderer. It was something that Lee remembered and the detail had emerged again. The only distinguishing features of Cosh Boy that Elodie could remember were his bright buttons, not an apron. So Bucke was as sure as he could be, that he was dealing with two different men here. Cosh Boy had probably been defacing library books with those juvenile illustrations, including drawings of a cosh and inadequate nudes, which might suggest a mental inadequacy of some sort. There had also been that gap between attacks. What did that mean? But the child-murderer seemed much less casual, more deliberate. Just as Constance had suggested – there were two of them, he was sure of it. Knowing that didn't make things any easier, though.

Hilda's murder had happened earlier in the evening than the other attacks but the location interested Bucke. The first one reported had happened off High Street when Sarah Rigby had been attacked. The other three, Lizzie, Elodie and Hilda – had all happened reasonably close together on the west side of the town centre. Was that important? Patrick had been found in this area too – where Bucke was now standing, in fact. A co-incidence? And what about the murder of Rhys Matthews, the carter? Did that fit in somehow? Or the deaths on the *Ann of Bridgewater,* come to that?

He shook his head. It was the old difficulty. He was responding to events; he felt unable to prevent them. The constables were watchful – much more vigilant than they used to be. But they couldn't be everywhere. So, did he have to wait for Cosh Boy to make a mistake before he could apprehend him? And in the meantime, someone else might die.

As he stood there, trying to see a pattern in all this mayhem that was gripping the town, Eliza Keast appeared, heading off along St Helen's Road. She was one of his most reliable informers and whilst she knew nothing for certain, she was certainly ready to speculate. 'I am telling you now, Inspector,' she said forcefully. 'These ain't the doin's of one of us. I'm not lying. This is outsiders, mind. None of us knows nothing. I can ask around, like I 'ave been doin', but you take my word. This is none of Swansea's work. I 'as 'eard of the old lady, Mr Bucke. Very sad that he 'as done 'er in but it might have been one of us young ones that he'd killed. I reckon that is what he wanted, but that would be no better, now would it? No matter what the toffs might say. If I 'ears anythin' I will let you know, straight off.'

He smiled as she walked away. He would never have anticipated this when he was younger and was about to start out as a policeman, but people like Eliza, were his people. Bold, unpleasant, immoral, common. But they were honest and they contained within themselves an essential human spirit. They fought, they argued, they survived and they passed on their inextinguishable qualities to their children. They were at the bottom of the social heap and they knew it; they could never escape from that fate. It wasn't about any qualities that they might possess themselves; their destiny was pre-ordained. But they laughed and scorned and mocked and then got on with their own lives. A long struggle illuminated by brief but brightly shining triumphs. And if their lives lacked refinement and sophistication who actually cared? Their friends? Their neighbours? Their family? Did it actually matter very much? If he was facing the possibility of oblivion, who should he rely upon for help? Lady So and So? Or Eliza Keast? Bucke knew that wasn't a difficult decision to make.

The death of the children troubled him the most. Those poor boys sacrificed for some unknown reason, and then the girl who had died with her mother as stowaways. What terrible cruelty. He found it difficult to shake away those images from his mind. He looked up and saw Cyrus Bishop leave the hospital, alone. What was he feeling at this moment? Bucke was not acquainted with him well enough to know. The vicar of Llwyn y Bryn was not someone he met very often. But he remembered all too well how he felt when his own wife died and he did not wish to revisit that dark and dangerous place. Perhaps Cyrus felt the same; perhaps he did not. But Bucke believed that he should be left alone. What he knew, what he suspected, what he thought, did not matter at a time like this. The vicar's life would never be the same again. In an instant and without warning, his life had changed. It would be best, he decided, if he went to see him tomorrow.

His head was full of murder and blood once more, but he was still haunted by that last meeting with Abramovitch. He could not trust him; he was evasive and devious, relying, Bucke felt, upon what he perceived as their ignorance – of his country and of his background. Perhaps it was a moment to challenge that. He needed to understand Abramovitch, if such a thing were possible, to understand the threat he claimed this man Czibor represented, the man who no one had seen and of whom Florian had never heard. He would go to see Constance, for he had an idea that he was interested in exploring, and as he told her, as she sat on the piano stool and looked at him intently, she was the only person he could trust to do it properly.

'Can you help me, do you think? I mean you don't have to. But it isn't dangerous, not this time.'

'Of course I will, Rumsey. As long as it does not involve posing in peculiar undergarments, with strings of pearls for Herr Goldman. It can be unreasonably cold in a photographer's studio, I believe.'

'That is not a gift that you should offer to strangers. That is a treat for myself alone.'

'And long may you believe so, Rumsey. And what is it that you would like me to do?'

'Investigation, Constance. Research. But secretly. I mean, I couldn't ask a constable. I need someone who can read, for a start.'

Twenty

'Well, well, well.' That had been as much as Cyrus had been able to say since last night when he had been called down to the hospital. What a strange turn of events. Poor old Hilda. Beaten to death on the street, as if she were nothing but a common prostitute. What a shameful way to go. If she had realised how far her social standing appeared to have sunk, thought Cyrus, that might have hurt even more than the blows that smashed her skull. But Hilda was dead and his marriage, that particular vale of tears, was over. And he had done nothing at all to bring it about.

'Well, well, well.' He sat in the cracked leather armchair and picked absently at the stuffing emerging through a cut in the arm. Yesterday he had been quite bewildered when he had received the news. He had been arranging his photographic cards, something he had always found inspirational, whilst Hilda had been murdered in the lane such a short distance from the house. How strange life could be.

Was this actually a sign from God? That he had been listening to him, all along? Surely not. Surely this wouldn't be God's way of saying to him, 'Pull yourself together. Of course I exist'? He didn't think that would be God's way, to arrange the death of his wife, no matter how much he had wished for it, in order to prove a point. But still, 'Well, well, well.'

He realised that he would have to learn how to behave in these new circumstances. What did grieving widowers do? What was regarded as an acceptable length of mourning, for example? There were many things he didn't know. And there was Faith too. He would have to tell her. He would write her a letter. He would have to find some words. That is why he had sent Lily home; he needed some time to himself, to think. He had had a piece of cod for dinner and the house still smelt strongly of fish. Had Lily done the washing up before she had left? She always had been a little slap-dash.

He would have to learn how to look after himself, too. It had been difficult since Lily had refused to live-in. A silly misunderstanding.

That girl got everything out of proportion, and she was certainly not as accommodating as Eunice with the laundry could be. He knew he would need some domestic help, but he was free to find it now. He could make his own decisions. No more deference, no more discreet settling of ridiculous shopping bills. Not such a bad thing at all. And yet at breakfast yesterday morning, everything seemed destined to continue unimpeded until the very end of time. And now? 'Well, well, well.'

Newspapers. Yes. He would have to put an announcement in the newspapers. Couldn't avoid that, people would expect it, especially since Hilda would be a news item. Was it an expensive thing to do? He would have to be sombre, of course; he would have to say the right things.

He just didn't know what they were.

Cyrus tried to remember if he knew anyone else who had lost their wife recently. He must settle down and think properly about it all, sensibly, maturely. He decided he would be required to offer forgiveness to the man who had killed her. It was what was expected of a vicar. Christian forgiveness, that sort of thing. Was he supposed to be angry, whilst forgiving? Or just irritated?

He would have to lead a service for her. People would expect a eulogy, too. He would write to Faith first, he decided. Before the story of her death appeared in the papers. Should he send her a telegram? Who could tell him the answers to these things? A telegram would be shorter than a letter, wouldn't it? He scratched his head and found hair in his fingers once again. He must be going bald.

Cyrus rubbed his abdomen. The pains were still there, sometimes worse than others, sometimes driving him urgently to the toilet. Perhaps now that Hilda had gone – he had to keep reminding himself of that – he would begin to feel better. He looked around for his snuff box, for he had long been convinced of its health-giving properties. He always thought his sermons were better with the encouragement he received from that special blend from Wilson's of Sharrow. Hilda used to object to him using it, said that he had sneezed all over the back of an antimacassar and stained it. That was, quite frankly, ridiculous, it always had been completely and utterly ridiculous. But it didn't matter anymore. He could take it as often and wherever he wanted now. Sneeze as much as he liked.

He couldn't see his snuff box anywhere but there was his packet of Roache's Liver Pills next to him on that battered arm of the chair. Hilda had always been very particular. He had to take one in the morning and one in the evening. If he was honest, he would say they hadn't made him feel any better, worse sometimes. In fact, now he thought about it, he'd only properly started to feel unwell after he'd started to take them. Nevertheless, Hilda had been very insistent that they were doing him good.

It wasn't important now. He realised that he hadn't had one last night or this morning. Did it really matter? He opened the packet. There were four pills left, rattling around in a thin coating of sugar, presumably added to make them palatable. It didn't. What was the point? He wasn't going to order any more, wherever it was Hilda that obtained them. He stood up and poured himself a large glass of brandy; it would settle his stomach anyway and with it he quickly washed down those four remaining pills and threw the box into the grate. He hadn't lit the fire: he would do that in a moment when he'd had another glass of brandy. There was no one to stop him now. What a strange day it had been. 'Well, well, well.'

*

It was early the next morning when Henry Fry hurried to the Vicarage in order to see Cyrus Bishop. He had heard of the terrible news of Hilda's death from his mother at breakfast and she was anxious that he should call on his way to the office, in order to offer his condolences. The man was going to officiate at his wedding, so it was the least he could do. He also needed to establish as subtly as he could, whether Cyrus was still available to do it. Harriet was, according to his mother anyway, already having anxieties. Knowing his mother, Henry realised that it might actually be her who was worried, but what he knew about Harriet made that seem very plausible. Of course, he had to have a conversation with Fanny about all this. He could not avoid it? But he was not sure how he could

241

broach the subject. How could he tell the woman he loved that he was soon to marry someone else?

The Vicarage was still dark when he arrived. Henry looked at the chipped, dark green, front door and realised that he had never found it a particularly welcoming place. It seemed to lack a heart. And warmth too, of all kinds; even Faith's enthusiasm for male visitors did not make it a comfortable place. Henry wondered if the whispered rumours about her were true. No one had seen her for quite a while now.

He knocked at the door and waited. Even the shrubs by the door seemed dry, lacking vitality. He looked at them carefully. They were lacking hope; any possible life-force had long ago drained away into the dust, like his dreams.

He knocked again.

There was no response. Henry knew that Lily didn't live-in anymore. There were rumours about her too, about an unfortunate incident which had meant that she had moved out, but there were always stories that seemed to attach themselves to the Vicarage. He was right, it had never been a happy place, for anyone it seemed..

Henry tried the door but it was locked. A flake of paint had attached itself to his knuckle. Perhaps poor Cyrus was in bed, shocked, confused, anguished. Who could blame him? He looked at the bedroom window above.

'Mr Bishop!' he called.

Nothing.

He looked into the reception room window next to the front door but he could see little through the stained, grey lace curtains. Henry walked around the house and into the garden. Here it was wet and heavy; just like those shrubs at the front, the rest of the garden also seemed to have given up. Spring would never arrive; this was a place of never -ending, unforgiving winter. Any hope of re-birth had long-since been abandoned.

And soon he knew that there would be no possibility of re-birth for Cyrus either. Henry saw him when he looked through the French windows. He was lying on the floor, his head resting on his outstretched arm. He knocked on the glass out of politeness, but he knew that there would be no response. Henry pulled out a rock that had been half trodden into the grass, smashed the small pane of glass next to the handle, and opened the window.

Cyrus was dead, his eyes staring sightlessly along his arm. Henry was not inclined to linger. He could see that the vicar had soiled himself quite expansively and there was vomit soaked into the threadbare carpet. Was this cholera? He stepped past the body and opened the front door, shouting loudly for a constable.

*

The police came to collect Cyrus Bishop, standing warily to one side, watching anxiously whilst Doctor Benjamin examined the body. He had been brought to the scene by Inspector Bucke. They were not the first to arrive, though. Constable Turner had smiled and nodded as they approached the front door. 'Let Herr Goldman in, sir. The photographer, sir. A picture tells a thousand stories, sir,' he said, smiling. 'It is the modern way, sir. Constable Leyshon is with him, makes sure he doesn't touch anything, sir.'

Bucke was irritated but had no wish to speak harshly in the presence of the doctor. He would speak to 'Page' Turner later. Who had authorised this? He paused for a moment and spoke briefly to Henry Fry, who had already written a brief statement about the discovery of the body. 'I thought it best to write it down. Not always something constables enjoy, I suspect. Here we are. I need to go to my office, Inspector. I have an appointment. If you need anything, you know where I am.'

Bucke was grateful for his good sense and nodded respectfully, before passing along the faded hall, with its scuffed parquet and into the lounge. There was a flash as they entered.

'Ah. Inspector Bucke. I have just finished. I will have the photographs with you this afternoon, assuredly. No charge, of course. This is just a sample of what I can do for you. At a moment's notice

243

too.' He moved to the side to avoid the legs of the tripod that his assistant was trying unsuccessfully to collapse. Goldman ran his head across his forehead, pushing his hair to one side. 'Come on, Horace, we are interfering with important police work. Get a move on.' Goldman stepped out through the French windows, with Horace stumbling behind him, overburdened and uncoordinated.

Bucke shrugged an apology to Benjamin, who shook his head and bent his thin frame over the body. He looked at Cyrus methodically and placed his hand on his neck. 'He has been dead for a while. Ten, twelve hours I would say.' He carefully rolled Cyrus on to his back and arranged him, ready to be wrapped in a sheet. Benjamin looked up at Bucke. 'I can see no signs of violence.'

Bucke gestured with his hand towards the mess on the carpet. 'And do you think ...' He left his question unfinished.

Benjamin shook his head. 'I don't think this is a case of cholera. Highly unlikely, in my opinion. I know it is our greatest fear, but I think not. It might be a sensible precaution to find out who washes his clothes, in case she is a transmitter. The vicar is undeniably dead and something killed him. There is plenty more work to be done on his body. The contents of his stomach will need to be examined.'

He stood up. 'The public analyst will have a busy time of it, I am sure. I shall go to the hospital with him. Come gentlemen,' he said to the constables. 'Let us put Mr Bishop in the wagon. There is nothing to afraid of,' he added, noticing their reluctance. He bent down and began to wrap the body. 'Someone should send a message to his daughter. Do we know where she has gone?'

As the wagon rattled away down the hill towards the hospital, Bucke spoke to Lily, who was waiting for him in the kitchen. Mr Bishop seemed as fine as a new widower could be when she saw him the previous afternoon, she said. She'd cooked him fish. He hadn't said anything to her about being unwell. He had told her that she wasn't required last night, and anyway with Cosh Boy on the loose, she didn't like walking home in the dark, did she?

'The thing is though, Inspector. Mrs Bishop wasn't done in when it was night time, now was she? So by rights, I shouldn't have been out at all. But I don't live-in no more, do I?' Lily returned Bucke's inquisitive look with defiance. Dark hair, dark wide eyes, pale skin – she was a young girl already well-practised in using her physical attraction to unsettle men. The washing? It was done by a girl who came in once a week, Eunice, she was called, but she didn't know anything else about her. She dismissed his question about Faith with a smile and a faint shake of the head. No, she wasn't sure where she was. Someone had mentioned Staines. Was that a place? she asked, with her large eyes feigning innocence.

Bucke was not inclined to believe her. He didn't much like Lily and he was sure she knew more than she wanted to say, but he would leave that for another day. He sent her home. He was confident that she would find a new position very quickly but he was sure she was someone who needed to be watched.

He was finally alone and ready to explore the house carefully without distractions. There was a story here, he was sure of it. He looked through what he regarded as the shabbily furnished bedrooms, and then stopped and corrected himself. How could he adopt such an attitude when the rooms were so much better than his own? Like his own room, these lacked love. They were bleak places. On the landing to the right was the main bedroom, dank and cold. He looked briefly inside a chipped wardrobe that smelt damp and rotten and which contained only Cyrus's vestments. The bed was grey, unmade, unwelcoming. Bucke wondered if Cyrus could ever have lived here alone successfully.

There was a door opposite that he pushed against but which was reluctant to open. He pushed it more firmly and whatever was behind it moved slightly. He closed the door and then pushed it harder until there was enough room to see inside. The dark heavy curtains were closed and the air smelt used and dusty but he could see enough to identify a room crammed with parcels and boxes. He stepped carefully through the room to open the curtains and reveal a remarkable collection of unrelated items, like a second-hand shop, though these items appeared never to have been used.

There were clothes still in tissue paper, so many shoes, brushes, tools and umbrellas. There was a stack of books, too. He picked up the top one. It belonged to the Swansea Free Library, labelled 'Reference Only' on the title page. It was 'Greenhouse Cultivation for Beginners.' The second volume, 'Celestial Bodies and the Planetary Orbits' - had the same inscription. This was Hilda's pointless treasure trove, each object only briefly holding her demons at bay, a perfect representation of a life without meaning – a room full of unused objects, trapped and abandoned. Faith Bishop had much to deal with.

In the third bedroom there was a thin, worn, virtually colourless rug by the side of the bed, unattractive and coarse. In the middle of it there was the shadow of a stain that he was sure was blood. How interesting. He bent down to examine it when there was a loud knock at the door. He sighed and opened the bedroom window and looked down at the front door. It was Alfie Woods, a young boy of indeterminate age dressed in a black torn jacket and a black scarf, a member of the Hat Stand Gang from St Thomas, who moved his attention to the bedroom in response to the creaking window.

'Inspector Bucke. I got a message for you. From Cocky. Wants to see you. He dint give me nuffin, neither.'

'Captain Colquhoun?'

'That's the one. Right away. Urgent, he said. He dint give me no money or nuffin.'

'Yes he did, Alfie. Stop trying it on. I shall be down directly.'

'Please yerself. Last time I am doing messages for the coppers, you watch.'

'We always give you coppers, Alfie,' replied Bucke as the boy disappeared from the garden. He shouted after him. 'Where is he, Alfie?'

'Up the police station,' came the muffled reply.

When he arrived at Tontine Street, it was soon obvious that Alfie had not been quite as efficient as the Hat Stand Gang always claimed to be. When Bucke went into his office he was greeted by the sight of

246

Captain Colquhoun relaxing in his chair and by an immediate question.

'Did that photographer man turn up, Rumsey? The Photographic Co-operative or something? The one on Wind Street? I picked up the news about Bishop from Constable Gill on Wind Street this morning and so I popped in to see Goldman since I was there.. He has been badgering me for a while about evidence and photographs and the like. Thought I would see how it went. Sent a boy with a message. Did he find you?'

That explained everything and Bucke explained how intrusive he found Goldman's presence.

'Yes, he does come over as rather obsessive and a little fussy. But I am sure photography will have its uses, Rumsey. It is up to us to learn how to use it most profitably. Don't worry about Goldman. If you had been there first, you would have been able to arrange things to your own satisfaction. I am responsible for that. But Goldman brought me the photographs just before you arrived. Very prompt. I suspect business hasn't been too good today but they are here. Have a look.' He pushed a large envelope across the desk.

Bucke was forced to admit that the quality of the photographs was very good and reluctantly he had to admit too that these images could be very useful. Together, he and Colquhoun could examine the scene carefully and talk about it. It wasn't as good as looking around the room in reality, but the photograph could be saved and shared. In this particular case there wasn't a great deal to see, just Cyrus, looking even colder in the photograph than he had in reality, in a dark and shabby room unnaturally lit for the camera. The photographs sheltered them from the smell of the dirty air and the pervasive bodily fluids.

'Unimpressive furniture, Isaac. I don't know why, but I expected better.'

'Indeed, though there have been some financial issues there, arising from Hilda Bishop's regular shopping visits to Swansea.' Colquhoun picked up another photograph.

'So I have heard.'

'Though personally I don't believe that can explain all of the obvious hardship in the vicarage. Never a happy household, as I understand it. I knew Cyrus Bishop vaguely. Mrs Colquhoun was on some kind of committee with Hilda. Helping orphans perhaps, I can't remember. Met them both now and again. There seemed to be some sort of issue with the maid.' Colquhoun scratched his beard. 'Lily, is it? Proper little missy that one. Stanley reminded me. She doesn't live-in following some kind of misunderstanding with Cyrus, they say.'

'I can imagine what that might have been,' nodded Bucke.

'Stanley has heard that young Lily has more money around town than might seem proper for a young girl in domestic service.'

'Trying to buy her silence, do you think?'

Bucke took out the remaining photograph from the envelope, one that looked beyond the corpse and at the fireplace. Not particularly useful, he thought.

And then he saw it. There, in the background.

He would have seen it had he examined the lounge before Alfie arrived, but that didn't matter. Here he was, in Tontine Street, and he could look carefully around the lounge and see in the grate, on top of the ashes, a small white box. How long it had been there he didn't know, but obviously after the last fire had gone out. He needed to see that box.

He went first to St Helen's Road. He would ask Constance if she would like to come with him. He respected her eyes and her perception. Of course, she was delighted to join him. Lessons were over for the day and a walk would be welcome. So together they walked up the hill towards Llwyn y Bryn and, arriving at the corner of Eaton Crescent, they saw a couple leaning very close together in a deep conversation on the other side of the road, wrapped up in each other, oblivious to anyone else.

Constance squeezed Bucke's arm.' It is wonderful to be in love, isn't it? No matter how old or how young. There is nothing better.'

'That is a rather interesting combination, Constance,' he observed.

'It goes to show that love has no boundaries, Rumsey.'

'Possibly so, Constance.' It was rude to stare and so they walked on. 'There is a notable difference in age between the two of them, you know,' he said finally.

'And does that matter?'

'I suppose not a great deal, though the young man perhaps should not be there. For many reasons, of course, but the most urgent one is that he might be seen, talking inappropriately in a public place to an older woman from the wrong side of town.'

'Who is he then?'

'Someone you know, actually.'

'I have to say that he did look a little familiar, but it is getting dark.'

'It is Henry Fry. The young man who found the body today. The young solicitor you spoke to the other week when Strick was unavailable.'

'Well I never. I thought he was engaged to Harriet Sullivan? They call her the Virgin Queen of Swansea. Wears it as a badge of honour and so, it is rumoured, remains reluctant to lose it. Unsullied and untouchable. She has a lot to learn. That isn't her, is it?'

'Oh no. Far from it.' Bucke smiled. 'That is Fanny Stevens. Better than a queen. She is the Angel of Swansea.'

'Who? I have never heard of her.'

'A singer. She is very good. We ought to go to hear her, though she sings at the moment at the Star, which isn't the most salubrious of theatres. More smoke in there than a bonfire. But the woman can sing. She has a bit of a past, as I understand it.'

'It doesn't prevent your future from being different, though, does it? Young Harriet's future had better be different or she will be sharing an unhappy marriage. And you think that young Henry is involved in some way with the Angel?'

'Who can say? But it is certainly a risk they are taking, being seen together like that.' He looked down at Constance. 'Love can make you take risks.'

She turned and looked at the couple, some distance behind them now. 'She has his heart. That is clear to me.'

'And her heart? Who has that?' Bucke asked.

She paused and peered again. 'No one, I'd say. It might be that she is damaged, Rumsey. She needs someone strong to repair her. I was fortunate. I was rescued by you. Not sure that Henry Fry is strong enough yet for a woman with a past. But you never know. She might just need to start again. Desperate for a second chance. She wouldn't be alone in that, would she?'

Bucke nodded. 'You are inventing all this, of course.'

'Of course I am. But not the part about you,' and she stretched up and kissed him briefly. 'Shameful behaviour in public, for which I apologise.' She turned for the last time. 'They have a difficult time before them I think. It will not be easy.' She watched them slip together into the shelter of a privet hedge. 'I hope one of your constables does not arrest them.'

Once they were inside the vicarage and the gas lights were flickering, Constance dismissed her natural curiosity about how other people lived and looked for any details that might help Rumsey. It was a gloomy place, cold and unwelcoming without a fire. Bucke examined the lounge closely and recovered from the grate the white packet that had so interested him in the photograph. It was an empty box of Roache's Liver Pills. He sniffed it and then looked inside. There was still white powder in it that looked like finely ground sugar. He didn't taste it though and put the box in his pocket. He needed to find out more and would take it to the public analyst for examination.

Constance, on her hands and knees on the floor, found the brandy glass that had rolled on its side under the armchair. It had been used recently. Cyrus had been relaxing with a glass and had suddenly died. A coroner would call it a 'Visitation from God.' Managing creation was probably hard work but for what possible reason had He taken time off to come to this soulless place, wondered Bucke?

Constance found further evidence in the study. In a battered shoe box beneath the desk, she found a large collection of the Parisian *cartes de visite*. She was amused and together they flicked through the neatly arranged collection of women dressed in the sort of unusual and uncomfortable-looking undergarments that Constance, and she assumed Rumsey, had never seen before. How many other people in Swansea had these things?

It was a question that troubled him for most of the night. Was this significant? Was it just two old men, Bishop and Barree, dreaming away their advancing years? Or was there a network to be uncovered? He would have to speak to Barree in the gaol, awaiting trial.

The following morning an opportunity presented itself to him, for he was called to Swansea gaol on another matter entirely.

There probably wasn't much that he could do, but there had been a death. John Neill, who was described by the governor as 'a professional tramp' had been found to be carrying 'the itch,' some kind of contagious skin disease. So he had been disinfected in a chamber of sulphur fumes. Bucke thought the chamber looked a little bit like a sentry box with a hole at the back, through which Neill could push his head. He was required to stand on two stones and between them was placed a bucket containing some red-hot coals. It all seemed rather unpleasant to Bucke, although he was assured that this was common practice. Then brimstone was thrown on the coals and the door of the box was closed to keep the fumes inside. Inside this box, Neill had died. The cause of his death was a matter for an inquest, all he had to attended for was to confirm that there had been no crime, as far as he could see anyway. Neill had complained about the procedure but no signs of burning had been found on his body when it was later examined. He had become unwell and was taken to the infirmary where he had died – of a bad constitution they decided. The heat had been too much for him.

It wasn't murder, though Bucke felt that it was hardly a procedure that should be encouraged, but then vagrants were universally regarded as expendable reservoirs of disease that must be dealt with. So since he was in the prison, he asked Major Knight, the governor, for permission to interview Louis Barree.

It had been Louis Barree's considerable misfortune that he should find himself in Swansea Gaol at the same time as Lemuel Collins, a neighbour of the Proberts, who had been sentenced to seven days for being drunk and disorderly on Portland Street. He was a man with an exceedingly quick temper and, it appeared, notable dexterity.

When they found Barree, it was obvious that a retribution had been delivered that was swift and forceful. There had been two blows to the head and some kicks which Barree described, delivered skilfully by Collins despite his chains, but apparently not seen by anyone else. Witnesses – including one of the warders - said Barree had stumbled in his leg irons and hit his head on a door. When Barree had fallen to the ground, someone – no one was sure who it was - had accidentally stepped on his groin. How regrettable, but these things happen in the most ordered of prisons, don't they? A frightful bruise had transformed Barree's right eye; it was now a swollen, livid, purple ball like a turnip and Bucke found it impossible to look at anything else whilst he questioned him.

Barree was not particularly co-operative. He was sullen and angry at the lack of personal protection and the appalling way no one was particularly concerned about his injuries. He told Bucke he was worried it might happen again and Bucke was, silently, sure that it would. He didn't think Barree would be any safer once he had been taken to Cardiff Gaol, as the Governor was trying to arrange. The criminal classes, Bucke knew, had their own, sometimes contradictory, moral code and Barree was a serious transgressor, whose crimes absolved his attackers of any guilt and, in their eyes, rendered them immune to prosecution.

'It is your *cartes de visite* that I would like to talk about, if I may, Mr Barree.'

Barree was disappointed, 'And so the assault upon me means nothing to you, or so it seems.'

252

Bucke ignored him. 'You have quite a collection.'

'A modest collection, Inspector.' He touched his eye gingerly, as if to draw attention to a detail that the police inspector had missed. 'I buy them solely for their artistic merit, Inspector. Of course if I had them with me in my current condition I should be unable to view them properly. Look at my eye! Please!' He banged his chained hands down on the table between them loudly.

'And tell me, Mr Barree. How do you obtain these cards?'

'A man brings them.' He paused and tried to look defiant. 'I do not know who he is. I do not know his name.' It was a petty act of revenge. 'Why is this important to you?'

'Because such things as this can lead to criminal activity, Mr Barree. Buying and selling can provoke arguments, threats, all kinds of things. Obscene material always has the capacity to fall into the wrong hands.' His gaze was uncompromising. 'Material like this can inspire many different kinds of unpleasant activity, Mr Barree. This is what I am supposed to prevent.'

'Well, I cannot help you.'

'Do you know where your gentleman obtains his material?'

'France, Inspector.'

'And do you know anyone else who was visited by this gentleman who you are not prepared to name?'

'Of course not. Why should that interest me?'

'Perhaps you met occasionally to exchange elements of your collections? Like-minded gentlemen sharing a hobby? That sort of thing?'

'You are being ridiculous now. You would be better advised to prevent the violence that is prevalent in our society. I am threatened on a daily basis and little is done to protect me. I must be transferred to Cardiff where matters are much more civilised, as a matter of considerable urgency. My eye, Inspector! Look at it!'

Bucke paused for a moment, wondering how much he could say and then realising that it didn't matter. They were alone. 'We live in challenging times, Mr Barree. And I think that you might have made them even more challenging for yourself. Your confession is the only glimmering candle of hope in this whole shocking crime of yours. Such retribution as this will always be waiting for you, wherever people know your name. And remember, rightly or wrongly, there will never be any witnesses to what might happen. This, I am afraid to say, is just the beginning.'

Barree looked at him without comment then briefly closed his eyes. Bucke left and walked across the town to the Swansea Free Library.

*

It took a while for Bucke to persuade Edward Bath to open the library merely for one reader, who was not in fact a member, and Bucke became increasingly exasperated.

He repeatedly emphasised the need for discretion. He did not want other library users to know about this exceptional opening, firstly because it was a sensitive criminal enquiry and secondly since it was probable that Cosh Boy was a member. So it must to be done quietly and he himself did not want to be seen doing it, either. So the library would have to be opened on a Sunday to give Miss Constance White untroubled access.

Of course, Bath said no.

A preposterous idea, against every possible regulation, to open the library in such a way. This person was not a member, either. It was only after Bucke talked at some length about the Chief Constable, about the extreme sensitivity of the task, and then finally mentioned how the Mayor might view his unwillingness to fulfil a vital civic duty, that Bath reluctantly acquiesced.

The idea of opening the library privately for Miss Constance White on a Sunday afternoon did not seem to trouble the normally taciturn

Mr Thompson, which surprised Bath but did not surprise Bucke at all. When Sunday afternoon came, he made the occasion very easy for her. He lit the small stove in order to drive away some of the chill that had settled upon the empty reading room and to drive away, as much as he could, the faint musty smell of old books and paper. He responded to her requests assiduously and did not ask any questions. He willingly brought her back copies of the *Times* and the local newspapers and watched her search for the sections featuring news from Europe. Thank goodness, thought Constance, that the section appeared always on the same page, thus saving her from wading through page after page of interminable parliamentary debates and even more uninspiring commentary.

Mr Thompson looked at her like a devoted puppy. He didn't know what she was looking for but then he didn't mind. He could think of no better way of spending a Sunday afternoon than alone in the library with an attractive woman and being, in his own mind, 'damned helpful.'

She began her research in September 1880 and found nothing of interest at all. The next hour took her deep into October and Mr Thompson was getting worried. He didn't want this moment to end so soon, but he also wanted to feel that when she found what she was looking for, he would somehow be associated in that success. He had started to pass the papers to her open at the correct page, once he knew where her attention was focused. She acknowledged his help with a smile. If only she would tell him, he thought, he could do so much more.

Eventually, Constance sat back and rubbed her hands around the back of her neck. 'Well, Mr Thompson, it looks as if I need to venture into chilly heart of November. I am so sorry about that. I had hoped my search would have been quite straightforward, but alas... You will be wanting to go home, I am sure.'

He shook his head gently; he wanted to do whatever he could. 'I have never found the month attractive and I regret that the arrangements in the library confirm such reservations, for our copies of the November editions are incomplete, particularly of the national papers. There has been some vandalism in recent months. Has Miss White considered August?' He looked at her hopefully.

Just because November was incomplete, was no reason to go back in time, thought Constance. But Mr Thompson had been so helpful, so anxious to find whatever it was that she was looking for, that she felt that for a few moments at least she should humour him. After all, it could be that the information Rumsey had been given was incorrect. And it couldn't hurt, could it, if she gave him a hint about what she was looking for? 'What we can do' – and his spirits rose when she said that – 'is that we can split August between us. We will get through it quickly then. I would be extremely grateful.'

'I would be pleased to offer whatever help I can in your search, but I do not know what…'

'We are looking for any references to a woman called Veronica Pesek, in any news reports from Central Europe.' He seemed to be waiting for her to say something, but she merely shook her head. 'I don't know why.'

Of course, Mr Thompson found it almost immediately. It had been reported on 11 August 1880. They checked the local Swansea papers too, but they offered no additional information, no surprise since they had merely copied it from the *Times*. But they had found it and after Miss White had left and he locked up the library, Mr Thompson was so very pleased, glowing with such pride and basking in the smile and the thanks she gave him. He found himself wrapped in a welcome, though unaccustomed warmth, that lasted throughout the rest of his solitary Sunday evening.

Twenty One

Henry sat in his office, staring out of the window and seeing nothing at all. Suddenly his life was a mess; a complete, unutterable mess. He knew he should marry Harriet because that was the sensible thing to do and who would argue with it? It is what everyone expected him to do, wasn't it? It was his middle-class destiny, expressing itself publicly for all to see. Harriet was a doctor's daughter and she was calling him to an inevitably respectable life. He would become middle-aged whilst he was still young. He could become a valued and admired member of his community, helping his neighbours, advising his friends. How would they see him? Informed? Intelligent? Wise? Reliable? Certainly a man for a crisis, someone always ready to dispense invaluable guidance, tinged with timeless wisdom. People would seek him out upon the recommendation of grateful clients. He would become a leading professional and he would grow fat, contented, and always respectable. He would have children who would be obedient and dutiful and who would marry well and give him grandchildren and he would retire and tend his roses and develop gout, smell old, forget things, become an expert on subjects he previously knew nothing about and then he would die.

Is that what he really wanted?

He could taste that life already. Whenever he saw Harriet, everything was controlled and measured. Everything was in its place, everything was predictable. He would have to learn to expect the average, to embrace the ordinary. How would Harriet react, if he tried to teach her some of the things that Fanny had taught him? He had no idea how much she knew about such adult secrets. Was their relationship to become something in which they could explore such secrets and enjoy them together? Or were these delights something about which Harriet would establish very clear boundaries? He didn't know the answer to those questions.

Perhaps Harriet might be a woman who as yet, had not discovered the possibilities of her desire, but if she did, she might be reborn. He had read a book about that sort of thing, though he could not remember the title. He sighed. He did not think that this was in anyway likely. She would not even hold his hand, which was a small thing he knew, but for him it was symbolic of so much else.

What Henry did know, was that the world was a very different place when he was with Fanny. The sun shone, the birds sang, there was laughter and joy and everything was possible. He was happy; he felt that he was his true self. That is what Fanny did to him and what Harriet did not. Age, appearance, experience – these things meant nothing to him when he and Fanny were together. She had become the fixed point around which his life revolved and happily so. When he was with Fanny, he was ready to surrender his individuality completely. He only wished to be part of her world.

This of course was his problem. A relationship with her would be scandalous. It would be described as wild and unseemly, a shocking rejection of everything that was right and proper. It might even lead to his own rejection by everyone around him. But the only time he ever felt happy was with Fanny. His dilemma didn't change. Was he prepared to sacrifice that joy for conventionality, as was expected of him?

He didn't think that he could do it.

He had to be fair to Harriet, of course. He had no right to make her suffer and there could be no grey area, no compromise here. It was one woman or the other – which meant one life or the other. And really he knew, that if he married Harriet, he would still go looking for Fanny. And if that happened there would be no winners. And therefore, what he was asking himself, he realised, was whether he was brave enough to offer himself to Fanny, and he knew that if he did, he would never need anyone else. He could not say the same about Harriet.

Henry watched a man get down from his cart and beat an intractable donkey viciously and to no purpose. The donkey would not move. It could not move. The load of rocks was far too heavy and unless the man removed some of them, the cart would never move again. Beating the donkey was irrelevant, almost certainly counter-productive. Henry could see that, but the driver could not;

he seemed oblivious to the emaciated donkey staring at him impassively whilst it bled. The man will have done it before, Henry observed. And he will certainly do it again, because that is all that he knows. But why? What could ever be the point? Someone should stop it. But no one will stop it, and so it will continue, in its eternal idiocy.

'Perhaps that donkey is me,' he muttered to the empty office. 'Beat me as much as you like. Beat me until I bleed, but you can't force me to pull those rocks.'

That, ultimately was the choice he had to make, a stark choice between respectability and happiness. In his mind there was no over-lap, they were mutually exclusive. There was no way in which he could have both.

'So choose, you bugger,' he said and then returned to the papers that were littering his desk now and had every chance of doing so for the next fifty years. He pulled out the file dealing with Constance White and her divorce. It was Mr Strick's case but he had been called again to his duties as coroner to deal with the unexpected death of Cyrus Bishop. A report from the public analyst had been requested, which could be very interesting apparently. and so Henry had once again to hold a meeting with Constance.

He was a pleasant young man, a little nervous, though not so much as last time, she thought. She could not doubt his appeal and imagined that, whilst he probably had a lot of learning to do, teaching him might appeal to some women. She remembered seeing him in furtive conversation with Fanny Stevens at the end of Eaton Crescent and wondering how such an unlikely relationship would develop. This added a new dimension to her meeting with him, for she felt that she knew one of his secrets.

Today she had been asked by Mr Strick to provide some examples of how she had been mistreated by her husband, which she had been happy to offer. Now she had to tell Henry Fry and she could see that he was terribly shocked by what she described. He sat wide-eyed as she talked of things about which he had no experience – the daily threats, the weekly violence and her struggle to maintain her self-respect in the face of such abuse.

259

Constance recognised that Henry seemed slightly more relaxed that the last time they had met, less intimidated by her femininity. Was that the word? It was the only one she could think of. She was quite happy to be completely frank with him. She talked about the soup incident when William had thrown a tureen at her and, this time, Henry was prepared to look at the puckered skin on her forearm. He screwed up his face, imagining how much it would have hurt. She talked about when he had thrown her downstairs when she was pregnant. He rushed to make legible notes as she spoke and then put down his pen. He looked nervously at her and Constance waited patiently for him to speak. He cleared his throat, rather more noisily than he had anticipated.

'It seems to me, and of course I am no expert in such matters, but I believe that under the terms of the Matrimonial Causes Act of 1878 you are, without doubt, entitled to a legal separation from your husband on the grounds of assault.' He coughed again.

'It is a start, I suppose. But what I want, and what I need, is a divorce,' she said firmly.

'Yes I know and I am sure that Mr Strick will be able to ...' He seemed distracted, his attention wandering away from his work. 'I am so sorry Miss White, and please forgive me for being frank, but I have a question for you. You don't have to answer it, of course. Well, it is more than one question but...'

'Mr Fry. What is it that you would like to know?'

'You see, it has nothing to do with your case. But there are a number of things I am trying to understand, and well, you see...'

Constance waited.

He swallowed, trying to draw together his courage. 'May I be candid?'

'Of course, Mr Fry.' She wondered where this conversation was leading.

'I mean, you are a married woman, Miss...Mrs Bristow.'

'A status you are being paid to resolve may I remind you.'

'Of course. I can see no difficulties with your case, Miss White. You merely need to show patience. But there are things that I do not understand, you see.' He ran his hand across his forehead, dispelling imaginary sweat.

He seemed a very young man again, thought Constance, trying to be grown up. His job sounded dull but it inevitably brought him into contact with every aspect of human life, even those he was not prepared for. She raised her eyebrows to encourage him.

'Miss White,' he began and then stopped. 'You see, what I want to know is, and please forgive me, but what I have to understand…'He stopped again.

She smiled at him. 'Courage, Mr Fry. Courage.'

He took a deep breath. 'Miss White. If I was a juror and I was listening to all that you have told me, this catalogue of woe, I would want to ask you, and I don't want to be offensive but what I would be wondering was…'He paused again. This was clearly something that was important to him.

'Mr Fry, please. You cannot shock me.'

'You have described a violent and unhappy marriage, Mrs Bristow – that is what they will call you in court, you know – well, the question is…' He closed his eyes and then finally seized the moment. 'Did you have relations with your husband whilst all this was going on?'

'But of course, Mr Fry. I was often angry and often made him wait as long as I could. But the answer to your question is, yes.'

'I see. But how could you? If he was being so violent? I don't understand.'

She smiled. 'Mr Fry. It is a woman's fate. And there are a host of things you can think about on such occasions. You would be surprised.'

'So…'

261

'So, it is an irrelevant question. The experience itself was tedious and irrelevant, though thankfully brief.'

'But if you had relations with Mr Bristow, then surely it indicates an acceptance of your marriage vows.'

'Or an acceptance of my fate, Mr Fry.'

Henry was thoughtful. He seemed to be considering whether he could ask her another question.

Constance felt she should take the initiative. 'What else is troubling you, Mr Fry?' She smiled sympathetically.

'You see, Miss White, what I am interested in – and purely for my own reasons, you understand, and you don't have to answer. But is it possible, do you think, for a woman to have relations with a man she does not love? Even if he is cruel and unfeeling?'

'Of course, Mr Fry. It happens all the time.' Constance couldn't decide whether he was relieved or shocked. 'Remember, women have just the same base needs as men. Please don't be shocked, Mr Fry, but it is true.'

'I am sorry, Miss White. I have been too forward.' His mind had been full of Jack McCarthy for days now.

'Don't be silly, Mr Fry. If you had asked me a question, I was not prepared to answer then I would not have answered it.'

'And so, you think that it is possible for a woman to still have relations with a man they didn't love, even if she knew another man who she did love.'

Suddenly she understood. 'There are some things a woman has to do, Mr Fry.' She looked at him carefully. 'A woman like the one you describe might, who can say, might even have relations with both men. It would not necessarily change her feelings about either man – neither the one she loved nor the one she didn't. Even men do such things.'

'But why?'

'Because we have to. Because life is complicated. You make a choice because you think it is the right choice, but you find out later that it wasn't. And the way things are, Mr Fry, there isn't much you can do to put it right.' She was aware that he was listening very carefully to her, for this conversation was very important to him, speaking directly to his anxieties and his circumstances. 'Think about my circumstances for a moment. I made a wrong choice when I was young and I paid a heavy price for that mistake, as I have told you. But in spite of all of that, I am profoundly lucky. Because it has enabled me to find true love when I wasn't looking for it. My marriage closed down but another door opened for me. But that does not happen to everyone.'

'So what you are saying is, that if, hypothetically, I was in love with a woman who loved me but she was having relations with another man, because she had to, then I shouldn't think much of it. Is that right?'

'I am not saying that, I don't think. You might still be very upset, but for her it might not mean anything at all. Nothing more than sneezing, perhaps.'

'And you don't think it means she doesn't love me?'

She chose her words carefully. 'You see, Mr Fry. I can speak from my own experience. When you fall in love, you realise many things. You suddenly know what love is, and there is no other experience like it. But you also realise what love is not, and in my case that meant that the whole of my previous life had been wasted. But as I told you, I have found love and that is why I am here, isn't it? For Mr Stick to set me free so that I no longer have to hide my love, though if I am honest, I am not making a very good job of that. But that is what I am paying for.' Henry looked at her, unable to say anything. She continued. 'Don't ever deny true love, Mr Fry. No matter how inconvenient it might be, or how wrong it may appear.'

'Life is not so easy for me at the moment, Miss White,' said Henry, looking at the desk.

'I am beginning to realise that, Mr Fry. It is easy for me. My husband has deserted me. Falling in love would never be enough to let me divorce him. But he has run away and that is an opportunity I am not prepared to squander. All I can say to you is that if you love someone who cannot be yours at the moment, don't dwell on it. Do not torture yourself with base images and fantasies, for they will come to haunt you. And always hope that in some way you cannot predict, that love will find a way.' She sighed. 'I don't suppose I have been much help.'

'Please, Miss White. I cannot thank you enough. You have been a great comfort to me. But, do you think that sometimes love can be inappropriate. Please speak truthfully, do not try to spare my feelings. I mean, if for example there was a great difference in age? Or in social standing?'

'Love is what love is, Mr Fry, and it can defy the logical part of your mind. These things you mention can be very difficult, I am sure. They shouldn't be ignored or dismissed as unimportant. But if the love is real and true, then they can be overcome.'

Henry looked out of the window. The donkey had gone but there was still blood on the road. 'The woman I love is older than I. She knows far more about the world than I.'

'Does that matter? If you love her?' She smiled at him reassuringly. 'Nothing is easy, Mr Fry.'

'But you don't understand, Miss White,' he suddenly blurted out. 'You don't understand. I am promised to another. What can I do?'

'Don't hurt the person to whom you are promised. She has done nothing wrong. If you know that the marriage isn't right, then do not go ahead with it, under any circumstances. Does she deserve such unhappiness. Does she?'

He looked straight into her eyes. 'Do I?'

There was a knock on the door and the clerk, Mr Sears, came in, smelling of peppermint and his face lined like an ancient leather-bound book of statutes. 'Mr Fry. Mrs Collins is here for her appointment. You are running late and she has been waiting for some time.' He looked at the young man disapprovingly.

'I am sorry, Mr Sears. I shall be with her immediately.' He looked embarrassed again now that reality had intruded. 'Miss White, thank you for your - '

'Don't mention it, Mr Fry. I am sure you will pass on the information I have provided to Mr Strick. I hope we have an opportunity to talk again soon.'

He stood up, unsure what to say. 'Please excuse me but...'

'Good afternoon, Mr Fry. I am sure Mr Sears will show me out. You are very busy.'

As she walked home, Constance realised that she could have predicted every word of that conversation from the brief glance she had been given of Henry Fry and Fanny together in the shelter of a hedge. She speculated too about what might happen next. Would it be love? Or sorrow? And for whom? For Henry? For Fanny? For Harriet? And she felt a wave of sadness pass over her because there might not be any winners at all. There was little anyone could do now to prevent the unhappiness for any one of them – or for all of them. No one would emerge from this unscathed.

She wondered how much of this should she tell Rumsey. It wasn't easy for her to keep things from him. But she had other things to talk about today. He was calling to see her after her next pupil and she could tell him what she had discovered from the newspapers.

*

Bucke looked carefully at the short article, as Constance had written it down in her book, in her neat and precise handwriting. 'Veronica Pesek. Well, well. A real person. That is the first surprise.'

'I copied it, word for word. It wasn't long. Not really of much interest to the *Times* reader in London, I shouldn't think. Look at what it says about her – *a beautiful woman of doubtful reputation*. Tactfully written, don't you think?'

'And her child, as he said. Eight years old. Rosa Budai. Does it say how she died?'

'It does further down. There.' She read it aloud. '*Her body, found hanging from her feet beneath the Széchenyi Bridge, split as if by an anatomist and her vital organs removed in a barbaric ritual.*'

A chill passed down Bucke's spine. He was reminded of what he had seen. 'But it doesn't mention Czibor, does it?' asked Bucke, reading through it again.

'There isn't much detail, It is a short piece, picked up by an agency and circulated to fill a bit of space. That is what Mr Thompson said. It is how the newspapers work, apparently. We only have the briefest summary. An unpleasant story just fill a space.'

'But it is enough for our purposes, I think. Abramovitch didn't think we could find out, did he? News from far away. How could we know? Why should we know? But look here, this paragraph, the one you have put a star next to. *The perpetrator is believed to have been her lover, the escaped Romanian spy called Ambrov who the authorities are most anxious to detain once more.*' He looked at Constance. 'Printing errors in the newspapers are not unusual, but…'

'It's him, isn't it? That's your man.'

*

Bucke's next meeting that afternoon was much more unexpected. He had walked slowly away from the inquest into the death of Cyrus Bishop with his mind trying to process the implications of what he had heard, at the same time as the information that Constance had found in the library was still swirling in his mind. He wondered why Abramovitch had said what he did? Obviously he didn't believe they had the means or indeed the sense to check his story. It was as if he thought he was untouchable. To talk about Veronica Pesek like that showed that he held them in contempt, and perhaps that he was proud of what he had done. That worried Bucke more than anything else. He had known they were dealing with a killer with an icy heart, a dangerous man who knew no boundaries. But at least now he knew who he was.

He was shaken out of his considerations by Alfie Woods, who had been sitting on the steps of the police station for over an hour waiting for him. He stood up as Bucke approached, looking around warily, to ensure that he was not being observed.

Alfie looked as he always did, frail and under-nourished, in his shabby black jacket with that tightly knotted scarf. Where and how he lived Bucke didn't know. He was an enthusiastic member of the Hat Stand Gang, running errands, taking messages and generally watching every development in the town carefully, in the hope of getting something, however small, from the margins. The gang were particularly unhappy at the moment, for they regarded the installation of wires to facilitate the telephone system as a serious threat to their livelihood and tried as hard as they could to disrupt its progress. Today though, Alfie seemed to be acting alone.

'Afternoon, Inspector Bucke. Been waiting for you, I have.'

'Have you indeed, Alfie? And why would that be?'

'On account of the fact that I have information for you, important information as I like to consider it, Inspector. As likely as not, you will be considering a reward, I do not doubt it.'

'Really, Alfie? Well that depends, of course, on the quality of the information you might have. An informant prospers or starves on the quality of the information they provide, Alfie. You must know that.'

'You what?'

'Tell me what you know and I will tell you whether it is valuable or not.'

'Oh, I know it is valuable all right, Inspector. Because I knows where Cosh Boy is hiding.'

Bucke was instantly alert. 'Really? And how do you know this, Alfie?'

267

'Cus I seen him.'

'And how did you know that this person you saw was Cosh Boy, Alfie?'

'Wouldn't you like to take me into your office, Inspector? So that we can chat nice and cosy, like?'

'I am fine here, Alfie, thank you very much. Tell me what you know and how you know it.'

Alfie looked irritated. 'It'll cost you. I'd rather talk about it in private. About the reward, like.'

'Is that a fact, Alfie? Let's see what you've got.'

'I'll need a shilling.'

'We all need a shilling, Alfie. Let me hear what you have to say and then I'll decide,' said Bucke patiently.

Alfie sighed. The adult world could be so disappointing at times and this was generally because they wouldn't listen to sense. 'A bloke I 'as been following for a while. Always thought he was fishy but I thought I'd bide my time, like. Wait until I was certain.'

'And how do you know that this is Cosh Boy? That is what interests me most, Alfie. How do you know?'

'A feeling, Inspector. Trust me, I know these things. Experience, you might say.'

'Might I indeed? And so you followed him, this man who you didn't like? Where did he take you?'

'It will cost you,' he said with little conviction. It wouldn't be silver, he was sure of that now. Coppers from the copper. Again.

'Alfie, please. What was he wearing?' asked Bucke.

Alfie made a face, as if this was an idiotic question. 'He was wearing clothes. Dark clothes. A coat? I don't know. Had pockets, I should think. You could keep a cosh in them pockets,' he said brightly.

'And was he short? Or tall?' asked an increasingly sceptical Bucke.

'Average I would say, Inspector,' said Alfie, nodding thoughtfully.

This was not at all convincing. 'And where did he go? You still haven't told me. Tell me that, Alfie,' asked Bucke. 'Because a less patient person than myself might think you were making all this up.'

Alfie relaxed. He was much more comfortable with this. 'Well see, Inspector, he went out on to the West Pier, Inspector. Right to the end until you can't go no further. That is where he is hiding. In that old warehouse there. What do they call it?'

'Giddings Sugar Warehouse?'

'That's the one. I has followed him out there a few times. Thought I'd tell you first, like, you being a decent sort of copper. Always fair, everyone says. But if yous don't go and get 'im, The Hatstand Gang will. Letting you have first dibs, see. Can't do better than that, can we?'

'Thank you, Alfie. That is very kind of you.' Bucke was not convinced. It all seemed very vague. Had someone put him up to this? Was he really ready to waste police resources on such a flimsy basis?

'A pleasure to do business with you, Inspector. That will be a shilling, like I said.' Hope lived forever in the small boy's breast.

'Perhaps we shall wait and see. If you are right, I will pay. After all, you said it was a feeling you had. You have offered me no evidence. But if you are leading me on, I shall come looking for you. Understand?' Alfie nodded, glumly. 'Here we are.' Bucke gave him a penny. 'Take this on account.'

'On account of what?' asked Alfie.

'On account of the fact that I am not sure I believe you.'

Alfie was affronted. 'Inspector! That is a terrible thing to say! You can trust me! Out of all the people in Swansea.'

'I hope so, Alfie. I do hope so. Now you scoot, lad.' Bucke paused on the top step, watching Alfie scurry away. How did the boy know it was Cosh Boy? That is what unsettled Bucke the most. Was Alfie being genuine? Or was he being used to lure Bucke out to the furthest end of the exposed West Pier? On the other hand, if someone was hiding out there, then he wanted to know why. And he didn't want the Hatstand Gang taking things into their own hands. Dangerous for them and additional work for him.

He opened the door of the Police Station and went inside. He would go out to take a look later, he decided. But he wouldn't trouble anyone else with it, not in the first instance. The constables needed to get out and find Abramovitch urgently and he didn't think it was something anyone should try to do on their own. It had become clear that the man had the potential to be extremely dangerous.

His plans were overturned immediately by Constable Davies, who was in his habitual place, leaning against the counter. 'That man of yours. O'Vitch. Done a moonlight, he has.' He shook his head sorrowfully at such terrible perfidy. 'One minute he was there and then the next he had gone. Not a word. On Saturday it was. Been meaning to tell you. Old man Mayhew is tamping. He stopped me on the street, he did. Castle Square, it was, but you'd expect that wouldn't you? That's where the Castle Hotel is, isn't it? But O'Vitch has paid nothing, see. Done a runner and owes him a small fortune.'

Bucke sighed. He hadn't really expected it to be as easy as he had hoped. 'Can't say I am surprised, Constable. I think he knows that this game is up, whatever his game might be.' He turned to Sergeant Ball. 'Stanley. Tell everyone to be extremely vigilant. I want this man found as soon as possible. I don't want him followed, I want him detained and brought here into the police station immediately he is found. Be aware, I think he could be dangerous, so I don't want anyone approaching him on their own, under any circumstances. Get as many of the constables as you can into the town centre. See if anyone knows anything at all'

'Inspector Flynn has deployed the constables throughout the town tonight anyway, something going on with the Militia he reckons, But I'll tell 'em, Inspector. We should be able to track the bugger down. Never taken to him,' said Ball. 'I don't suppose he will be wanting this now, will he?' He took a box from a shelf behind him and withdrew from it a square of material. 'Dropped this the last time he was in here. I was going to give it back to him.'

Bucke leaned over and took it from the sergeant. It was, as he suspected a handkerchief, and in the corner there was, carelessly embroidered, the word PESTH. A matching piece to the one he had in his office, displaying the word BUDA. This wasn't really evidence of much at all, but for Bucke it was sufficient; he knew without a doubt who had killed those boys.

Davies nodded wisely. 'To be honest, we'll all be pleased to see the back of him, I'd say. Wandering around everywhere. Always turning up. I reckon he was following me.'

'I didn't think he walked that slowly,' added Sergeant Ball as he flicked through the ledger.

Bucke smiled as Davies struggled to understand what Ball had said. 'You check the lodging houses and the hotels, Evan. This is really important. See who has recently taken a room or a bed. Abramovitch might have left town, in which case you will be wasting your time, but I doubt that very much. I think he is still here, and we have to find him. You understand, Evan? We need to find Abramovitch urgently, but you mustn't approach him on your own. Understand?'

Davies nodded wisely. 'Funny, isn't it? How things work. You know, like, my sister's husband's cousin, you know Harri, the one with the beard?'

Everyone else started to shuffle, returning to their tasks, their interest in what Davies had to say dissipating immediately. Bucke could feel himself becoming irritated with his obvious procrastination. There were enquiries he should be making.

'I've been meaning to mention this, like, but you know, like, it's been so busy, hasn't it just? But anyway, this Harri – he's not my cousin, obviously, not even related, me mam says, but anyway, he works at Neath Station. You know, the railway station.'

For some reason Bucke decided to hear him out. He was sure he

271

would regret it.

'Well, he was there when that Irish pal of ours turned up. O'Vitch. The one you want me to ask questions about. Him.'

The station started to fall silent. 'What do you mean, Evan?' Bucke asked.

'Well, he got on the Swansea train there, didn't he? A couple of weeks ago or something. All his luggage was waiting for him. It had been sent from somewhere foreign. Been there a while. In the corner of the luggage place, that's where it was. Most stations have them. So it was there, waiting like, and then O'Vitch turned up to collect it, like. And do you know what? He turned up dressed ordinary like, just like any old worker. And then he went to the gents with a suitcase and he come back dressed as a proper toff. That's what our Harri said anyway. And then he got on the train, with his luggage. Hell of a fuss, shouting and everything and that is how he is here in Swansea. The O'Vitch man. Not our Harri. Not his luggage, was it? Been meaning to mention it. Rum do, isn't it? Not surprised you want a word with him. I wouldn't be surprised if he didn't pay the proper train fare. Looks that sort to me.'

Twenty Two

Giddings Sugar warehouse was damp, dismal and derelict. There were very few people who could ever remember it being used. Its brief moment as a vibrant business enterprise had long since been forgotten. It stood on a cracked battered quayside, thin tough weeds clinging in the cracks against the winds, surviving, just, the tides that occasionally swamped it. It had become an overlooked feature of the shoreline, a place where no one ever went. It had the smell of neglect etched into those abandoned stones; there was a scent of death in its hollowness, for it had come to the end of its days.

The warehouse had never been anything other than a doomed venture. How could Swansea ever hope to compete with the established sugar importers of Bristol? So it was never a success, never profitable, the investment in the building never justified. And now it was an empty shell, an unwanted, unpleasant ruin that only the very bravest of adventurous young boys visited for a dare. There were just pigeons and gulls, and the rats that fed off their nests.

Bucke circled it cautiously. There was little evidence of its past as a thriving place of trade and it had long since been ignored, even by those drunken sailors who had lost their vessel and neither was there an appetite amongst the local people to pillage the ruins for any more building materials. It loomed darkly against the sea, a long building, constructed from local stone. Once the windows had been salvaged, the lintels and cills had been taken and many, though not all, of the holes left behind had been inadequately boarded up some time ago, with wood that was now wet and rotten.

Parts of the roof were still sufficiently intact to provide occasional shelter, though there were significant gaps which had allowed the rain do its work on the floor of the loft, so that had consequently collapsed in places. There was still a double wooden door in the gable, over which there was a rusted hoist. Bucke saw a grey gull with the cruel eyes of a hangman sitting on the metal arm, a looped rope reaching downwards, creaking and swaying in the wind. Must be a bird from Gower, thought the inspector. They always seem to be the most sinister, for some reason. He shook his head, to remove such a ridiculous fancy from his mind, but with little success.

In the twilight gloom this was a sinister place. It stood above a greasy sea, the dirt and debris washed down by the river, gathering together and sliding thickly against the quayside. The clouds were building once again out in the bay, the light to the east contrasting with the threatening darkness approaching once again from the west. It would rain later, certainly. It was cold and it was not a good place to be. Bucke looked at the building thoughtfully.

Was this really where Cosh Boy lived, Bucke asked himself? It seemed very unlikely. Perhaps he had been there, once and for some unknown reason, but he couldn't live here, could he? He examined the outside of the warehouse once more. He wasn't sure that he wanted to go inside on his own. He had brought an oil lamp with him, as well as a truncheon, which he took from his belt, taking comfort from its weight. But still Bucke felt exposed and vulnerable.

At the end of the building there was a door. Bucke noted that the hasp was broken. He pushed at it with the end of his truncheon. It creaked ominously and the bottom caught against the floor, sticking briefly. Bucke stayed outside for a moment longer, looking back towards the town. The lights from the public houses were bright and appealing, suggesting warmth and companionship, but they seemed such a long way away. He felt very alone, as if he had drifted out of his own life, into a time and a place in which he did not belong. He should have brought a constable with him, he realised that. He would never have allowed a constable to come here on their own. And so why did he think he should do so?

He picked up the oil lamp, lit it with a match, and then pushed the door open a little further. He looked at the floor. It seemed that someone might have trailed some rain in on their boots, for the entrance was wet. He didn't think it could have crept in under the door, but he might be wrong. As he stared into the threatening interior, he wondered why anyone would ever want to live out here. He told himself not to be stupid. Someone who wished to remain hidden, that was obvious. It had so many advantages; the most important being that only rarely did people come to the Giddings Sugar Warehouse. But it still appeared empty. There couldn't be anyone here? Could there?

Bucke stepped back from the door and then held up his lamp. There was no obvious source of light within. Perhaps Cosh Boy wasn't here yet. He would surely need a lamp or a candle at the very least. There was nothing to smell either, except neglect and the sweet decay of the sea. Another seagull squawked suddenly and flapped off into the wind. Bucke should not have come alone, he knew that for certain. It had been stupid and reckless and he felt exposed. He should have gone looking for Abramovitch.

There was a noise inside, as if something had fallen. What was there inside that could have made a noise like that? A bird? An animal? He walked through the door. There was rusty bracket screwed on to one of the loft supports and he hung the lamp on that. He didn't want to walk around the warehouse in a pool of light, advertising his position. He wanted to keep his hands free, too. He moved away from the lamp into the darkness, allowing his eyes to adjust to the gloom that seemed to make the air thicker, his long truncheon held in both hands in front of him. The place still seemed, abandoned, neglected, although there seemed to be a pile of old stained rags behind the door.

Was that really paraffin that he could smell now? Why would there be paraffin here? Was someone once trying to keep warm? He took another cautious step. There was an undeniable trail of water leading further into the building. He couldn't see where it was going, so he followed it cautiously.

There was a square wooden structure in front of him, though it was difficult to distinguish properly, next to the open steps that led to the loft. It must have once been an office. He took precise slow steps towards it, pausing after each one. It was getting darker.

Suddenly he turned quickly, sure that he had heard something behind him. Nothing appeared to have changed.

What would he do, if he wanted to hide here, he asked himself? He would want to be enclosed, he thought, but not so that someone could creep up on him silently. He would need to be able to get away quickly, too. He wasn't sure that the office would have been a good place; too easy to be trapped inside. But he approached it carefully, nonetheless, each of his steps sounding like a dropped hammer. He lit a match and looked through the glassless window of the office. For a brief moment it was like daylight. The room was empty. Shelves that might once held ledgers had been stripped out, presumably taken for firewood. Their brackets had gone too, leaving behind the regularly spaced holes, like empty, black eyes. The water stains had disappeared this far into the warehouse. There were no signs that anyone had ever tried to live here. He shook out the match and listened for a while, waiting for the light from the match to leave his eyes. Suddenly he was aware that the oil lamp had gone out too, and the far end of the warehouse was now completely dark. Had someone extinguished it? Or had it just failed? He could see nothing. He could hear nothing.

He looked up the steps. They seemed secure enough, but he tested the third step with his truncheon as a precaution. It was sound. It was just as dark in the loft, it seemed, despite the holes in the roof, which he assumed were directly above those large and extended wet patches in the ceiling. The steps led to a black square, threatening and dangerous. Was the floor of the loft strong enough? Would it take his weight? He had come so far there was nothing to be gained by retreating now. He carefully walked up the centre of the staircase, pausing after each step. When he eventually reached the loft, he was sure he would be able to stand quite comfortably in the middle, although the pitched roof meant that the usable space was limited to that central part which ran from gable to gable. He stopped before his head reached the level of the floor, where he thought he might be at his most vulnerable. He could see very little and to abandon caution at this stage would be foolish. If he struck another match, he would just make himself easier to see. Why did he think someone else was here in the warehouse with him? He was uncomfortable; uncertain. Perhaps he should leave now and come back with support.

He took off his hat and scratched his head. Why had the lamp gone out? Lamps did go out by themselves. Of course they did. All the time. He was just being over-dramatic. Stupid thoughts were going through his mind and there was no one here with him to soothe those anxieties. No one would see what he did, no one would think he was stupid, because no one else would know, but once the idea had taken root in his mind, he could not shift it. So he put his hat on the end of his truncheon and pushed it up slowly through the opening into the loft.

There was a sudden shift in the air above him as something smashed into the truncheon from the side, just below the level of his hat and knocked it from his hand. He staggered on the stairs, keeping his balance by grabbing at the remaining steps above him, as his truncheon fell into the darkness below.

A silent figure was now standing above him at the top of the steps, striking down at him with what seemed to be a staff, though Bucke was unable to see any details. He instinctively moved his head to the side and the staff caught him sharply on the shoulder. The momentum of the blow knocked him off the steps and on to the ground below. The attacker ran down the stairs after him, his boots confident on the steps. Winded though he was, Bucke had to get up; no one ever won a fight by lying on the ground. The man swiped at him horizontally again and Bucke was able to dodge beneath the weapon and ram himself into his chest. He could feel leather, cold against his face. It was an apron, he was sure of it. They both fell backwards and Bucke gasped, 'You are under arrest!' The man laughed and hit him on the side of the head. Bucke reached up and tried to grab his beard, but there wasn't one, just a thin stubble, coarse and sharp. The man seemed to be thin and strong and he wrestled himself free of Bucke's grasp to slide off into the darkness. Bucke could not see where he was. Damn! thought Bucke. I had him in my hands!

He pulled himself up and tried to still his breathing so that he could hear any movement in the darkness that enveloped him. Everything was silent. He panted involuntarily and then stopped himself. He moved carefully – desperate not to reveal his position. He felt around on the floor but could find neither his truncheon nor the staff the man had used, if he had dropped it. Where was he? Bucke felt something against his right leg. It was the staircase. He blinked rapidly to try and adjust his eyes. He was sure there was a shape to his left. Had it just moved? He moved backwards to place his back against the side of the office. His assailant would have to come at him from the front, so he might have a chance.

Then he could smell them; fumes, drifting from the door he had used, making the air denser, forcing him to cough. Then he saw a flame, small but vigorous. Suddenly it caught and blazed up. The rags. The paraffin. There was light now too. Hazy and obscured and he could see no one in the building. The flames were spreading now, seizing upon dry and ancient timber and turning wet wood into acrid smoke. Bucke knew that he had to go into the loft and escape from there, he would never get past the fire. He ran up the stairs and saw the loft filling with a dark smog, forcing its way through the cracks in the floor. This wasn't safe either; the floor would soon collapse. At the far end there was a faint licking of flame where the fire had found something to its liking. He ran to the other end, to where the double doors opened in the gable. He kicked at them but they wouldn't open. He kicked again and felt sure they had weakened but perhaps they were seized up through lack of use. He knew that if he forced them open the air might well feed the flames, but he had no choice; this was the only way out. The smoke, streaming quickly, was getting worse and he couldn't stop coughing now. He peered around for something, anything that he could use to force the doors..

What was that? A heap of rags? No, for there was a protruding leg. He bent down and exposed the body of Alfie Woods. He had been strangled. Bucke could see in the light of the flames that a thin cord had been twisted into his neck, his eyes frozen in a terrible stare of fear, flickering as if moving for the final time. Poor Alfie. He had been tricked too, an expendable messenger, doomed from the moment he had been recruited. Bucke in his anger ran into the door with his shoulder. He was sure that it had moved. He kicked it as hard as he could with the flat of his boot, twice, and the rusted iron hasp fell finally from the rotten wood. The doors creaked but they opened reluctantly and as the fresh air entered, re-arranging the smoke, he suddenly felt an increase in the heat behind him from the grateful flames. He didn't have much time.

Bucke grasped the rope hanging from the hoist and pulled it inside. He hoped it was strong enough. He picked up Alfie – who might still be able to help him, for the last time, and looped the rope under his armpits. He was as gentle and respectful as he could be, and even if it did not matter at all, it was important to him. Then he lowered him slowly to the ground. The weight of Alfie's body held the rope a little more steadily which allowed Bucke to climb down it slowly. His weight however started to buckle the hoist above him, and this made his descent to the ground faster but more dignified than he could have hoped, until it snapped and he fell the remaining three or four feet. As he landed, he immediately covered his head with his arms to prevent injury but fortunately that falling metal arm landed with a clatter, a short distance away.

The warehouse was properly ablaze now, with flames shooting high into the sky. The dry wood was crackling and stones began to fall as their wooden supports collapsed. He hoped that the constables could see it and react. He released Alfie and picked him up. His own body was starting to ache now from the blows and the tension and he walked slowly, as far away as he could, though the heat constantly stretched out its fingers towards him, as if trying to pull him back. He laid the body on the quay and sat down, waiting for his colleagues to arrive. He remembered suddenly that they might be delayed. James Flynn had heard that the Militia were heading to Wind Street tonight and had directed most of the constables there as a precaution. Bucke sighed. It was a sensible decision, but it meant that support might be longer in coming; he hoped that there wasn't some kind of riot. A little too early for that, he decided. He closed his eyes briefly as stinging smoke drifted into them and then looked at Alfie's body. There seemed to be so little of him. Another incomplete life snatched away. Why? To what purpose?

He touched Alfie's head, silently promising to find justice for another Swansea child, another child from Fanny Steven's song, another child lost in the dark unforgiving wood that Swansea had become. Bucke realised that he knew nothing about Alfie – where he lived and who he lived with were mysteries that would all too soon be revealed, so that he could make his visit and deliver the terrible news of another child murdered.

The fire was roaring now; he couldn't understand why it was burning so fiercely when it was, he had thought, so rotten. But there had been that scent of paraffin which he should have taken more seriously. He was sure that he could hear police whistles. But in the light of the fire he could see no one at all. That hadn't been Cosh Boy in the warehouse, it wasn't at all as Elodie had described him. This wasn't her lump of lard. It could only have been one other person. Recently clean shaven – stubble, not a beard - quite strong, determined. 'And someone who wants me dead,' said Bucke to himself. 'Czibor? Of course not. A man who does not appear to exist?'

The fire erupted again, like an explosion of laughter, sending a huge plume of flame into the dark sky, the wood splitting and fracturing noisily, bathing everything in an infernal red light, the heat flashing over his face in a wave. Welcome to hell, it said. They must be able to see it from the town centre. How could they not? They could probably see it in Port Talbot.

Elbows on his drawn-up knees, he put his head in his hands. Bucke was exhausted, drained by his sudden brush with death, and his mind was wandering. His shoulders were starting to ache properly now. He knew he had been drawn into a trap to facilitate his own murder and that he should never have considered coming here alone. He thought about Alfie Woods again. The boy had been nothing other than entirely disposable. He had been sent with a false message to lure Bucke to the warehouse, killed to ensure his silence and then his body would have been lost in the fire. Who would have looked for it? He shook his head, trying to clear his mind. Who had done this? Could there now be any doubt about that? And what did that mean? That suddenly Abramovitch considered him to be a credible threat?

He didn't know the answer to that, and he moved his shoulder tentatively, trying to ease it. But he had another, even more pressing question that required an answer. If Abramovitch was the man, and he was sure that he was, where had he gone?

Twenty Three

They hadn't bothered to use the fire engine when the warehouse burnt down. Inspector Flynn decided that it was far too difficult to get the machine out to the blaze at the furthest end of the West Pier and really, it didn't matter a great deal either, since it was a derelict building, unwanted, unsightly and surrounded by water. It was much safer to let it burn itself out. A job that needed to be done that was suddenly, and helpfully, making its own arrangements.

Bucke, smoke blackened and weary, had thought it was a good decision too, though he would have appreciated a ride back to the police station. He had become angry with himself for having Abramovitch in his grasp and losing him, angry that he could not yet bring him to justice for the murder of Alfie – and goodness knew what else. He needed to rest.

Strangely there was a fire the next morning too and they didn't use the fire engine for that one either.

As James Flynn later observed, the drama all began when the Militia went out drinking. They knew something was going to happen in the town, it just didn't happen on Wind Street where they had expected it to happen. They had been a celebration, of course, for the Royal Glamorganshire Light Infantry Militia had plenty to celebrate, since they had kept Swansea safe for quite a few weeks now. Their skills too had been finely honed on the edges of the Brecon Beacons and news of their gunnery precision had, they were sure, spread envy and terror in equal measure amongst all potential, craven, European invaders. This was a very special moment indeed.

They enjoyed wearing their impressive uniforms, confident in the allure that they gave them, their capacity to make the female heart flutter was undeniable. There were confrontations with lily-livered local youths which were only be expected and some desultory blows were eventually exchanged as the evening wore on, but Inspector Flynn's decision to place as many constables as he could spare in the town, particularly on Wind Street, whilst depleting resources, ensured that the police cells were not overcrowded. There were few arrests, which suggested to Flynn that the police operation should be regarded as a success. The evening therefore lurched quietly towards its natural and unimpressive conclusion, dribbling away into unconsciousness and vomit, and the constables could return unscratched and unmarked to their beats.

Captain Mayer thought it had been a jolly good evening all round as he wandered home with exaggerated care to his room in a lodging house at 7 Somerset Place. Good for the men, he thought. Learning about each other, sharing an experience they can remember with pleasure when they find themselves under fire, or when they were going hand-to-hand with foreign johnnies in a conflict both necessary and righteous, before laying down their lives for victory and an honourable mention in dispatches. Things became particularly hazy for Captain Mayer when he found himself on Victoria Road and stumbled over the slippery rails of the tramway, glistening and shiny in the damp air, but decided that he must have been buffeted by a sudden gust of wind. A woman spoke to him from a doorway on Adelaide Street but he wasn't quite sure what she said. When he turned towards her, too quickly, his vison became, unexpectedly, much too fluid and he fell backwards against the wall. He really ought to be home. That was probably where the woman had gone too, because he couldn't see her. And then suddenly he found himself quite unexpectedly on Somerset Place. Best collect himself. Be the Militia captain in control. A leader of men, exuding quiet authority. Colleagues envied him that gift, he was sure.

He was fortunate that the door was still open and the hall was empty, so no one saw him walk into the newel post. Neither did anyone see him walk up the threadbare carpet on the stairs as if he was dragging his feet from dangerous quicksand that clutched at his thighs like a lover. His key seemed initially much too large, but somehow he managed to open the door to his room and he was so pleased when he closed it. He had to lean against it for a while since everything was turning around so quickly that it made his ears ache. He thought about locking the door but he had dropped his key and he could not see it anywhere. Later. He would do it later. Captain

Mayer remembered that his dog, Wellington, was in the room somewhere but he couldn't see him. He decided that the best thing he could do was light a candle – then he would be able to find him. It wasn't that dark in the room at all, but with a candle he would be able to see Wellington, for sure. The coal fire was still smouldering and he managed to light the candle from the embers and he placed it on a small chipped table near the window. He hadn't taken the dog out with him. Had he? Surely not. He picked up the candle again and took it to the bed to see if the dog was sleeping underneath, but he couldn't see him. Where was the wretched creature? He sat on the bed and started to unbutton his tunic but the buttons must have swollen whilst he was out because they seemed too big now. Start with the trousers he decided and lay back on the bed, the ceiling swirling around as he fumbled at his waistband. This had always been a tricky belt, he decided.

Wasn't Captain Tomlinson coming to collect him in the morning? Or was it Sergeant Tomlinson? Couldn't remember a damn thing, if he was honest. Was he was a corporal? Best get a bit of sleep. Couldn't have other ranks finding him not properly prepared, now could he? Did he still have that bottle of whisky? Where was it? A night cap would be nice. He started to tug at his belt once again.

*

Mr Tomlinson arrived early the next morning on the mail train. He was a solicitor in Cardiff, a humourless man with a long mournful face. He was always serious, his face permanently impassive, and he was believed by younger colleagues to have been born middle-aged. But he was never out of work; he always had cases to conduct, for whilst his colleagues found him dull, he was unwaveringly meticulous and thus popular with his clients. On this occasion he had been engaged by the landlord of the Black Lion Inn in Brecon.

Militia men taking refreshment whilst on manoeuvres had boisterously wrecked the snug of the Black Lion in the belief that they would never return and that their anonymity would grant them immunity from prosecution. Tomlinson was here to take Mayer back to the Black Lion to see if some amicable figure for compensation could be agreed, without the need for expensive court proceedings and unnecessary publicity.

But when he arrived at 7 Somerset Place and walked cautiously through the open door, he was rather alarmed by a smell of burning which seemed to pervade the whole house. No one else was around but he was sufficiently alarmed to try and find out where it was coming from. He walked upstairs, calling out 'Good morning. Captain Mayer? Good morning.' As he approached the landing, the smell of burning material was stronger and dark wisps were emerging from beneath the door of a bedroom. He shouted more loudly now. 'Fire! Fire!' and pushed opened the unlocked door to the room.

Tomlinson was horrified. The room was full of dense choking smoke, though he could see that some of the bed appeared to be on fire, before the fumes forced him to retreat. With great presence of mind, he immediately closed the door, shouting 'Fire! Fire!' even louder than before. A man, evidently dragged unhappily from his bed, with tousled hair, wearing a grubby vest and desperately tying a rope to hold up his trousers, appeared at the bottom of the stairs. 'For God's sake mun, what's all the noise by 'ere, then?' His attitude changed immediately he saw Tomlinson standing at the top of the stairs, coughing and then calling. 'Quickly! The room's on fire! Get everyone out!'

The man was happy to devote himself to rousing the other inmates of the house, whilst Tomlinson carefully wrapped a wet handkerchief around his month, entered the room and extinguished the flames with bowls of water from the washstands in the adjoining rooms. He opened the windows to disperse the smoke and, as police whistles began to sound in the street, he was able to see the dreadful scene in the room. On the floor, near the window, lay Captain Mayer, quite dead, and close by was the body of Wellington, the dog. Mayer was partially undressed. He had taken off his coat and waistcoat, and indeed had unfastened his trousers, but they were still entangled around his feet. When Doctor Rowlands later examined the body, he said that it was clear that Mayer had been dead for a few hours and Inspector Flynn, who also attended, was happy to speculate that the

285

unfortunate captain, had, for whatever reason, incautiously placed his candle on the bed, which had consequently caught fire.

'This, Doctor Rowlands, is Captain Mayer, the paymaster of the Glamorganshire Light Infantry Militia. Thirty two years old, I am told. Sad loss to the force, I am sure.' Flynn stood up straight, with his hands clasped behind his back. He could see that Doctor Rowlands, nervous and uncertain, was not well experienced, so it was his job to guide him, he decided.

'A most unexpected loss, I am sure.'

'Aye, lad. And I have to tell you that I am of the opinion,' said Flynn as he surveyed the room and noticed the overturned whisky bottle near the edge of the bed, 'that in the act of undressing, the Captain must have fallen asleep for a short time, and, when he woke up, he recognised that the room was on fire and so he tried to reach the door.' He looked at the body, still on the carpet. 'I would say, however, that in his efforts to do so, either because his feet were entangled in his trousers, or possibly from the effects of the smoke, he fell to the floor, and was unable to get up again, and was thus suffocated. How does that suit you, Doctor Rowlands?'

'Suits me fine, Inspector. I am sure you know this sort of business better than I ever will. Apart from the face and one hand being slightly scorched, there are no external marks of injury on the body. So I think we can agree that he was suffocated. The evidence of the witness and of the hostel owner would certainly support that view.'

'Absolutely. Good work, Doctor. Done well.' Flynn laid a large hand on the doctor's shoulder and gave it an encouraging squeeze. 'I shall inform the coroner immediately.'

Tomlinson had already given a statement to the Inspector and he was standing on the landing, leaning against the banister. This was most inconvenient, he thought. It made the issue about compensation far more complicated than it should have been, though of course there was always money to be made. The landlord's case was a strong one and this unfortunate death would do nothing to make it any weaker. This was a case of law, not of sentiment. There was the sound of boots outside. The Militia had arrived.

Flynn felt considerable exasperation at the amount of time they were all spending on what was, in the end, a self-inflicted tragedy. He had heard that Mayer had been drinking with soldiers and then there were naked flames, and nightcaps, by the look of things. How could anyone expect that combination to end happily? He knew that it would happen again, just as so many things happened when militiamen went to Wind Street, or indeed on manoeuvres in the hills outside Brecon. Toy Soldiers, that is what they were. The lead soldiers he had bought his nephew for Christmas were more impressive, he thought, and certainly more intelligent.

*

Constable Davies enjoyed some parts of his job. Naturally, the assiduous investigation and careful questioning that Inspector Bucke had tried valiantly to instil in the constables might not have been for him. But leaning against a doorframe and gossiping was his idea of a good day's work. The rare occasions when this produced important results was sufficient for Davies to justify the wasted hours he spent listening to shopkeepers talking about their mothers-in-law and informants offering him irrefutable evidence that Fenians were hiding in the cellar of the Mackworth Hotel . But today provided a moment that could have justified such indolence for many months to come.

Davies was on duty, happy to offer comfort to the public in Castle Square merely by his reassuring presence. He was listening with barely half an ear to Sally Solomon, the cockle seller, who claimed to know who Cosh Boy was, when he saw a man who looked vaguely familiar emerging from Pratt and Reece, the gunsmiths, on Castle Street. He looked around him, seemed to pat his left breast as if checking for something, perhaps inside a pocket, and then walked away briskly. Who was it? A bit scruffy. Dirty clothes. A peaked cap like sailors wear but much too big for him, which meant it hid a lot of his face. But there was no denying that he looked a bit familiar. He tried to remember who he had seen recently who looked like that. A wagon passed down the street and obscured his view and by the time he could see again the man had gone. Was it that man? The one with the

287

Irish name who claimed to be proper foreign? What was his name?

Davies strolled down to the shop, trying to remember. He casually raised his foot to move on a stray, emaciated dog that proceeded to snarl at him over its shoulder as it shuffled away, and then managed to put his boot down straight into the malodorous gift it had left behind. 'Oh!' he said, irritated, and, of course, the name came back to him then. O'Vitch, that was it. And they were supposed to be looking out for him. He remembered that they were not supposed to go after him on their own but Evan Davies could sense the kind of triumph that would make his mother proud and, in the hope that their shine would grant him even greater authority, he rubbed at his buttons with the cuff of his coat before entering the shop.

He was very disappointed. He had been mistaken. It wasn't O'Vitch at all. Mr Pratt showed him the register. It was another odd name, one Davies realised he had no hope of ever getting his tongue around. He looked at the letters and then looked at Mr Pratt who shrugged. 'Said he was Polish. A sailor. From Danzig he said. Nice enough, for a sailor. Buying a present for his brother, he said. Better than a bag o'cockles. I reckon.' He gestured irritably at Sally peering through the window,

'And how did he say his name, then?' asked Davies, with notebook and pencil at the ready.

'Szarmach. Least ways that is what I heard. Asked him to write it in the book for me,' said Mr Pratt defensively. 'Nothing wrong in that, is there?'

Davies shook his head. It definitely wasn't O'Vitch and he was particularly disappointed. He could have had the credit for tracking down a particularly dangerous villain. The man had given an address on Carmarthen Road and when Davis had seen him he had been heading in the wrong direction but perhaps he had more shopping to do or something.

Davies went outside and decided not to mention this back at the station. They might laugh at him again. He looked around. It was very quiet at the moment, nothing happening anywhere. He decided that he would go back to the Station House and have a little rest. It was on Caer Street, so it wasn't far away and no one would miss him for half an hour or so.

*

Still aching from the fight the night before, his shoulder tender and bruised, Bucke attended the inquest held on Alfie Woods. He had a duty to attend, to report what he knew and to respect the incomplete life of another lost Swansea child. The grandparents were there, Wyn and Maria, and he wondered when, if ever, he had seen a couple so ground down by their daily experience as the Woods. What had happened to Alfie's parents no one ever explained, but the two of them had taken on responsibility for Alfie at a time when they were finding it difficult to look after themselves. This explained why Alfie had appeared to run free, always looking for a chance – an errand, a single coin - and everything he earned he handed over to his grandmother without question. How much had he been given to lure him to the warehouse, Bucke thought? Enough, certainly. The three of them, grandson and grandparents, obviously spent all day is pursuit of whatever they could find – a penny here, a farthing there - with no plan, with no concept of the future, merely with a determination to survive today, to earn enough money for a jug of drinking water, wheeled through the streets in a cask from a clean spring in Mount Pleasant; to earn enough to buy green meat or a rotten rabbit from Mabe the butcher at the end of the day when the market was closing; for Wyn to try, and then fail, once more, to get a day's work on the docks, whilst Maria scratched away at the slag heaps for scraps of coal that would do very little to keep them warm.

It was a shocking way to live, a way of life as far removed from daily life in Sketty as it was from village life in India. What could Alfie have become if he had been given a chance, Bucke wondered? He was intelligent, resourceful and adaptable in ways that his more privileged contemporaries could never match. Yet it mattered for nothing. He was dead, murdered, and as Bucke looked into the eyes of his bewildered and grieving grandparents, he could see without doubt their future. They would die, very soon, very quickly, and within days of each other. They had given everything they had, their devotion and all their energy, to Alfie. And now that he was gone, what had been the point of any of it? They had lived on the very edge of destitution for so long, but with a purpose. Now that purpose was gone and so had their reason to live. It was a tragedy, Bucke knew it.

Doctor Benjamin had carried out the post mortem and gave his report clearly and succinctly. He estimated Alfie's age at around thirteen. He was thin, largely malnourished and the doctor confirmed that he had been strangled. There were the bruises left by adult sized fingers all over his upper body and there was that thin cord pulled horribly into his neck.

Mr Strick turned his long mournful face towards Bucke, who told him all he knew at that moment. Alfie's life meant that he was everywhere and nowhere at the same time. The constables hadn't noticed him and it seemed that no one knew anything about him loitering around the old Sugar Warehouse. Bucke reported that he had brought him information about the assailant known as Cosh Boy, but that it was his belief that a trap had been set for him by someone as yet unknown, who had attacked him, after presumably murdering Alfie to cover his tracks.

Strick shook his head at the terrible state of affairs in the town. He hoped fervently that this spate of murders of young boys would be properly resolved soon. He looked significantly at Bucke and hoped that he would at the very earliest opportunity, be able to confront the murderer here in the court.

It was a pointed comment which Bucke understood entirely. A small town and a murderer of children on the loose and the police apparently unable to do anything about it. He needed information, just one piece of information, and he would catch Cosh Boy and that is why he had gone to the Sugar Warehouse. But it hadn't been Cosh Boy waiting for him, had it?'

He stopped for a moment outside the Town Hall; the South Dock unusually quiet today and rubbed at his strained shoulder. If

Abramovitch was still in Swansea, there were so many places where he could hide. Doctor Benjamin came down the steps and stood next to him. 'These are terrible days, Inspector. Poverty, disease and death stalk the streets of the town. It cannot possibly go on. And it won't.' He turned towards Bucke and looked straight into his eyes. 'The day is coming, and it will be with us very soon, when the poor will rise up. Only then will we see true social justice in the town.'

'And you really think that this will happen? That there will be a revolution, here in Swansea?'

'Of course, Inspector. I do what I can to help the poorest children, but it is not enough. There are too many desperate people. When you look at those like the Woods, could you blame them if they were to rise up? What have they done to deserve the life they have had?'

'You must continue to help the children, Doctor. As must we all,' nodded Bucke. 'Violence has every chance of making things worse for them, not better.'

Benjamin turned on him angrily. ' What do the prosperous people know? What do people like you really know?' Bucke thought it was a ridiculous thing to say, given the nature of his work, but allowed the doctor to lecture him, for in his own eyes, Benjamin was the only one who knew the truth.

'Behind all the streets and the shops, and the comfortable homes, hidden away from sight, there are the slums. They are a disgrace, a terrible stain upon this town, a weeping cancer. People like you know nothing of them. You never go near them, not to where the poorest of the poor live, poorer than the rats that crawl through the sewers. The children are lost in filth and moral degradation, covered in festering sores. The constables only go near them in pairs, I know that for a fact, Inspector, for these are wretched places that poison and destroy the soul. Alfie died, like all the other boys died, working to support a family that should be supporting him. How many children die working in the copper works or in the mines or on the docks? Answer me that, Inspector.'

'And you think I don't know these things, Doctor? Is that what you are saying?' But Benjamin was not listening.

'There will come a time, Inspector, and it will not be long, before those bred in the squalor of those degraded streets and alleys will rise up and slay the well-to-do, who in their wealth have no thought for the poor creatures of the slums and do not see that they are rich only because so many others have nothing. It cannot go on. And it will not.' Benjamin suddenly grasped Bucke's forearm, his eyes alight with conviction. 'It is capitalism, you see. It is a system that enslaves the poor. It produces internal tensions which will eventually lead to its own destruction. Listen, Inspector, please. I have something at the school you must read, a fascinating book that will change your life, as it has changed mine. A philosophical work and it is hard going in places but certainly worth it. *Capital* it is called, by a German philosopher called Marx. It will open your eyes, Inspector, I promise you.' He turned to leave but there was another point he needed to make. He placed himself in front of him and lowered his voice. 'Listen carefully to my words, Inspector. The day will come when you and every other policeman will not be seen as the enforcers of law and order as you believe, but rather as the protectors of an unjust system, designed entirely to exploit and suppress the poor. There will be a revolution, I am sure of it, and you must think carefully about which side you will be on when it happens. Come up to the school, Inspector and I can show you the book. I read it most nights and it has changed my life.'

Bucke smiled to himself and remembered the last time he had been asked which side he would be on, when the world as he knew it started to fall apart. The Church of Our Lady of Mumbles, and that hadn't ended well at all. He watched the doctor walking away, a man of passion and conviction. Perhaps it was good to feel so strongly about these things. His ideas gave him a purpose to his life and his mission amongst the children in the town was so very important. He tended the sick, often without charge and raised money constantly to keep the school open and to feed its children. Bucke wondered however how far he would be prepared to go in his support of them.

Twenty Four

When Amy went missing on Saturday, Sarah was terrified, though she tried her very best not to display her overwhelming panic, as if by suppressing it she could prevent it from disabling her completely. What had happened to Amy? Had someone taken her? Had the child-murderer returned, this time for a girl?

She had to remain calm; she had to assess things carefully. Would Amy voluntarily run away? That did not seem likely. Had they argued about anything? No, not at all. Amy was a particularly devoted and dutiful child. Had she shown any desire to return to her old life? That seemed unlikely, too. Would she have just abandoned her pram and her doll like that? Of course not. So, as she told Inspector Bucke, the inevitably disturbing conclusion was that she had been taken, which in its turn raised so many other questions in a town as anxious and fearful about its children as Swansea was.

Bucke was absolutely sure who had her, though he decided not to tell Sarah. Abramovitch was here to obtain a child and it seemed that he had found what he was looking for. Sergeant Ball deployed as many constables as he could spare to look for her, to ask questions. Sarah walked the streets too, trying to convince herself that when she returned to Elephant Court, Amy would be there waiting for her. She asked the children at The Ragged School on Monday, but no one had seen her at all. Myra Kealey had been waiting for her to call and there was nothing to suggest that Amy had planned to disappear. The children were frightened and excited at the same time. They were eager to abandon school to look for her, afraid that she had fallen or was trapped somewhere. Perhaps she was lost, one of them suggested, but Amy knew the streets of Swansea better than most. The haunting fear of the child murderer could not be so easily dismissed, by anyone.

On Saturday morning, Amy had gone out to play. She was going to call for Myra, for it was time for another Dolls Day Out, though she also really wanted to see if Black Bart would allow her to push him around in the pram. She doubted it, but it might be worth a try, if she could catch him. She had promised Sarah faithfully that she would be home when she heard the clock strike twelve. She enjoyed counting up to twelve and when she got home she was going to practice her reading in the afternoon, to maintain the excellent progress she had made in such a short time.

Sarah had not been initially concerned when she didn't come home on time. Perhaps the two friends were both wrapped up too deeply in the game they were playing. But by 2.00 pm she was walking around the town and by 4.00 pm she was sitting in the police station.

She hadn't found anyone who had seen her. Amy had said that she was going to Myra's house but the Kealey's hadn't seen her. Myra was particularly disappointed because Amy had promised to show her that their names contained the same letters. So it seemed that she had disappeared somewhere between Elephant Court and Greenhill.

On Sunday, feeling alone, bereft and extremely tearful, Sarah did the journey repeatedly, trying different routes. And then, in the St John's graveyard, behind a memorial, gaunt and shattered like a broken tooth, she found the pram. Amy would never have left it behind, not with the ribbons still attached and, more importantly, with Sarah Dolly still inside. Someone must have taken her. She pushed the pram to the police station where she presented it as evidence, then left immediately, for she had no desire to talk to Sergeant Ball and exchange with him happy memories of her abandoned life.

She hurried home, walking quickly up the stairs, past Jack, not wishing to talk to him. Sarah did not feel that she wanted to acknowledge him, let alone confide in him. For his part, he seemed reluctant to acknowledge her too, and ran down the stairs, taking less care than would normally be recommended. Then after pacing around the lonely room for ten minutes with the rescued doll in her arms, she felt she couldn't stay there any longer. She needed to do something, anything, to persuade herself that she was actively looking for Amy. Walking the streets had to be better than waiting, and so she walked for hours, fruitlessly and alone, deceived by fate. How could she have been so presumptuous to have considered that happiness and fulfilment could ever be hers? After all those grim years? Eventually, exhausted and forlorn, she went to see Constance and sat on the piano stool and wept.

*

Amy sat sullenly in the corner of the room, the cold from the dirt floor seeping slowly into her bones. She was tethered to the window frame by a long piece of grubby rope and, try as she might, she would never unpick the knots that held her. The rope had been carefully attached to a broad leather bracelet which, in its turn had been stitched together to tightly circle her wrist. She did know where she was, though. She was in Mariner Street, in the house outside of which she had once seen the two women who had snatched her, bullying a soldier. Jack McCarthy had just turned up too, the man who lived on the other side of the stairs. She did not like any of these people. The man especially, because he wouldn't let her look out of the window and had made her sit on the cold floor, but it was the other man who bothered her most of all, because he said that he was her father.

She had seen him before, too. At Riley's Clothes Cart and at the school, but he had looked different then. Now his clothes did not seem to be so clean. He didn't look like a toff any more. He was ordinary and his face was dirty. Amy remembered him looking at her. She didn't like him at all and she thought that was odd, because she had always thought it would have been nice to have a father, but not this man. This man told lies.

'Look at me very carefully,' he said. 'I repeat. You are my daughter. I am your father. You have forgotten, but it is true.'

If he was a nice man he would not have let Vinegar and Milford steal her from Sarah and then keep her here. Sarah was her best friend ever and looked after her all the time, like no one else ever could. She refused to reply. This could not be her father. He was lying, she knew that he was.

He held out a doll to her. 'You love this doll. This is true. I know that it is. It was your favourite. You had one that is just the same. Think about it. You will remember. We called them your twins.

Perhaps you have lost the other one I gave you to keep safely. It does not matter. You have others at home.'

She put her head down. If he was her father, why had he given her to these two women? They had tied her to the window and that was very cruel. If he really was her father he would stop that, straightaway. Wouldn't he? And anyway, how could this doll be better than Sarah Dolly? How could anyone think that was possible? This one was thin and floppy and the legs looked as if they were about to fall off. She wasn't going to look at it.

'Do you remember your name? You are Chana. Think. Remember.'

'I am Amy,' she said defiantly.

Abramovitch smiled. 'But before, you were Chana. You lived in a big house, far away. With me.'

He was wrong. Why was he saying these things? She had never lived in a big house. 'I didn't. I lived with Auntie in a shed and now Sarah is my best friend.'

'We are wasting time,' interrupted Jack. 'Does it matter who she is? Do you want her or not?' He pulled her up and dragged her dress from side to side to expose her shoulders. 'Look. Marks on her shoulder, like you said. I can't do no better than this. Girl. Scars. Right age, just about. Available.'

Abramovitch ignored him and instead grasped Amy's hands. She tried to pull them out but he was too strong. 'Think carefully. When you came here, to Swansea, on the ship, you had a bright shiny jewel and two pieces of wood with some paper wrapped around them.' Amy shook her head. 'Yes, you did. What happened to them? I want them.'

'I have never been on no ship. I want to go back to Sarah, she is my friend.'

Smiling, Abramovitch turned to McCarthy. 'This is the girl. I am sure of it. She just needs help with what she remembers. She looks so much like her blessed mother.' He stroked her cheek and Amy pulled away. 'I shall take her. What is your fee?' McCarthy shrugged, refusing to commit himself. 'The heftel and the scroll are not so much a problem. It is the child that I need. This is the daughter. It is very clear to me. This is Chana.' His smile was like a knife. 'Thank you, Jack. I shall get you the money.'

'I want £25.'

Abramovitch laughed. 'I see. I give you £20.'

Jack considered. 'I will take £23. But I want £5 of it now.'

'Of course, my friend. Goodwill is so important to me.' He threw a small purse to Jack. 'Here. The rest you get when you give Chana to me. I do not want her yet. She is happy here, I think. I will get the money very soon. £17, I think. I will send you a message.'

'That should be £18, I think.'

'Ah yes. My mistake.' He shrugged. 'It is a great deal of money, Jack.'

'But not to a man who wants to get his daughter back.' Abramovitch seemed happy with it though, and that worried Jack a little. Perhaps he should have asked for more. 'What are you going to do with her? Not that it is any of my business, Mr Abramovitch.'

'My name is Szarmach, Mr McCarthy. I am a sailor from Danzig. In Poland.'

'That's not what the newspaper says. Is it? Your name was all over it.'

'How do any of us know what is true? You can tell the newspapers anything, Mr McCarthy. Do not trouble yourself. They sell words in ink on paper. They do not sell the truth.' He looked round the room, as if addressing a meeting. 'Look at me now. Look at my clothes. I am the sailor, Szarmach. Or I am Abramovitch. Or am someone else.' He smiled again. The more he smiled, the more alarming it appeared. 'I will take the girl home with me. She is the daughter I seek. She is a great heiress and I shall teach her to be Chana once again.' he smiled. 'For a short time, I think. There is much sickness in my country.

297

There are swamps. We have many diseases. Children, they die. And then her inheritance? Well, a man must be ready to accept his responsibilities.'

Jack was convinced now that he should have charged more.

Abramovitch pulled a cloth from his pocket and unwrapped it. Inside there was a large pendant. 'You can do so many things with glass these days, do you not agree, Jack? Chana, think carefully. Do you remember bringing something like this with you on the ship? It is so beautiful, isn't it?'

It caught the inadequate dim light in the dismal room and reflected it in so many different colours. There was green, blue and a striking red. Amy could not take her eyes away from it. But she knew she had never seen it before.

Jack looked at him carefully. 'I don't think you are her father at all. I mean, let's be honest. If she was your daughter, then you would be the heir or whatever to this estate of yours, not her. You would come first, now wouldn't you? Not her. Not your child.'

He shrugged. 'My country is strange, Jack. This girl is the daughter, Chana. The one I have been seeking. How I love her.' He smiled, and rubbed his hands down the greasy fabric of his trousers.

Amy wasn't following this very well and was confused. She was a child - her words were not as well developed as her instincts – but she knew beyond anything else, that all this was wrong. He said he was talking about her and about what she used to be, but she knew it wasn't her at all. And if he was her father, then she should feel something about him, shouldn't she?' If he was her father would she have found him so unpleasant? If he was her father why did she think he was a stranger? Why was he a toff one day and then a dirty sailor the next? Those weeks she had spent with Sarah were starting to feel like a dream. Such happiness wasn't intended for her. It belonged to others. Now she was the old Amy again. The proper Amy. Wary, hesitant, suspicious. It would be better, she decided, not to say anything. Family? What was he talking about? She tried to step back as he bent down again and held her forearms but she could not pull herself away.

'You will come with me, Chana. Everyone has missed you very much. They talk of nothing else. Five long years you have been away. We have a long way to go, on a train perhaps, or a boat and then a train. But we will have plenty of time together, so that I can remind you who you are. Because you are Chana. You are a princess. So many dolls will be yours. We have suffered so much without you, but finally we shall be back together.'

'I like Sarah.' She couldn't stop herself.

'Sarah is nice sometimes, Chana, but not all the time. I know her. You didn't know that, did you? But I do know her. I went to see her this morning and she said she didn't want to see you again because you belong to me and she doesn't like you.' He bowed his head slightly, as if in apology.

He was lying, she knew it. 'I like Auntie too.'

'But at home you have so many aunties. So many. This auntie of yours was kind, was she? Well, we shall reward her too. How do you like that? She must have been a very good friend. But not Sarah. Oh no. She was very cruel. She said she didn't want you anymore.' He picked up his large cap from the table and appeared to study something inside it.

He was lying, she was sure. What he was saying didn't make any sense. When was she cruel? Never. Amy said nothing, biting her tongue. She wished she had never said anything. She looked into the corner of the heartless room, as if looking for some impression, some vision, of this lost life he spoke about, full of aunts and treasure, but she could find no trace of it. There was just a battered rag doll, its limbs barely connected, about which she felt nothing at all.

Jack picked her up roughly and put her on a chair. 'So we are agreed. She stays here – or somewhere else – until I have the money. Prevents any misunderstandings, in my opinion. Don't you think? She ain't yours, I am sure of that. You are not fooling me. But you want the girl, so she is yours. But only when you have settled the bill.' Jack looked at the heftel as he wrapped it up. 'Will you use that thing of

299

yours to raise the money?'

Abramovitch shook his head. 'With the heftel, Chana claims the inheritance. The estates and the vineyards, the railway, all those things that are ours by right. The heftel proves who Chana is. It is a valuable thing, it is rubies and diamonds and garnets and it shines, full of light and promises. It is an object of beauty, as you can see. But what it represents is more. It is her inheritance and it is the proof that is needed that she is Chana. Her inheritance is the richest part of our kingdom. And I should have it, for it is mine. And it is Chana's, in addition.' he added, as an afterthought. 'She inherits much wealth with this heftel, but if disease should take her... As I say, life in Romania can be so fragile.' He added, without expression.

Jack was barely following what Abramovitch was saying, his eyes drawn to the pendant. 'Valuable then, you say, this jewel thing?'

Abramovitch smiled. 'Of course, Jack. But I am not a fool. This has been considered. There is no honour amongst people like ourselves, as well we both know. And so I have had a copy made. Of glass, Jack,' he smiled. 'So no good for you to steal this thing from me. It is a cheap copy, but it will be sufficient, because it will be enough to prove that Chana is the one. Who knows what has happened to the real one? Perhaps you might look for it here in Swansea. You may be lucky.'

Jack had no idea of when Abramovitch was telling the truth. Was this really a copy? Or was it the real one and he was trying to trick him?

He continued. 'But when I return to Romania, I say to them all. It has always been like this. Did you not know? So strange. For it has always been made of glass. It is a symbol, it is not a jewel, it was never precious. And so it will be true enough, if people believe it. Just like the girl. If they believe she is Chana, then that is who she will be. Do you see that, Jack? It does not matter what is true. What matters is what people believe. They are different things. And I will make them believe. And so Jack, I will take this girl of yours and I will make sure that everyone understands she is Chana, I told you. And if the child should die without an heir, then the estates of the Abramovitch family will pass to a faithful relative.' He stopped. Perhaps he had said too much? Did it matter what this man thought he knew? He smiled a twisted, cold-eyed smile.

Jack suddenly thought he understood what Abramovitch was doing, if that is who he was. It didn't matter whether Amy was the right child or not. Everything he had done, that Jack knew about anyway, like the newspaper and his presence around the town, was to ensure that there wasn't a right child anymore. The right child had not emerged, despite all the noise he had made at a time when the young seemed under threat and, as far as this man was concerned, whoever he was, that was obviously good enough. He knew that there was no evidence to show that Amy wasn't Chana. And he could actually create evidence that would prove she was. Jack was interested in how he operated, that was all. The games that he was playing were interesting. But Jack didn't actually care what they were.

'Whatever you say. I'll bring her to the Vaults on Saturday night and we can carry out the exchange then, when you have the notes. But don't you do nothing funny, like. Won't work with me, Mr Abramovitch.'

'My name is Szarmach, Jack. I am a sailor. I come from Poland. I told you.'

'Whatever you say, Mr Abramovitch.'

He smiled. 'And how do you know my name is Abramovitch? I asl you before. Which one, my friend, is a lie? Abramovitch? Szarmach? Or something else? Is the heftel glass? Or real?'

'Turn up with the notes, that is all. I don't have time for your games.'

'And if I don't?'

McCarthy gestured towards Amy. 'This one will be in the North Dock. She knows who I am.'

'And?' Abramovitch replied. 'This should concern me, you think?'

'Got something in common then, haven't we? I don't care neither.'

Amy heard. At school one of the boys said that was what happened to her brother last year. She was determined that it wasn't going to happen to her. But the rope attached to her wrist she could not budge, and the red mark the bracelet had caused was very sore.

Jack scratched his head. 'You are trying to play games with me, mate, and I don't like being messed with. This ain't your daughter. I know that for sure.'

Abramovitch smiled. 'She will suffice. She has lived here for enough years and no one knows who she is. So she can be Chana, for as long as she needs to be.' He was pleased with himself. He liked playing his deceitful games. 'And do you know? I have always thought that sometimes it is better to be an uncle. Don't you think so? All the pleasure and none of the work.'

*

When the men had gone, Bridget and Selina did their best to cheer up Amy, though they did not release the rope that tied her to the window frame.

'Now come on, missy,' said Selina. 'There is no reason to be glum. That gent, what's his name? Starmack or some such,? He says you are a princess and that. Wish I was a princess. Got to be better than this,' she said, gesturing vaguely at this desolate room, as if she too had once had something so much better that had been her birth-right and which had been stolen from her. 'What do you think, Bridge?'

Bridget pulled up her skirt and scratched her thigh. ' I mean, I don't think he is your Dad, if I think about it, but he seems nice enough to me and that is a lovely bit of jewellery he has got that he says is yours. Bet there is plenty more like that where you are going.'

'And the doll,' added Selina.

'Mustn't forget the doll, must we?' Bridget picked something out of her hair and threw it on the floor.

'I want to see Sarah,' said Amy, defiantly, sitting cross legged on the dirty floor.

'I am sure you do, my lovely. We knows Sarah, don't we, Sel? Nice old stick is Sarah. Known her years, we have. I mean we can't let you go. Jack would likely be very cross and you wouldn't want that, now would you? But we can have a word with her, can't we, Sel? Don't cry. It's not so bad, is it? You being a princess. You will have all airs and graces, you watch. Born lucky you is, I reckon.'

'I want to go back to Sarah.' Amy was trying to be brave but her defiance did nothing to lift the misery from her.

'Tell you what we will do.' Selina crouched down before her. 'I shall go and have a word, on the quiet, like. Tell her you are not in no danger, tell her that she is not to worry, Can't say fairer than that, now can I?'

'But I want to see her, now. I don't like sleeping on my own. Sarah holds me tight.'

Bridget was running out of patience. 'Well none of us can have everything, can we?'

'I can take the rope off you for a bit,' soothed Selina, 'if you promise, with no word of a lie, that your ain't going to do no running away.'

'No. I want to go back to Sarah.'

'Problem that is, isn't it?' Selina shook her head. 'Let's see if you feels any different tomorrow, shall we? Have a drink of water.'

Twenty Five

The *SS Polaria* came in on the tide early on Wednesday and Inspector Bucke was there, along with two constables and hundreds of spectators, to watch its arrival. It was only its second journey and it still carried into Swansea a sense of excitement and novelty. The ship was sleek, modern, still shiny and the steam tug, *Cruiser,* respectfully edged it slowly and precisely into its berth in the South Dock.

Bucke could not deny that this was an impressive sight, an iron steamer built in Newcastle for the Cambrian Line, 300 feet long, two masts with their fascinating tangle of ropes and its black funnel, now quiet, only barely tarnished and with a broad white band shining brightly in the morning sun. This was an emigrant ship from Hamburg and it was lined with people sailing to America for a new life. There were over seven hundred people on board, from Germany, Eastern Europe and Russia, and that was why Bucke was there, for their presence in town would bring with it complications he would have to manage. The *Polaria* would be here until Saturday whilst it loaded a cargo of tinplate and 850 tons of coal and Bucke knew that it would be the last chance for the emigrants to feel dry land beneath their feet before they spent two weeks on the Atlantic. There might be excitements.

Now resident in the South Dock, Swansea had a new international village, which had the fascination of strangers speaking exotic languages previously unheard in the town, strangers who might be innocent and inexperienced and ready to be fleeced. Bucke spent a great deal of his time dealing with foreign sailors, always so excited to be in the town after dangerous weeks at sea. But this was different. These were ordinary people running towards a dream – or running away from a nightmare – who might never have left their small home village before, wherever that might be. They had boarded the ship in Hamburg for a new world, but Swansea would be the first place they would see after they travelled towards a new life.

He looked along the quayside. He could see too many familiar faces for his liking, all too ready to help the excited but apprehensive passengers looking down from the deck, to offer guidance, commodities and services. He saw Vinegar Bridget and Milford, up early to offer to sailors the kind of comfort that only they could provide and advertising themselves with bright umbrellas. Young boys, probably part of the Hat Stand Gang, were on the prowl for all opportunities, eyes flickering in their search for unguarded items. A small market had already sprung up on the quay. Riley, Mrs Raatz and Isaac Siedle all selling second – hand clothes and shoes, ideal for Atlantic storms, or so they claimed. Mrs Raatz, however, had an advantage and was already shouting out loudly at the passengers, in what Bucke presumed was Yiddish. Dai Potato was there with his cart; he must have lit his oven very early and the warm smell of those earthy delights drifted insidiously along the quay and up on to deck. Haynes the Baker was there too, with a tray of pies, for the food in steerage was notoriously spartan. A seedy-looking man who Bucke did not recognise, with a dirty flat cap rammed on his head and a shabby jacket held together by a single, oversized, button, was sitting on a stained barrel, offering currency exchange.

The *Polaria* kissed the side of the quay and then stilled itself. Those involved in its manoeuvring were very skilled and Swansea's finest gangways, sturdy and canvas-sided, were attached in an instant. Soon a surge of men forced their excited way down on to the quayside; it was early in the morning and there was an unfamiliar town to be explored. After that first rush had descended into the embrace of the temporary market, Bucke walked politely up on to the ship, smiling, nodding, raising his cap to those stragglers leaving for the town after that first impatient surge. He watched the crew hurrying around, opening portholes and hatches to encourage a flow of air to release the smell of all those bodies crammed closely together down in the darkness of steerage. How brave these people were he thought. Ready to sacrifice everything for the hope of a better life in a country far away about which they knew so very little. Everything packed away in a single battered trunk, with the address of their second-cousin in New York scribbled on a scrap of newspaper representing their dream of a better life.

Bucke was fascinated by it all, by all these remarkable human stories contained within this one ship but, for now, his presence here was a matter of business. He had come to see Captain Winckler.

They had met before, when the *Polaria* had docked in Swansea on its first voyage, and Bucke had warmed to him from the first moment. Winckler was a tall man and particularly dignified, with a grey nautical beard and sharp blue eyes, which held an obvious sympathy for his passengers, many of whom, he knew, had experienced anguish and tragedy before they had arrived in his care. He respected their courage and they, in turn, responded to his natural authority. In that small, fragile, sea-borne community, his authority was absolute and he exercised it with tolerance. His striking uniform of dark blue cloth with gold lace trimmings was the perfect expression of his position and a symbol that had already steadied and then quelled disputes in his ethnically-diverse floating village. He was waiting for Bucke on the bridge and greeted him warmly. They stood together, looking down at the deck where daily life continued amongst those not going ashore. Washing, talking, praying, eating, staring. Some were reading, others seemed to be asleep. Mothers fed their babies, children played. It really was like a village, and one that contained so many diverse elements.

'Of course, Inspector Bucke, as you know, I am happy to accept those of your town who wish to come aboard our ship as visitors and to see, if only for the briefest moment, the diversity of people that we carry across the ocean. It is a remarkable thing that we do. But please, Inspector, I can assure you. I am ready to deal with stowaways. I have been at sea for many years now. They would eat our food and do nothing in return, so I do not want them. There are no spaces on the *Polaria* for more stokers or firemen or maids, whatever made-up skills they claim to possess. All stowaways we will find, and then put them ashore at our convenience, not theirs. I can tell you that I have a small number of places for paying passengers, but I must insist on cash; I will not accept promises. None of this is your problem, but I tell you so that we can understand each other. I shall, quite naturally, return your ruffians to you. When you find any of mine then I am very happy for you to keep them too.' Winckler inclined his head and smiled. 'For some of them, your cells will provide better accommodation than the homes they have left behind.'

Together they watched as early visitors were greeted courteously and taken on brief tours. Bucke also saw an impromptu meeting which seemed to be taking place on the deck, where a man he thought he recognised, together with a thin woman, was waving a piece of paper emphatically. The sailors in front of him appeared unmoved.

'I have told them all, Inspector Bucke, as clearly as I can. But naturally with the number of different languages we have on board, it is impossible for me. I must rely upon the passengers translating for each other – and sometimes they do not do it very well.' He lifted his hat and scratched the top of a forehead so deeply lined, it seemed to be decorated with stray lengths of rigging. 'But I have told them all, I promise you. The *Polaria* does not wait. We sail on Saturday evening. If they are in the cells of the police station, no matter what their misdemeanour, we do not wait. We sail.' He extended his hands, palms up. 'Only a fool would say that there will be no difficulties of course, on your side and on ours. But I tell them. This is your town and they must follow your rules. They walk, they feel the ground, they are a long way from home and of course now perhaps they do not even have a home. Many of them do not sail before, or even leave their village. And for some they are nervous and do not want to leave the ship, for now it is their home. But others are greatly excited. And I tell them. Stay close to the ship and guard your money, for I sail on Saturday. It is clear to me that sometimes they do not know life in towns or life in seaports. They live in a small village until the trouble came, whatever it was. And now they are at loose in the world.' Winckler sighed.' There are times when this is like taking many children on a journey who cannot look straight ahead but are always looking to the side.'

Winckler handed over a small sum of money with which to reimburse shop keepers for the inevitable petty pilfering that would occur with people who might be bewildered by a different currency and an unfamiliar range of shops. 'If you do not need it, then please keep it for next time,' he smiled.

'I suspect I shall need it,' Bucke replied. Captain Winckler would be visiting Swansea regularly and these visits needed as much good will as they could both establish. Bucke was pleased to hear that Winckler intended to stay on board to supervise the loading, for then the ship itself would be one less thing he needed to concern himself with and he would be a reassuring presence for any new crew members, who would always know where to find him if they experienced any misadventures of their own in Swansea.

He told the captain that he hoped they would one day take a drink together. Winkler shook his hand. 'Of course, that would be a pleasure. If you can return, perhaps tomorrow or Friday, I have some excellent coffee here on the *Polaria*. I do not appreciate alcohol on my ship, when we are doing work such as this. Too many troubles.'

'If I do come back, Captain Winckler, it will be because your visit will be progressing smoothly.'

'Well then, let us hope that I do see you. I have some stories I am sure you would find most interesting, Inspector.'

'That would be a great pleasure. I hope that your visits to Swansea don't give you too many new stories with which to entertain any future visitors.' Bucke was sure that together they could manage the visit successfully. He understood why Burgess and Co. of the Exchange Buildings and other local businesses were eager for the *Polaria* to call regularly, and knew they believed that it was his responsibility to make sure there was no interruption to either their trade or their profit. But he also recognised that Swansea was still a deeply unsettled town, disturbed by the murders of children and women. The racial tension potentially to be introduced by the *Polaria* was the last thing that Bucke needed at the moment. But he was more confident than he had been before, that his constables would be able to deal with it.

He asked Captain Winckler to be vigilant and inform him immediately if a man with a child, perhaps eight years old, tried to come aboard. He might acquire a woman who would pretend to be his wife, That was always a possibility. But it was the man who he was interested in. He thought he was more likely to try and pay for a crossing, rather than stowaway, particularly if he did arrive with others, but you could never tell. Winckler listened carefully and then nodded. He didn't need to be given a reason and for his part, Bucke knew that he could trust him.

As he left to return to his duties on dry land, Bucke paused on the deck to listen to English voices which seemed out of place in the bewildering mix of languages on the ship. He watched the first mate, a compact, impassive man called Overath, pretending to be the captain, whilst the two people who he now recognised as the musical entertainers, Minx and Stinx, tried to negotiate their way on board.

'My dear boy, there has been a dreadful misunderstanding. Wholly understandable, without doubt. I certainly don't blame you. These things happen, of course. All the time.' Stinx waved a piece of paper, which had already been deemed to be inadequate. 'You are doing your best, of course you are. Who could say otherwise? It is just that it is so damn confusing, I know that, of course I do. And irritating. I am sure you don't mind me saying.'

Overath said nothing.

'I say, old chap, you are following all this, aren't you?' There was a hint of anxiety creeping into his voice.

The German officer still chose not to speak.

'You see, this is quite straightforward, Captain. One's money-man has been known to be a touch tardy, don't you know? Irritating at times, if I am allowed to speak honestly. It has happened before with these blessed banker's draft things. I do apologise.' He looked dismissively at the piece of paper in his hand. 'Seems to me, and of course I am not a bean-counter myself obviously, heaven forbid,' he laughed but still elicited no response. 'But you see, it appears that he has not provided me with a proper piece of paper, merely the draft of a draft as I understand it, as I am sure you are aware yourself.'

Stinx smiled rather desperately and looked around, nodding at Minx, who said nothing and averted her eyes. 'Quite obvious, if you look at it carefully. Should have noticed, of course. My fault entirely. Not a man for paperwork, myself. You see, he employs his nephew. Bit of a favour I imagine but he's not terribly sharp. That is what has happened, I can see it clearly. I will get it rectified at the very soonest, you can trust me. It is just a piece of paper, after all. So if my wife and I could leave our luggage in our cabin, I will go and get the bankers draft immediately. Back straight away. Shouldn't be an issue. Have to go there anyway to tell the bank to transfer my dear wife's inheritance to America. You do have a private cabin for my wife and myself don't you? Poor Dora. Has issues with her chest. A martyr in my view. Can't share accommodation. Sure you understand. Not fair on the others. Infections, that sort of thing.' He nodded wisely and smiled patronisingly. Bucke was fascinated by such insubstantial bravado.

Overath decided finally to speak. 'I need money. Not a piece of paper. Money. You do not have money.' By the merest inclination of his head he indicated to two deckhands that it time for the visitors to leave. Stinx did not catch on immediately, convinced by his own powers of persuasion, but his self-belief quickly dissolved like a morning frost in the sunshine.

Bucke heard him ask loudly and foolishly, 'Don't you know who I am?' The only possible answer was that they did not and that was the most desperate truth of all, for no one knew who Stinx was. He knew Stinx as a second-rate music hall entertainer who would forever be a nobody, trying always to convince himself that he was a somebody. Bucke watched him bundled easily down the gangway, still shouting loudly over his shoulder to Overath, offering to entertain the passengers – two shows a day, evening and matinee – in return for a private cabin, and by the time he reached the dock he was ready to perform merely for a place in steerage. Minx displayed rather more dignity and walked steadily down to the quay, leaving behind her the only means of escape she would ever have and knowing too, that the *Polaria* represented an escape that would never be hers.

As Bucke walked back through the town he saw clumps of emigrants gathered together on street corners, wondering what to do. Some of the younger passengers were very excited by the freedom that Swansea offered to them. They had been on board ship for a short time only and there was a much longer stage of their journey to come, but they were aware that they had already left their old life behind them. Now they were Citizens of the World, mature and experienced travellers with the wisdom that had previously eluded them, until they put to sea on Saturday evening.

As both Bucke and Winckler had anticipated, the rest of the day gave some of them ample opportunity to show that they believed they had a licence for the kind of behaviour they had never previously embraced. They giggled together, looked for drink, laughing at the grey and tired people of Swansea. They hired cabs and were over-charged for trips around the town. They marvelled at how black some of the buildings were, coughed exaggeratedly in the smoke that wafted into their faces and ate exotic food like pasties and cockles. There were the occasional fights and scuffles with local boys looking to prove themselves, who were absolutely convinced that everything that was said in Polish or German or Yiddish was a calculated insult, designed to undermine their manhood; sometimes it was.

The constables had already been encouraged not to over-react and Bucke had urged them to keep the peace whilst minimising arrests, though of course, if any of them were themselves assaulted there was no possibility that it would be ignored. It troubled Bucke that at some point, either now or on a future visit, a *Polonia* passenger would be gaoled for the stupid drunken moment and the ship would depart without him and there was nothing that Bucke could do to prevent it. Where would such a thing lead, he wondered? Vagrancy? Crime? His money, perhaps his life savings or borrowed from a money lender, would have been spent on a passage that he had now lost. He would emerge from gaol, no matter how short a period of time it might be, penniless and homeless in a foreign country where he could speak little, if any, of the language. It was an alarming prospect, yet human nature being what it was, it was inevitable.

*

Constance was hurrying home as quickly as she could, taking a route that would avoid the groups of emigrants standing outside pubs. She had been out to Mumbles along the tramway to see Mathilde Barree, who had given up her house on Cradock Street and moved out to Thistleboon to try and set herself up as a teacher of dance and

311

deportment. She had to do something to support herself after her husband's disgrace. Whether there was sufficient demand for lessons in deportment in Mumbles was something that Constance doubted, but perhaps it represented something more important, a sign that she was taking the initiative and trying to order her life and her future. Constance knew from her own experience that this was an important decision.

Elodie had been there too, so it had been quite a sociable evening, even if Mathilde had never been the easiest company at the best of times. Elodie was full of gossip about her engagement to Fred Goodman at Singleton Abbey and their wedding preparations, though she had one particular irritation which had almost derailed the plans completely. And now Constance was rushing home, for she had arranged to meet Rumsey briefly there as he passed by, monitoring all those passengers ashore from the emigrant ship. She needed firstly to reassure him of her safe return and then, secondly, to tell him what she had heard.

Elodie's fiancé, Frederick, who, in Constance's considered opinion, was nowhere near good enough for her, was an enthusiastic collector of those Parisian *cartes de visite* she had seen at the houses of Cyrus Bishop and of Barree himself. Fred had made the mistake of showing them to Elodie, in the expectation, perhaps, that it might encourage her to review the contents of her wardrobe. Only a very stupid man would think that might happen, thought Constance.

Elodie wanted to know where he got them from. And so he told her, as he threw them one at a time on to the fire; Jack McCarthy. 'They were such a silly thing,' Elodie said, shaking her head in disapproval. 'But you can be sure that he will be buying no more of them.' Constance didn't recognise the name but she knew that Rumsey needed to know it. She was sure it would mean something to him.

She had got down from the tram on Oystermouth Road to walk down Richardson Street and, as she crossed Oxford Street, she glanced casually to the right towards the Agricultural Hall. In the gloomy light of a gas lamp a few yards away from her, she saw a man with his hand raised, ready to strike at the slumped figure of a woman, her hands on her knees. Obviously he had already hit her at least once and was so locked into his moment of triumph, so lost in his ecstasy of violence and obscenities, that he did not know that Constance was behind him. There was no time for thought. Constance fumbled with her umbrella but it slipped through her hands and it dropped to the floor. She had no time to pick it up so she reached around his neck, pushing her fingers into his nostrils and then pulled him backwards.

It was so unexpected and so painful that he could not resist and the man fell, his arms flailing, and knocking past Constance, hit the floor with a considerable thump. She looked around for her umbrella, with which to hit him again, but she couldn't find it, so she kicked him in the ribs, a little ineffectually since she was hampered by her heavy skirt. She put her fingers in her mouth and whistled; there was an unpleasant taste on one of them but this was not the time to be fastidious. She had learned to whistle like that from her daughter, Agnes, never realising at the time how useful a skill it would one day become. She whistled again, a little louder. She knew it wasn't a police whistle but she hoped it was shrill enough. She kicked the man again, who rolled away and dragged himself to his feet. She was sure he must be Cosh Boy and stared at him, wondering what he would do. She whistled again, though her mouth was suddenly dry with fear and the sound was feeble.

The man realised that he had to run. He didn't have time to deal with either of the women in case the police arrived quickly. Why one of them had possession of a police whistle was a puzzle to him. He glared at Constance and then wiped away blood from his nose. 'Bitch!' he shouted viciously. He had been lying on the umbrella and Constance picked it up. It was broken, the spines bent. She could hit him with it though, and she brandished it above her head.

He turned away from her and walked straight into the other woman, who slapped him across the face, a resounding impact that echoed off the walls like a slamming door. 'You devil!' She grabbed at his jacket to restrain him but he backed away and, as the umbrella came down sharply upon his head, he pulled himself free and ran away along Oxford Street into the darkness.

'Thank you, missus. You saved me,' said the woman.

'Think nothing of it,' said Constance, wiping her fingers discreetly on her dress.

'We was so close to catching the bastard too. But I reckon you saved my life. Not that there is many as reckon its worth saving, but it means something to me. My head don't half hurt though.' She touched an ugly weal above her left eye. 'I'll look a hell of a state. Not good for business, either.' She looked more closely at Constance. 'I know who you are. Ain't you that piano teacher? Rumsey Bucke's fancy woman?' Constance smiled in the gloom and nodded. 'Lucky cow. He is a decent sort he is. You don't want to be letting go of him, now do you?'

'I have no intention of ever letting him go, Miss…'

'Eliza, I am. Eliza Keast. Your Rumsey knows me, don't you doubt it. Here, I has got a present for him. Just the thing, for a clever sort like him.' She held out her fist which she then opened dramatically; she was pleased with herself. There, in the palm of her hand, was a brass button. 'Pulled it off the bugger's coat, didn't I? Not sewn on proper or I would have had the bastard. Looks like a soldier's button, I reckon. You tell your Rumsey that, my love.'

There was the sound of police boots approaching from town. 'About time too.' She turned towards them. 'Where the hell have you been then? Oh no, it's you,' she said to the policeman as he came close to them. 'Constable Smith. PC 43. I should have guessed. Always late, this one.' She looked conspiratorially at Constance. 'Won't get much sense, either. Now you listen up to me, young Smithy. We had Cosh Boy here, we did, me and this lady, and she is a lady, so you best shape up or there will be trouble. You could have had him too, if you had got your arse here in time. Look at the state of my head.'

'For goodness sake, Eliza. What nonsense are you talking now, eh?'

'Where's me nose warmer?' Eliza produced a stubby pipe from a pocket on a skirt. 'I reckon I am gonna need it. Now you listen to me, Smithy…'

Twenty Six

It was, unquestionably, a fine day for soldiery. Notwithstanding the sad circumstances in which the regiment found itself, it was a perfect opportunity to remind the people of Swansea that their safety was guaranteed, when such an impressive body of men was stationed amongst them. Precision marching would make young female hearts quiver and the arms of old service men spring instantly to an arthritic salute, their heads nodding in admiration. Young men, consumed by envy, would beg to become recruits. All this would be Captain Mayer's final gift to them. He would be so proud. And then, in the late afternoon, there would be much drinking to be followed, with luck, by spirited and manly confrontations with callow civilian youths on Wind Street.

The Militiamen smartened themselves up as best as they could and gathered, as ordered, on the narrow parade ground at the barracks, eager to be set loose on the town as soon as was decent. Then they wandered loosely to the cricket ground at St Helen's, where Colonel Ballard would attempt to form them into something vaguely dignified. The formalities and gravity of the funeral would be enhanced by the kind of lustre their brightly-buttoned uniforms would inevitably bring to the occasion.

At the police station on Tontine Street however, the atmosphere was much more brisk and purposeful. Last night had been an unexpectedly informative evening, for which Bucke was especially grateful. The things Constance told him were extremely precious. Jack McCarthy's enterprise made him a person of particular interest and, after informing Captain Colquhoun of his plans – and thus ascertaining that none of his own associates had mentioned the trade to him - Bucke set up a surveillance programme to watch McCarthy and find out what he was doing. It would be a mistake to question him too soon, before they had a chance to uncover a trade that had the potential to lead to a very seedy network.

The greatest triumph though, was the button ripped from Cosh Boy's clothing, which matched exactly the one recovered in Tower

Lane after the attack on Sarah. It was a breakthrough, Bucke was sure. He knew it was Cosh Boy, not a copy-cat. His behaviour, as described by Constance, certainly seemed consistent with the details Elodie had reported. He realised that if he wanted to find a soldier, then a funeral escort by the Royal Glamorganshire Light Infantry Militia, would be a good place to start.

He had set off walking very briskly down to the cricket ground, since he needed to get there before they marched off for the service, but he was picked up by Payne and Gill in the police wagon which was sometimes, though not always, quicker than walking. Today, however, the roads were reasonably clear and he arrived just as Ballard was about to inspect his troops, badgered into line by the loud, but rather portly, Sergeant-major Mills.

Bucke jumped from the wagon before it had stopped and ran towards the parade, shouting. Ballard turned, confused and irritated, at such an offensive civilian intrusion. 'Colonel! A moment please, if I may.'

Ballard blustered, his fantasy of military competence suddenly disrupted. 'This is most irregular, Inspector! This is a solemn moment for the Militia. We must mourn the loss of our good friend and respected colleague Captain Mayer, and it is not for you to interfere!'

'Please,' soothed Bucke. 'I understand your concern, of course I do. You may know, actually, that I was once in the army myself. Served on the North West Frontier. Saw action, in fact.' He paused. 'I did not serve in stores and provisions,' he added, lowering his voice just sufficiently to make his point effectively. 'That's always disappointed me. I am sure you understand."

Ballard's administrative experience could provide no comparison and he knew it; in these circumstances he could hardly sustain his illusionary reputation as a man of action. 'I was about to inspect the troops on parade on this tragic occasion and –'

'Excellent. I'll come with you,' said Bucke, taking his arm.

'But you cannot, it –'

317

'Have you done this before?' asked Bucke.

'Inspector, please. I must protest...' but as Bucke led him closer to his troops, he realised that further protests would be classified as weakness by his men, who were watching the policeman carefully.

Sergeant-major Mills stood at the end of the first rank of men, puzzled at the Inspector's presence and unable to understand what had happened. 'Sir! Ready for Inspection! Sir!' He clicked his heels and then watched, bemused, as the colonel and a police inspector passed along the line and examined each man in turn. He saw Bucke working his way carefully amongst them, assessing each man precisely, his hands clenched behind his back, whilst Colonel Ballard admired their polished shoes. He saw Bucke stop in front of John Elias, who looked straight ahead, standing up straight with his chest out and who had formed his face into the sort of sneer suitable for an upstart civilian in an embarrassing uniform.

'We have met before, haven't we? Friend of Richard Walters, as I remember. His case comes up next week I believe. Not looking good, so I have been told.' Bucke shook his head, sadly. 'Tell me soldier,' he asked, 'Would you agree that there appears to be dirt on your trousers? Do you think that the crease could be a little sharper? I do.'

'Sir!' replied Elias emphatically, still staring ahead into the far distance.

'Thank you, Inspector, said Ballard, ineffectually. 'Thank you, Private – '

'Just one more thing,' asked Bucke apologetically. 'There is a thread on your jacket; in fact, you are missing a button. Am I right, Colonel?'

Ballard was angry with the private for leaving the Militia open to such avoidable criticism. 'Well, soldier?' his face reddening.

'Sir! Came off, sir. Whilst I was saluting, sir. Here it is, in my pocket, sir.' He put his hand swiftly into his tunic pocket and produced the button. Bucke put his hand into his own pocket and withdrew the button lost by Eliza's attacker. Side by side he could confirm that they were the same. He was certain that he was looking for a member of the militia. He wished that he had looked at these artificial soldiers much sooner.

'Re-attach it immediately, soldier,' said Ballard, seeking solace in trivial authority. Bucke noticed that Elias winked at him in response.

At the end of the parade, Bucke asked Sergeant-major Mills if all of the soldiers were present. He stood to attention. 'Sir! One soldier is missing, sir. George Thomas, sir. Ill, sir. Damaged his hand, sir. On gunnery practise. Can't sew his buttons back on his tunic, sir. Came off in manoeuvres, sir.'

'Did they indeed, Sergeant-major.' Bucke was immediately interested. 'Where does this George Thomas live, Sergeant-major? I need to know immediately.'

'If there is a problem,' interrupted Ballard, 'I am sure the Royal Glamorganshire Light Infantry Militia is more than capable of dealing with it.'

Bucke shook his head. 'That won't be necessary, Colonel. This is a police matter. Where does he live? Tell me.' He called the constables over to him, as Mills looked at Ballard, who appeared confused and blustered ineffectually once again.

'Really, Inspector. I cannot see – '

Bucke was becoming frustrated. He was running out of time. 'Tell me, or I shall arrest both of you in front of the parade,' he said calmly, knowing that he had little basis in law for what he had threatened. 'It really is up to you. Constable Gill and Constable Payne are ready to escort you to the police wagon.' He smiled and raised his eyebrows, waiting to hear their decision, then again, dropped his voice slightly. 'They do carry handcuffs, you know,' he said and smiled again. 'Constable Gill, if you please.' The constable produced a pair of handcuff from his tunic, nodding at Colonel Ballard with a smile.

Mills coughed. '17 Vincent Street, sir. Lodges with Mrs Humphreys. The lady wife's cousin, sir.' He glanced guiltily at Ballard, since in his own eyes he had sacrificed his self-respect for the good of the regiment. 'Begging your pardon, colonel, but it had to be done. Couldn't have you arrested, sir.'

Mills watched Bucke hurry away, then he called the Militia to fall in line, in order to march impressively to the Argyle Street Chapel so that they could parade behind the coffin of Captain Mayer, whilst real life unfolded elsewhere.

The police officers urged the horse along, anxious, for reasons they could not explain, to arrive at the lodgings of George Thomas quickly. Of course when they arrived, he wasn't there. Their wagon was suddenly surrounded by young boys, some of whom had slipped silently out of Vincent Street school in an excited anticipation of drama and had given themselves immediately to pinching and prodding the horse in an attempt to upset it, watching the policemen as they knocked on the door of number 17. But George Thomas had gone. The landlady, the rotund and florid Mrs Humphreys, had never anticipated that she would see Inspector Bucke standing in her very own house, as large as life. What would the neighbours say? So she was eager to help in any way that would ensure the officers left her home as quickly as possible. 'I told you, Inspector. You can't see Mr Thomas because he is not here. He is out and I don't rightly know when he is coming back, do I? You'd best be going down the market, if I was you. Probably having his boots heeled or something, I shouldn't wonder. If you goes now, you might catch him, I'll be bound.'

Bucke nodded and smiled, apparently grateful for her advice. 'And do you have a key to his room, Mrs Humphreys?'

'I do indeed, Inspector Bucke.' He said nothing in reply and looked at her significantly, waiting.

She shook her head. 'I don't think he would be very happy, see, if I let you into his room and him not there. Sure he wouldn't,' she added for emphasis. 'Very particular, is Mr Thomas.'

Bucke sighed. 'Mrs Humphreys. You have two choices. Nothing at all complicated. You see, you either give me the key or we break down the door. It is quite simple, really. I never seem to have a great deal of time, and today is no exception. So what is it to be?'

She looked alarmed and rested her hand on the stained kitchen table. 'You can't just break down a door…'

'Constable Payne. If you could be so kind. Force open any locked doors upstairs, please. Use as much force as is required.'

'Yes, Inspector Bucke. I'll break 'em all down, don't you worry,' he said with enthusiasm, eager for action. 'I will break 'em all in and then you can decide which one interests you most.'

'Here is the key,' said Mrs Humphreys, pulling it out of her apron pocket.

'Damn,' muttered Constable Payne.

She was mortified at the sight of constables trampling up her stairs in their large and noisy boots and she sat on the kitchen bench and slumped forward on to the table, horrified and breathless at this terrible turn of events. She heard Bucke ask her where he had gone but all she could do was shake her head. 'What shame he has brought on me. I should never have taken him in,' then she recovered herself slightly. 'I don't rightly know where he was going. I hope them coppers of yours don't damage nothing.'

Payne called down the stairs. 'It is open, Inspector. Not much to look at, but you might be interested…'

What Bucke saw was a mean room, untidy and dirty. There were, scattered across the simple unstable washstand, some of the Parisian cards that seemed to be following him everywhere. Next to the bed were plate illustrations that had obviously been torn from art books in the library and featured illustrations from classical sculptures, on to which Thomas had added his own crude enhancements. There were two piles of library books, one in the corner of the room and the other beneath the window. There was certainly plenty here that Bucke would like to talk to Thomas about. There was also his uniform, of course. Constable Gill found it bunched up in the bottom of the wardrobe and pulled it out so that he could hold it up for Bucke to examine. The bottom and back of the tunic were tinged with mud and there were three gaps in the button display marked by broken black threads as if, Bucke thought, there were once flowers on the uniform that had been eaten by slugs.

'He's our man,' said Payne. 'Now where is the bugger?'

There was a shout outside and Bucke looked out of the window and down on to the street. The boys around the cart were waving and a couple were pointing up at the window at which he was standing. He looked along Vincent Street. A rather flabby-looking man had paused at the far end, obviously examining the scene and paying particular attention to the significant details of a cart outside his lodgings and the shouts of 'Police! Police!'

'He's at the end of the street.' Bucke studied him quickly. 'Not tall, a little stout. Black coat, long, down below the knees. No hat. Has something under his arm. Might be a book. He will run, that is sure. He can't go back down Vincent Street – that's a dead end. So he will have to turn down Argyle Street. Let's go. Blow your whistles, let's make him panic a bit. You two go after him. I'll cut through where I can and try and head him off.'

In fact, Bucke's brief descriptive details were not required. The constables merely chased the man who was running away and Bucke, for once, was in luck. A brewer's dray was delivering to the Badminton Hotel on the corner of Vincent Street and Thomas avoided the obstruction by running down Argyle Street towards Oystermouth Road.

Payne and Gill raced after him, blowing their whistles and shouting. The boys around the police wagon joined in, not wanting to miss out on any excitement. So a crowd chased after Thomas, whilst Bucke ran down Burrows Road and cut across Upper Fleet Street to intercept him. Bucke knew that Thomas had a significant head start and that he therefore had to be considerably quicker to catch him. There had been heavy winds yesterday which had, as always, blown sand along the streets that ran at right angles to the beach. As Thomas tried desperately to run faster than he ever had before in his life, he skidded on the dry sand, lost his footing and crashed to the ground. He pulled himself to his feet and set off again, but one of the boys chasing along, and who had easily left the constables behind, tripped him up. The boys were indifferent to his offences; they merely wanted to see him caught, in the hope that there would be a fight. Thomas banged into the wall, cursing, and swiped out ineffectually at the boy and then set off again, his face red . He realised that he had no plan, no idea where he could go to find refuge. The docks? The Barracks? He was sure the police officers were gaining on him but he dare not look back. He could see the Mumbles tramway at the bottom of Argyle Street and he could smell the sea on the air. If he jumped on one of the trams would it help? He had nothing to lose. He slapped again at the small boy trying to trip him once again and managed, fortuitously, to catch him on the side of the head. That will teach him, he thought.

Then, as he reached the next junction, a policeman appeared in front of him. 'Stop!' he commanded loudly. Thomas tried to swerve around him but the officer was too agile. Bucke realised that this flabby figure was Elodie's lump of lard, there could be no question of that. He grabbed Thomas by the spongy waist like a rugby football player and bundled him to the ground. Thomas found himself winded, face down and with his hands held firmly behind his back. He wasn't really sure how that had happened. He was aware of more footsteps now.

'Cuff him, Constable Payne,' he heard the policeman say, and his hands were dragged roughly into position and he felt the cold handcuffs enclose his wrists, clipping the skin. He was caught and knew that struggling would hurt, so he tried to relax as much as he could. All he could see were the grains of sand on the ground, some of which had worked their way into his eyes, making them sore.

'There we are,' said a voice. 'Shall I go back and get the wagon, Inspector?'

'Yes, thank you, Constable Payne. That would be very helpful.'

There was a child's voice, then. 'Are you going to hit him now?'

'No, son. There is no need. We have arrested him and we shall take him to the police station to talk to him about some of the things

323

we think he has done.'

There were groans of disappointment but Thomas knew that he wouldn't be in the police station for long. Once they knew what he was doing, once they knew he was clearing up the filth from the streets, they would let him go.

'He dropped this book.' It was another young voice, but he could not turn his head to look. 'Had a look at it. Pictures of tits. Rubbish, it is, Not like the real thing. If he'd wanted to see some he should have talked to me. I got sisters.'

'Thank you for picking up the book for me, Eddie. That is very helpful,' said the policeman.

'Don't mention it, like. But I reckon you would be better off looking for the bastard who killed our Alfie, not chasing fat book stealers.' Thomas would have hit him if his hands had been free. That is what the insolent urchin deserved, a proper thrashing to teach him a lesson.

He was surprised that his visit to the police station did not live up to his expectations. The police wagon on which he was taken had been followed by the gang of boys and, as the news spread, people came out of their houses to shout and spit at him. Then, once in the station, the police seemed, to his way of thinking, curiously reluctant to listen to him and put him in a police cell, which seemed rather unnecessary and, if truth be told, rather uncomfortable.

Later in the afternoon, when those two inspectors spoke to him, they started to talk to him about library books, which seemed a bit strange, because surely they were not that important? And then they talked about his collection of those little visiting cards. He had two copies of some of them they said, and they wanted to know if he ever met anyone else who he could swap them with. Perhaps they had cards of their own that they wanted to swap? He didn't know, but this was a decidedly odd way of improving your collection, if that is what this was about.

But then things took an unexpected turn. They wanted to know about those young boys who'd been killed. He was happy to tell them that he knew nothing about them. Not his style, not his work, but they didn't seem to believe him. He did admit to killing that old lady in Llwyn y Bryn but that was a mistake and he was sorry about it. These things can happen in the heat of a moment. It was the filthy whores he was after and he was sure they would understand. But one of them, the older one, not the one who had caught him, said he was going to be moved to Cardiff and that he would be hanged.

How could that be? After all he had done, he was going to be punished for one little mistake? The woman shouldn't have been walking on the streets alone, should she? And anyway, they didn't do that sort of thing to soldiers, did they?

They were just teasing him, that must be the case. But they still wouldn't let him go and they put him back in the cell, which was, he thought, very uncomfortable and cold too. They said they would arrange his transfer to Cardiff in the morning and, when he thought about it later, he decided that it was probably a good idea. Cardiff people would certainly be more sympathetic. They would definitely appreciate what he had been doing. They would probably want to help him with his work. The Swansea police force appeared unaccountably interested in other issues which he found hard to digest. How could that be? He was Cosh Boy, he had been in the papers. Didn't that count for something?

*

Events however did not allow Bucke any moments to either consider or relax. It became a very busy afternoon indeed. It began when one of the younger emigrants, who Bucke believed was probably German, although it didn't really matter, had an encounter with Eliza Keast. Bucke certainly admired his courage in coming to the police station and trying to explain, in a foreign language, that he had been defrauded by her. Constable Gill brought her in but she denied, first of all, that she had taken money from him, and that then she had thrown him to the ground and walked away. Eliza spoke loudly and aggressively with a great deal of arm-waving, though both Bucke and Gill found it hard to concentrate on what she said when that lump on her head had such a magnetic fascination. The boy might have had a chance if he had paid Eliza before he had changed his money at an extortionate rate with the money lender on the quayside. But all Eliza had in her purse were English coins, no foreign currency, and they could have come from anyone.

It was an expensive moment for him and Bucke hoped that he had learned something from it. He was sure that Eliza had done what the boy claimed but there was no proof. Nonetheless, he warned her, in spite of her mock innocence, that she had been very lucky. Another man might have pulled out a knife and stabbed her. She shrugged. He hadn't done that, so she had no cause to worry.

'And thank you for the button, Eliza,' he added as he took her to the police station door. 'You have done well and I am very grateful.'

'Don't mention it. Hope you have got the bugger. People are talking. '

'Yes, I believe we have. I might need you as a witness you know, when he comes to court.'

'Been in court before, you know. Won't bother me.' She walked down the steps on to Tontine Street and then turned to look back at him. 'And I tell you what. You look after that young lady of yours, inspector. She's too good for you, and that's a fact,' she cackled.

He did not have too much time to reflect upon her advice because he saw Constable Smith dragging Lyndon Griffin up to the station, who was complaining and resisting but he was not strong enough to break free. Smith's pox-marked face was red with exertion as he pulled Griffin through the door that Bucke held open. 'Thank you, Inspector,' he panted. 'I caught this one nicking again.'

Griffin went over and sat on a bench along the wall, drawing into himself. 'You hurt my arm,' he said sullenly.

'Well, you should have come quietly then, shouldn't you?' Smith pointed at him for emphasis.

Sergeant Ball left his place behind the counter and went to sit next to Griffin, to stop him trying to get away. 'What you been doing, lad?' he asked quietly.

'I done nuffin,' he muttered.

The boy was dressed in the dirtiest clothes Bucke could imagine. Lyndon had acquired some shoes from somewhere since the last time he had seen him, but they were not a matching pair. The waistcoat that hung from his thin shoulders was serving as an inadequate hiding place for a number of small, angular shapes that made his chest look like a badly carved tree trunk.

Smith sighed. 'This is Lyndon Griffin. I think we have all met him before.'

'I haven't been nicking nuffink. A man asked me to take them things to the post office.'

'What did he want you to take to the post office, Lyndon?' asked Ball.

'Them boxes. They got stamps on them.' Bucke noticed that his head occasionally twitched involuntarily as he talked.

'You nicked them,' insisted Smith. 'You were trying to sell them in the market. I saw you.'

'That man give them to me,' Lyndon insisted.

'May I look at one of them please, Lyndon?' Bucke asked gently, holding out his hand, knowing what the box would be before he saw it.

He turned it over in his hand. Neatly and securely packaged, clearly addressed. 'Can you read, Lyndon?' The boy shook his head. 'It says Roache's Liver Pills. Here.' He pointed at the words. 'Do you know what they are? ' The boy shook his head again.

'He was trying to pass them off as boxes of sweets. I watched him.'

'A man give them to me. To take to the post office. They has stamps on them.'

'And so that is why you were selling them, is it?'

Lyndon shrugged. 'I didn't sell nuffink. Search me. Ain't got no money.'

'Not a good day then, Lyndon,' said Ball gently.

The door to the police station opened again. An untidy and gaunt figure stood there, his hands on his hips. It was Idris Morley, a man who usually idled around the market looking for casual employment. 'There he is, the little bugger. He stole my boxes. I was on my way to the post office and I dropped them. That little urchin there offered to help me pick them up but then he buggered off with some of them. I tell you something, my lad. Doctor Benjamin isn't going to be at all happy about that, is he? Think on that, sonny.' He looked around the room at a group of policemen who had suddenly gone very quiet.

'Good afternoon,' said Bucke warmly, as if he was greeting some long-lost friend. 'It is Mr Morley, I believe. I am so glad you have called in this afternoon. Do you know something? I think it would be a really good idea if the two of us had a little chat, in my office. That would be nice, wouldn't it? Don't you think?'

Twenty Seven

He spent a long time with Lily, listening, waiting, probing. She cried quite a lot, her wet, worried eyes darting everywhere, seeking solace and comfort which today, like most days, were impossible to find in the police station. She was a pretty girl, although rather shallow to Bucke's mind, flighty too. Her clothes were more expensive than anyone would have expected and she wore jewellery when it wasn't necessary. Lily was an illusion, without substance, Bucke thought. She was young, she was frightened, she was alone and she told him everything. It was a sorry story, but he believed that it was true. Stupid girl, he thought. Stupid, stupid girl. He hadn't known about Faith's child, that was news to him. But he had known that there was a baby farm in the town and finally he had a lead. Her sister, Margaret Grove, had passed the baby on, though Lily wasn't sure where. That wouldn't be too difficult to unpick.

The day was, as Sergeant Ball later described it, 'rather lively.' A couple of emigrants were brought into the police station, bruised and drunk in the middle of the afternoon, after a visit to what was either an illegal drinking den or a brothel. They were put in the cells for their own safety, whilst Inspector Flynn went outside to disperse their assailants, who were hopeful of an early release so that they could resume hostilities. Constable Payne, who later released them from the cells, made it clear in emphatic sign language that they should spend their last night in Swansea on board the *Polaria*. It had to be better than spending the night in the cells and running the risk of an appearance in the Police Court on Saturday, just hours before the ship steamed away.

Late in the afternoon, a group of young men from the *Polaria* had crowded together inside Haynes the Bakers and the proprietor claimed very loudly that some of his pies had disappeared. There was little proof that anything had happened and no witnesses at all. Haynes ranted and railed, declaring that he would never let passengers from the ship inside his shop again, or indeed ever again serve any member of an unsympathetic police force. It might have happened and it might not, but as Inspector Flynn observed, Haynes had been charging the emigrants inflated prices anyway, which, he added, was rather unsavoury, rather like his pies.

Perhaps this comment inspired Constable Smith, who later cautioned Mark Lawrence for obstructing Temple Street with his wheelbarrow containing a tin of warm baked faggots. When he complained that he had stood in that same place for four years, Smith replied that his faggots tasted like it as well and threatened to confiscate his wheelbarrow.

Nevertheless, it seemed to Bucke that the visit of the *Polaria* had, generally, been quite successful, though he never felt sufficiently relaxed to spend that happy hour or two listening to Captain Winckler's stories. Everything seemed to have been generally good-natured and, once the ship had gone, he would visit his small list of deserving places, where he would quietly distribute some small considerations, courtesy of the captain. There were other positive things to cheer him. He had detained Cosh Boy and he had made significant progress with the Parisian visiting cards and now he had a lead about the elusive baby farm.

Was Abramovitch connected to any of this? Or entirely unrelated? He didn't know, though he thought it was unlikely. But Bucke was still haunted by their failure to trace Amy; haunted once more by the Fanny Stevens song, *The Children of the Wood.* Was Amy just another child lost in the forest, in danger from those who should have been protecting her? He was sure that Abramovitch had her. It was the only thing that made sense. But where? Was it wrong of him to believe that they were still in Swansea? But he dreaded the feeling of guilt that swept over him in a wave whenever he saw Sarah forlornly walking the streets. He needed information and he still had nothing to go on. Bucke had convinced himself; Abramovitch must have her. He'd been looking for a girl, hadn't he? Was this a coincidence?

He went to see the public analyst, Mr Williams in Richard's Place, a short, dark, studious man with his eyes deep-set and his brows angled downwards, which gave him a permanently mournful look, an expression that invariably suited the news that he had to deliver.

Today was no different, though Bucke had known for some time what the analysis of Cyrus Bishop's stomach contents – and those liver pills - would show.

Now, he had to talk to Dr Benjamin.

*

The doctor was, not unexpectedly, aggressive. 'I cannot be blamed, Inspector, if my medication is misused by others. I would be very surprised if an overdose of my entirely wholesome pills caused the vicar's death. There must have been an unusual underlying medical condition. No other adverse reactions have been reported and sales continue to increase. I did not kill Cyrus Bishop. My pills did not kill Cyrus Bishop. If he was killed, then someone else did it, and I will not be held responsible.'

Bucke sat opposite him at the kitchen table, leaning forward, resting on his elbows, as always with his fingers intertwined. 'Hilda Bishop killed her husband, Dr Benjamin. She poisoned him with arsenic.'

'Congratulations on a successful investigation, Inspector. And what has this to do with me?' His anxiety was obvious. Bucke had told him immediately he entered the empty, echoing Ragged School, that he had come to talk about Roache's Liver Pills and that they were implicated in the death of Cyrus Bishop. But how did Bucke know that he was their manufacturer? That had unsettled him.

'She sent her housemaid Lily to Moses Davies on the High Street to buy arsenic powder. She said it was for the rats in the shed. Unusually, Hilda sent money to pay for it. Then she rolled your pills in it. Hilda made sure that Cyrus took them regularly, Lily said, though she swears she didn't know they were dosed with poison. It was a low dose but it accumulated over time. Not a happy relationship, it seems.'

'I am sorry to hear this, but as I said, you must know that you cannot hold me responsible in any way for any part of this domestic tragedy. 'He tried to look impassive but a clear expression of his relief passed across his face.

'Oh I am quite aware of that, Dr Benjamin. But you see, the circumstances of Cyrus Bishop's death led me to examine the nature of your pills. I have to say that Jonathan Williams, the public analyst, was not at all complimentary about Roache's Liver Pills. He said that they contained nothing of value at all. Organic matter was the only way he could describe it. Said the main ingredient appeared to be shreds of grass.'

'They are a natural product, Inspector. And surely the point is, that if people believe they are good for them, then they will help, won't they? Do you find that is in some way unacceptable, Inspector?'

Bucke screwed up his eyes briefly and scratched his nose. He shook his head. 'Except that all the claims on your box are entirely unfounded.' He took a box from the pile on the table and turned it round in his hand. '*a sovereign remedy for bilious disorders, liver complaints, dyspepsia or indigestion.*' I might ask, who says so?'

'This is entirely unfair, Doctor. If people believe –'

'It is a lie, Doctor Benjamin. The whole box is a lie.' He put it back on the pile. 'You are trading in unproven products, making spurious claims, taking money from strangers.'

Benjamin sighed, then folded his arms. 'I don't do this for myself, Inspector. I do it for the children. The small profit that we make helps the school.'

'But it doesn't make the pills more wholesome, does it, doctor?'

'It helps the poorest children in this drab little town. Surely that is enough?'

Bucke waited, watching Benjamin's eyes that glanced rapidly around the room. 'And who is Roache?' he asked eventually.

Benjamin laughed. 'You see, Inspector. There you have it. Proof. It is a name I invented from the letters contained in the words *Ragged School*. Because that is what the whole of this has been for. The sole benefit of the school. The children have nothing, and if those who are more wealthy and more comfortable, who do not know what real sickness is like, who know nothing of grinding poverty, who have minor ailments that owe their origins to over-indulgence, if they believe that my pills are effective, then surely, Inspector, it is right that they contribute, however little they know of it, to those who have nothing at all.'

'But what are you selling them, Doctor? Along with these baseless claims?'

'Hope, Inspector. A dream of health that they do not deserve. That is all. Pills rolled in American sugar, sold in boxes. No money stolen, all orders fulfilled.'

'And the pills? Tell me about those,' asked Bucke.

Benjamin waved his hand dismissively. 'As I told you, they are entirely natural, Inspector. I can see no point in you detaining me here any longer. I have matters to attend to.' He stood up, inviting the Inspector to leave.

'You see, Doctor. I have spoken to Idris Morley. A very interesting conversation. It was, shall we say, very revealing.'

Benjamin's face changed immediately, his confidence evaporating. Suddenly he seemed very young.

'There is more that we have to talk about, isn't there?' Bucke waited for his confession.

He sat down. 'Everything that I have done was for the best, for the school. I want you to know that. It wasn't about me. I had to buy the boxes and the sugar and I had to employ Mr Morley. Then there was the advertising, which isn't cheap...' He was running out of words. 'You must understand, Inspector. It was for the children.'

'Shall we talk about the pills, Doctor?' asked Bucke, gently. 'Or should we call them pellets?'

Benjamin sighed. 'Whatever pleases you. I couldn't afford a pill-making machine.'

'And so what did you do?'

His head dropped, he covered his face with his hands and refused to talk.

For a moment, Bucke felt sorry for him. He had invented a world within his head, in which the needs of the school justified everything that he did, perhaps because there was no one close to him to tell him that what he was doing was dangerous and wrong. He knew that there were dangers in loneliness. Bucke knew that he himself had been lucky to escape from them.

'Let me help you,' Bucke offered. 'It has been a really simple business, as far as I can see. And I am afraid to say that it was probably your idea, not the idea of Idris Morley. He has never had an idea in his head for the whole of his life. No, you devised it, because you couldn't afford a pill machine. But you needed something small and round. So you sent Idris Morley out and about, didn't you? I am sure at the time that it made perfect sense to you.' Benjamin turned his head away, refusing to acknowledge Bucke's presence. 'He went up on to Townhill and down into Cockett and collected rabbit droppings from the warrens. That is what he told me. Sometimes sheep droppings too.' Bucke held up his finger and thumb to indicate their perfect size. 'Round, dark and pill-sized. You must have thought they were perfect. Did you?'

Benjamin stood up and turned away, gripping the edge of the cold sink behind him with two hands.

'Then in the evenings, Morley tells me, you roll them in trays of sugar and flour and then pack them in boxes of twenty, with the recommendation to take one in the morning and another in the evening. Ten days supply. So your customers would have to order more to see any effect. And is it any surprise, Doctor Benjamin, that people are anxious to talk to you? There have been reports of gastric discomfort and disturbance that are being linked to your pills.'

Benjamin turned around sharply from the sink. 'I have no shame, Inspector,' he said, trying to sound brave. 'Everything I have done has been for the poorest victims of a wicked society. It was done for the oppressed, for those who have nothing. And if a few wealthy people have been to the privy more often than usual? So what?'

'You seem to think that you can create your own morality, where the ends are always justified, no matter what you do. It was wrong and reckless.'

'If there are those who are so stupid as to believe advertisements and then buy pills on a whim, then why should I care?'

'Because you are a doctor. That is why,' said Bucke firmly.' Because health is your responsibility. You take an oath, don't you? You cannot abandon that oath simply because it doesn't suit you and then invent a reason why it is permissible.' Benjamin looked back at him with a blank expression. 'This trade of yours needs to stop immediately, doctor. Please understand, I cannot protect you from the consequences of what you have done. And, if word of your actions was to spread, your reputation would be in shreds and no one can prevent that happening. Then your position in Swansea, or indeed anywhere, would be impossible. I hope you can see that. And it would be a consequence of what you have done. Don't forget, Idris Morley has already been to the police station and has been questioned and you can be sure that he does not want to face any consequences alone. The first thing he will do in court – and he has done it to me already – is that he will blame you. He will say that he relied entirely upon your professional knowledge. Because you are a doctor, remember?'

Benjamin looked away, as if persuading himself that Bucke was there by not looking at him and by not speaking.

Bucke continued, regardless. 'I shall not take you to the cells. I shall accept your word as a professional person that you will stay available for me at all times, whilst I take advice about how to proceed. As we both know, there are impoverished people in this town who need your services and you cannot provide them from a police cell. If the public knew that you had been kept in the police station you would have no future here. The constables would know. Some go home to their families and they will advise them not to buy any more of your pills. So I will trust you, but you are to remain in Swansea and report to me at Tontine Street every day. Do you understand?'

Benjamin still said nothing, standing by the sink, trying to look defiant with the debris of his enterprise before him on the table.

As he left the school, Bucke wondered whether he would ever see Doctor Benjamin again.

*

It had been a long day and a busy one. He knew that he had to be around town, supporting his constables on what was not only Friday night, but also the last full night of the *Polaria's* visit. But he needed to speak to Constance and so he called on her before inviting her to join him on his patrol. It was a fine night, dry and crisp, and they walked together along Oystermouth Road for a short distance, the occasional lights of the town sparkling in reflection on the dark sea.

She listened in disgust to the Liver Pills. 'He is such an intense young man, Rumsey. Fervent and rather unsettling at times. Convinced that he is right about everything. And lonely too, I think.'

He told her about Lily. What did she think? That she was a child, not a criminal as such but a child, who had never considered the consequences of her actions. A magpie attracted to the bright and shiny, but never knowing the price of such things. Bucke nodded in agreement. Terrible things had happened, but Lily was too trivial to see them and soon she would appear in court.

Constance, looked at the sea, at the waves rolling into the shore. 'The other thing you need to consider though, is this. Faith Bishop's child. It was sold – probably to a woman who could not have her own. And in the circumstances, how do you know whether or not the child is better off? Given the choice between a life in that vicarage, with those people, or a life with a childless couple desperate to love a baby? To be frank, I would have taken my chance.' She raised her hand. 'Yes, I know what the law says, Rumsey. I know that. But it doesn't make it right, now does it? What are you going to do if you find Faith Bishop's child? Give it back to her?'

'I don't know, Constance. I really don't. But I have to make sure that no children are being murdered.'

'And perhaps someone should make it easier for the poor to bury their still-born too,' she said. Her voice softened slightly. 'And still no news of Amy?'

'None at all.' Bucke paused and shook his head. 'The child haunts me, Constance.'

'I must go and spend some time with poor Sarah tomorrow. I haven't seen her since Wednesday. What about Black Bart? Perhaps he can find her. He is devoted to her.'

'Worth a try, the police haven't a clue, I can confirm that. We work largely on information and we haven't had any at all. Yet something, and I don't know what it is, tells me Abramovitch has her and that she is still alive and is still in Swansea. But at the moment, I feel that a cat has more chance of finding her than I have.'

On Saturday morning Constance looked for Sarah but couldn't find her. She went to her room, something she didn't like doing because it was an unpleasant place and she was not sure about the neighbours, but Sarah wasn't there. She must be out walking the streets again, Constance thought, trying to manage those consuming fears and her deepest sorrow. She went to the Ragged School on Back Street to see whether Sarah had gone there for some reason, but there was no sign of her. The school room was unexpectedly open and she wandered through the building, which had a strange, empty feeling for a place that was always so lively and busy. It reminded her of her husband's school in the days after he had disappeared, a shell, suddenly without a purpose. The kitchen was untidy, an indication that Sarah hadn't been there. The cupboard doors were open and there were small boxes on the table with a thin covering of a white powder that looked like sugar. Constance was sure someone had been here recently – there were doors open and a couple of chairs overturned. There was no sign of Black Bart there, either. She went outside and closed the door. She decided she ought to tell a constable that she had found the school open, though she didn't expect him to know anything about the missing cat.

Twenty Eight

Fanny went home after the rehearsal, very tired and very fed up. The orchestra – though who could have ever thought they were worthy of such a name – had been ponderously unmusical and she and the drummer, the only one amongst them with a semblance of ability, exchanged long-suffering glances as their level of incompetence prolonged the rehearsals beyond all patience. Because she was singing in Welsh and the players couldn't speak it, they were unable to pick up any clues from the lyrics. They had been there all morning and a large part of the afternoon and it was not the way Fanny wished to spend her Saturday. The manager, Melville, had cancelled her evening performance as a result, with the warning that if the orchestra didn't improve, Fanny would have to sing unaccompanied. She had done it before but she knew that the musicians desperately needed the fee, so she agreed to wait a little longer. She hadn't seen Henry either, not for a few days now, which didn't help her mood. He had been busy with a complicated dispute about shipping contracts and there had been some family events that he was required to attend.

Fanny was jealous, there was no other word. She was excluded by circumstances from too many aspects of his life; she was second-best, she knew that. She had merely a walk-on part in his life and could never be centre stage, never allowed dialogue, destined always to wait in the wings and watch, only occasionally allowed to perform in the chorus. And however much Henry said that he wished it were otherwise, this was how it was and this was how it would be, she was certainly aware of that. What did they say? Like it or lump it? That was just about right.

So she had to know her place until perhaps Henry tired of her, or he married. She paused and looked over to the Bethesda Chapel, grey against a grey sky, where a man was busy tidying up a grave. Our final destination, she thought, mine just as much as it is for anyone. And what would anyone say about her when she got there, if anyone ever remembered her? That Fanny could always be relied upon to make the wrong choice? It would be an appropriate epitaph, without a doubt.

She clumped wearily up the stairs to the room, which she knew would offer neither comfort nor solace, merely more of an endlessly bleak winter. She just wanted to rest. Fanny pushed open the door and walked straight into Jack who was waiting for her, his arms folded, his chin at an aggressive angle.

'You have been seeing someone, haven't you?'

'Please, Jack. I don't have time for this.'

'Answer me. You have been seeing someone. I've been told. One of my customers, Maldwyn something or other. Took him some cards and he told me a lawyer or some such has been hanging round the music hall. You have been seen with him.'

'What's it to you? You don't care.'

'Where's my cut?'

Fanny sighed. 'There is no money, Jack. That is not what it is about. Never has been. Leave me alone, Jack. I am tired. You don't care for me, you never have. Am I not allowed even the briefest taste of happiness, without you demanding most of it for yourself?'

He pushed her against the door, the noise echoing through the building. 'Don't you remember what I said?' She could feel his breath on her face, an angry force pushing her backwards. 'Well? Do you remember? About your nose?' He held her shoulders harshly against the rough wood. 'I could do it so easy,' and he made as if to head-butt her, stopping just short of her nose. Instead, he put his head to the side of her face and bit her ear harshly. 'But I got something better, just you see,' he whispered. Jack stepped back and then dragged her roughly to the table. 'Here. Look. Read it. Your little boy.' Fanny didn't want to look but could not stop herself as he forced her head down towards a copy of the Telegraph, open at the Family Announcements.

Dr and Mrs Charles Sullivan are pleased to announce the marriage of their only daughter, Harriet Rose, to Mr Henry Dodswell Fry on Saturday 16 April

Fanny stopped reading and screwed up her eyes, her face and her spirit hardening. She struggled free from his grasp and looked at him defiantly.

'The boy. Lover boy. Getting wed. How I laughed when I saw it.' Jack grinned. 'It will be such a happy day!'

'I knew,' she lied.

'You still owe me, Fanny. You know you do. You work for me. And you have been working, Fanny. I know that. So you can settle with me later. You never know, I might pay Mr Henry Dodswell Fry a call. There are things I reckon he don't want others to know, don't you think?' He picked up his large shabby satchel in which he normally carried his *cartes de visite*. 'I got a meeting down the Vaults now but I will be back. You have a sit down. Put your feet up, Fanny. Read the paper.' He closed the door noisily behind him and Fanny sat down on the bed, her head down, her eyes closed, listening to his feet on the stairs. Everything seemed so utterly pointless.

When Jack McCarthy left the building, Constable Morris, behind the wall of the burial ground and looking as inconspicuous as a constable in working clothes could ever look, turned and bent down, as if he was tending to a grave. Then he stood and began to follow him cautiously. Morris noted that he was carrying a satchel, presumably full of cards, he decided. The streets were quiet and Morris maintained a suitable distance, though it did not seem that McCarthy was paying much attention as the daylight began to fade and his long strides were stretching out the distance between them. To Morris, he appeared determined and confident, excited, even. Perhaps he had a big sale ahead of him, Morris decided, and was eager to seal it. He wondered where McCarthy was going and he shortened the gap between them as much as he could so that he didn't disappear.

He turned into Mariner Street. This was a surprise. Morris had expected him to head to one of the High Street pubs. Who lived on Mariner Street who could afford Jack's cards? Morris crossed over to the other side of the road and watched McCarthy shoulder a battered, water-stained wooden door and then slip inside. Morris stepped out of the shadows into the road to get a better look, though it was gloomy and detail was hard to make out. He was sure he knew the house. It was the one Vinegar Bridget and Milford used, where they pillaged drunks and sailors. He had been called there before, hadn't he? Some sort of disturbance?

He watched for some time, getting cold, wondering what was going on until, in the window, and barely through the grimy glass, he could see the face of a child, a girl. She was gesturing at him and her mouth seemed to be shaping the word 'Help!' Suddenly the face disappeared, dragged away, he suspected. But it was enough. He stepped back inside a doorway. The child had been a tiny thing, he was sure, a scrap with bright eyes. Couldn't tell her age, not from this distance and through that glass. But all the constables had been told about the missing girl, Amy with the pram. He walked quickly back to the High Street and then the short distance to Tontine Street. He threw open the door of the police station and shouted loudly. 'Inspector Bucke!'

He came quickly from his office and listened carefully to what Morris reported, and then called together the three other constables, available and still unassigned, before the habitual excitements of Saturday evening began. There was, he realised, no time to implement an elaborate plan; he knew they had to act as decisively and as quickly as possible.

There were five of them and they walked briskly to Mariner Street, sometimes breaking into a trot. This was no time for subtlety. Directed by Morris, they burst straight in through the door, snapping the tenuous grip of the rusty hinge. It was dark within, but Vinegar Bridget and Milford were easy to see, despite their dark clothes, sitting at the table and drinking what smelt like cheap gin from a jug.

Bridget stood up in shock. 'What the hell is you doing? You fair give me a fright, you bastards!'

Bucke grabbed her and pushed her against the wall and some more of the thin plaster fell off in flakes.

'Where's the child?' he demanded. 'I know she's been here. Where is she?'

'Leave her alone, copper!' shouted Milford. She stood behind Bucke and tried to pull him off but Morris and Payne grabbed her and pinned her back into her chair.

'Tell me, Bridget,' he continued. 'A young child. An abducted child. You have kept her here and I want her back! Where is she?'

Bridget and Milford exchanged a look and Morris, seeing it, knew that they had got them. Their instant denial that followed was unconvincing.

'You have been keeping her here,' went on Bucke. 'This is a serious offence. Abduction? Kidnapping. What do you want to call it? Tell me. '

'Where is she?' added Morris, his arms pinning Milford's elbows. 'How long do you want to be inside, you mutton? Weeks? Months? Years? Tell me!'

Bucke pushed Vinegar against the wall again. 'I don't have time to wait for someone like you. She was here, we know it. I want her back.' He knew that he had to give an impression of certainty, to suggest that he had evidence. But he was working on instinct.

'She is not here,' said Bridget, 'even you can see that, copper.'

'Has Jack got her? Where is he taking her?' He felt Bridget shake in his hands. She couldn't stop herself. He knew about Jack and that shocked her.

'Tell him, Bridge,' said Milford, unsettled by the prospect of imprisonment. and realising that they no longer had any choices.

Bucke's face went closer still. 'Tell me, Bridget.'

She turned her face away. 'You tell him, Milford.'

'No. You tell me,' said Bucke and when she sighed he knew that he had beaten her.

'He is taking her to the Vaults. Selling her to a foreigner down there. Says he is going to take her away to be a princess. Lucky little bitch.' Bucke released her. He knew he was right; he knew who had Amy. 'We been looking after her, that is all,' continued Bridget. 'Haven't done her no harm, honest. Nice little thing she is. Fed her and everything, even when she said she weren't hungry.'

'You've been farming babies, haven't you? We have been looking for this place. You could be in serious trouble.'

'There are them who has been hanged for such a thing,' added Morris.

'I never killed no kids, copper. Honest. We just buried the dead ones. Sold some, Jack did. But we never killed none. I wouldn't do nuthin' like that. Nor Sel, neither. Not a word of a lie.'

Bucke, still angry, turned and considered the two of them from the door. 'I am coming back for you two when I have got the child. Don't either of you go anywhere.'

*

In the back yard of the Albany Vaults, Jack McCarthy counted out the money before he handed over possession of the rope that tethered Amy. The money was right; he had been prepared for an argument but it didn't look as if he was going to get one. He really should have asked for more. Abramovitch took the rope from him. The end was plaited into a short piece of chain which, in turn, was attached to a strap that he now buckled tightly to his wrist.

'Pleased to do business with you, Mr Abramovitch. A pleasure.' He saw elements in Abramovitch that he recognised. He was cunning, resourceful, untrustworthy. He rather liked that, for he hoped that he was looking at a version of himself. 'Let's do it again sometime.'

'I sincerely hope we do not have to do so,' replied Abramovitch, testing the strength of the rope and watching as Amy slumped to the floor of the yard once again, her head down, a girl of spirit and intelligence, reduced to a possession that could be dragged, bought and sold. She was a commodity and she looked crushed.

'Is this what you came here for? Have you got everything that you

343

need? Is there any more help that I can give you?'

'I told you before. The heftel is very precious. It is worth much money but since I cannot find it I shall use the glass one. It is an irritation only. It will suit my purposes.' Abramovitch pulled on the rope experimentally once more. Amy toppled over into the dirt. 'If you do find the heftel after I have gone, then you are a very rich man indeed. Perhaps it has been buried in the sand somewhere. Or it was lost at sea.' He smiled another of his joyless smiles. 'So I wish you luck.'

'If it is here, then I shall find it,' nodded Jack. He was very interested in the possibility of hidden treasure. 'I know the beaches.'

'The scroll too has been a problem for me,' continued Abramovitch, 'but I have to accept that it has gone somewhere that I will never know. I cannot have a new one made, that is impossible. But I shall not worry about such things. I have a girl. A Swansea girl, a Romanian girl, brought here by your honourable sea captain. She is a key to a new future.' He looked at Amy sprawled on the floor reluctant, it seemed, to sit up again. 'I told you, there can be no inheritance without proof and Chana is the proof that I need. She inherits. She is the only heir. The one we have been seeking. There is much rejoicing. All is hers, but then she dies. A tragedy. Everyone is so sad.' His smile was a death sentence. 'Chana, she dies so unexpectedly. What is to happen to her glorious inheritance, I wonder?' He shook his head in anticipation of the grief he would one day experience. 'Come Chana, together we shall return to your home. Remember, you are a princess. You have been gone too long – five long years. Your people are waiting for you.'

'And how have you planned your journey, exactly?' asked Jack. Abramovitch shrugged. He did not trust Jack and would never consider telling him any of his plans. 'It is just that I have a business colleague arriving tomorrow on the tide. Frenchie, Captain Morin. I can get you places on his ship, for a price, of course. Nothing to worry about. He goes straight to France. You can trust him.'

'That is kind of you, Jack. But I have already made my arrangements. There is a ship waiting for us, even now. My name is

344

Szarmach. A sailor. I am dressed for work.' He used his free hand to push his scarf inside his drab buttoned waistcoat and then tried to settle his jacket around him, which seemed to sag a little on one side. There was something heavy in the pocket.

Jack found it hard to believe a word he said, a quality he admired in a man. 'Well, the offer is there. Care for a drink, Mr Abramovitch? Celebrate a deal well done?'

'Thank you, but no. We shall leave. I have no plans to go into the public areas of this town of yours. Chana and I will leave through the gate here.' He pulled his large seaman's cap down to his eyebrows, refused Jack's offer to shake his hand and dragged Amy through the gate and on to York Street. He was going to the High Street Railway station, but not directly. He needed Jack to think he was going to the docks, as any sailor would. So Jack could tell whoever he wanted. Let the police search the wharves and the ships. But he would only go so far and then double back along the Strand.

Abramovitch shortened the length of the rope to make it less obvious that Amy was like a dog on a lead by pushing it into the canvas bag he was carrying. 'And let me make one thing clear to you, Chana. You are now from a rich family. I shall be teaching you how to behave as we travel home. You must always pay very close attention. So now come with me. And if you walk properly, the rope will not hurt.'

*

Fanny ran down Wind Street, her eyes obscured by her tears. Henry had gone now, she knew it. She had lost him. Why had she been so foolish to dream? A man stepped out in front of her and she almost crashed into him. 'Alright, lass?' he asked. 'I am looking for a bit of companionship. I has a bit of cash.' Fanny shuddered and ran around him. This was her life, her fate, her future. How could she have been so foolish to believe that she, of all people, could ever be happy? That she could be loved? Respected? Her future had been snatched away, not because of who she was, but because of what she was. She flung open the door to the Albany Vaults and stood, dramatically, in the doorway.

What on earth was she doing here? She really didn't know. Somehow she needed to confront Jack McCarthy. And what if he attacked her? Hurt her? Maybe even killed her? Did that matter? She realised that at this moment it didn't matter at all. She walked slowly to the counter, put some coins on it, pointed at a bottle and then drank a glass of brandy in one gulp; of course, it was good for her voice, made it smooth but gave it power. She had believed so many lies, why not this one?

She leaned her back against the counter and looked contemptuously around the room, glaring at the leering faces that had turned in her direction. She could not see Jack, but everyone could see her.

'Get 'em out, doll!' a sodden voice shouted, coloured by smoke.

There were sniggers from this ragged audience, but Fanny knew that she could command them and all the yearning of the past few weeks, the urge to find something better and the terrible feeling that she might be too late, that what she had was all that she was ever likely to have, surged through her. Everything she had ever wanted and wished for, had been consumed by the bitter disappointments of her life and by her awareness that she had been offered other roads to take that she had not chosen and on which now she could never hope to tread. And now she was here, in this filthy, stained inn, that would smell forever of sour beer, surrounded by drunks and tarts. She could see displayed before her their brutish and shallow lives, barely lived, at the very edge of society, where everyone tried to survive by exploiting the desperate needs of others. But suddenly a calm settled upon her at the greasy bar of this squalid place, at this rat-hole of broken dreams and wasted lives.

She would sing. She didn't know what compelled her, but she would sing. And she chose *Bugeilio'r Gwenith Gwyn*, the piece that had so disjointed the orchestra earlier in the day. It was called *Watching the White Wheat* in English and everyone knew it – apart, of course, from the orchestra - and at that moment, nothing spoke to her more clearly and more truthfully than this old Welsh song. *I fondly watch the blooming wheat. Another reaps the treasure.*

346

She began and Sally Solomon the cockle seller, standing by the bar, took her basket and placed it on the floor to listen. Suddenly the purity of Fanny's voice, the melody and the words, settled upon them all unexpectedly, for she expressed a longing that all of them shared, for something better than a life that had brought them here to this place. There were many there who did not know what she was singing – but the raw emotion swept them along. They were not just listening to her voice; they were listening to her heart, feeling their spines shiver with the passion in the air. Most of the woman knew the song and joined in, their voices lifting ever upwards in hope, and then falling away, descending into despair. These were women who sat on the laps of drunken strangers rummaging in their pockets for lost coins. And they knew there was another world in which they could never hope to live. The sailors were bemused by this sudden collective longing, feeling suddenly very out of place as the women sang of love that would always be denied to them. She changed the words very slightly as she sang

For in thy bosom, thoughtless man

My heart's true key thou bearest.

Fanny held the final note defiantly and then finished the song. She had laid herself bare in this awful place. No burning tears. They would come later, when she was alone. She stared at the room, at these men who did not deserve to know the anguish that lived within her soul.

'Well bugger me. Look who it is.' Jack was standing, leaning against the door that led out into the yard. 'The Lawyer's Whore. What's wrong? Can't find him? Or has be kicked you out?' He came and sat at a table in front of her, his eyes all the while focused on her. 'Still, you are back where you belong.' He took a drink from his pot and then spat it out on to the floor in a thin stream that washed over Fanny's boots. 'Maggie,' he called to the barmaid, 'your beer is shit.'

If he thought that he could puncture the mood in the bar, then he was wrong, He had intruded upon such a rare moment of reflection and everyone turned to look at him. There was no agreement, no laughter. Only silence. Fanny walked over to him, the fear and humiliation of her life finally finding an expression, and she slapped

347

him hard. He fell off his stool and she threw his beer over him. Still the bar was silent.

He rose, his waistcoat soaked in spilled beer, and hit her, his face rigid with hatred. The rest of the bar still watched. Fanny might have the voice of an angel but that counted for nothing, for this was how purity like hers was treated in Swansea. He grabbed Fanny and dragged her to the door and pushed her outside on to Wind Street. Jack stumbled after her, swearing.

'Steady on,' a feeble voice called after him but he was never going to listen. In his mind, his inability as a pimp to control his woman had been displayed publicly and there was a price that Fanny had to pay.

She slipped on the cobbles, fell on the ground, and Jack kicked her in the stomach. That was just to start. He watched Fanny curl herself into a ball. He decided to kick her again and after that he would pull her to her feet and start on her properly.

Suddenly someone pushed him in the back and he staggered away, barely managing to keep his feet. He turned round to see a well-dressed young man helping Fanny to her feet. 'Have a care, sir,' he said. 'Such behaviour is entirely unacceptable and constitutes a criminal offence. But in the first instance, Mr McCarthy, you are answerable to me.'

'Henry! No!' gasped Fanny. 'Just leave. Don't get involved.'

'But I am involved, Fanny. It is my choice. I have been looking for you. I need to talk.'

Jack looked at him with scorn. 'So this is him then, is it? The great Henry Fry. Too posh to be Harry, then?'

'Be careful, sir. I shall not allow such an assault upon the woman I love to go unpunished.'

'The woman you love?' Jack laughed riotously. 'Do you know what you are saying? Do you know what she is? She is a whore, Harry. That's what she is. A piece of mutton, a hedge-creeper. Yours for a shilling. She needs a beating, so you watch carefully whilst I do it.'

'And I tell you, sir, that you shall not.'

'Henry! Don't! Leave it alone! Go back to your life and leave me to mine!'

'I will never do that, Fanny. Never!'

Jack pulled out a long, ugly knife. 'Here we are, sonny. It is time to run along home. So stand aside or I shall cut out your heart. Be a good little boy and bugger off, or you are dead.'

'Henry!,' shouted Fanny. 'Please! Go! He means it. Go back to Harriet! This isn't for you!'

He did not move and held Jack's gaze. 'I must tell you that I boxed frequently at school. I had quite a reputation. I was no stranger to success.'

'And I have killed three men.' Jack waved the knife at him, as if bidding him goodbye.

Henry saw the proof in his eyes and was terrified, but he could not back down now.

'Jack! Leave him alone!' cried Fanny as he moved towards Henry, forcing him to back away along Wind Street. She saw a clay beer pot lying on the ground, picked it up and smashed the end of it. She pointed the ugly-looking spikes at him. 'I am warning you, Jack. Leave him be. Let him go.'

Police whistles seemed to be sounding some distance away, perhaps on High Street, but Jack was not distracted. He held Henry's eyes, smiling with malice, for Henry looked ridiculous in a traditional boxer's stance so rarely seen on Wind Street. He was leaning forward but steadily moving backwards before the blade. Jack switched suddenly and faced Fanny briefly, who also involuntarily took a step back. He continued to make false movements and laughed as Henry stepped back again, this time his back against a stationary brewer's dray, drawn by a large cart horse standing impassively, like a sculpture. At the end of the passage a small crowd from the Vaults watched the confrontation, unsure about whether they should risk an intervention.

Jack came a little closer. 'Look,' he said. 'Look at the knife. I shall split you open like a fish, do you understand? Nice and sharp it is. Won't feel a thing until you see your guts on the floor. Bet you will try to pick them up too, try to put them back inside. Won't work, sonny. You will die. Sure as an egg is an egg.' He raised his eyebrows and smiled. He could hear the police whistles again, but he knew that he still had time.

'No, Fanny!' shouted Henry suddenly. 'Don't! Stay back!'

Jack turned sharply and then stepped to the side as Fanny lurched towards him with the jagged clay pot. 'You will have to do better than that, whore.' He looked at her with scornful contempt. 'You wait there. Let me deal with the boy first.' He turned back to Henry who, in terrible fear, swung a punch at Jack's head as he dodged away from the horse. He missed but caught his shoulder. Jack laughed but lost his balance and stumbled into Fanny and, trying to regain his balance, staggered into the flank of that large cart horse, still standing immobile between the shafts of the dray. The horse shied, Jack fell to the ground, and in regaining its position, it stepped on his head with a terrible crunch. Henry watched with horror as the hoof slid off Jack's forehead, that cracked and oozed like a squashed egg, and then, unable to avert his eyes, saw the horse tread on him again, this time in the mouth, with a horrible cracking of teeth. Quite unexpectedly, and as the whistles got louder and the boots of the policemen could be heard, Jack McCarthy was dead.

Henry and Fanny stared at each other, stunned at how a life had ended so quickly and how their own lives had, potentially, been transformed. Horror, elation, relief, fear – all the emotions were clearly visible on their faces as Inspector Bucke arrived, with four breathless constables.

He looked at Jack, with one blank eye staring at the horse's abdomen above him. 'Damn! Damn!' he cursed. He turned to Fanny and Henry who were holding on to each other in shock. 'The child!' he demanded. 'The child! Did he say anything about a child? A girl?'

'Please accept my sincere apologies, Inspector,' said Henry, a little pompously, 'but I appear to have been present during an altercation

350

in which a man has met with an unfortunate death.'

'Did Jack McCarthy mention a young girl before he died, Mr Fry? Did he speak about a man called Abramovitch? It is vitally important,' said Bucke. 'Please try to remember.'

Henry was flattered that Inspector Bucke knew his name. 'We didn't speak a great deal, Inspector. He was intent on killing me and I defended myself.'

'I killed him, sir,' said Fanny. 'It was an accident but I am responsible –'

'Hush, Fanny,' interrupted Henry. 'No, Inspector Bucke. I hit him in self-defence. He attacked my…' Henry struggled for the right word and then blurted out all that was in his heart. 'My fiancée. With that knife you see there,' pointing. 'Isn't that right, Miss Stevens?'

'Yes it is.' Fanny was stunned, barely able to speak in the face of this bewildering turn of events.

Henry continued. 'I struck him a glancing blow, he lost his footing and he fell under the horse, as you can see.'

Bucke looked at the scene before him and shook his head. He had been so close to Amy and now she had gone. 'He was with no one else? No man? No young girl?' He turned to Fanny. 'And you saw nothing, either, Miss Stevens?' Fanny shook her head. 'Did Jack McCarthy say anything to you recently about the girl? Amy? Sarah Rigby's girl? Anything? Did he tell you where he was going tonight?'

Fanny spoke quietly. 'All he said was that he was meeting someone here. I knew that Amy has gone missing but he never spoke to me of her. He has been very violent towards me,' she added as an afterthought.

'He was an unpleasant and violent man, Inspector, who has made numerous threats to my fiancée. As you know, I am a solicitor at law and I acted in self-defence. That cannot be doubted. I shall represent myself in what is likely to be a brief case in the coroner's court,'

'And fighting in the street is an offence, Mr Fry. You, of all people, will know that.'

'Of course. But I have every right to defend myself and indeed to come to the assistance of another, in this case the woman I love.' He spoke with a confidence Fanny had not properly seen before. 'You, of all people, will know that,' he echoed.

'It is all about circumstances, Mr Fry.'

'Indeed it is, Inspector.' Henry put a protective arm around Fanny's waist.

Bucke, frustrated by his inability to question McCarthy, had no inclination to deal with an increasingly confident solicitor, and certainly not in public on Wind Street. He needed to act, for Amy might not be far away. He turned to two of the constables and sent them back to pick up Milford and Bridget and take them to the cells. He sent Morris into the Vaults to see what he could find out and he sent Smith off to the docks in possible pursuit of Abramovitch. Why had he come to this end of Wind Street if he wasn't planning to escape on a ship? Gill had turned up in response to the whistles and he was told to guard the body until the police wagon came. McCarthy's head was a horrible sight and the barmaid from the Vaults came out with an old blanket that they used to cover it. Bucke himself took Henry and Fanny back to Tontine Street. They wouldn't cause him any difficulties and it would give him a chance to consider his next steps.

As they walked up to Castle Square Fanny whispered to Henry. 'Am I your fiancée, do you think?' she asked.

'Well, if you are not, then I have been lying to the police. Could make things a great deal worse,' he smiled.

'But what will happen now?'

'Don't you worry. Nothing very much. Self-defence, after all. Everyone saw it. I will either be discharged or I might have to do a month in gaol. You will wait for me, Fanny? Won't you?' He squeezed her hand. 'Who would have thought that this would happen? We might have to move away from Swansea. Start again somewhere new. But we will be together. Strange, isn't it? Your Jack has given us a future. We should be grateful.'

Twenty Nine

The trail had gone cold. Amy had been taken to the Vaults and had been handed over to Abramovitch, but Bucke had no idea where he had taken her. Police constables were patrolling the streets, asking questions but to little effect. He questioned Henry and Fanny to find out if they had seen anything but they were unable to help him. Neither of them knew anything about the girl. Bucke had been so very close, but he had lost her again. He finished his meeting with Fanny Stevens and told her to keep herself available; she was an important witness to what had happened on Wind Street.

Fanny left and, as she closed the door to Inspector Bucke's office, she saw Sarah Rigby sitting tensely on a wooden bench in the lobby. 'Any news, Sarah?' she asked. Sarah shook her head and Fanny sat down next to her.

'It's been a week now.' She bit a lip that was already sore and cracked. 'Amy could be anywhere. He could have fallen, she could be trapped, she could be hurt. Anything.' She did not want to consider anything more serious, but she had started to confront the horror. 'I want to believe that someone has taken Amy, but no one has seen her. I am desperate, Fanny.' She closed her eyes and clutched Fanny's hand. 'I can't stay here, she announced suddenly. 'There is nothing they can tell me.' Sarah drew in her breath loudly and then bit her lip again to hold back the tears as she walked quickly out of the police station.

Fanny decided she should let her go. There was nothing she could say that could make her feel better, she knew that. There were some sorrows that could not be shared, sorrows for which comfort and solace can never be found. She leaned back on the bench and put her head against the wall. What was she going to do? She could feel the tears filling her eyes, and she did not cry very often. She saw Sergeant Ball behind the counter watching her, pretending to be busy. She asked if she could see Henry Fry but Ball refused. 'Come back tomorrow, Miss Stevens. In the morning, if you please. I should be able to slip you in then.' Fanny smiled thinly and went towards the door that led to the darkness of Tontine Street; the constables returning from their fruitless search for Amy, stood aside to let her pass.

Once she was outside the tears came, properly now. Perhaps it was for the best. This was a relationship that could never prosper. She knew it was not what Henry needed. He would soon tire of her, she was certain. The loss of his family, his status, his career was a huge price to pay, and she was sure that he had neither the strength nor the experience to end their relationship himself. Fanny stared into the night at nothing at all. Now that Jack had gone, so suddenly and unexpectedly, she had a chance to cut herself free from everything and start again somewhere else. Without making a conscious decision, she started walking briskly back to Elephant Court. The streets were quiet and she saw no one she knew. There was a squabbling crowd of drunks outside the Full Moon public house but she crossed to the other side of the road where the gas lamp was broken and no one saw her

She had a carpet bag under her bed into which she stuffed some clothes and her tattered newspaper cuttings. She then recovered a dirty linen bag that was tied out of sight to the leg of the bed against the wall. Her money; the money that Jack hadn't known about. It wasn't much, but it was a start. She grabbed her umbrella and left the room without a backward glance, clattering swiftly down the stairs. She was going to High Street Station in search of a London train. Fanny had a sister in Pimlico. She hadn't seen her in years but no one in Swansea knew anything about her. She'd get work in a music hall, there were lots of them in London, and she would be able to get her own place in a week or two. Would Henry come looking for her? Well, he couldn't until his court case had reached its conclusion. Her trail could have gone cold by then.

And then she stopped at the entrance to the station and leaned against the wall. *Why am I doing this?,* she asked herself repeatedly. *Why? Why?*

And the answer came quickly, unbidden. *Because I love Henry, that's why. Because my life has always been chaotic. It always will be. This is who I am.*

How could it ever think it might be different?

And so, because she loved someone - a man, a boy, so much younger than her, innocent, intelligent, trusting – because she loved him she was running away? How could that be? How could that make sense? *Because I am Fanny Stevens.* What other reason could there ever be?

She went to the office and bought a ticket. A single ticket to London on the last train of the day, change at Cardiff for the 10.30 pm to Paddington. Third class. 20s 7d. Seven hours. She would sleep on the train, if she could. The Angel of Swansea was flying away and she wandered down to Platform Two to wait for the train that was coming in from Llanelly. Fanny looked absently around her. The station was smoke-stained and dismal, with gas lamps casting lonely, fragile, barely-glowing pools.

And then she saw her, in one of the distant puddles of yellowed light. Amy. Unmistakably Amy. With a man. Was that the one who Jack met, the one with the strange name? Abram or something? Ovitch? Was that it? He had Amy. How? That didn't matter. She saw the girl drift away from him and then she was suddenly pulled back, He had her on a lead, like a dog, attached to his wrist by a chain or a rope. She sat down at his feet, her head bowed. They were waiting for the train, due in fifteen minutes. Fanny looked around but could see no one else. What should she do? She walked quickly out on to High Street. The police station was on the other side of the road but Sarah was there, walking the streets aimlessly as she had done for the past two days. She waved at her. 'Amy! She is in the station! A man has got her! I'll go to the police.'

Sarah's eyes opened wide and immediately she ran into the station, whilst Fanny approached a constable who had just emerged from Tontine Street. Fanny didn't know him but she had to assume that he was competent. 'Hurry!' she called. 'Waste no time! I am sure Inspector Bucke is in the police station. Tell him that the missing girl Amy is in on Platform Two. Quickly! Before the Cardiff train arrives!' Constable Payne paused. 'Now!' shouted Fanny. He weighed up his options, turned and ran back inside. 'It will need more than one of you!' she called after him and then waited for a moment or two to see if he emerged, She decided however that it would be better to go and support Sarah in any way that she could.

When Fanny got back to the station she could see the distant confrontation between Sarah and Abramovitch at the far end of the platform. He wasn't beneath the light anymore so she could not see him and she was not sure what to do. It was with relief that she heard the running footsteps of the policemen approaching her.

Sarah stared steadily ahead in spite of her breathlessness, whilst Abramovitch pointed his gun straight at her. His hand did not waver, did not move. 'Sarah,' whimpered Amy. 'Sarah.' It was the first time she had ever seen Amy distressed and it cut her heart in two. She tried to recover her composure after running so quickly.

'You are nothing,' sneered Abramovitch. 'You have nothing. I have the girl. I can shoot you – and I will. Now leave.'

'I won't leave because you are wrong. I have everything,' replied Sarah. 'Because I love. And I have the one thing you will never possess – Amy's love. She is not your daughter and we both know that and I know she will hate you if you shoot me.'

Abramovitch shook his head faintly. 'This is real life, not a story book. Do you think I care? She is evidence, that is all. And when she has proved that she is Chana, then maybe she has an unhappy accident and so then the estate passes from her to her uncle. So why should I give her to you? Nicolae, her father died in the house when it was burnt and so everything is hers and so I had to come here to collect her. My duty. One sickly orphan from Swansea will not be missed. You have many.'

'She is not an orphan.' Sarah knew. She did not need proof. Amy was her child, the one she had given away seven years ago, she knew it for certain; deep within her soul, she knew. Nothing else could explain her feelings. She had found her daughter again and now, not even death, could be worse than losing her again. 'You will never escape. Not now. The police are coming. I can hear their boots.'

'You lie.'

357

'Listen,' she said, taking a step towards him.

'You stay. Or the child dies.'

'Sarah,' sobbed Amy.

Sarah took another step. 'You can't get away. The police -'

'Never underestimate the stupidity of your policemen.' Then he heard them. He snarled and dragged Amy back into the shadows. He didn't want to shoot, not yet; he didn't want anyone to know where he was, but he was angry with himself. Coming to the station had been a stupid mistake, a foolish miscalculation. He had not expected that the police would have found him. It was too obvious and so, surely, the last place they should have looked. Surely they should have decided he was too clever to use the train? Jack had offered to arrange a place on a ship for him but he hadn't trusted him. Perhaps he was right to do so. But had he indeed betrayed him? Or those vile women who had kept the girl? He backed away from Sarah, pulling Amy with him, his gun still steady. 'You stay where you are,' he called.

He needed to bottle up his anger, it was stopping him thinking properly. He needed to remain calm, but that was very difficult. Everything had been carefully planned; it should not have gone wrong. He had bought tickets in the morning and he had entered the station unseen this evening through the sidings at the end of Pottery Street. So how did they know he was here?

The platform was quiet, as far as he could see beneath its inadequate lighting. He could not see Sarah and wondered if she was trying to circle around him. It was being imprisoned in Budapest that had ruined his plans, had delayed him unnecessarily and for such a long time – that, and his desire to find Ovid's scroll. He had been too ambitious. He was never going to find the scroll now and a forgery was too complicated to arrange. He should have kept it simple – find a suitable girl in Germany or somewhere and return in triumph with her and the glass heftel. But no, he had wanted the public acclaim for recovering the scroll, the national rejoicing might even have become the basis for a career in politics for the kind of national hero he would have undoubtedly have become. The idea of fame had been too seductive; he should have concentrated on inheriting the estates. Now, though, he needed to concentrate on getting out of Swansea.

His mind was working fast. The train was no longer a viable option if the police had indeed arrived. He needed to get out and lie low for a while as Szarmach the sailor. He could try a ship. Or a cart to Neath or someplace with a station. He could walk, even. He was trying hard to persuade himself, not very successfully, that this was merely an irritation. Take the girl, go back across the tracks. Get out of the station and he could slip away. He had to dispose of Amy now, since she would only slow him down. He needed to get back across the Channel and then he could find another girl. That wouldn't be too hard. Paris was full of them. Or there was London, too. He would find one there, too. But he was angry with himself. After all he had achieved, how could he have got it so wrong?

Abramovitch still watched out for Sarah but still couldn't see her and so he then dragged Amy further down the platform. If Sarah stepped into that pool of light there he could shoot and then run across the tracks. But he needed to stay silent. He would deal with Amy, quietly, when he was out of the station, but he could not do that when they were tethered like this. Not now. He needed to concentrate. If he had her, it might inhibit the police. He leaned close to the sobbing child, smelling her fear. 'Shut up or I shall kill you. Understand?' There was a shout from the far end of the platform, down at the entrance.

'He is there,' Fanny shouted. Bucke stopped by her side, looked at her luggage and gave her a quizzical glance.

'What are you doing here? I thought I had told you…' He left his sentence unfinished as he looked along the platform into the gloom. He glanced at Fanny briefly. 'I will deal with you later. Stand here,' he ordered her. 'Like a passenger. Put your bag by your feet. Look normal. When the train arrives you climb on board. But please try to look normal, for god's sake.' He turned away but then turned back with an afterthought. 'The train isn't going anywhere, so you stay on it until I come to get you.' He looked at her, briefly, with more sympathy. 'And thank you for what you have done,' before he sent

Payne off to find the station master. He pulled the constables into the shadows, whilst they listened to what he had in mind.

Bucke was energised. Finally he would be able to assert some control. The station would soon be his, secured and arranged as he required, and the constables could be deployed as he wanted them. At last, he had what he had been waiting for. He could slowly force Abramovitch under his control and make him to go where he wanted him to go. But his priority had to be to save the child. Too many children had died since this man had come to town.

Mr Prosser, the Station master, was initially confused by the group of policemen in the shadows of Platform Two but he was sharp enough to understand and implement Bucke's careful intentions. 'The Cardiff train is coming in from Llanelly in 10 minutes, I believe, Mr Prosser. Where would that be?'

'On Platform Two, Inspector. This platform here. As normal, Inspector.'

'Do you have another passenger train available, Mr Prosser? An empty one?'

'I can provide you with an additional train, Inspector,' replied Prosser after a moment's thought.

'Good. What I would like you to do, Mr Prosser, is to direct the train from Llanelly on to Platform One and keep all passengers on board, even if they wish to get off. But do not announce it. Not at all.' Prosser nodded. 'I would like you to bring the additional, empty, train into Platform Two now. Tell the man at the end of the platform, the one dressed like a sailor, the one with the little girl, that it's the Cardiff train. Let him get on it, if that is what he wants. Once he is on the train we shall have him. That train is going nowhere. Close off the station entrance- don't let anyone else on to any of the platforms until our business is concluded.' He looked at Fanny again. 'I shall speak to you later, I promise I will. In the meantime, you get on the train, I want him to think you are an ordinary passenger. Then stay there.'

The station was his now.

Abramovitch had not moved. Was he trapped? That was his greatest fear, but he still thought he could get away, even if the child slowed him down a little. He could use a train to hide his movements. A plan was forming. He watched figures slipping occasionally out of the shadows at the end of the platform, down near the buffers. The station was a terminus and trains could only arrive and depart in one direction. He smiled. He didn't have to leave that way though. He had come in to the station across the tracks. He could leave that way too. It was darker, and it was more complicated, with sheds and machinery. He could lose them, he was sure. Then, as if to illustrate how cluttered a station could become, he was aware of the sound of an engine behind him and smiled with relief.

A train with five or six carriages rattled slowly and noisily along the rails on to Platform One until it squealed and squeaked itself stationary just before the buffers. Nothing dramatic happened. No passengers got off the train, as far as he could see. No one got on. In the gloom it looked empty. Abramovitch couldn't remember the timetable well enough to know its destination, but then, there was the sound of another train behind him. This one reversed in slowly next to him, dragging its carriages with it, and a man in an official-looking hat appeared on the platform, pointing at it, shouting '7.20 train to Cardiff! Platform Two for Cardiff!' So near and yet so far, but he dare not board it, not now that the police were here. He would be trapped if that woman told the police where he was. There was no where he could hide on a train, was there?

The train seemed empty and perhaps it was not a popular service, and not knowing made him feel a little uncomfortable. He watched a woman with a bag and an umbrella climb on board. It must be the Cardiff train, as the railway man said. He tried to guess what the police would think. Did they really expect him to climb on board this train? Is that what they believed? They were so stupid they might well think that he would do so. There was no need for him to be so nervous. He could cross the tracks quickly before either train pulled out and escape into the town. So he started to drag the reluctant Amy down the line to the darker end of the platform.

Bucke crept along the wall by the side of Platform Two, peering into the darkness in front of him, looking for Sarah. He found her about half way along. She seemed to know who it was before he said anything. She spoke over her shoulder.

'He is there. I can just make out the two of them. It is that Abramovitch man. He seems to be moving down the platform to the back of the train.'

Bucke put his hand on her arm. 'Sarah, please. You have done well. Now let me deal with this. I have my men with me. This is no job for you.'

Because it was dark, he could not see the exasperation in her eyes. She turned round to face him. 'Deal with it properly, Rumsey. Save Amy. Save my child.'

He looked briefly surprised, but he did not have time to respond to what she said. A slip of the tongue in her distress, he felt, and he led her back towards the entrance hall.

'Please be quick. He says he will shoot Amy. I am sure he means it.'

'He has a gun? Thank you for telling me. The constables and I will cross the tracks and work ourselves along the other platform. We will get him, do not fear, Sarah.'

'I care nothing for him. I want my Amy back.'

'I know. And you shall have her. Move further back down the platform for me please, Sarah. Shout out if he comes back towards you and we are not in sight.'

He told Constable Davies to guard the entrance hall and prevent anyone going on to either platform. Then, with the others, Bucke ran on to Platform One, past the engine with its smell of oil and steam and coal, and past the carriages where passengers pressed their faces against the steamy windows to catch a glimpse of this unexpected excitement. When they reached the rear of the train they jumped on to the tracks and Bucke held them back. He was sure they had overtaken him.

'Is that him there?' asked Gill, pointing through the gaps between the carriages, at a vague shape on the other platform.

A shot rang out, the bullet striking one of the rails and bouncing off into the darkness.

'Spread out, constables! Keep down.' Bucke jumped forward and slid behind the train. 'Abramovitch! You are under arrest. Throw your gun down on to the tracks, now.' There was another shot, a defiant reply. There were the sounds of movement on the platform behind him and, as he looked along the tracks he could see that the constables had crossed the rails and were crouching low against the edge of Platform Two, ready to mount it on his order. He knew though, that he had to be the first. He turned and went down to the couplings between the last two carriages and used those to climb on to the platform. He was close to Abramovitch now, who was wrestling with a recalcitrant Amy, dragging her roughly by the rope. Morris, who had been watching Bucke, instructed the other constables to climb up and then spread out behind him. There must have been a noise, a footfall, a loud breath or something, because that was when Abramovitch heard them and turned to stare defiantly down the platform.

'I shall tell you this so that you understand clearly, Inspector, sir.' He pulled Amy up against him and pointed the gun briefly at her head. 'I do not find it hard to kill children. I have done this already. And I shall do it again. You policemen, Inspector, sir, must walk away slowly. Or I shall kill this child. She is not important to me. When it suits me, I can find another.' Yet in spite of his defiant words, he stepped backwards towards the engine. Bucke matched his steps. Abramovitch was being driven back towards the entrance hall, which was not the direction he wanted. Very suddenly, he really was starting to feel trapped. 'You need to understand. This child is nothing to me. She is vermin.' Again Abramovitch, perhaps unconsciously, retreated a little further. He was next to the engine now. 'You must walk away, Inspector, sir. Or she dies.' He knew that Amy was all he had and even she might not be enough to take him to safety. He decided that he had to kill her quickly in front of the police, to cause shock and confusion, and then out-run them. He couldn't see an alternative. But he would somehow have to get the rope unbuckled from his wrist, and he did not have a free hand.

He was running out of platform now and was effectively surrounded. Bucke could not be sure what his intentions were but the priority had to be Amy. And Bucke did not blink. He did not react. He dare not indicate that Sarah was behind Abramovitch, creeping slowly towards the steam engine. He wasn't sure what she was doing either. 'Mr Abramovitch, you cannot escape. You are trapped here on this railway platform. Killing the child would be a futile gesture. It would achieve nothing. I am arresting you. Please listen carefully. Your case is serious and the charges against you are very serious indeed. You will be charged with five murders, do you understand?' Sarah had reached the footplate now.

Abramovitch laughed. 'Is that all, Inspector, sir? You know so little.'

'I believe that you have killed others too, but I will charge you in the first instance with the murders of the young boys, Dolphin, Mazey, Connor and Woods and that of the cab driver Iestyn Godfrey.' He knew he had to make this last as long as he could, to give Sarah more time to do whatever she was doing. 'Shall I tell you what I think, Mr Abramovitch. I think you came to Swansea to find the child Chana, and you expected it to be easy. When it wasn't, when Felton Butler was dead and the family had fallen apart, you were ready to take any child. No one would ever question her and anyway you planned to kill her soon enough, whether she really was Chana or not. This isn't your daughter, because you are not a father. That has only ever been a pretence. You are here to secure an inheritance.'

He tried to focus entirely upon Abramovitch and not watch Sarah climb up into the panting engine.

'So who are you? The wicked uncle? Is that it?' Once again, he felt as if he was living through the terrible details of *The Children of the Wood*. 'You see, I know there never was a Hungarian. There never was a man called Czibor. It was you. You murdered in Hungary and then came here, first in secret, and butchered those first two boys, didn't you? Is that the kind of thing you like? Is that what gives you pleasure? And after you had done that, you went to Neath and then came into this station on the train, for everyone to see, as if you had only just arrived.'

Sarah had now disappeared from view.

'It is my duty to caution you that you must be very careful in what you say, for what you do say I shall have to repeat and it may be used in evidence against you.'

'Go to hell, Inspector, sir. Now. Go completely to hell. Back away or I kill the child. As you say, I have done this before. Only this time, Inspector, you will have to watch.' He pulled Amy close to him and pushed the gun harshly into the side of her head. For the first time, he didn't have a plan, other than flight. He had to kill the child, shock the policemen, and then improvise. But there was still the lead that joined them.

Suddenly a tremendous hiss of steam shot out from a valve and engulfed his legs. Abramovitch screamed and the gun was thrown involuntarily from his hand and clattered down on to the track as the steam spun him around. He released Amy, who ran towards Bucke to the extent of the rope that tethered her. Bucke grabbed it and held it tight, standing in front of Amy and taking the strain. Constable Morris was quickly at his side and used a pocket knife to cut through it. When the leash was severed, both Bucke and Abramovitch fell backwards, the rope snaking away with the release of the pressure. At the same time, the train began to move slowly. The rope whipped itself into the wheels of the engine, and the coupling rods that joined the driving wheels drew it into their mechanism, turning Abramovitch around and pulling him with it. He was dragged inexorably towards the train as it moved away along the platform, hissing and snorting like a long-tethered bull that had just been released.

Abramovitch fumbled desperately at the buckle on the strap at his wrist, but the chain was secure. 'Help me!' he shouted, struggling to keep his footing, unable to resist he power of the engine. Bucke ran to his side to try and help him, but the rope was disappearing into the train so quickly and, like a snake, would not stay still.

'Quick Morris! Cut the rope!' But it had become very short very quickly and Abramovitch was screaming now. Morris could do nothing to stop the train eating up the rest of the rope because he could not hold it steady for long enough cut it quickly . Bucke barely noticed Sarah jump down from the cab and run back past the desperate man without a glance, to sweep up Amy and hold her tight, never to let her go, sheltering her face from the horror that was unfolding. The station master and the engine driver raced past them too, to climb on to the train to stop it, but it was too late and Bucke, desperately holding on to his elbow lost his grip and had to watch Abramovitch being eaten beneath the wheels.

He was pulled off the platform and, still screaming, Abramovitch was hauled into the iron wheels and then slowly but methodically destroyed by the heavy machine. It was a terrible sight. The wheels were spinning in the blood, briefly unable to grip. The smell of that blood, mixed with the axle grease and the smoke and the steam would stay with Bucke for the rest of his life. The clanking of the couplings and the grinding of the wheels were the sounds of the train consuming a man, flesh and bone.

The driver stopped the train. There were now ten yards of the track that looked like an extended butcher's shop. The head seemed to have disappeared, though there were clumps of gore that might once have formed some part of it. Then, as Gill leaned, white-faced against the wall, Bucke saw an unmistakable lower jaw, still with three teeth properly embedded. Someone would have to clean it up, but it might be best not to involve Gill.

This was the man he had fought with in the warehouse, he knew that as soon as he had held on to his arm, in his vain attempt to prevent a dreadful death. Everyone would say that he deserved it. But he had left behind so many unanswered questions, not least, who was he? Was Bucke's story correct? Did that come near the truth? How would he ever know? What did he want, and most importantly, how many people had he killed, and why? He had killed at least four innocent boys. What had they done to be selected for a cruel death? To Abramovitch they were merely human material, neither useful nor valued, just disposable. But to what end? Bucke sometimes thought that his life was composed entirely of unanswerable questions. Was this really the answer that had eluded him over the past weeks? That two deaths in the town had been caused by a fat soldier and the others by this vile length of pie filling spread along a railway track? Was that it? But why?

How had Abramovitch arrived in Swansea? Things started to fit together if you believed that he arrived unnoticed on a boat – like the *Ann of Bridgewater* - and then into the town with full-fuss on that train from Neath. If that was the case, it was all part of an elaborate deception. Was he really here to look for his daughter? Did he want Amy for who he thought she was? Or because she seemed to be the right age? The real Chana had died or disappeared, Bucke was sure of that. But now Abramovitch had been ground into pieces so small that each piece of him was not substantial enough to offer a word of explanation, nor even an individual letter.

'Can I let the Cardiff train go, Inspector?' asked Mr Prosser, interrupting his thoughts. 'It is a little late but it should make the London connection if it has a decent run.'

Bucke nodded 'Yes, we have what we want. We have the child. Let it go, Mr Prosser. And thank you for your help. You did good work tonight.'

Prosser tipped his hat with pride and so, with metal rolling against unstained metal, the train pulled out of Swansea High Street station, the passengers disappointed that the entertainment had finished so suddenly and with little explanation. They had hardly seen anything at all.

Bucke went to Sarah, still entwined with Amy, their shared tension and fear washed away by their tears. He felt he was intruding, but he had to ask her. 'What happened, Sarah?'

She pulled her wet face briefly away from Amy. 'I pulled every lever that I could. My father was an engine driver and he showed me how to drive one. This was an old train. Or my father was with me.'

She shook her head. She had more important issues to think about.

A child needed to be loved, and Amy would be loved, always. She was her daughter and she had given birth to her. That possibility would have gnawed at her forever, unless she accepted it now and always, as an indisputable truth. Amy occasionally emerged from her shoulder and tried to wipe away Sarah's tears. Sarah knew she was such a wise girl, although she had so much that she needed to forget. She also knew that somewhere else, they could both forget so many things and start again, anew and together.

Sarah gasped, composing herself. 'Rumsey I must have your help. Please. The ship to America, sails soon tonight. I want to be on the *Polaria* with Amy. I knew that if I got her back this is what I would do. Please will you help me?'

He knew better than to suggest she waited and think very carefully about such an enormous decision. He knew that she had dreamed of this for a long time. It was a chance, suddenly presented to her, and she had to seize it. He nodded. 'Of course, Sarah. But if this is what you want, then we must move. We haven't much time. You will also need money, you know.'

'Constance knows. It is in the piano stool.'

'Very well. Let's go. We will use the police wagon. Morris!' he called. 'This is yours now, I have business. Re-open the station. Turner! Deal with the body, if you will.' Then he spoke to Gill, who still looked very pale. He needed something to take his mind off the scene. 'I must escort Miss Rigby and Amy to a different part of town. In my absence, could you get Fanny Stevens from the train please? . Tell her I will see her in the morning. Then you go home, constable. You don't look well.'

Gill looked in every compartment of the empty train, but Fanny wasn't there. She had disappeared.

*

Fanny sat in the cold, unheated and uninviting waiting room alone, waiting for the last train to London, dabbing away the tears that still crept down her face, with her wet handkerchief. She had watched the last train of the night from Cardiff to Swansea depart. She had thought very carefully about getting on it and returning to Swansea before anyone knew she had gone, to accept whatever might happen next. But she had made up her mind. And she realised that the further into the journey she went, at each separate stage, she had been more certain that she would never go back.

It was dark on the station and there was little to look at, but she was lost in her memories, smiling at the image of young Henry Fry facing a raucous audience from his place in the stalls at the Star Theatre and trying to calm them for her. Or the look of horror on his face when he saw the dead cat someone had brought in and threatened to throw at a conjurer. She remembered too, the feel of his young body, the tenderness of his hands.

A doomed love? But a wonderful one, the best moments of her disordered life. She knew that it was time to move on. By killing Jack, however accidentally, Henry had set her free.

Now London was waiting. For the Welsh Nightingale, perhaps? London, the capital of the Empire, the centre of the world. Or merely another place in which she could get things monumentally wrong? Her life had been littered with mistakes and missed opportunities and there was every chance this was to be another, eager to be added to that long list.

She had been a bird that sang in a cage, hanging outside a dirty window beneath grey heavy clouds. And every day, imprisoned as she was, she sang to make other people feel better, no matter the cost to herself. But now? Someone had left the door open and the nightingale could fly away. And would the bird stay free? Or would it inevitably climb into another cage?

Henry might come looking for her one day. He could find her, too; he was very determined and resourceful. And he would find her living with some vile petty criminal, because that is what she did, and every night she would sing simple songs loudly to drunks and wonder what she had done to her life. And then what? What would Henry do?

She had crossed from one train to another when they were side by

369

side at High Street Station in Swansea, helped into an adjacent third class compartment by a flirtatious travelling salesman who had thankfully disappeared into the Cardiff night after she had politely declined his offer of a drink at the Station Arms before her train departed. 'I am meeting a friend. Such a man,' she had said. 'A captain in the Dragoons.' It was a lie that usually worked. Encounters like this had been her life once before. They would return, she knew. Henry had once told her that he was worried that she would find a dragoon. She squeezed her eyes shut for a moment. Why did he always think he wasn't good enough for her?

Fanny had known that when she had slipped secretly from one train to another she had made a choice. One of those train lines represented staying in Swansea; the other something else, something unpredictable. She could never know what would have happened if she had stayed on the first train and had then been escorted back to the police station. The rail track that she was on now, led to a completely different place. And, no; there could be no going back. The thought that she could have climbed onto the last train to Swansea and returned was a delusion. She had made her choice. For better or for worse that choice was hers, and hers alone.

She rubbed her side, still sore where Jack had kicked her, then picked up her bag and went outside to stand on the platform to wait for the train. It wouldn't be long.

Thirty

They chased Nora Leary through the *Polaria*. They didn't really have time for this, since they were sailing in ten minutes, but it was never going to be that difficult to catch a woman who did not understand the layout of the ship. Nora had been desperate to find somewhere to hide but she'd been spotted trying to climb into one of the lifeboats and so had run. Initially she seemed to be trying to go down into the hold, screaming as she almost fell down the stairwells. Then she went back up towards the deck, the baby clutched closely to her breast. She stopped; a breathless, wretched, tearful woman, drowning in despair.

An elderly Russian woman, moved by her distress, reached out to her in a narrow passageway to lay a kindly hand upon her cheek and brush away a tear. In response Nora tried to force the baby on her, pushing him on to the old woman with both hands. She shook her head regretfully and held up her hands in refusal, then indicated with her head that the officers were closing in on her. She ran up once again and found that she had been driven back on to the deck. Now the men edged her slowly towards the gangway that was still in place. Nora turned around, bewildered and trapped and so she backed away until she found herself pressed against the port-side gunwale, with nowhere to go.

Nora stood, panting. The sea was calling to her, offering a route to America, but they were now going to put her off the ship and sail away without her and her son. She looked at the officer closest to her, a tall man, strong, good looking – a representation in her eyes, of the life her son was now to be denied. 'Please take him. Please. He is a good boy. A lovely boy.'

The sailors stood back from her in a semi-circle. Nora looked at each of them in turn, at their uniforms which suggested an ordered, purposeful life, nothing at all like her own. And here on this ship, soon departing for another world, where there could have been another life for her and her son, all Nora's hopes had crumbled into dust. 'Please take my son. He is a good little boy,' she repeated. 'Please give him a chance.'

Captain Winckler was anxious about the time he was losing. They really needed to get the *Polaria* out to sea. As far as he knew, all his passengers were back on board and all the crew were present and at their posts, apart from two drunken stokers who were snoring in their hammocks. He was running out of patience, and he was a patient man. Where was Inspector Bucke? He had sent a message to ask him to hold the ship for as long as he could, whilst he collected the money for a new paying passenger. Why a policeman had to do such a thing he could not understand, but perhaps it was one of their duties in Wales. But if he didn't return soon, then they would sail regardless. That woman with the child, pacing the quayside below would be left behind. And then this, when everything had been going so well.

'Madam,' he said. 'Please. You are distressing yourself. Let us perhaps talk about this.' He could always put her on the tugboat and have her brought back once they were in the open water. He started to move towards her. Nora gasped, turned and held her baby over the side of the ship. 'Come near me, take one more step – and I will drop him over the side.'

Winckler stopped, horrified by the woman's fragile grip on her son. If the ship rocked, or if she was startled by something, the child would surely fall. 'Please, madam. There is no need.' He gestured quietly to his officers and together they took a step backwards. 'You are over-wrought, I think. We understand your anxieties.' He wasn't sure what he could say or what he could do. 'I have some clothes in my cabin that my own son no longer requires. I am sure they would be ideal for your delightful boy. What is his name, madam?' She stared wildly at him, saying nothing.

The steam tug was ready, waiting for the signal, but Winckler could not leave, not with a woman threatening to throw her child in the dock. He could hear a noise from the quayside, shouting and a distant whistle, and Overath, mouthed '*Polizie,*' hopefully, though he could see nothing. It might help if the woman thought the police had arrived, but not if the child went into the water. 'Madam,' he said quietly, 'Let us think carefully. All of us. I cannot allow you, in your unhappiness, to harm an innocent child. I would never be able –'

372

'Don't you dare come near me!' shouted Nora.

'Captain Winckler.' There was voice behind him, speaking in German, and he turned slightly, unwilling to surrender eye contact with the woman, hoping that it was the thing pinning the woman to the deck. 'Captain Winckler, please captain.' It was that couple who had always been in the same place on the *Polaria,* at the stern looking out to sea together, at the wake the ship left behind, quiet and self-contained, looking into their past, he always thought. He was sure he had never seen either of them at any of the social events he had attended on board. The man spoke again. He was an elderly man of quiet dignity, spare with fair hair, thinner than he would like, in one of Mrs Raatz's old tweed suits, that was slightly too large and so hanging from him in genteel poverty. 'My name is Otto Haller. This is my wife, Elsa.' She smiled and bowed her head. She was small and trim, much younger than her husband. Her once attractive face had a haunted look, her dark eyes deep with sorrow. 'We come from a village near Dusseldorf. We will take the child, if it is permitted. We lost our own son some months ago. There is a hole in our hearts and perhaps this poor Welsh child can fill it for us. Tell her that we will take the boy from her. We will offer him love and he will share our new life. Please ask her. We will call him Felix, like our own son. Please ask her for us. We cannot yet speak English. Please tell her though, that we cannot pay for him. We have no money.'

'I don't think it is money she requires, *Herr* Haller.' Winckler assessed them carefully. He knew he was under pressure to get the ship off the dock and there was a real temptation to accept the offer because it was expedient. But he saw in their eyes that they were genuine and that unexpectedly they had been offered an end to the grief that haunted them. There would be a woman somewhere on board who would be able to act as a wet nurse for the voyage. He would willingly pay for that himself.

A new beginning? It was the dream of everyone on the *Polaria.* Sometimes it came true. He nodded to the Hallers. '*Danke.* I shall put your offer to her.'

It was a relief, a solution, but Winckler still saw it as a tragedy. He watched a mother handing over her son, knowing that she was unlikely ever to see him again. He watched his sailors, who now started their practised duties with relief. These were the physical duties they were used to and were much less complicated than the emotions of departure and separation. They started to throw down the ropes and the tug built up its steam. Nora, crying now, consumed by both terror and relief, and holding on to each final, precious moment as long as she could, allowed Winckler and Overath to lead her gently to the gangway, whilst the stewards ushered the Hallers and their new son, a Swansea child, quickly out of sight.

The gangway could not be detached whilst Nora was escorted each agonising step of loss down to the quayside, where Sarah and Amy were waiting, anxiously looking back towards the town, and sensing the imminent departure of the *Polaria*. There would be other boats, surely, wouldn't there? thought Sarah, who smiled unconvincingly at Amy, who smiled in return, though not in anxiety, but in perfect trust. Sarah was aware that there had been a commotion on board but she could not see what it was and she saw the woman brought down from the deck, sobbing dreadfully. Probably a man, Sarah thought. It was always a man.

There was a shout and she turned. Rumsey and Constance were running along the quay. The crowd stood back, wondering what further entertainment the *Polaria* could offer. A woman running? Without shoes? How scandalous!

'Here! Quickly!' said Constance breathlessly. 'You must go.'

Bucke passed her the cloth bag from the piano stool – her savings. 'God speed, Sarah.' He bent down and took Amy's hand. 'And you too, Amy. You are a very special girl, a very brave girl, and we shall miss you terribly. Look after Sarah for me. I know you will.'

Amy looked at him, puzzled, as if she had realised for the first time that she was leaving.

Constance picked her up, still slight but ready now to grow and to blossom and hugged her. 'You are a wonderful girl. A treasure.'

Constance was crying now. 'Our gift to the New World.' She put her down gently and then she and Sarah embraced.

There were shouts from the ship. Nora Leary, who had delayed the departure of the *Polaria,* was sitting on the quay and crying loudly. The gangway was finally loosened. There were more shouts. Men in uniform on the ship were waving at them.

Sarah held Bucke's forearms and looked into his eyes with unexpected intensity. She shook her head, very faintly. 'Thank you, Rumsey. For everything. For the big things and the little things. Everything. You know something? I have always…' She stopped, left the sentence hanging, unfinished. She bit her lip, took Amy's hand and they ran up the gangway. Sailors tried to stop her but she ignored them. There was a gap there now as the ship floated free and the tug took up the strain. 'Quick Amy! Jump!' The gap was increasing. Amy jumped and landed on the deck, suddenly giggling. Sarah followed her and was caught by two sailors. She rattled her money bag in their irritated faces as the mate approached and, at that moment, Sarah Rigby knew that she had done it. A new life was calling to her. What it would be, what it might hold, she could not know. But it would be her life and she would be able to share it always with Amy.

On the quay, Rumsey and Constance saw the distance to the ship gradually increase. Oily water appeared, widening from a ditch, to a stream, to a river. They looked for Sarah and Amy but could not see them, for the ship was lined with people waving excitedly and saying goodbye to their European past, ready to brave the Atlantic in springtime for the endless possibilities of the new world. There was a chill wind and Constance took his arm and pulled herself closer to him as the *Polaria* was drawn out of the harbour.

'She loves you, you know.'

There was a long pause and he continued to stare out to sea, a pause so long in fact that Constance thought she had said the wrong thing.

'I know,' he said eventually. Then he turned to her and put up his hand to rest it gently on her shoulder. 'But Sarah knows that I have you, Constance. And she also knows that nothing else matters so much to me as you.'

*

Later as the *Polaria* was released from the tug and they pulled away into the Bristol Channel heading west, Sarah and Amy stood at the stern, holding hands and watching the glimmering lights of Swansea fade away, a life left behind, with all those regrets and that anxiety and that terror now replaced by hopes and possibilities. Sarah had borrowed a pair of scissors from a lady sitting on the deck and knitting, who watched curiously as she cut slowly through the leather bracelet on Amy's wrist and then threw it over the side. Amy, too, had been set free.

The two women had smiled at each other as Sarah returned the scissors, and perhaps they recognised that this voyage was a shared journey into the unknown, something that might draw them together. They both laughed and showed mock alarm as the ship lurched slightly, for out in the channel the sea had become a little rougher now.

Sarah could not believe that she had finally done it and that Swansea, for good and for bad, was behind her now. The people she knew, those she hated and those she loved, were left behind and who could know what lay in front of her. Was it really true that she would never see its streets again, those streets she had walked endless for days? She could not comprehend that thought, for she was exhausted by the terrible fusion of emotions that had consumed her in those recent hellish days and she held on to the gunwale for support as her legs shook briefly.

Then Amy squeezed Sarah's hand and she looked down at the little girl, dragged away suddenly from her thoughts.

'Sarah? Where are we going?'

' We are going to America. Together, Amy.'

'Is it a long way? To America?'

'Yes, Amy. It is. But we will be together and everything will be

376

fine. A new country. A new life. I promise.'

Amy looked thoughtfully at the grey sea, then she turned her head decisively to look at Sarah, who was smiling down at her. 'May I ask you something, Sarah?'

'Of course you can, Amy. What is it?'

'I think I would like to call you, Mummy. Can I do that?'

It was a few moments before Sarah found the strength to answer. 'Yes, Amy. You can.' Her voice was shaking. 'I would like that very much.'

Epilogue

Hannah stood up and sighed, running both hands down the small of her back. It wasn't much fun being old. No one had ever told her it would be like this. She looked at the clock. Another few minutes and she would turn the radio on. She had always listened to the news at midday. A ritual really, but sometimes she wondered why she did it. It always depressed her. And they never told you what you wanted to know. Perhaps there were things they weren't allowed to say, but her grandson Gareth was out in Korea and they never told you anything about him. Nevertheless it was time to turn the radio on, to give the valves a chance to warm up.

How much longer did she have? Hannah had wondered about that a lot since Emrys died, two years ago. Every day was a bonus, she supposed, though not one that was necessarily welcome. She still missed him, but he was buried just a short distance away in Danygraig cemetery and she visited him most weeks, which was a comfort, of sorts. He had been a good husband, kind and thoughtful. A good father too, always close to the children. But quiet sometimes, when a cloud might settle over him. She had known what it was, of course; the First War. It was always a war, for wars seemed to haunt her life. Emrys had fought in the Dardanelles and had brought back shadows with him. She knew when to leave him be, when his happy stories of marching through tomato fields in Bulgaria were replaced by something darker. The loss of their son, Gwyn, in the Second World War had brought all the horror back to him and his last few years had been difficult ones.

She went over to the sink to fill the kettle. It always seemed strange to her. Emrys had talked about his service in the Balkans and had always struggled to pronounce the names of some of the places he'd been. There were times he liked to talk about the countryside and the churches but he couldn't say the words, and yet for some reason, she always felt confident enough to correct him, as if she knew how to say them. She didn't know if she was right but they sounded right, that was the point. How could that be?

There had always been strange wisps of memory in her mind that came back to her when she least expected it. Hannah had never understood them, but now as she got older they seemed to return more frequently and much more clearly than ever before. They seemed like memories but she knew they were only dreams. Vivid dreams, but dreams nonetheless. They couldn't be anything else. Shadowy figures, dark alleys, a ship. They were quite disturbing images and the only thing that could comfort her was holding that old necklace of hers that she kept in a box on the mantelpiece.

That was a strange thing too. It had always been with her. Her mother had never said where it came from. It looked impressive and it seemed quite old too, but it was probably just paste. Or glass. It was certainly pretty, especially when it caught the light. Her daughter Pam used to like to wear it and now her granddaughter Alison did too, when she was playing her elaborate games, even though it was heavy and hurt when it bounced against her.

There was something on the news about a rescue. Hannah hadn't really been listening, but it was one of those words that oddly set her mind off on one of its wanderings, far away from Swansea, to another place. Words like *rescue* did it, or *nephew* or *venue*, words that ended in that particular way. When she heard them she always persuaded herself that the scar on her shoulder would start to itch. No one could ever say how she got it. It happened when she was a child, but mum had always changed the subject. *Queue*, that was another of those words.

It was very odd. And she didn't have to hear them, just thinking about the words set off the pictures in her head. It had to be a dream or a nightmare. It couldn't be real, she had been brought up in Port Eynon and the place in her dreams wasn't a bit like Port Eynon. A dark street. Running down to an oily black sea. Then flashes and noise. Shouts. A man holding her tightly. Must have been her father, because she knew he was kind. There were steep cobbles and a big ship. There was a fire and she could smell it. Her shoulder and arm felt sticky. Then the pictures stopped and she could never go beyond that point, no matter how hard she tried. It was quite a puzzle. Could dreams have smells? One of her earliest and most traumatic memories was being told that her father, Rhys, had been killed on his cart. Someone murdered him when he was taking seaweed to Swansea. They never did catch the man who did it. Mum married again, a man called Ernest, but Hannah didn't like him much. But those dreams that came back to her were always far more vivid than the moment when she received the news about her father. She had always felt guilty about that.

She sighed and leaned against the sink listening to the kettle humming and looking out through the window. The garden was a bit untidy since Emrys had died. She ought to do something about it but it needed too much bending. It was odd, really. She had lived here in Danygraig in Swansea ever since she was married, which was more than fifty years ago. She had survived the air raids, she was proud that she had waved at Churchill when he came to see the damage, her children and her grandchildren and now her great granddaughter had been born here. But she had never properly felt at home in Swansea. It was hard to explain. She had always been dark, though there were more grey hairs these days than she liked, and she had always been very striking. Quite a catch, according to Emrys. He said she was 'exotic,' whatever that meant, smiling at the thought. But the children in Port Eynon had been quite cruel sometimes, calling her a gypsy, telling her she didn't belong there. She had spent many days talking to a fragile untidy doll in a made up language. She must have had quite an imagination. Perhaps that explained the dreams.

As she got older it seemed that she could remember things better, things that she had forgotten. She hadn't thought about some of these things for years and suddenly they were so vivid it was like yesterday.

She had lots of unanswered questions when she thought about it. Why was she called Hannah? She had asked her mother why she had chosen the name but she just shrugged and said that she liked the sound. And then there were those two pieces of wood she kept in a drawer upstairs, never wanting to throw them away. They were really old. She remembered that they once had a long piece of paper wrapped around them but the dog, a terrier called Snapper, had run outside with it in the rain, the thing had got wet and it had all fallen apart. Her mother said that was hers too, like the necklace, but she had no idea what it had been. But she always wondered, why were they hers and not her mother's? Where had they come from? And why? Perhaps she should have been more persistent.

The kettle was singing loudly now. Alison would be coming for her dinner, full of news about her morning in school. She would eat her cheese on toast quickly and then run back to the school in time to play skipping games in the yard. Hannah always loved hearing her talk. It was such a pleasure. Sometimes she saw in Alison's dark eyes and a complexion a shadow of herself and it made her feel proud that part of her would live on into a future that would be so different from her own ordinary life. Being old wasn't much fun and it came upon you far too quickly. But it was good to be a great-grandmother.

Afterword

This is quite obviously a work of fiction, though it has within it certain elements that are true and which, in my mind, help to anchor the story in nineteenth century Swansea. All the locations are authentic, apart from Giddings Sugar Warehouse. After all, you can't go around in novels burning down real buildings just because it suits. So that has been invented, along with the West Pier. Most of the other places you can find, if you have a mind to.

The central part of the story, the search for a lost heiress in Swansea isn't true. Neither is the story about the militia and nor is the part about Fanny Stevens, though her repertoire is authentic. Cosh Boy isn't real either. However, I have tried to create an authentic picture of nineteenth century Swansea by taking details from the historical record, as reported in the local press. The story is set in February 1881 but I have integrated a number of genuine news items from different times during the century.

Louis Barree was arrested and convicted in 1844. Captain Diogene Morin refused to remove his money from a drunken woman's mouth in 1873. I should also make it clear that, as far as I know. he was never involved in some kind of prototype for an adult-orientated Top Trumps card game.

Ann Wood, eight years old, died collecting cinders on the Hafod slag tip in 1876. Neither the first, nor the last, Swansea child to die in its industrial wastes.

The migrant ship *SS Polaria* under Captain Winckler did call at Swansea en route from Hamburg to New York in the late 1870s.

The manslaughter of Lizzie Grimshaw by members of the Militia happened in July 1881 and Veronica Pesek and Rosa Budai were murdered in Pesth in 1885.

The *Ann of Bridgewater* was abandoned by its crew in a storm off Rhossili in 1899 and the story of the bodies found on the *Maryland* dates from 1901.

The name of the Ragged School lives on in Swansea in the name of a local amateur football team. The school did important work, often as a soup kitchen, eventually relocating from Back Street to Pleasant Street in 1911, where the fine red brick building can still stands, with its benefactors remembered on corner stones that you can still see.

The idea of animal droppings disguised as pills was an urban myth that had some appeal in the nineteenth century, when medication was frequently sold through unregulated advertisements in the newspapers.

The Roman poet Ovid escaped execution by Emperor Augustus and was instead exiled to Tomis in 8 AD. His verse drama *Medea,* of which only a couple of lines have survived, is considered to be one of the most important missing pieces of Roman literature.

I like to think that the occasional references I have included to Romanian history are largely accurate. However, they are spoken by Abramovitch and you can't believe anything he says. I picked up his name from Isaac Abramovitch, who was arrested in April 1904 for acting suspiciously in Swansea Market. His defence, that he was assessing the feasibility of establishing a boxing booth, was dismissed and he was imprisoned for three months. I have always thought that was a little harsh.

Most of the other characters have been invented, though poor Eliza Keast was murdered on the Strand in 1906. James Flynn and Isaac Colquhoun were both successful and respected police officers. Constance Bristow was the abandoned wife of an abusive headteacher. Rumsey Bucke was a police Inspector who was dismissed following accusations from a disaffected constable that he had once stolen a yew tree. I wanted them to find happiness together and within the narrow confines of my books I think that they have. In real life it is highly unlikely that they ever met.

Harry Boston, the Singing Painter – 'Artiste Extraordinaire'- was one of my ancestors. His talent was the brightest of all shooting stars, illuminating the music halls of the early twentieth century in south Yorkshire all-too briefly. His act remains an achievement that none of his descendants have ever been ready to emulate.

Nellie Damms, who is referred to by Sarah with regards to curtaining material, was my paternal grandmother, a market trader, also in south Yorkshire.

The newspaper vendor, Paul Roe, was created to remember my uncle who died of Covid 19 and to whose memory this book is dedicated.

Patagonia Jack
By Geoff Brookes

In the next novel in the series, *Patagonia Jack,* Swansea is excited beyond measure by the visit of the Prince of Wales to officially open the new dock. But there are other forces at work in the town…

Craven went to the door and looked up and down Gloucester Place. He knew he had seen him before, there was no question of that. But when? Not recently, he was sure, but then he didn't have a good memory for faces. He assessed the street for the final time, confirmed that there was no one there and decided to shut the hotel for the night. He bolted the door and then climbed the stairs with a flickering candle in a saucer and with his cashbox under his arm. He sat on his untidy bed covered in stained, dark blankets and, as he always did, checked under the pillow. Yes the gun was still there. It had been his habit ever since he returned to Swansea to keep a revolver there, just in case. After all, he'd done some things in his life, here and there.

Craven stood up and stepped across to the window to look down on the Seamen's Mission to see if that man was hanging around there, whilst he removed his breeches. As he pulled them down to his ankles and stepped out of them, the man from the bar slid silently and unseen from beneath the bed and blew out the candle. As an exasperated Craven struggled to turn to see why the light had disappeared, the man threw an arm around his neck tightly and then pulled him close. He whispered in Craven's ear, the hissing sound of death.

'Remember me now, Fred? Remember? You knew I'd come for you.'

Look out for this gripping story from Geoff Brookes, author of 'A Swansea Child.' Published by Cambria Publishing